the FORTUNATE ONES

the FORTUNATE ONES

CATHERINE HOKIN

GRAND CENTRAL
PUBLISHING

NEW YORK BOSTON

Grand Central Publishing
Hachette Book Group
1290 Avenue of the Americas, New York, NY 10104
grandcentralpublishing.com
twitter.com/grandcentralpub

First published in 2020 by Bookouture, an imprint of StoryFire Ltd.
First Grand Central Publishing edition: July 2021

Grand Central Publishing is a division of Hachette Book Group, Inc. The Grand Central Publishing name and logo is a trademark of Hachette Book Group, Inc.

The publisher is not responsible for websites (or their content) that are not owned by the publisher.

The Hachette Speakers Bureau provides a wide range of authors for speaking events. To find out more, go to www.hachettespeakersbureau.com or call (866) 376-6591.

Library of Congress Cataloging-in-Publication Data
Names: Hokin, Catherine, author.
Title: The fortunate ones / Catherine Hokin.
Description: First Grand Central Publishing edition. | New York : Grand Central Publishing, 2021. | Summary: "Germany, 1941. When Inge - all blonde curls and good manners - first locks eyes with Felix, she knows instinctively that he's off limits. Her staunchly proper parents will never approve of a working-class Jewish boy for their precious only daughter. But that doesn't make their first, shy kiss less significant, or the moment they're torn apart less shocking. The next time they see each other, it will be across the packed courtyard of a Nazi concentration camp - Felix in the prisoners' ranks and Inge on the arm of her new, Nazi husband. Inge never knew that her father's 'party loyalty' would extend to marrying her off to a cruel Nazi officer twice her age, who sees his new wife as just another thing to control. She has always been a good girl - a silent wife - but when Inge sees Felix that day - beaten, bloody and brave - she knows she can't stay silent any longer. She must save him, whatever the cost, whatever her husband or even her country might do to her later."—Provided by publisher.
Identifiers: LCCN 2021006857 | ISBN 9781538705018 (trade paperback)
Subjects: LCSH: World War, 1939–1945—Concentration camps—Germany—Fiction. | Holocaust, Jewish (1939–1945)—Germany—Fiction. |
GSAFD: Historical fiction. | Love stories.
Classification: LCC PR6108.O39 F67 2021 | DDC 823/.92—dc23
LC record available at https://lccn.loc.gov/2021006857

ISBN: 978-1-5387-0501-8 (trade paperback)

Printed in the United States of America

LSC-C

Printing 1, 2021

For Claire, Daniel & Robert—my Three Musketeers

the
FORTUNATE
ONES

CENTRAL REGISTRY OF WAR CRIMINALS AND SECURITY SUSPECTS (CROWCASS) No: 15540 (SN)

1. **Document Title:** Sachsenhausen Konzentrationslager (KL), Oberführer Dr. Maximillian Eichel.
2. **Period Covered:** October 1942–February 1945.
3. **Source of Testimony:** Isaak Zeitelbaum, Prisoner, Barrack Eighteen, Sachsenhausen KL.
4. **Recorded by:** Felix Thalberg, Assistant Clerk, CROWCASS.
5. **Date of Testimony:** 12 September 1946.
6. **Form and Content:** Testimony regarding medical treatment of prisoners by the aforesaid Dr. Eichel.

Notes:

1. Our source, Sachsenhausen inmate Isaak Zeitelbaum, as identified above, was unable to sign this testimony as a consequence of injuries received during the relocation of Barrack Eighteen/Nineteen prisoners from Sachsenhausen to the Ebensee Konzentrationslager in April 1945 (document **15562 (EB)** refers). An audio recording is available.
2. Barrack Eighteen referred to in this testimony has been identified (with Barrack Nineteen) as the center for the *Operation Bernhard* counterfeiting program at Sachsenhausen KL (document **15560 (SN)** refers).

I, Isaak Zeitelbaum, make under oath the following declaration:
I was deported to the Sachsenhausen concentration camp from the Judenhäuser district of Mitte, Berlin, in October 1942. Because

of my skills as an engraver, I was interred in Barrack Eighteen and given the status *Jewish: Special Prisoner.* A month after my arrival, I suffered an ear infection and was sent to Barrack One of the infirmary block. Because of my status, I was placed in an isolation room. There was a larger ward on the same corridor which the orderlies called "Dr. Nadel's Playroom." When they said that, the orderlies mimed giving an injection. They told me that I was a lucky man: only Barrack Eighteen and Nineteen patients were given the correct medical treatment and guaranteed a return to the camp.

In October 1944, I became ill again and was returned to the infirmary. All three blocks were overcrowded due to a typhoid outbreak, so I was placed in a ward with inmates from the wider camp. They were forbidden from speaking to me; a guard was posted for the duration of my stay. Each morning, orderlies forced the other patients out of their bunks. Anyone who could walk twenty paces unaided was sent to the Playroom. In the four days I was there, twelve men were judged fit for transfer. I do not know what happened to those repeatedly judged unfit. One night I heard the orderlies refer to the Playroom's doctor not as Nadel but Eichel: I then understood that *Nadel* was a nickname, meaning needle. According to the orderlies, this doctor's specialty was testing stamina drugs to see if they were safe for use by Luftwaffe pilots and also measuring which substances could stop a heart the quickest. His preferred method was injections. Dr. Eichel came only once onto the ward. He was very tall, with dark blond hair and a friendly manner. He walked around the beds, patting the patients and smiling. He did not approach me once he knew I had Barrack Eighteen privileges.

In November 1944, I was asked to work on a set of false passports and identity papers for a number of SS officers, including the doctor and his wife. I remember her photograph: she was very young and very pretty. For his set of Italian passports, Dr. Eichel ordered that we use the name *Ago,* which is Italian for needle. The orderly who delivered Dr. Eichel's request thought this was a very amusing joke.

PART ONE

CHAPTER ONE

October 1941, Berlin

Hardenbergplatz was packed with people pouring in and out of Zoo Station, jostling for their little bit of space. It was too early yet for the cinema and theatergoers with their overloud, *look how daring we still are* voices. These bodies were hunched, their faces too set for anything as frivolous as make-believe.

Felix leaned against a wall pasted with rules and reminders and watched the crowds come and go. Everyone was preoccupied, part of the bustle and separate from it. Rushing to shifts, stumbling from shifts, minds on lines that grew too long and shops that grew too empty. Running through the Party meetings still to fit in, the donations to scrape together, the right people in their housing block to smile at and slip a cigarette to. Looking loyal and staying safe. Felix knew the drill: he lived it.

He shivered and wished he'd brought a scarf. Barely halfway through October and snow was already nipping in the wind. Last month, everyone was obsessed with milk and where all the cows had gone; this month it was coal, or rather the lack of it.

"Maybe we should move, Arno. Find somewhere smaller and easier to heat." A sensible suggestion—his mother's always were. He should have added his voice, propped up her idea with neighborhoods they might like, or might at least be able to afford, but his father's hands shook like leaves and the moment to step up was gone.

"Hush, my love. I'm sure there's no need to go. We won't talk of it again." A kiss for Arno, a smile for Felix. A whisper that was half apology, half excuse. "It's understandable. He does so love the garden here."

Neither of them prepared to voice the truth: that Arno never went to the garden anymore.

There was still no sign of her. Felix blew on his fingers and stamped his chilled feet; the soles of his boots were wearing thin as slippers. Maybe there would be coal in the shops tonight; there had been rumors all day of new supplies. Even half a bucket would make a world of difference. Felix imagined his mother's face if he could promise her enough hot water to cook and to bathe, and resolved to make time to get in line before his air-raid duties began. Taking one burden off her would make him as happy as finding the coal.

The station disgorged another wave into the silvery afternoon. Most people streamed past without looking up, but some glanced at Felix and glanced again. *Who had the time to loiter these days? Or the business?* He could hear the questions ticking. Stand here much longer and somebody would nudge somebody else, would catch an eye, would draw attention in that oh-so-subtle good-citizen way that let the informant walk on with conscience clear.

Felix scanned the crowd for his mother's green hat and checked his watch again. Half past three. He was a little early, she was a little late; their usual pattern, but it always unnerved him. Meeting to share the walk home on the couple of occasions a week their shifts lined up gave him a sense of normality he needed more than any eighteen-year-old should.

Another look his way. Time to find a new waiting spot. Felix turned his collar up against the cold and dodged across the sprawling square, patting his pockets to check his papers were safely in place. Everyone did the pat-down now, the action grown as involuntary as sneezing. He pulled at his collar again so that the *Hitlerjugend* pin sat a little higher on the lapel. Whatever else the red-and-white diamond might be, it was some protection against prying eyes.

"Felix! I'm late: forgive me. Frau Clasen surprised us all with twins, and her husband cried more than the babies."

She was finally here, in a breathless rush, the wind tugging at a hat that was already losing its battle against her mass of frizzy curls. His shoulders relaxed as she stretched up to hug him.

"Two little boys. Such a chubby pair, no doubting who their daddy is. Still, he was nothing if not grateful. Look." She showed him her bulging string bag. "Sausages, potatoes, onions. No waiting in line tonight—for dinner at least." Another generous patient padding out their larder.

Although she shrugged away any claim to it, Felix knew Kerstin Thalberg was one of the best-loved midwives at Berlin's Charité hospital, and her family ate better because of it.

"Good." He looped her arm and steered her toward the broader streets fanning out from the station. "Let's take the longer way home, walk along the Kurfürstendamm and admire the wonderful windows." A joke even the turned-down heads would find a smile for. The state of the Kurfürstendamm's great department stores was Berlin's worst-kept secret: towering displays packed with goods and every packet empty. *Good for morale* was the official line; *propaganda for the foreign newspapers* more truthful.

"If you like, if you don't freeze to death first. Eighteen years old and you still can't remember a scarf."

He grimaced as Kerstin reached up to ruffle his hair and sent a gaggle of chain-smoking factory girls into a fit of giggles and winks. When Kerstin's smile faded just as quickly as it had come, the girls' amusement was instantly forgotten.

"Not too long, though, Felix. I don't like your father to be alone once the blackout starts. If there was to be a raid…"

Another unspoken worry, one more in a growing list. If there was a raid, would Arno venture to the communal shelter in the apartment block's cellar? Without Felix or his mother to claim their three spaces, would Blockwart Fischer check to see that he came?

"It's not likely there will be. There's been barely any bombing since the summer." She chewed her lip; he hated when she did that. "But we'll go quickly, I promise."

He patted her hand, awkward at this role reversal, and led her toward the brightly lit windows whose lights would soon disappear beneath chink-proof blinds.

Kerstin tried hard to play the familiar game. She pointed out the perfume bottles filled with neon-bright water and the cleverly painted cardboard handbags, but it wasn't long before she was tugging on his arm and chewing her lip again.

"We should hurry; we've still a way to go."

Before he could answer, a shout cut through the rumble of people and trams, and a gap opened up in the crowds.

Kerstin's voice dropped. "Felix, come on now. Please."

Another shout, this one guttural and harsh. The gap widened. Felix stepped forward, craning for a clearer view. Two green-shirted *Ordnungspolizei*, batons raised, rearing over a crumple of dusty rags. Not rags: a man, tumbled half into the road, his patched black coat bunched around him. An old man judging from the thatch of gray hair beside the policemen's boots. Felix winced as the batons crashed. The heap shuddered at the impact but made no sound.

"What did he do?" Felix wriggled forward, pushing against the tide.

Kerstin's hand shot out, grabbing his elbow with a ferocity that made him jump. "What does it matter? Do like everyone else: keep walking." Her pace picked up and, because she held him so tight, so did his.

"But they'll kill him. He's an old man. What can he possibly have done to deserve such a beating?"

One of the policemen pushed at the body with his boot, turning it beetle-like onto its back. And there it was, the answer, stamped onto the coat's stained front: a star, its yellow points cutting across the limp body.

"Is that it? Really? Is that all it takes now to make everyone blind?"

He spoke too loud: heads turned, including the two green-shirted thugs, bored of their easily squashed quarry.

"Move." Kerstin's nails dug through his sleeve. She wrenched him into the press of people, wrenched him harder when he tried to look back. A ripple behind them suggested he had roused the attention she feared.

"In here, quick. Straighten your tie. Don't speak." A push of heavy glass and the street disappeared, its clamor deadened in the plush of thick carpets and a piano's soft playing. Café Kranzler. The domain of the wealthy—wartime or not. Felix had often looked through the windows but never dreamed of entering.

"What are you doing?" Felix stared openmouthed at Kerstin as the maître d' approached, all draped white linen and oily hair. "People like us don't come in here."

"Exactly. We don't need to be people like us right now; we need to be people like them." Kerstin frowned away his protest and took the situation so calmly under control, Felix understood exactly why frightened mothers-to-be always asked for Frau Thalberg. Kerstin smiled; Felix copied her.

The maître d' bowed a fraction of a bow, keeping at a pointed distance. Kerstin set her shoulders, smiled wider and ignored his supercilious look. She kept smiling as the excessively curling hand shooed them through silver-laden tables, past swastikas pinned to fur, not fraying wool. Not a flicker as he seated them at a table so close to the kitchens it would be nobody's choice and dropped menus onto the spotless cloth as if he offered Bibles to the heathens. Not a waver until the rigid back spun away. Then the mask cracked so quickly, Felix grabbed Kerstin's hands across the table to stop her sliding beneath it.

"Pour me some water." She drained the glass, waved for another. "I knew he couldn't refuse to let us in: even if we are a little worn, we're clearly respectable, but those brutes outside? They wouldn't dare try. Thank God it wasn't the SS or the Gestapo you decided to rattle; they'd be welcomed in here with open arms." She tugged at her hat, began digging in her bag. "What were you thinking of? Why did you make a fuss? It's simple: whatever happens, don't stop, don't look, don't ask. You've been told it often enough."

"He looked like Father." Felix didn't mean to say it. He hated that tears sprang at once into his mother's eyes. He hated that he'd dragged them into this place they had neither the clothes, the money, nor the ration coupons for. A place that was filled with people he despised and feared in equal measure. He hated more that he had done nothing to help the old man, and everyone else had behaved the same. "I'm sorry. I'm so sorry."

Kerstin nodded, rising as she finally located the faded cosmetic purse he knew held nothing more than a gap-toothed comb and a lipstick stub. "I know. It's all right. Find something on the menu that won't cost us a ransom while I tidy up." She tucked her purse into her pocket and clamped her smile back on as a waitress hovered.

Felix opened the menu, closed it again. Two cups of ersatz coffee: whatever the menu offered, what else could they afford? He watched his mother moving confidently through the room. *She always fits in, wherever she is.*

"There's a path through everything, Felix. You just need to find it." Sitting by his bed, stroking his hair. Six years ago, when his world was reshaped with words he didn't understand. Three years ago, when his father came home from the university white-faced and jobless and wouldn't get out of bed for a week. "Things might feel confusing, or frightening, but, whatever comes, we'll meet it together, as a family. Nothing is ever hopeless." He wondered if she still believed that.

The waitress came closer. She had the swanlike neck and light step of a dancer. Felix picked at the napkin by his plate: it was folded so tight the cloth had stretched into cardboard. Without thinking, he pulled out the nub of pencil he always carried. A few strokes and he had the almond-slant of her eyes, the slash of her cheekbones. A few more and he caught the long curve of her neck and the swoop of her loosely tied bun. A smudge here and there and the mouth softened, the eyelashes fanned.

"What are you doing?" Kerstin was back before he could cover the damage. "Now I must pay for the linens as well?"

But the waitress was smiling. She swept up the drawing with the menus, shaking her head as Felix tried to apologize and order the cheapest thing she could bring. A moment later she was back, balancing a loaded tray, ignoring their protests as cups and cakes slid onto the table.

"A thank-you, for the drawing. My husband will love it. He's always writing, asking for a photograph, and who has the time? There are people here with so much money they'll never notice a little extra on their bill. Enjoy."

Scents rose up so rich and thick, Felix's arguments dissolved. Coffee. Real roasted coffee, not the bitter dried-out tang of barley or acorn. And vanilla, fragrant with the memory of hot days and carnivals, cut through with the fruity bite of cinnamon as if Christmas had dropped into the middle of summer. He cut a small piece of the torte, took a tentative bite. It slipped into his mouth silken and creamy. No sand, no sawdust, no money-saving tricks. Icing kissed his lips with sticky sweetness, crumbs melted into butter on his tongue. *With jellies soother than the creamy curd, and lucent syrups.* A line taught long ago, some English poet he doubted any school permitted nowadays. The memory caught in his throat, flew back to a childhood when cakes were everyday pleasures and summers all tasted of ice cream.

"It's hard, Felix, I know. When you remember." It was his turn to well up with tears as Kerstin continued. "You are so good: you never complain; you always do what is needed."

He blinked furiously and buried his face in his coffee cup, unable to trust his voice. What was there to say, or do, different than he did? What would be gained by complaining? He was luckier than some—he tried every day to remember that. This redrawn world he'd been consigned to had closed the doors of university and art school, but Kerstin had called in favors and got him work at a newspaper office. It was on the bottom rung of the print workshop, barely an apprenticeship, but it was a skill; it was money. He was good at it, a fast learner with an eye for detail; everyone said so. There could be a future in that, if there was a future in anything. He might have to fight, of course: the blood rules were hazy when it came to battlefields. He tried not to think about that, and he couldn't ask Kerstin, or anyone else, for fear of drawing attention. Still, it was three years until his call-up; with a bit of luck the war would be done by then.

The cup rattled, dark spots splashing the tablecloth. He let his mother take it and wrap her fingers around his until they stilled, the way she did with his father.

"I know what it costs you. The way I push you to fit in."

No, you don't; no one does. Felix swallowed hard. How could she know when he never said? And how could he say? Everything Kerstin did, she did out of love: if she knew how much he struggled, she would never forgive herself. So he hid it. He hid it so well, there were days when he felt as if he was nothing but a bundle of unspoken words. Whatever Kerstin told him to do to blend in, he did it. He put on his *Hitlerjugend* uniform and sat in lectures where people labeled the same as his father were classed as inhuman. He went to his *Flakhelfer* training sessions and studied his aircraft charts, next to boys who would beat up Arno without a second thought, who would expect praise for it. Who would expect Felix to join in and beat him up too if he refused.

In his outside world, he said as little as he could and then he came home, and he said what she needed. His life had turned into a tightrope, balanced between the fear of speaking and the fear of staying silent with every word measured. What good would it do

Kerstin to know that? It was six years since the race laws had become Germany's new bible and assigned categories to Felix and Arno that he still couldn't fathom, despite all the diagrams the National Socialist Party produced. The Party had set out their ideology as clearly as a math problem: this plus that equals good, this plus that equals bad. Felix looked at the bloodline numbers and the pictures beside them—monster-shaped drawings of old men with hooked noses and bulging eyes—and felt as much connection as he would to a spaceship full of Martians. He had a label; he knew that. What he didn't know was how visible it was. Which teachers could see it; which of his gradually shrinking circle of friends. He didn't know who checked; he didn't know how much it mattered. He didn't know anything at all and yet he had to walk through his days as if everything made sense.

He looked up into his mother's warm eyes and six years of confusion spilled. "How can Father be Jewish now when he never was before? He keeps Christmas; he loves it. He goes to church when Grandmother and Grandfather Müller visit—or he did. He became a Lutheran, I remember that, even though he said all religion is pointless. How can he be Jewish *and* a Lutheran? And even if he is a Jew, what does that have to do with us, with me? And why does it even matter?"

His mother lowered her fork, glanced around. No one appeared to be listening. She answered in a whisper anyway. "Why does it matter? Because the Party says it does. What other answer is there? As for who is Jewish and who is not: that is at *their* choosing. It has nothing to do with which church you attend or which holidays you keep. Your father's father was Jewish and so were three of his grandparents and that, under the Führer's new laws, makes him a Jew. Whatever he really is, whatever he really feels or does, makes no difference to anything."

Felix knew the formula; he'd heard it time and again, seen it on the posters plastered across the city and around his classrooms. The magic number three. In fairy tales that number granted wishes; now it brought a change in race that had somehow bled down to him. Arno had three Jewish grandparents; that made him a Jew. Felix had only one but that was enough to fix him with the Party's new label: *Mischling*. Mixed blood.

Kerstin had given up trying to eat. He should stop talking, he always had before, but there was a different air about this place, so cushioned from his everyday world, which loosened his tongue.

"Why didn't you leave him? When the laws changed, when the university didn't want him anymore and he lost his job, why didn't you leave him? Plenty of women like you, who married Jews before the law forbade it, did; the group leaders crow about it. Or why don't you leave him now, when he hides all day and is afraid of his own shadow? The rules are tightening—you must have seen that. Soon you won't be entitled to anything but Jewish ration cards, won't be able to shop until everyone else is done. How will we manage then?"

Her face collapsed so quickly, he might as well have hit her. "Mutti, I'm sorry. Forgive me. I shouldn't have said that about leaving him. I shouldn't have asked. It was wrong."

If she was angry, she covered it well. "No. It wasn't. You're not a child; you have the right to ask whatever you want. But I don't have answers that will make sense of it, and I can't make it all better anymore." Her face was so worn, her voice so tired. He wanted to stop her, but a dam had broken in Kerstin too.

"I've tried so hard, Felix. Pushing on as if everything was normal, turning you out every day like a good German boy; trying to protect you. I didn't know what else to do and yet I'm scared that I've failed. To them, you're a *Mischling*. What if, despite all I've done, nothing but that ever counts?"

How he hated that word, especially on her lips. *Mischling*. Did it even exist before 1935? Before the Party cooked up their new laws and decided to run the world by manufactured rules of race that made sense to no one but them? Before they began looking for Jewish blood everywhere? One Jewish grandparent, or two, or three; full-blood or mixed blood, in the first degree, or the second, which was the way they categorized him. No matter what you were before, you were Jewish now, and whatever flavor they stuck you with, it meant the same: you were different, you were subject. Too much of the wrong blood and you might be dispensable.

Kerstin was still talking, tears thick in her voice. That his unflappable mother was on the edge of crying in public was enough to make Felix wish he'd never started this.

"...Joining the *Jungvolk* and the *Hitlerjugend*, becoming a *Flakhelfer*. Whatever you had to join, to stay in school, to find a job, to melt in with the masses and keep you safe, I thought it was for the best. Finding the path, remember?"

He nodded, took her hand and prayed she wouldn't let the tears flow and tip his world further off balance.

"Please God, the path I've pushed you down is a safe one. As for me: leaving your father isn't just wrong, it's impossible. I love him. Whatever else changes, that does not." Finally, a smile, although it was a weak one. "Even Herr Hitler cannot break that."

Oh, but he can. He squeezed her hand, grateful she was looking down, for he had no smile to offer in return. Kerstin could tell herself she had the strength to hold their world steady, but Felix knew how easily it could fall. Every *Hitlerjugend* meeting started with a list of the latest neighborhoods targeted. He had seen the mounting suicide reports and the rising list of "relocations," a term he didn't understand but sensed meant nothing good. Every one of those resettled removed people was loved by someone and they were still snapped from their lives as easily as a child breaking a twig. He looked at her white face and retreated back into silence.

"We need to go, Felix; this has to wait." Kerstin tore a square of paper off one of Herr Clasen's gifts and wrapped the last sliver of cake up as carefully as if it was one of her newborns. She got slowly to her feet. She looked lost.

"I love him too, Mutti." He didn't know what else to say. Nothing would take his words away or bring the café's magic back.

"I know you do, and now he needs us to go home and take care of him. Whatever the rights or wrongs of this, Felix, remember that: your father needs us both."

It was as close to a rebuke as Kerstin would get and it set his skin smarting.

"The nonsense they feed us at meetings, I don't believe it. I'd never say or do anything to hurt him, I promise."

She linked her arm through his as they emerged from the now heavily curtained café into an eerily darkened street and rested her head on his shoulder.

"You're a good boy, Felix. Whatever else wobbles, I've never doubted that."

Berlin in the blackout. A different city entirely from its daytime face. Streetlamps turned off or filtering a watery blue. Darkness so thick it sat on the skin, hobbled feet to a snail's pace, muffled any thought of speaking. They waited a moment in the doorway, eyes narrowing as they adjusted to their new navigation tools. Bodies and buildings had disappeared. The flare of a cigarette swapping between mouth and fingers had to do for a man. Here was a car reduced to a tiny yellow rectangle; there was a woman reduced to the reflective gleam of a blackout badge. Dots and dashes picked out in a phosphorescent Morse code warned where the pavement ended and the road began. Light dipped and darted in points and patches, red and yellow and blue and white. Everything solid was stripped back to a silhouette. Everyone complained about the blackout, but not Felix: there was a strange beauty to be found in its simplicity.

Progress was slower now, paced out in stumbles and wrong turns. The twenty-minute stride from the café to their apartment in Wilmersdorf shortened to a shuffle, stretched to an hour. By the time they reached the block, Kerstin's hands were shaking, her key fumbling in the lock.

"Frau Thalberg and young Felix. Good evening. You're out late tonight." Herr Fischer, the building's designated Blockwart, lurking in the stairwell, ears alert as a Doberman's. His notebook was at the ready, his chest thrust out so the swastika pin on his lapel was unmistakable even in the gloom.

"We were caught out by the blackout, Herr Fischer. It slowed us. Nothing to concern yourself with." His mother's tone was politer than Felix could have managed, but it didn't stop the hand barring their way.

"But that is my job, Frau Thalberg. To concern myself."

No, it isn't. It's your state-sanctioned pleasure. A rubber stamp on your snooping. But Felix caught his mother's eye and kept his mouth shut.

"And, dear lady, I regret to inform you, but there is a problem. Your blinds have not been drawn. As I'm sure I don't need to remind you: that is an offense."

It was too much: Fischer's smirking face and *forgive-me-if-it-pains-you* tone, his greasy head tipped just so. Felix stood straighter, unfolded his new inches.

"It is an offense if there is light showing. Which there is not. Our apartment is easily visible from the street and it's in darkness. As you will see if you care to step out with me this time and check?"

Herr Fischer's answering smile was as polite as Kerstin's. "What a lawyer you would make, young man, if any school would admit you. Then let us not say offense; let us call it an oversight. Which I tried to remedy, as is my duty. I knocked, Frau Thalberg, a number of times. Is your husband away? I confess, I find that hard to imagine—I so rarely hear him go out. To be honest, I have been wondering if there was something amiss."

Kerstin's hand curled around Felix's again, this time to hold back his fist. "Have you? How kind. No, Herr Fischer, he is not away; he does not go out. As you well know. Since you and your kind started stamping people like cattle, any pleasure to be had in strolling the streets has rather vanished. Now it is, as you said, late. You have had your fun. There is no offense—we are all agreed on that—so let us pass. Please."

Felix laughed; he couldn't help himself. At his mother's elegantly measured rudeness, at the Blockwart's dropped jaw.

"He will make me pay for answering back." Kerstin's hands trembled as they swept up the stairs.

"So what if he does? You're more than a match for him. You were wonderful. Father will be . . ." Felix stopped. *What will Father be?* Not proud, not now. Terrified? Silent?

"Waiting, Felix. He will be waiting."

He nodded. The third possibility, the more soothing choice. And the right one.

Arno was sitting, as he always was, hands in his lap, staring into space. Felix hung back in the chilly corridor, watching as Kerstin flitted around, pulling the blinds, lighting the soft lamp placed at Arno's side, opening his book at the page he had been stuck on for a week. There was love in every movement. It shone from Kerstin and reflected back from Arno as he watched her, as he closed his eyes at her kiss.

How could I have questioned this? Felix hovered beside the Führer's portrait they kept on display in the hallway in case of visitors, not wanting to intrude. This was all so wrong. His witty, clever father chipped away, bit by bit. His job gone, his friends disappeared, even his name altered to fit this twisted new reality. *Arno Israel Thalberg: Jew.*

When Felix had seen Arno's papers and asked about the addition, Kerstin had batted his question away. "It's the law: Sarah for Jewish women, Israel for Jewish men. It's a name, nothing more. Not worth the upset."

If it's not worth the upset, why did Father cry? Felix had kept quiet, added her non-answer to his growing pile of uncertainties.

Now, as if he was a child again trying to hide, he buried his face in the coats hanging on the rack. Arno's smelled musty, as if it hadn't been worn in ages. Felix rubbed the heavy tweed between his fingertips. Arno didn't go pottering in the gardens anymore—did he ever leave the house? Had Kerstin got him as far as the park on the weekend, or had he refused? Felix couldn't remember. He ran back over the last few weeks, his stomach sinking. Never mind the apartment—Arno barely left his chair.

Felix pulled the coat off its hook, desperate to do something to make amends for upsetting his mother. He would persuade Arno to go for a walk. A short stroll around the silent streets, nothing more difficult. That would pull him out of whatever this darkening mood was. They would talk, like they used to. Nothing serious: books, that was easy, and Felix would describe the café and the cakes and his drawing. He would make his father laugh—he used to be good at that. A bit of a prod, that was all Arno needed; it wasn't as if he was ill. Felix shook the dust from the heavy material, the plan so clear in his head, its success was a certainty.

"Vati, I have an idea. You'll like it, I promise." He was half in the sitting room, the coat outstretched, before he stopped. He was a fool. The tightly drawn stitches puckering the thick cloth were proof of that. How could he have failed to realize what the last law the Party brought in actually meant? A sudden memory hit him: Kerstin, six weeks ago, sitting with her sewing box and weeping, blaming her tears on a badly pricked finger. Another explanation he hadn't questioned, although he knew it was nonsense. Six weeks. Plenty of time for him to notice the rash of yellow patches blooming across the city, but not enough apparently to make the connection with his father's blank stare.

Felix looked at the coat that swung from his fingers, its star twisting like a scrap of forgotten bunting. *He looked like Father.* He retreated.

Too late. His father's face crumpled.

"Put it away, Felix. There's a good boy. Go to your room now. Leave him to me." Kerstin's voice was as gentle as the way she wrapped her arms around Arno.

Felix crept along the corridor, hung the coat up, closed his bedroom door against his father's sobbing. The day fitted around him like jigsaw pieces. The old man, the crowd's indifference, the Blockwart's furious insulted face, Arno's isolation. The weight of all these unfathomable laws that turned stars into weapons and made new people when there was nothing wrong with the old.

Felix unpinned the *Hitlerjugend* badge from his lapel, ran his finger over the red-and-white enamel, traced the swastika's raised edges. Pressing it into his palm, he glanced around the room. At his blue *Flakhelfer* jacket flung across a chair, at his *Hitlerjugend* tie curled in a knot on the floor. He'd gone blindly about, doing what his mother wanted, trying to grasp the world's shifting shape and where he stood in it, and it was clear all the time. Printed for everyone to see. *Kerstin Sophie Thalberg, née Muller: German. Arno Israel Thalberg: Jew. Felix Gerhard Thalberg: Mischling.* His mother could call him German; she could find him any number of uniforms to wear. It was all window dressing. Felix Thalberg was his father's son: one day, one unstoppably coming day, nothing else would matter but that.

CHAPTER TWO

November 1941, Berlin

Yellow. That would be cheerful. Or the deep blue Liesl had in *her* bedroom. Even white. Anything but this prissy, unadorned, little-girl pink. Inge leaned closer to the fire's crackle and surveyed her room. Nothing had altered since she was five years old. Not the ruffles cascading over the counterpane. Not the dolls arranged stiff-skirted around the cupboard tops. Not even the discarded dress that Mother had the nerve to call new. Every year, the same drooping florals and lace-edged collars repeated in a larger size as if Inge was a set of Matryoshka dolls. A child's room, a child's clothes. No cosmetics on her dressing table either—Heaven forbid Mother would allow anything so unpatriotic in the house. Briefcases full of lipsticks had flooded the country since the fall of France, but Grete Ackermann's barricades were unbreachable. "Faithful German women do not cover themselves in trinkets and paint. Decent German men do not expect them to." Sometimes Inge wondered what the point of all Papa's money was.

The one thing in the room that said eighteen not eight was the gold-stoppered bottle of Arpège, and that was only tolerated because Max had bought it. Inge didn't really like the perfume; its heavy floral scent clung too thick, but she wore it anyway; Max noticed if she didn't. Besides, Liesl said Arpège was the last word in sophistication.

Liesl, her closest friend since kindergarten, said a lot of things, especially about Max. "Divine, darling, simply divine. Those cheekbones." The way she'd said that had made Inge laugh: fingers lifting an imaginary cigarette, eyebrow arched, voice a Marlene Dietrich drawl. "And that mouth. You are a lucky girl, Inge Ackermann."

Was she? Inge hadn't known the answer to that a year ago when her engagement was arranged, and she didn't know it now, with her wedding merely weeks away. Max Eichel—Oberführer Doctor Max Eichel, to be correct, which—given his position and her role as his wife—she would need to learn to be. Transformed from family friend to fiancé almost before she realized. "How things were done," according to Mother. His father and her father were old friends and business acquaintances, both the families were equally wealthy, both members of the Party since its earliest days. Max Eichel was, as Mother repeated, a very suitable man. And as good as a stranger, although no one but Inge seemed bothered by that. "You've always known him; don't be silly" was Mother's tight-mouthed response.

It was true, she supposed. Their circles had overlapped for years, and she must have seen him plenty of times, but Inge couldn't remember meeting Max properly until her fourteenth birthday. He was twenty-nine then, already a doctor, rising through the ranks of the SS Medical Corps and far too glamourous in his black uniform to speak to a flustered teenage girl. After that, Max disappeared from Berlin, gone to take up a hospital post at a clinic in Austria, according to Inge's father. A posting he said was an honor and would see Max's future position in the Party assured.

When Inge was sixteen, however, Max returned to Berlin and suddenly became a more regular fixture, singling her out at dinners and picnics and family gatherings. Their conversations were light, forgettable things. She found him perfectly pleasant; she seemed to amuse him. There was a supervised courtship that felt awkwardly staged, and an elegantly phrased proposal in front of the whole family that seemed better suited to a film. Liesl thought it was *sublimely romantic.* Inge said yes; of course she did: who turns a man down when their parents are already clapping? When the toasts were done and the ring presented, she had tried to air her doubts, but the moment for wavering was gone. She wasn't sure if it had ever existed.

"He's almost twice my age, Papa. He could have his pick. Why would he want to marry me?"

Her father had smiled and patted her cheek and swept away any discussion. "Because he's going to be an important man to the Party, my dear, and that needs the right wife. Which is what you, a good German girl from a loyal family, will be. His connections will help my business; you will be well looked after. It's the best thing for all of us; don't let me down."

A year on, the dress was almost finished, the flowers were ordered, and Max, although charming and undeniably handsome, was still a complete mystery. Like all men, Inge supposed, except her elder brothers, Eric and Gunther, and they were far too annoying to count.

"You are such a little innocent. It's what makes you so valuable." Liesl again, when Inge confessed that her courtship was a public thing conducted in respectful pecks and other people's conversations and she had no idea how the divine doctor's kisses tasted. "But he's not. You'll need some tips before your wedding night."

A swiftly thrown pillow had put an end to that. Liesl's stories were as lurid as they were unbelievable and did not bear hearing twice.

"No more nights away from home for her, Karl. I won't have it." That was Grete, four years ago, white-faced and shaking, berating her husband before he had time to drop his briefcase and remove his coat. A storm breaking over Inge's head all because she had stood in front of her mother in her newly acquired BDM uniform and asked why her brother Eric had told her M stood for mattresses. "It is her duty to be part of the *Bund Deutscher Mädel*, I know that. I won't stop her attending the sports meetings or the housecraft sessions or any of the other activities suitable for a properly raised girl. But the summer camps? No. The junior camps were one thing, but now she is fourteen, they stop. The girls who go aren't safe; they are prey and they are ruined. You've seen what that Liesl's turning into. And no *Reichsarbeitsdienst* for her either. You have the money—pay off whoever you need to or, better yet, find her a husband. Inge is a good girl; I've worked hard to make her one. She will serve her country best as a wife."

Grete's foot went firmly down and Inge's life—and the path that led to Max—was inescapably mapped out.

Some days Inge envied her brothers: there might be dangers to face, but the army still promised them a kind of freedom. Surely not even the Führer, who had once patted her braids and called her a "pretty little maiden" when she presented him with a bunch of edelweiss, could set rules as rigidly as Grete Ackermann.

Inge stared at the dolls and the flounces and wondered if marriage might be a good thing after all: at least once she swapped this house for Max's, she could order some adult clothes and color her rooms how she chose.

"Fräulein Ackermann?" The knock was so tentative, it set Inge's teeth on edge. "Fräulein Hüber is here to collect you." It was Hannah, her head poking tortoise-like around the door. This latest maid was a nervous scrap of a girl and so skinny it was almost an insult. Didn't she know good German girls were not meant to diet? Stick-thin bodies made unhealthy babies and nobody wanted that.

"Pack the new dress and the blue strapped shoes. And don't let the fire go out: I don't want the room freezing when I come back." Was that a frown? Mother was right: the war had made it impossible to find good servants.

Leaving Hannah to sort out her jumbled clothes, Inge ran down the curved staircase, hoping to see Liesl waiting in the hall. There was no sign of her.

"In here, Inge. Don't dawdle." Mother had pounced. Inge scuffed across the marbled floor, gritting her teeth against the coming lecture. "I'm waiting." Grete sat on the far side of the drawing room, perched on a lemon brocade sofa as if its padding was fashioned from concrete. "Straighten your back, Inge. Hold your head up. Why must you slouch like a degenerate?"

Liesl, who was nestled into the armchair with her legs happily if indelicately crossed, pulled her mouth into a perfect copy of Grete's pout. Inge snorted, turned the laugh too late into a cough and sank onto the chair opposite her mother, pulling herself up as Grete's eyebrows flew. Liesl was impossible. Nothing about her manner or her costume came even close to Grete's standards. Inge could see her mother's thoughts grinding. Liesl's black beret, artfully framing elaborately rolled bright-blond bangs, would be *frivolous*. The cherry-red coat, which only a girl confident of a driver would risk in a Berlin winter, would be *attention-seeking*. The lacquered lips and penciled eyebrows, however, would be *beyond the pale*. Inge swallowed a giggle and forced herself to focus: the more attentive she acted, the quicker this would be done.

"You should not be attending this dance, Inge; you know my views. Young engaged women have no right to go socializing without their fiancé or their father present. Your father, however, is far too soft and I am overruled. That does not mean you may do as you please. There is to be no alcohol. As for the dancing, I assume the gentlemen who are attending are of the right sort and there will be chaperones?" Grete glanced at Liesl, who answered with the sweetest smile.

"I am sure everything will be done just to your liking, Frau Ackermann."

Inge refused to catch Liesl's eye.

"Good. You will permit no more than one dance per partner, and you will keep that partner at arm's length. Do not stay until the end; even the best of our young men can grow foolish near drink. You must be back at Liesl's by eleven thirty and back here in the morning by ten." A pause, but Inge knew better than to think Grete was done. "I cannot fathom why you have to stay overnight. It is barely half an hour's drive from here to the hotel; we are quite capable of sending our own driver if Fräulein Hüber is permitted to stay out longer than I consider wise."

Inge willed Liesl to ignore the insult: if this wasn't carefully managed, the whole excursion could slip away. Luckily, the front door flew open before she could get out a tentative "But, Mother…" Father, home in time to throw her a lifeline. She leaped up, ignoring Grete's clipped sigh. "Papa! We're in here; come and join us."

Karl Ackermann strode in, dripping snow all over the silk-threaded carpet, waving aside the maids fluttering in his wake. "*Schatzi*, you are a sight for tired eyes. Your poor papa has worked his fingers to the bone today."

Inge laughed as he stripped off thick astrakhan gloves to reveal fingers as plump and pink as sausages. Whatever her father's suite of factories did, they did it without Papa's hands getting dirty.

A kiss on the forehead for her, another brushed across his wife's limply extended hand; a glance at Liesl that lingered a little too long. "So, are you girls ready for your treat?"

Grete sniffed. "I was just explaining to Inge that I see no need for her to stay out overnight."

Karl's smile barely reached his lips. "Nonsense." He shrugged off his coat, ignoring the maid who stumbled as she caught its weight. "If Gruppenführer Hüber is kind enough to extend his hospitality to his daughter's dearest friend, who are we to refuse?" A flick of his fingers and his wife was silenced. "Your father has been very generous to my business, Fräulein Hüber. Please thank him most kindly for me."

Grete's face flushed a blotched scarlet as Karl lifted Liesl's manicured fingers slowly to his mouth and kept them there. The room grew silent.

Inge shifted from foot to foot. She ventured a smile at her mother but was met with a look of fury that immediately dissolved any sympathy. No wonder her father was such a flirt—her mother was such a misery. Still, Liesl could have withdrawn her hand a little quicker, or dropped her eyes at least.

"Liesl, perhaps we should be going?"

A cough from Karl, a giggle from Liesl, a flurry of goodbyes; only Grete stayed silent as the girls left the room.

"Your father is a complete sweetheart. Your mother should try harder to please him, or someone else will. These devoted Fatherland wives with their dull dresses and plain faces and their medals for motherhood haven't a clue what their husbands really want. Make sure you do better with Max."

Inge shook her head at both the words and the accompanying wink. She knew she should call Liesl out on her behavior: every time her friend and her father were in the same room, the atmosphere thickened. She might be an innocent, but she wasn't a fool.

"Now, *Schatzi,* don't frown, don't be cross. You know me: I like to shock. I never mean any harm." Liesl tucked her arm through Inge's and displayed her most charming grin.

What could Inge say that wouldn't sour the evening? Besides, the car was waiting, its engine growling in the ice-sharp air.

Inge hopped over the running board and into the car's cigar-scented warmth. Nothing was going to spoil tonight. The snow flurries had stopped before her shoes could spoil; there would be dancing; there might even be champagne. Liesl would lend her lipstick, and real silk stockings, and a far better dress.

The driver swung the Mercedes down the drive, catching her eye in the mirror as he purred the car through the double gates and into Charlottenburg's leafy streets. He was very attractive in his black coat and polished cap.

Liesl leaned forward and began a giggling conversation. Inge sat back against the butter-soft leather and let weddings and her mother and her friend's shortcomings wash away in the glamour of a gleaming Mercedes and a uniformed smile.

*

Liesl's home, a double-fronted three-story house that mirrored Inge's own, was in its usual state of elegant disarray. Chandeliers blazed on every floor, despite the blackout; a row of Mercedes idled on the drive while their chauffeurs lounged and smoked; laughter and high-pitched voices poured out of the front door, which stood open as if it was summer.

"Perfect timing—they're on their way out. Their plans will be of far more interest than ours." Liesl slid out of the car, her loosened coat falling open, her dress hitched up. Their driver, who had flirted as happily with Liesl as she had with him, stood watching, his eyes on the inch of pink flesh visible above Liesl's stocking tops.

Inge kept her own coat tightly wrapped. The air had crystallized into snow again and fell in soft flakes against fingers and cheeks. The girls shrieked, grabbing each other as they ran up the short flight of steps and into a hall as bright as day. Light enveloped them. It flashed from the low-slung chandeliers, bounced off the narrow-arched mirrors, glimmered from the silver-etched vases that clustered across every surface. They stood for a moment blinking and unnoticed. Guests milled around the checkerboard flooring, finishing brandies, calling for wraps, squealing in mock terror as a gust of wind whirled in. The overheated air prickled at Inge's nose, pungent with perfume. Citrus and musk floated from bared shoulders to mingle with the heavy scent breathed out by a forest of roses.

"Only my mother could demand fresh flowers in winter. Who knows how many greenhouses Father had to empty of useful things like food to get them?"

Anyone who didn't know Liesl would hear a complaint, but Inge knew better. The Hübers might live life at a pitch that left little room to monitor their daughter's doings, but the bond between the three was strong, and Inge envied it.

On cue, Frau Hüber caught sight of them and flew across the floor, a vision in butterfly-printed chiffon. "Jürgens, sweetheart, the girls are here." She swooped first Liesl and then Inge into an Acqua di Parma embrace and then held them both at arm's length. "Darlings, look at you. Liesl, that coat is too perfect and, Inge, your skin: it's smoother than cream. If only your mother would lend you to me—oh, what my dressmaker could do. One afternoon at Romatzki and you would be the toast of Berlin."

Inge reddened, imagining Grete's horrified reaction. Her discomfort went unnoticed.

"We've had the loveliest gathering. Freddie made us all sidecars, just like they drink in Paris. Well, I wonder…do they still drink them in Paris, now that it's occupied? Goodness, what a thought. Anyway, you know everyone?"

A vaguely waving hand did for introductions, not that Inge needed them. The evening-suited and uniformed men were the stalwarts of her father's social circle and known to her since childhood. Friedrich Flick and Wilhelm Zanger, who owned the few factories in Berlin her father didn't, or so he liked to joke. Minister Goebbels with his twisted leg, who never stopped talking and had no sense of humor. Those faces she knew, but not the slender girls draping silver furs around backless dresses. These immaculately polished beauties had little in common with the women Inge had expected to see, the ones who came to all the Christmas and May Day celebrations. They were austere and a little bit frightening, like Frau Goebbels, or tall and athletic and sporting the dirndl dresses and high-crowned braids that were Grete's idea of perfection.

"These parties, always such a mix. Not your mother's thing at all, I'm sure." Frau Hüber moved seamlessly between the girls and her guests, shooing them to the waiting cars as Inge craned for a closer look. "Now, there is a stack of canapés left if you want them, or Cook will make you some supper, unless you have dinner plans of your own, of course? And you are going to the Kaiserhof, to the Schäfer boy's leaving dance? How lovely. We will be at the Adlon, a late one no doubt, so don't wait up. You have Anders to drive you?" A barrage of questions, but no care for the answers. As Liesl had remarked more than once (and sometimes, to Inge's surprise, rather sadly), Christa Hüber had treated her only child more as a sister than a daughter from the moment Liesl could mix a passable martini. "Goodbyes now, everyone, or we'll be late. Blackout driving is such a bore."

Farewells were breezed through, car doors slammed, tires crunched across gravel; the house sat suddenly silent.

"Well, that's done. They won't be back till dawn." Liesl's voice was curiously flat, but she rallied before Inge could comment. "Are you hungry? No? Good."

Even if Inge had been, there was no point in saying anything; Liesl was already halfway up the stairs.

"We don't have much time, so I've laid some things out. Try on whatever you want, but I think the plum silk would work best for the Kaiserhof: the pearl trim means you won't need a necklace. And then the blue crepe. It's a day dress and a little plain, but that's not a bad thing. The black suede wedges would work for both. What are we going to do with your hair? There's no time to curl it, so maybe a half-roll would do best."

"Liesl, slow down. Why do I need two dresses?" Inge ran after her into the bedroom and came to an abrupt halt. The room looked like a pack of puppies had rampaged through it. Dresses puddled across the bed, there were shoes scattered all over the carpet, and hairclips and earrings glittered across every surface like rhinestone confetti.

"What?" Liesl followed her gaze. "I had to try out all the different combinations. The maids will deal with it—"

Inge cut in before she could start rattling again. "Why do I need two dresses, Liesl? We're only going to one dance." Liesl's grin was not reassuring. "What are you up to?"

"Giving you a little fun. Here, try this on and I'll explain." Liesl plucked a dress from the pile and threw it to Inge, waiting while she shucked off her thick wool skirt and jumper. "Dear Lord, your underwear. Promise me there'll be less fabric for Max to wade through on his wedding night."

Inge ignored her, distracted by the swish of soft pleats falling around her hips.

"That's perfect; you should keep it. There's a coat somewhere the same color—take that too. That shade of blue turns my hair yellow. Now try on the plum."

The mention of the second dress woke Inge back up. "Not till you tell me what's going on. You can't change our plans now, Liesl. I have to go to the Schäfers' party: Mother will interrogate me on every detail."

"And you'll be able to tell her whatever she wants to hear. We're going to the party—who said we weren't? It's only that, once you've memorized everything and we've made sure to be seen, we'll go on. To Hella's Ballhaus."

"You can't be serious!" Inge let the plum dress fall. Even she had heard of Hella's: Eric and Gunther had been there, although they swore her to secrecy when she heard them discussing it.

"Why not? It's all arranged. We take the second dresses with us, mingle for a bit and then change in the restroom. No one will notice—they'll be too busy emptying Herr Schäfer's pockets at the bar."

"But… Hella's? They play jazz. Swing. You don't know what sort of people will be there."

Liesl grinned. "Which is precisely the point! Look at you, shivering and pretending to be shocked. You can't fool me with your wide eyes—I've heard you complain about how stuffy it is at the Kaiserhof. Do you really want to spend your whole night dancing poker-stiff waltzes with men twice your age? Don't you get enough of that now? Don't give me that look. In two months, you'll be married, and all this will be done. No more sleepovers, no more sneaking off for ice cream in the park. Max will demand all your attention and then you'll be buried in babies. This could be our last chance for an adventure. Don't you want that?" Liesl's hands were on her hips. Inge had no idea how to answer.

All of this, finished? How could that be? And buried in babies? That wasn't the plan. Except it was. Inge had been so busy thinking of marriage as an escape, she'd given no thought to what it actually entailed. She looked at her reflection. The blue dress was very pretty. She flicked out the skirt and tried to imagine herself dancing. She didn't know the steps; she barely knew the music: it had been banned before she had time to take notice.

"Even if I agreed, how could we do it? Get from one place to the other, I mean. We can't go wandering about in the blackout—it's dangerous."

"We won't need to. Anders will take us to the Kaiserhof, wait while we do our bit, and then take us to Hella's. It's a hop away, no distance." Liesl paused. "He won't be wearing his uniform. He'll be coming in too." So there was more to this than a friends' final fling; Inge should have guessed this was all about Liesl. Some things never changed, no matter how prettily they were packaged.

"You've done this before, of course you have, and with him."

If Liesel heard the disappointment in Inge's voice, she ignored it. "How else can we be alone? Father would kill him if he knew. But you matter more than Anders: we can make him stay in the car if you want." Liesl's batting eyes were so ridiculous, Inge couldn't help but laugh. "That's better. It will be fun, I promise. And we won't get caught, I promise that too."

Inge shook her head, but they both knew she was beaten.

"You'd promise me anything to get your own way. Stop talking and let me try on the other dress." She was only surprised the servants didn't come running at Liesl's ridiculous shriek.

*

Relax. An impossible instruction, but Liesl kept repeating it. That and *talk to as many people as possible, get noticed.* As if she needed to invite attention. The plum-colored silk was too striking, Liesl too loud. The newly called-up boys swarmed like monkeys; their girlfriends joined ranks and grew ominously quiet. *Calm down.* More unwanted advice as Liesl swapped encouragement for clipped tones and pulling hands.

Dresses off, dresses on and into the waiting car, Liesl determinedly deaf to Inge's chafing. "The party has spilled into half a dozen rooms; everyone will assume we're somewhere else. And no one will care enough to check."

The car crawled through the blind streets and pulled to a halt in front of a courtyard edged by a straggling garden. Inge could barely see the club's doorway for the milling crowd.

"We have to line up?"

Someone laughed; someone else muttered about rich kids slumming it. Inge shrank into her coat and longed for her little-girl bedroom.

When they eventually made it inside, there was no cloakroom, no coat check, no circling waiters. The walls were half covered in dingy paneling and half painted in a curious deep pink decorated with silver streamers that shimmied with the dancers. The dimly lit dance floor was a heaving mass of whirling skirts and blurring feet. It set Inge dizzy, desperate for air.

"Breathe. Give it a chance." Liesl's hand dropped on her shoulder, steadying her this time. Inge closed her eyes, blanked out the bodies. "Listen to it." She didn't need to. She felt it. The music, creeping up through her toes and into her legs, pushing under her skin, bubbling through her blood till she brimmed with it. "Don't you love it?"

Inge opened her eyes, her body not dizzy but fizzing.

"What if the police come? Surely this is forbidden." She knew it was; now she knew why. There was nothing ordered here, nothing that answered to rules and measures. This music didn't wait for people to take notice—it grabbed its listeners by the throat.

"There are spotters outside. One sight of a uniform and this becomes the most traditional club in town. Come and dance. Don't say you can't. Follow my lead. It's easy."

It wasn't. There were too many hops and twirls and unexpected kicks to make it easy, but Inge started to get it. When Liesl told her to stop thinking and loosen her hips, she got it even more.

"You're a natural."

Her hair had shaken out its pins, she was sweating and gulping ice-cold beer like a workman. She didn't care. No one cared.

"There's no waiting to be asked. It's so much simpler." There were groups on the dance floor, couples, even people dancing alone and perfectly happy. The whole thing forming and re-forming in a twisting kaleidoscope. "Though some people still do it the old-fashioned way. Like him. He's been watching you for the past hour." Liesl nudged Inge's attention toward a brown-haired boy sitting quietly at one of the long trestle tables. Dark trousers, white shirt, loosened black tie. Nothing out of the ordinary, nothing to mark him as any different from the other boys milling around, sharing their cigarettes, offering toasts. Except the way he stared at her, as though he was learning every detail.

"He's gorgeous, Inge. Don't just stand there all frozen. Smile, or wave. Or go over." Only Liesl could be so cavalier.

"Are you mad? He could be anyone. Besides, even if I wanted to, which I don't, I'm about to be married."

"Which is all the more reason. Max isn't here, Inge. No one is. You don't have to be you."

Liesl was on her feet, pulling Anders away from his drink. "We're going to dance. Let's see what lover boy does."

"Liesl, no." But she was already swallowed up. Inge twisted in her chair, fiddled with her glass. He wouldn't come over. If he did, she didn't need to speak . . .

"You dance like you were born to it."

"It's the first time I've done it." She meant to say something dismissive, not give him this opportunity he immediately seized.

"Then it mustn't be the last. Will you?" His hand was out, almost touching hers. There were stains on his fingers, inky-blue splotches. A clerk of some sort, no one she was used to.

She hesitated, but the music cutting across the floor tugged at her feet.

"'In the Mood.'" He said it in English, a little clumsily, but that he used the language was unexpected, intriguing. "Everyone ought to dance to it, at least once in their life." His smile was so sweet and the music so stirring, it was hard to refuse.

Inge let him take her fingertips and weave her through the dance floor's crush. She picked up the rhythm at the same time he caught it. He was good. Quick and light. He didn't spin her too fast or catch her in too close, not until she was ready.

A glance around and there was Liesl, winking and laughing. The music grew faster. Inge stopped looking. She let the dance floor shrink to his clever feet and confident hands and those eyes that crinkled when he saw she was laughing. Spin after spin, hair undone and flying, and then the lights softened, the music shifted and mellowed. The move into his arms just another dance step.

"'Mondschein Serenade.'" His voice a whisper, warm on her cheek. The music lapped, moving them closer. Their feet slowed, shrank their little circle even farther. "Felix. Felix Thalberg. In case you were wondering."

She nodded, lifted her head from where it had dropped onto his shoulder. She started to speak, but somehow his mouth was on hers and whatever it was she meant to say flew away in the press of his lips. When he let her mouth go, she pulled him back to her.

"Inge! Where are you?" *Why was Liesl's voice so loud?* "We need to leave, right now!"

Somehow, without her noticing, the music had stopped, the lights had come up.

"What is it?" Felix surfaced, bleary-eyed. People were darting about, grabbing coats, calling for friends.

"You have to move. There's an air raid. There's no shelter here." A girl jostling past.

Inge could see Liesl on the stairs, scanning the floor. She needed to move, but her body was liquid.

"Come with me." Felix was suddenly all quickness, his eyes wide and alert. "I know a place a street away."

"No. I have to go. I can't get caught here."

His grip was too tight. "What do you mean? One shelter is as good as any other."

She shook her head, untangled her hands; she really should be running.

"Well, if you won't come, at least tell me your name. Promise me I'll see you again."

What to say? She shouldn't be here. She shouldn't be doing this. What if word got back to Max, to her father? She didn't know this boy, didn't know who he knew. She really should be running, but his eyes were so hopeful, and she could still taste his lips. A second's hesitation and then a name came tumbling.

"Hannah."

He waited.

"Hannah Hüber." A nonsense-sounding name, but he would hardly come looking.

"Meet me then, Hannah Hüber. On Saturday. I'll be at the Tiergarten at three. At the café by the Neuen See."

Liesl had seen her; she was coming over. There was no time for this. Inge nodded and gasped as his mouth swooped once more onto hers. She pulled away reluctantly and ran.

"Hurry up, for goodness' sake. We have to get back to the Kaiserhof before their shelter closes. If we aren't seen in there, we'll be in serious trouble."

Liesl's panic pushed her up the stairs, into the waiting car and a too-fast, too-silent journey, twisting back into their gowns as Anders leered through the mirror.

They tumbled back into the Kaiserhof just in time: the hotel's cavernous, elegant shelter was still open. There was studied boredom, there was calm; there were waiters on hand with endless champagne. She was safe.

CHAPTER THREE

December 1941, Berlin

She wouldn't come, Felix was certain. He'd raced to the shelter on Wednesday night bubbling with the thought of her and now Saturday inched closer and his hopes had all unraveled. He'd barely slept. He'd botched his work. The only thing he could hold in his head was Hannah. That line, woven into so many films and books, he'd always thought it was meaningless: *I've never met anyone like her.* Well, this time it was true. Hannah Hüber was no everyday girl. She might dance as well as any girl in the Ballhaus, but she didn't fit there. Her hesitation at his ink-stained fingers, her pause before she surrendered her name. Everything about her placed Hannah a step away from the factory girls and typists he usually spun across the dance floor. Even the dress she wore: it slid around her like water. Felix knew next to nothing about clothes, but he could tell when they weren't made over or mended. The material's blue shimmer gave her the air of an ice queen. And the scent of her when the music dropped her into his arms. "My hair doesn't even smell clean, never mind look it. This stuff won't rinse." Kerstin's continual complaint as her frizzy mane turned to straw from the hard soap that was all anyone had to tackle skin and hair and clothes.

Everyone in Berlin was dried-out and dusty, but not Hannah. Her blond curls fell against his shoulder in a tumble of apple blossom; her wrists and neck breathed out violets; her mouth was softer than butter. *Perhaps she was a tailor's daughter?* Four o'clock in

the morning and the thought jumped him half out of bed. Tailors
had skills they could barter, and they must need all sorts of soaps
and lotions in their line of work. Her smell, her beautiful clothes...
yes, that was it: she was a tailor's daughter. It made perfect sense.

Felix burrowed back under the blankets as the cold bit, pulling
the evidence around him. She'd been desperate to run when the
sirens had sounded, which was understandable, but equally desperate to avoid a local shelter. Perhaps she lived in Mitte itself then,
somewhere close by the Ballhaus. He didn't know Mitte well, apart
from his forays to Hella's, but he knew it was an area where lots
of Jewish tailors lived, where they had been moved to once other
neighborhoods closed their doors.

More and more pieces fell into place. She must have a strict father
and a short enough journey to get safely home before questions were
asked. No good girl could risk getting caught near Hella's. And as
for a Jewish girl, which Hannah the tailor's daughter from Mitte
must surely be, well, she would have more to fear than most if she
was caught in the wrong shelter or out on the streets in the blackout.

He clutched his pillow as Hannah's life filled out. Perhaps she
was an only daughter, or an only child like him. That would account
for her reticence: she lived a sheltered life. She said it herself: she'd
never danced like that before. What if Wednesday was her first
time at Hella's? The sheer wonderful luck of it: her first visit to
Hella's and he had been there. He hadn't even planned to go on
Wednesday; he rarely went midweek. In the end, he'd given in to
his workmates' pushing because he couldn't bear another closed-in
evening with Arno. But he was there, and so was she, and that must
mean something, surely?

"I wasn't supposed to be at the picnic at all. I was meant to be at
home, keeping company with Aunt Trude. But the day was pretty,
and she was cranky, so I went where I shouldn't." His mother's tale
about meeting his father, trotted out at birthdays and anniversaries.
"And there he was and there was I: right where I was meant to be."

The story made him blush when he was little and made him sad now, but Kerstin still smiled when she told it. "Me for him and him for me and no one else ever needed." Which nothing changed and never could. There was beauty in its certainty. *There he was and there was I.* There was magic in that.

Felix got out of bed and pushed the curtain aside, just a fraction, just enough to see that the clouds had lifted and there were stars dusting the sky. Maybe, with a little more luck and a little more wishing, she might actually come.

I won't go. From the moment she jumped into the car, until they were safe inside the shelter, Inge repeated her promise. She wouldn't meet him and she wouldn't tell Liesl he'd asked. Liesl would tell Anders—she was enamored enough to want the whole world to be in love—and what Anders might do with that information was anyone's guess. Inge had seen him, watching them, storing it all up: that wasn't a boy who planned to stay long as a driver.

No meeting, no telling and no thinking about Felix Thalberg in any way at all. Not about the curve of his lip and the way he bit it when he bounced her back toward him in that first spin. Or about the way those lips pressed against hers, first soft and then so certain. And definitely no thinking about the way that he held her, as if she was breakable and unbreakable all at once. Felix Thalberg had no place in her head. Who was he anyway, besides some good-looking boy with inky fingers and clever feet? And who met boys in dance halls and thought that held any meaning? Girls with no pedigree and no prospects; girls who thought a clerk from Mitte was a catch. "It was nonsense. He was a nobody, taking advantage. There's nothing to say. I'd rather forget it." Any other night and Liesl might not have been so easily cheated, but the dash to the Kaiserhof had unnerved her too: she could pretend the whole thing was a lark, but her knotted fingers said otherwise.

No more Felix Thalberg and no more Liesl, not for a while at least. Liesl was teetering toward disaster—Mother was right. Inge had had an adventure; she'd had a lucky escape. The best thing now was to focus on the wedding.

She managed it on Thursday. She managed an interest in the merits of orange blossom over rosebuds and lace gloves over satin that relaxed Mother's mouth almost to a smile. She managed it again on Friday. Not one complaint about aching shoulders and sticking pins as the dressmaker fussed and commented on Inge's constant yawns and drooping eyelids. Nerves were blamed and Inge agreed: what else could account for these wide-awake nights? Not Felix Thalberg.

Every time his face swooped into her muddled thoughts, she changed its contours to Max. She was getting good at that. As the dressmaker said, all brides grew nervy and restless as their wedding approached: whoever heard of a dress being let out? It was merely the strain of the wedding that kept her awake on Friday night, that had her still counting the hours away as dawn approached. Saturday's coming meant that in exactly one month's time she would become Frau Eichel. There was to be a celebratory dinner, the last time the families would meet before she swapped one set of parents for two. What bride would sleep before that?

She wouldn't go to the Tiergarten. Even if, by some unimaginable chance, she wavered, Saturday would be far too busy with menus and flower arrangements and rearranging the rooms. Except it wasn't. Mother had the whole event running like clockwork before Inge was even up. By noon, the house was polished and perfumed, the kitchen instructed and the servants set. Nobody needed her. Father disappeared to his club; Mother announced she would spend the afternoon resting and urged Inge to do the same. Grete had picked out her dress, given instructions to Hannah on how her hair should be arranged. There was nothing to do and it was so hard to settle, especially when the skies were bright blue, and it hadn't snowed since Thursday.

Inge pushed open the window so she could better see the little knots of people bustling past the ice-frosted trees on Platanenallee. A little air would be nice, and there were so many pretty parks in Charlottenburg, why venture farther? A walk then, no need to disturb Mother; it was not as if she would be gone for long.

Inge put on Liesl's blue coat; the color really did suit her. She added a navy velvet hat—not the most practical choice, but the soft material flattered her thick eyelashes and turned her skin ivory. A short walk through Charlottenburg. No need to go as far as the Tiergarten or the little café by the lake, although she knew the route and the timing was right. But she wouldn't go there; she was certain of that.

The unexpected sunshine had bundled Berlin into its coats and filled the public gardens. The café was fogged with steam, musty with damp wool. There wasn't a seat to be had. Felix clutched his tray and pushed his way out onto the empty veranda, his eyes watering as the temperature shifted. An hour until sunset and the wind was picking up, blowing the lake's gray surface into ripples and whirls. It was too cold to sit outside, but he didn't know what else to do: what if the crowded café unnerved her?

He put the steaming mugs onto a table and pushed his hands deep into his greatcoat pockets, checking that her present was safe. The ersatz coffee was thin and bitter and there was no point in asking for milk or sugar—not that any girl in Berlin would expect to be offered those. Behind him, the café door opened and immediately slammed shut in a burst of complaints. He must look quite mad, standing outside with his two mugs, all alone. Perhaps buying two was tempting fate, a sign of overconfidence. Not that he felt confident. He felt foolish, and cold.

"Felix. I'm late. I'm sorry." She had the softest voice. He'd barely heard her say a handful of words at Hella's and not any of those his name. How quickly the cold stopped mattering. The magic had worked: she was here, hovering on the veranda steps like a frightened fawn.

"You look lovely."

Her mouth pinched. He should have started simpler, opened with hello. It was the color of her coat that caught him off guard, the same rich shade as Wednesday's dress. Prussian blue: he knew it from the printmakers. She looked like a duchess from an old painting. Now, instead of moving toward his arms as he had dreamed, she was frowning, shifting from foot to foot and staring at his uniform. Perhaps she thought he was a soldier.

"I'm in the *Flakhelfer*. I have to be on air-raid duty at the Zoo Tower in a while. Not yet." Still watching, still silent. One more wrong word and she would bolt like a rabbit. "I bought coffee. It's warm—at least I hope it is."

That brought her closer. Her nose and cheeks were tipped with pink and her eyes, which he should surely have remembered were as vivid as her coat, shone diamond-bright in the cold. She took a mouthful of coffee, spluttered and put the mug back down; it must have been hotter than he thought.

The heavy door flew open and slammed shut again with a crack that made her jump and edge back toward the steps.

"This was a mistake. I shouldn't have come."

"No, wait. I have something for you." She paused long enough for him to pull the paper from his pocket and smooth it out so she could see the figure dancing across the page.

"Is that me?" She took the drawing, turned it toward the light. "You drew this?"

He nodded. There it was: that perfect smile. He could have somersaulted over the railing.

"It's so clever." She traced a gloved finger over the swinging hair and spinning skirt, the closed eyes and open mouth. "I look so alive, like I'm still moving. I look beautiful."

"Because you are." This time, her mouth widened. "Do you want to go for a walk?" The steps to the lakeside had begun to ice over. He put out his hand. There was a pause, just long enough for him to bite his lip, and then she threaded her fingers through his.

"Should I expect you to spin me around?"

"I could." He grinned and bent in a bow. "I could dance you around the lake if you like."

"A walk will do." But she was still smiling, and her fingers were woven tight through his.

They walked a little way in silence, trying to find their rhythm, but the pebbled shore was slippery, more treacherous than it looked. After two or three stumbles, she shook her head.

"Over there. Let's sit for a minute. If it's not too cold." There was a bench tucked into the shadow of the fir trees, a picnic spot on sunnier days. They picked their way over, sat down. She shivered and let him pull her into his shoulder. "Who are you, Felix Thalberg, beyond a dancer? Are you an artist?" She was so close, he could smell spring in her hair again.

"I wish I was. But no, I'm a printer's apprentice."

She was waiting. He didn't know what else to say. He was so tired of labels and all that they carried. He didn't want to swap stories and share miseries, not yet. Right now, with her body so close and her face so lovely, he wanted to forget the weight of their lives and be Felix and Hannah and no more than that.

He tried for a less wistful tone. "Art school didn't happen, but it's no worse for me than plenty of others. The war's taken a lot from everyone. You must have had your own share."

Was that a frown? He knew he should ask its reason, but her mouth was barely a breath away and he was done with talking. He moved his shoulder and brought her upturned face a little closer. She didn't pull back. She reached up her hand, cupped first his cheek and then the back of his neck. His lips were on hers; hers were answering. The kiss enveloped him, and hardships and Arno and the whole muddle of life melted away quicker than snowflakes.

He had no idea how long he was lost in her. The sky was dark, and the air was freezing, and her hat and their gloves were lost by the time they surfaced, gulping for air. All the tightly wrapped layers between them and yet he felt he'd learned every inch of her. His head was stuffed with snatches of poetry and declarations from movies that would make him sound insane if they tumbled out. And promises it was too soon to make, but how he ached to be making them.

"We must meet properly. Do this right." She wasn't looking at him now; she wasn't soft curves anymore. "What's the matter?" Her mouth was open, but not for him.

"I have to go."

No. Not again. Not another flight—that would take his heart this time.

"What is it?"

She was rigid, peering up through the trees at the café's partially obscured veranda. Felix could see a man, his body glimpsed in snatches as if he was pacing. He was tall, dressed in a long black coat and a cap with a peak. He turned suddenly and the light still spilling from the café window caught across the cap's silver facings. An SS officer. No wonder she was afraid; anyone would be afraid.

"It's all right. He's not looking for us—why would he be?" But she was up, poised behind the bench, her body pulled away so fast he could still feel the weight of her. "Hannah, please."

Her eyes were blank, not even a last glance for him. One more look at the café and she was gone, running through the trees as if hounds chased after her.

"Hannah!" His voice cracked like a gunshot in the frosty air.

The officer turned toward the cry. What on earth had made her run? Was she in some kind of trouble? *Was there a star on her coat?* Now he thought about it, he couldn't remember. It could have been hidden by her scarf. Or maybe she was like him and hadn't been forced into one yet, or she was brave or foolish enough to ignore the rules. Whatever it was, it didn't matter; all that mattered was getting her back.

He cried out again. "Hannah!" Shouting like that with an SS man so close was dangerous and attention-attracting, but Felix didn't care.

There was no answer; there was not one blue glimpse of her—with the lamps all turned off, the trees had closed up solid as a wall.

He called out one last time, his voice breaking. The SS officer stopped. He stared out toward the lake and then he turned, pushed open the door and disappeared into the café. A few seconds later, the blinds rolled shut. Whoever the man was looking for, it wasn't his Hannah. *His Hannah.*

Felix slumped forward, head sinking into his hands. She was his—every kiss had told him so and now she was gone again, and he had no more to go on than the first time she ran. He sat until the sky was sullen and swollen with clouds and the lightless café swallowed up. He was late for duty. He would be reprimanded or punished if weasel-faced Schneider was in charge.

What did it matter? He had let her go again. Hannah had come to him and he had let her go. Whatever stupid, pointless punishment Schneider devised, Felix deserved it.

Six o'clock. Far later than it was meant to be. Inge inched open the gate. The house crouched; blackout-ready. She stumbled around the driveway's dark edges, the scramble home still clinging in a heart-hammering chaos of canceled trams and wrong directions. A few minutes' luck was all she needed. An empty hallway, an empty staircase, the quiet of her bedroom and the chance to craft some story that might make sense of what had happened. Not what she had done with Felix: that made perfect sense. Thoughts of him and her and the sensations still holding her body were enough to make this evening's dinner impossible. Not Felix then, but this fear that had a name she couldn't face. The prowling man. It couldn't have been him, it couldn't, and yet the coat, the tall pacing figure . . . the way it moved. It wouldn't let her go.

She sidled up to the door, her breath ragged. It wasn't locked; maybe that was a good omen. Inge leaned into the glossy surface, craning for voices or footsteps on the other side, but the thick wood refused to give the house up. Her luck would hold; it had to. One push, a sprint and then safe . . .

"Fräulein Ackermann, please. You have to wait here. Your mother was most insistent." Skinny little Hannah, standing sentry in the too-bright hallway, a red welt engraved across her cheek.

Inge wavered. The maid would need to move to fetch Grete; the stairs were still in reach. Inge took a step forward, but Hannah held her position and reached into the pocket of her apron. A small bell. Grete was ready for her: Inge should have guessed. One sharp shake and there she was.

"An explanation, quickly." One look at her daughter, however, and the imperious tone collapsed. "What have you done? Where is your hat? Why do you look so . . ." Grete pounced before Inge could conjure up any answers. She wrenched Inge's arm behind her back and half flung her toward the staircase. "Get up there, out of sight. Now."

She's afraid. The thought was so bizarre, Inge froze.

"Inge, my dear. What has happened? Are you hurt? Have you been attacked?" A second figure appeared in the doorway, his black uniform starkly outlined by the pale lemon paint. Max.

All her fears were real. The drawing hidden in the bottom of her bag lit up in her mind like a searchlight.

Max's hand replaced Grete's as Inge's knees buckled. "My poor girl. Come and sit by the fire. A brandy, I think, for whatever shock this is. And for you too, Frau Ackermann." Steering her to a chair, plumping cushions, pouring brandy.

Inge swallowed the liquid in a single gulp, only remembering to cough when his eyebrows arched. Was that a smile?

"Another one perhaps? You barely tasted that." He was playing with her, as if he knew all about her and Liesl's tasting games. She had a sudden urge to call his bluff, but the thought of that was unimaginable.

She put the glass down; it rattled against the polished table.

Max pulled his chair closer. "Come now, you are shaking. And still so cold." Her hand was suddenly inside his. The afternoon's echoes were so strong and her skin so alive, she jumped.

"Don't be nervous. I'm sure there's no need." He cupped her fingers, cradling them. This was not the measured touch she was used to, the quick transfer of gloved hand to uniformed elbow. This was intimate, sure of itself. His finger traced her palm. She jumped again and tried to pull away. If Max held her any longer, Felix's touch would vanish.

"Look at me, Inge." A finger under her chin, tipping it up. Grete gasped, but Max ignored her. A quick glance and turn away was all she intended, but he wouldn't let her head drop. "Look at me."

Blue eyes flecked with hazel, high cheekbones, narrow mouth. A beautiful face. Felix had a beautiful face too, but his was open: he lived in his eyes, in his smile. This one was far more careful, far more watchful; a more complicated thing all together. For the first time, she lingered on the shape of Max's lips and wondered at his kisses. He smiled.

"Good. Now, tell me: what happened this afternoon?" His voice was so gentle, it was almost hypnotic. But he couldn't know, or he would have challenged her.

She spoke quickly, leaving no room for questions. "I went to the Tiergarten. To meet Liesl. I couldn't find her, and I panicked.

It got dark and I got lost. I'm sorry." If she could hear the lie, so could he, but he stroked her cheek and smiled again.

"A simple mistake then. Nothing to be concerned about." He dropped his fingers from her face. "I was there myself today, at the café by the lake. I had to remind them about the blackout, which was quite an irritation." It was him on the veranda; of course it was. Inge swallowed hard to stop her confession tumbling.

"You are very pale." His other hand was still holding hers, the fingers weaving. "That's enough of this for today. You should rest a little. But, Inge? Will you make me a promise?" He waited; she nodded. It didn't matter what he wanted, as long as he released her. "No more wandering. There are too many undesirables still to be dealt with and you are so trusting. I will speak to my staff, arrange a companion. Whatever it is you want to do, let me know and you can do it. Are we agreed? Good girl. Go and rest now. Tonight is, after all, a celebration." He let her hand fall.

Inge rose; Grete followed. Max nodded them both away.

"Hannah, draw Fräulein Ackermann a bath and lay her dress out." Grete's voice hardened the moment the door swished shut. "Get up there now. Move." She pulled Inge stumbling behind her and shoved her into the bedroom. "You little tramp. Did you think Max was fooled? Did you think I was?" The blow caught Inge around the back of the head, where it wouldn't leave a mark. "Who is he? Some driver like Liesl chases? Or some little nobody you met when you *weren't* at the Kaiserhof? Did you honestly believe no one noticed your vanishing act that night?"

"How did you know?"

"How do you think? Max."

Inge sank onto the bed as Grete's face twisted.

"What? You thought it was a coincidence he decided to drop in, without warning, hours before tonight's dinner is due to start? He mentioned Wednesday's dance, oh so casually. How—or so the gossip, which he would, of course, never pay attention to, said—that you were there one minute and gone the next and then suddenly popped up in the shelter like a genie from a bottle. He was most *amused*. He kept telling me that. And then he asked where you were today and knew I had no hope of answering."

"I don't understand."

"Then you truly are stupid." Grete sat down so quickly it was as if she had deflated. "This is not my fault. I have done everything to keep you safe. This is all your father's doing, and Liesl's. Well, you are done with her. Max watches you, Inge. He knows where you are, what you are doing. He is in the SS; you are going to be his wife. What did you expect? Do I have to spell out everything? Stop crying, I won't have it. All the honor he brings this family and you risk it, for what? Some seedy little fumble in a park? Do you want to ruin us all? Do you want to see your father's business destroyed? Well, I hope your boy is worth it. I hope he comes from a good family and can give you a good life. What do you think: can he?"

Inge wanted to say yes. She wanted to tell Grete about Felix, about his crinkling eyes and the way he made lava bubble in her veins when he touched her. About the way she thought she could love him, if it was only them, a boy and a girl meeting and no businesses or family standing to care about. That was the truth. She wanted to say that a humble clerk from Mitte was worth far more than factories and money and that he would keep her happy and safe whatever was coming. Except maybe that wasn't the truth. Perhaps there was more to Felix Thalberg than his heart-stopping kisses and his artist's eye, but, if so much truly hung on her marriage, was she really brave enough to find out?

The moment passed. Inge said nothing; Grete finally unbent.

"Then perhaps we are safe. Max has his suspicions, but whatever he went to the Tiergarten to see, he didn't. No more needs to be said than that. He's older—he will chalk these last few days up to a young girl's nonsense, provided you snap back into line. No more

Liesl, and no more going out alone until you are married and Max's problem. Now get ready. I expect perfection tonight, nothing less."

Grete slammed out.

Inge's first instinct was to pull the drawing from her bag, to pull Felix back around her, but Hannah was watching, and Hannah was Grete's. Instead, she moved blankly through the next hour. Into the bath, into the flower-sprigged dress. She let Hannah gather her hair in a simple braid; she left her face bare. Everything done, Inge sat on the bed and waited for her summons. The little girl back in her room again.

CHAPTER FOUR

February 1943, Berlin

My Dearest Hannah,
Have I already told you they are my favorite words?
My dearest Hannah, it's your Felix. What are you doing
right now? Are you staring out of the window, same as me,
watching the snow falling? This winter is never-ending. You
would laugh if you saw the way I come to work, so bundled
up I would bounce if I tripped. You must be the same,
although it's hard to imagine your blue coat all wrapped
over with blankets and your curls hidden under scarves like
a babushka. You would still look beautiful, I'm sure of that.
So what can I tell you that you won't already know?
All anyone talks about beyond the weather is the shortages,
and you don't need to hear about those. I'm so bored with
the moaning. I've decided I'm going to choose one thing a
day and remember it as hard as I can for five minutes and
then that's it, no more thinking about all the things we don't
have. Today I picked oranges. I don't know why, but today
I miss oranges. And I miss you, always you.
I wish I knew you were safe. It's so hard to find out any-
thing; no one trusts anyone else and nothing is what it seems.
The "relocations"—I daren't call them anything else—have
increased, although everyone pretends they haven't. There are so
many apartments suddenly available, what else can it be? No
one does anything or says anything: it's as if we're all paralyzed.

I see them sometimes, Hannah, when I'm on the early shift: the quiet lines shuffling by. The elderly and the ill; all clutching their precious cases. How do they choose what to take? How does a life get so reduced? They don't look up. What would we do if they did? Smile, or say goodbye? The guards would be on us in seconds. Amon (from the typesetting room, I've mentioned him before) says there's nothing to worry about. He says the old and the sick are off to some new Jewish facility in a place called Theresienstadt, where there are hospitals and decent houses. Perhaps he's right—that's what we print anyway. I don't know. There are rumors; you must have heard them. Shootings and round-ups, and piles of cases left at the Anhalter station that never follow their owners. Who knows what the truth is; who would dare ask? Please God you are safe…

"Thalberg, for goodness' sake. Every time I turn my back, you're at it again. Stop scribbling. Do you want to go and explain to Van Beck why there's no ink and no paper left for his proper writers to use? No, I thought not. Your break is done; get back to work."

Wilhelm, the permanently miserable printing-floor supervisor, made a grab for the letter, but Felix was too quick. He shoved it in his pocket, trusting the ink was dry, and headed back to his section, Wilhelm's daily dose of insults chasing after. Felix had stored up plenty of responses far cleverer than anything the plodding supervisor could invent, but there was nothing to be gained by using them. As Wilhelm told him every day, "There are plenty ready to snap up your post."

With his twenty-first birthday approaching, Felix already lived under the shadow of an imminent call-up. Now they were taking boys as young as seventeen—whose blood the Fatherland presumably valued more than his, even if it was just to spill it—he was even more vulnerable to a belligerent dismissal. Threats and insults and too much work was the pattern of his days and nothing to be done about it.

Felix turned back to his desk. In the short time he had been away, the photographs awaiting his attention had spawned across three tables. Row after row of glass plates fixed with negatives that would all need to be painstakingly checked before the etching process could begin. Heaven forbid one of the endless images of Hitler or Goebbels or another flag-waving rally should reach the readers anything less than pristine.

Felix picked up his magnifying glass and adjusted the lamps so his eyes wouldn't be stinging by the end of the day. Finishing the letter would have to wait. Not that it mattered. Not that this one was going anywhere different from the one before or the one before that. They were all unsent, all folded away into the tin that used to house his toy soldiers and hidden behind the brickwork in the alcove that was now his bedroom.

My Dearest Hannah. He may as well be writing to a ghost. Hannah Hüber had disappeared. She had vanished into the trees in the Tiergarten over a year ago and there had not been a trace of her since.

Felix finished one photograph and moved to the next, his eye so tuned to the patterns of the dots and what would reproduce and what would not, he could sort them like a robot.

Hannah was lost. He blamed Arno. No, he tried not to blame Arno. It didn't work.

"He's missing, Felix! Gone, goodness knows where, and he doesn't have his coat. Which means he doesn't have his star, or his papers."

All Felix had wanted to do that miserable Saturday night was fall into bed and get the last hours of darkness done. A few hours to sleep and escape his misery and then back out to search for Hannah. His shift had been brutal. Schneider had pounced on

Felix's lateness and his snarled apology. When Felix had argued against his punishment, because he needed to fight with someone, Schneider had happily made it worse. Ten hours consigned to the top level of the Zoo Flak Tower, staring at a sky everyone knew would stay empty, until his eyeballs felt like they were coated in ice. Felix could barely see on the long walk back, but Kerstin's tear-filled panic had sent him out again into the silent gardens and alleyways. It took him over an hour to find Arno. His father was curled under a tree, weeping and shivering and long past explaining why he had finally ventured out.

It was another hour before Felix could persuade Arno to trust him and move. By the time he had shushed his sobbing father up the stairs, convinced at every step that Blockwart Fischer would swoop out and snatch them, dawn was breaking.

That night was only the start of it: Arno couldn't be left. First he was terrified, then he was sick. So sick, it was weeks, almost February, before Felix could do more than sprint between the apartment and work and his *Flakhelfer* duties and any pharmacist who could still find him medicine. Thoughts of Hannah never left him, but he was too exhausted to do anything more than long for her. Then Arno was better, but Kerstin was worse. Her shifts on the maternity wards were reduced, her wages cut in half and ration cards stamped with a J swapped for their old ones. She grew frighteningly thin. They were all thin now and struggling with the days. Air raids were coming, or rumors of them were, and even rumors set the sirens wailing, howling across the city like an orchestra of cats. Night after night, everyone was shocked awake, sent stumbling into shelters made acrid with fear and then forced to sit and endure the breath-choking wait for the rumble that could be thunder or engines or the end of it all. Berlin became a city of sleepwalkers.

There were very few babies to be delivered on the hospital wards now—what pregnant woman could stay sane in Berlin through this? Anyone who could go was gone and anyone who was left had no place expecting a hospital's care: nature would do what it did anyway, and the beds were all for the wounded. Kerstin offered to work in any ward that would take her, but there were plenty of nurses not married to Jews to fill up the slots. The Thalbergs' meager pot of money shrank, and Felix added apartment hunting to his daily list, shouting at Arno this time when he whimpered about moving.

When he finally found somewhere, in the run-down tenements at the edge of Wedding, he could have wept as Kerstin praised him and refused to admit how much she hated it. "Four rooms might be squashed into two, but at least there's spare furniture for the fireplace." Sometimes he wondered how she could keep up the act.

It was summer before Felix could turn his dwindling energies back to Hannah. He tried to find her. He haunted Mitte's crammed-in streets so often he was mistaken for a Gestapo spy and narrowly escaped a beating. Even when he explained himself, no one would listen. Everyone was looking for someone; plenty didn't want to be found. "If this girl is hiding, let her hide. What is she to you anyway?" As if he knew the answer to that.

He couldn't find her; he couldn't stop looking. He'd turned to writing letters and wondered if he was starting to go mad.

"Thalberg." He jumped, dropping his magnifying glass. Wilhelm again.

Felix nodded to the plates he had already worked through. He couldn't risk another reprimand. "I am almost done here, Herr Overseer. Most of the pictures are useable."

The older man rubbed at his spectacles. Felix waited for a barbed retort; sat up straighter when it didn't come.

"I'm not here about that. There are men upstairs, asking for you. Do you have your papers?"

Sweat popped up in little beads across Felix's forehead; his hand trembled when he tried to mop them.

"It may be nothing, but there are rumors of... well, I don't know what exactly, but tread carefully when you speak to them." Wilhelm hesitated. "Someone said they are sweeping the factories, looking for all the Jews who've slipped through before."

So it had come at last.

Felix tried to stand, but his legs wouldn't listen. "I have permission. To work here. I'm not a Jew. I am a Mischling second degree. No one has ever asked for me before."

Wilhelm shrugged. There was sympathy in his eyes, but not enough. "Like I said, it may well be nothing. But I wouldn't keep them waiting."

One step and then the next, up the winding stairs to Editor Van Beck's office, refusing to think where the journey might really be heading. In the last corridor, he passed a group of about twenty men, lined up, expressions blank. No one looked at him. Wilhelm left him at the glass doors. Inside, he could see two men waiting: one seated, one standing. Felix had expected uniforms, but both men were dressed in well-cut civilian suits and heavy tweed overcoats. Gestapo. Bile rose in the back of his throat.

As Felix entered, his rubber soles squeaking a fanfare, the seated man glanced up.

"Felix Gerhard Thalberg?"

He nodded, stumbled on a yes and wondered if he should have said *Heil Hitler*. Too late to add it now without sounding guilty.

The man scanned him, assessing his details as if he was one of the photographs piled up in the print room. Light-brown hair, blue-gray eyes, medium build; Felix went through the checklist and wondered if he had passed.

"Papers."

Trying to keep his hand steady, Felix handed over his identity card, which the man barely glanced at, and the *Blut-Zertifikat*, which spelled out his ancestry.

"She didn't divorce him then."

It wasn't a question. Felix stayed silent while the second man, who had the slightly broken look of a boxer, joined his colleague at the desk. They turned the flimsy paper over and inspected the family tree printed on the back, the catalog of everything Felix was and everything he was not.

"Second degree. Not German, as I gather you like to pretend. Your mother shamed you."

Whatever they wanted him to say, he wouldn't say it.

"Well, Felix second degree, your work is done for today. You need to come with us now."

Sweat prickled across his back. He could feel his bowels churning, his bladder burning. This couldn't be right: surely there were rules, procedures to follow. Time to pack a case at least. He tried to think of a question that wouldn't end in a beating, but the seated man spoke first.

"There's just one thing. Your father, Arno: where is he?"

"What do you mean?" The question caught Felix off guard.

"Concentrate, Felix, there's a good boy. It's a simple question. We have your father's name, but no place of work, which makes us wonder what the problem is. I'll ask you again, where is he?"

The quiet lines of the ill and the elderly. Felix swallowed, but no better words came.

"He is at home." Fingers tapped on the table. "He has been sick."

"Since the war started?" The boxer-man laughed; the seated man didn't. "He isn't registered with a hospital. He doesn't seem to be contributing to the community or the country that cares for him. We are struggling here, Felix, to understand exactly what he's been doing. Can you shed any light for us?"

Maybe there was a right answer, but Felix couldn't find it. "He is a good man. A kind one. He has had some difficulties. That is all." Everything out of his mouth making things worse.

"Well, as long as he is good and kind." His interrogator scribbled a note on the clipboard. "Difficulties, you say? Then we had better solve those. You have been a very helpful lad, Felix. Off you go." Dismissed. Added to the end of the silent line, marched out and into the waiting truck while the rest of the building looked the other way. It was all Felix could do not to sob like the child they'd turned him back into.

"Women and children to the right. Men to the left. Papers ready. Keep moving."

Felix clambered from the truck, picking up his pace as the guards funneled them past a line of straining dogs. His group merged with another and another until there wasn't a recognizable face left. "Where are we?"

The man half running at his side frowned. "Levetzowstraße. The synagogue. Or what was the synagogue. Don't you know it?"

Felix was saved from another answer he didn't have by a volley of orders.

"Get in line. Papers ready. No talking."

A moment's milling in a bottleneck outside the heavily guarded door and then they were pushed through into a narrow corridor lined with rows of evenly spaced desks.

"One at a time. Keep moving." Uniformed soldiers waited, pens and rubber stamps and piles of thin cards looped with string laid out neatly in front of them. "Name? Certificate? Put this on. Go through the double doors. Move."

He was processed in less than a minute. Still reeling from the speed of it all, Felix hung the white card stamped with a large green *J* around his neck as directed and let the crowd carry him to the next set of guards. Everyone was hung with a label and marked like a package ready for mailing. One or two of the cards were plain white, but most were stamped like his, with green or yellow, red or pink. Before he could even think what it meant, he was swept through a set of wide square doors into a hall that might once have been spacious but now crawled like an anthill. Galleries rose on three sides of the high-ceilinged room, their wooden balconies still patterned with gilding. There were tiled mosaics on the few patches of the floor still visible. Narrow fluting columns rose up in front of delicately arched windows that should have flooded the building with light, except they were filthy, engrained with dust so thick it acted like shutters.

More people poured in. Felix peered around, looking for somewhere he could sit and regroup, but there wasn't a chair or a piece of furniture to be seen, only straw-filled sacks and closely guarded nests fashioned from blankets. He shifted as more bodies surged in behind him. There was barely room to stand, let alone sit. His heart was fluttering; his teeth beginning to chatter. He didn't know where he was meant to be; he could barely breathe. The stink of unwashed clothes and unwashed bodies and the acrid bite of ammonia rose up like a wall. He twisted around, tripped over an outstretched foot, tried to apologize, gagged and knew he was close to tears again.

"Don't worry. As soon as it gets dark, they'll ship the next lot out. You should be able to bag yourself an inch or two, at least until morning." A man in dark overalls grinned up at him and offered Felix the thinnest cigarette he had ever seen. "Here, take it. I've no idea what kind of leaves we're scraping up now, but at least it smokes the stench out."

Felix grabbed it and took a long drag, not caring that it made him cough till his eyes streamed.

"There you go. You won't be able to smell a thing for an hour or more. Save your life that will. So, you're clearly new—are you alone? We heard it was all factory round-ups in today."

Grateful someone was taking an interest, Felix managed to stop spluttering.

"There were others from my workplace, but I lost them."

"Then come and make some new friends. I'm Efrayim. Sit. Join us."

Efrayim made a space among the red-labeled men on the floor and rattled off a list of names Felix couldn't catch. He introduced himself and accepted another cigarette and a mouthful of slightly brackish water. Now he had time to look, he could see the hall was more ordered than it had first appeared. The largest groups were arranged along one side. Those people were marked in yellow and had cases with them, most of which had been used to build makeshift screens. The majority of the women and children sat on that side. The people wearing red stamps, who were mostly men, were huddled in the center; their groups were smaller, their conversations more intense. He could see a few cards marked with pink, but not many, and even fewer green or plain ones.

"What is all this? The colors and the groupings? And what did you mean *shipping the next lot out*? What is everyone doing here?" A couple of the men closest to him turned and glanced at his card. One spat; both turned their backs. "What did I do?"

"Probably nothing." Efrayim shrugged. "Do you know this place? Have you ever been in a synagogue? No, I thought not. Not practicing then and no doubt you don't work or mix with Jews?"

Felix's lowered head was enough of an answer.

"You don't know anything, and yet you still got snatched like the rest of us. What are you: first degree or second?"

"Second." In this place, the declaration sounded like a boast.

"That explains it. This building used to be one of Berlin's finest synagogues, until the Party seized it. For the last two years, it's been Berlin's finest deportation center. As for the cards, they're easy. It's a classification system so the guards can see what you are and determine where you go next: yellow for Jew, red for communist and Jew, pink for homosexual and Jew. Green must mean mixed blood. I've not seen many of those, but you get the idea: whatever the color, it's always Jew. It's a simple system, like marking cows or sheep. They're nothing if not efficient, Hitler's boys."

The flimsy card pulled at Felix's neck as if it had transmuted to metal. "What do you mean, where I go next? Where will they send me?" His voice was as thin as a mouse; he couldn't tell if Efrayim's was exasperated or worn out.

"I don't know for sure, Felix—no one does. You're young and fit and your diluted blood doesn't seem to threaten them quite as much as our thicker stuff, not yet anyway. So maybe the army, or maybe home, if there's someone to shout for you. As for the rest of us? All I know is people disappear and no one writes home from wherever it is in the Reich that Jews are welcome."

Someone cursed, Efrayim turned away, but Felix sat forward: finally, there was something he knew about and could share, information that might help.

"The old and the sick go to a place called Theresienstadt and get looked after. There's hospitals and good houses there. That's what we were told at work anyway."

The fist flew so fast, he didn't see it coming.

"Mendel, back off! He's a kid, a Mischling. What does he know? He probably thinks Jews are beneath him, same as the rest of Berlin."

"I do not." There was blood pooling in his mouth and one of his teeth felt loose. "I might not be Jewish, but I don't look down on Jews—I know they're no different than anyone else. The girl I love is Jewish."

"Then God help you, Felix my friend, for you'll get no peace there." But Efrayim was smiling and no more fists came his way. "So, you don't class yourself as Jewish, fine, but you don't need to be blind. Theresienstadt: some kind of Jewish paradise? You truly believe that? Think about it: why would the Nazis build such a place? We are vermin to them and no one I know looks kindly on vermin. No, whatever they told you, wherever they send our people, it's not to be looked after. Not how you mean anyway. We disappear without a trace, as if we'd never been." Efrayim broke off.

Across the hall, a baby was crying, and a group of children was playing catch with a hat.

"They want us gone, every last drop of us. Full blood, mixed blood; a body full or a splash so diluted it would take generations to trace it back, it doesn't matter to them. It's still Jewish blood; it's still the wrong sort. They'll work through us all in the end. Maybe someone will come for you and take you back to your charmed life, please God they do. But it will be a reprieve, Felix, not a rescue. Remember that. Know your enemy the way they know you."

There was a sudden bark from the rear of the hall, a flurry of instructions that had women and children clambering to their feet.

"The kitchens are open." Efrayim didn't move. "Go if you want. There's not much and what there is isn't worth eating. Most of us let the children go first. Have another cigarette instead."

Felix took one, but he moved away from the group to smoke it, and no one called him back.

The crush of people and noise was too much. He went up to one of the galleries and found a quiet corner. It wasn't long before the families trooped back, the adults gray-faced, the children whimpering. Guards wandered among the curled-up bodies, kicking open a suitcase here, another there; helping themselves to the contents. Felix could see no logic in what they were doing and no particular anger.

At some point, as darkness fell and he could no longer see his wristwatch, more guards arrived, rousing sleepers, marching them out. The soldiers moved quickly, separating mothers and children, the old from the young, the able from the not. This time, he could see there was logic, but there was still no discernible anger. Everything was done as clinically and efficiently as the way he separated the good negatives from the bad. Weeping, begging, reasoned questions: whatever the herded groups tried to do, they were simply ignored as if their voices worked on a different frequency. By the time dawn broke, Felix felt he had lived a dozen lives and run out of tears in them all.

"Green and white. Line up. Get moving."

Felix scrambled to his feet, hands flailing as the floor lurched. Three days with nothing but water and the occasional cigarette had left him light-headed, his limbs disconnected. His one miserable foray to the kitchen had merely proved Efrayim right. There was nothing there but a thin soup to feed hundreds of people and too many hollow-eyed children waiting.

Felix had kept himself largely to himself since that first night, only venturing to the hall when the misery of not using the over-flowing toilet grew worse than the misery of using it. Every night, groups swept out; every morning, more squashed in. The floor was as much a sea of discarded cases as crammed-in bodies. Last night he had stumbled over a tattered bag in the dark and found a heel of bread. No one saw him scoop it up. It was in his pocket in seconds and gobbled up as fast. If he found another today, it was his, regardless of who was watching.

"Green and white. You are called. Move."

He scrambled across the floor toward the main entrance, no longer careful of untucked hands or feet. There was no sign of Efrayim anymore, or his companions.

The line Felix was pushed into was short, already moving past the rows of desks, and the processing out—because that was what it seemed to be, although no one explained anything—was as quick as the processing in. After so many hours of dusty twilight, the morning seemed unnaturally bright. For a moment, Felix wondered if he was free, but another truck waited. This journey was a shorter one, the landmarks more familiar. Felix watched the trees in the

Tiergarten flash past, the swastika flags waving on the Brandenburg Gate. He wasn't foolish enough to ask where they were going.

"Papers ready. Line up to the left."

There were no dogs this time, just guards directing his bleary-eyed group to a four-story building squatting on the corner of a narrow, nondescript street. Felix stared around, trying to get his bearings. He knew this one—it was Rosenstraße. The building was some kind of welfare center for the local Jews; it was one of the first places he'd gone looking for Hannah. He was processed again, everything the same, and pointed toward another set of double doors. This time, Felix was ready. He steeled himself, holding his body tight against the expected crush; the reality waiting inside left him just as confused. The large room was busy, milling mostly with men, but there was room to move. There were still sacks of straw for sitting on rather than chairs, but there was a table laid out with jugs of water and plenty of cups. Above all, it was quiet and, although by no means fragrant, the air was lighter. He could breathe.

"New arrivals over here." The skinny man calling out had a yellow star fixed to his chest, but he clearly had some kind of authority: none of the lolling guards looked up. "Take this." He handed Felix a battered spoon. "There will be food served for this level at noon. It's nothing much—cabbage, a little sausage, some bread—but there's enough to go around."

Nothing much? Felix stared at him: he'd described a banquet.

"Are you Mischling first or second degree?"

"Second."

The man consulted what appeared to be a plan of the building. "You need to go to the third room on the right down that corridor. There's not so many of you, so you should find yourself a space. Do you have Aryan relatives outside?"

Felix nodded.

"Good, let's hope they can speak for you." He was clearly being dismissed, but Felix wasn't ready to go.

"I don't understand. Is this another deportation center? Is everyone in here Jewish?"

The man sighed. "They're Jewish enough. Whether it is a deportation center remains to be seen. Everyone in here is what the Nazis call a 'privileged' Jew—a strange choice of words and no doubt it amuses them. It means mixed blood, married to an Aryan or a veteran of the last war. Till now it has also meant safe, so all you'll hear is complaining. If there's much more arguing over who has the most rights, I expect the Nazis will be happy to drop the privileged bit. I tell them, but who listens? The old ones are the worst." He nodded toward a group hunched in the corner. "They don't seem to understand when to keep quiet."

The complaints ran on, but Felix had stopped listening. Arno. One of the men flapping his hands and talking, a white card around his neck, was Arno. Felix garbled some thanks and dodged his way across the floor. As he grew closer, he realized the men weren't talking to each other as it first appeared but babbling to themselves. There was a wide space around them.

"Vati, Vati. It's me. It's Felix."

Not a sign of recognition.

He hunkered down and took Arno's hands; they were as crisp as parched leaves. "It's me; I'm here. I'll look after you."

Arno kept muttering. Felix could make out Kerstin's name, but not much else. He stayed kneeling, cradling Arno's hands, not knowing what else to do. When the shout came that food was being served, the room shuffled itself into orderly lines, all except the old men, who stayed ignored in their corner.

He hasn't eaten. No wonder he's confused. Felix wrapped an arm around Arno's shoulders and pulled him off the floor. It was like scooping up a blossom. The others were clearly as helpless, but Felix was forced to ignore them: as frail as Arno was, after three days without food himself, Felix barely had the strength to deal with his father's needs, never mind a stranger's. He followed the lines into the allocated dining room and sat Arno down. Two plates appeared, both carrying limp cabbage, stringy sausage and a slice of dry black bread. It smelled like heaven. Felix could have crammed the whole lot in his mouth, but he fed Arno first and made him drink two cups of water.

Color pinked the old man's cheeks. He looked at Felix and suddenly his eyes brightened. He grabbed Felix's hands and began laughing and crying, calling for Kerstin.

Someone farther along the table tutted. "A little dignity, please. We aren't children or animals. There's no need for hysteria."

"Be quiet!" Not Felix—although he meant to say the same thing—but one of the women serving. She waved everyone to silence. "What's that noise?" The people closest to the windows put down their spoons. "It sounds like shouting."

Felix shushed Arno and strained to listen. There was some kind of commotion out in the street. Shouts that soon swelled to the rhythm of a chant: "Give us back our husbands!"

A middle-aged man in a suit that had seen better days began to laugh. "Listen to them: they are shouting for us!"

A crowd began to gather at the window, jostling for a view. Felix untangled Arno's clutching hands and ran to join them. The narrow pavement opposite was filled with women, bundled into headscarves and lumpy coats, lined up in neat rows and all shouting up at the building. As men spotted their wives and began waving and hugging each other, the women grew louder.

Felix pushed closer to the window, suddenly saw Kerstin and cheered as wildly as the rest.

"Our wives. They are mad." All the men were saying the same, their voices a mixture of fear and pride. "The SS will shoot them."

But they didn't. They didn't do anything. By the end of the day, hundreds of women were squashed together and calling for their men.

"Even Hitler can't ignore this. All these German women, some with sons at the front, who would dare hurt or upset them? They'll have to let us out now. They'll have to!" The cry ran through the building until everyone was beaming.

The women's chanting went on into dusk, continued as the sky grew darker. And then it stopped.

Felix ran back to the window, fearing the worst as air-raid sirens ripped across the city.

"It's a practice. They're doing it to drive the women away. Or to cover up the shooting." They weren't. The first blast threw everyone back from the glass.

"They'll take us to the shelters, surely?" They didn't.

All night, Felix held Arno tight as planes droned across the sky and the bombs thudded. Explosions lit up the clouds with angry red smears. The shock rippled through the floors and walls, rattled bones and teeth and turned the air to plaster dust. By morning everyone was gray, covered in powder and turned to ghosts. The bombs stopped with the dawn, but exhausted ears kept hearing them. Finally, as the sun limped into the smoke-stained sky, there was silence. And then the chanting began again, seeping through the building like medicine.

"They're back. Our wives are back."

The guards didn't even try to stop the cheering.

Three more days and nights with the pavement packed and the guards gave up. The desks reopened. Felix clutched Arno to his side as they waited for their turn. When they reached the front of the line, the guard barely looked up.

"Take this discharge sheet. Both of you report to the police station in Oudenarder Straße at two o'clock tomorrow for your labor detail. Go."

"I thought I'd lost you." Kerstin clutched the two men to her and could barely speak for crying; the women around her were all the same. "A week and nothing and then your father was taken and I finally got word you were both here. All our men gone from us. We had to make some kind of a stand. We were so afraid the whole time. We never thought they'd listen."

Felix nodded and focused on Arno, who was shaking with shock and couldn't walk without stumbling. He couldn't take any of it in. How could it only be a week? That was nothing, the blink of an eye, and yet he felt old and like an outcast in his own city. It wasn't just the raids, although they had left their stamp everywhere. Kerstin said the worst damage was to the south and west, but Berlin's core was shaken. Even in Wedding, the sky hung acid yellow with smoke, and glass crunched like frost on the pavements. Berlin had been pounded into a new shape and so had Felix.

It will be a reprieve, Felix, not a rescue. The warning whispered along streets where he couldn't meet anyone's eye, through the dinner Kerstin tried to make into a celebration, through a sleepless night. Through an impossible morning he spent trying to imagine how to get Arno to the police station. What could he say? *If we don't go to the appointment, they'll put you in a labor camp.* He knew better now. If they did go, if anyone saw the state Arno was in, being sent to a labor camp would happen anyway. He couldn't take Arno and he couldn't go alone: all they would do is ask where Arno was. So Felix said nothing and, when the knocking rattled the door, he went to answer it as if the visitor might be a welcome one.

"You failed to report. You must both come with us." Not a soldier or a green-shirted policeman, but a young man not much older than himself, wearing the silver flashes of the SS on his gray uniform.

A printer's apprentice and a crumbling ex-lecturer and they send the SS. What a threat we must be.

Felix waved Kerstin back from the doorway.

"I will come, but my father is unwell. Could he perhaps report another day?"

There was a snort of laughter from a taller man leaning against a sleek black Mercedes. Felix hadn't noticed that, or the two trucks idling their engines. There was nothing to be gained by worrying about them now.

"I apologize: we've caused you inconvenience. I am sure he could manage it tomorrow. My mother will bring him."

A louder burst of laughter this time. The car door slammed and the tall man sauntered over. There was something familiar about his loping stride, but Felix couldn't place it.

"Well, you *are* priceless." He was older, more confident, and the flashes on his black uniform were crested with oak leaves. "Here's me thinking this would be an utterly tedious day, making sure the last of you slippery little people were all accounted for. Not my kind of thing at all, rather a demeaning duty to give a doctor, but what can you do when someone asks a favor? A dull day is what I expected, and then you pop up. So, let's have it again: Papa is poorly?"

Felix prayed Kerstin, who was still hovering, would stay quiet. This man was dangerous; his too-alert eyes and languid manner reminded Felix of a panther.

"Well, call him out, let me have a look. Not you. You stay here. Mama can fetch him."

Whatever Kerstin said to try to calm Arno, it hadn't worked. One look at the two uniformed men and he shook so hard the air seemed to shiver.

"Oh, dear. Yes, I can see you wouldn't want him brought in. Not many factories would line up to bid for those doddering hands." He cast an eye over the junior officer's clipboard. "There's still too many left to do today—let's make this one easier. No more deportation stations or selections..." He paused as if he was weighing the matter.

There's no emotion. There's no anger. We're nothing to them. Their indifference is more dangerous than hatred. Felix blinked.

The SS doctor grinned as if he could read Felix's thoughts. "You're a bright one, aren't you? Why don't we send you to Sachsenhausen then, see what you're made of? Into the first truck, off you go. As for Father, he needs a different kind of care. Second truck. Theresienstadt. Come on now, get moving."

Felix heard the coat stand rattle as Kerstin crumpled.

"What about our things?" A pointless challenge, but anything to win more time. "We don't have our cases packed."

There was a pause and then the doctor roared with laughter. "You are right, where are my manners? What would you like to take from this little palace? Your silver? The family jewels?"

Felix rushed back in and grabbed two coats, flung one around Arno.

"Quickly now, the clock is ticking." Kerstin bundled scarves around them, swept up spoons and cups and wet shirts from the fireplace. She stuffed as much as she could in their pockets while the doctor whistled and tapped his foot. "Right, that will do. Playtime over. Your turn now, Schmidt; I've more important things to get on with. Load them up."

Schmidt saluted. "At once, Oberführer Eichel." He took Arno's arm and began lugging him along the path.

Felix lunged down the steps and tried to make a grab for his father. "You can't do this!"

"Oh, but I can." Eichel's crisp tone pulled Felix around. There was a pistol pressed hard against Kerstin's temple. "Such ingratitude. We gave you another chance, even though you are Jews and we don't have to do anything, no matter how much your wives and mothers bleat. All you had to do was to keep your end of the bargain, come to your appointment—a civilized request, surely? But no: you'd rather tell me what I cannot do. Well, here's the thing." Eichel turned the pistol on Arno, who cowered. "I can do whatever I like. I can kill her, or him. I can make you choose who dies first. Or, as it's a sunny day and you've rather entertained me, I can send you both where I suggested in the first place and let you take your chances. Give dear Mama a reason to live. In fact, as you're so full of orders today, let's make the choice of what happens next yours, not mine. How would you like that?"

Kerstin had sagged to the ground, her skirt caught up, her head lolling.

Eichel spread his hands. "Be a good lad for your mother now and sort this out. I'm waiting."

Felix looked at Arno, whose eyes had gone blank. A bullet today would be kinder than whatever was coming for him, but how could Felix make that choice? That same bullet would kill his mother.

He stared at Eichel, drinking in every detail. "We'll go. Both of us."

"Excellent. Maybe it will turn out to be the right choice, who can tell? War is a tricky thing—the strangest people survive it. Now, why don't you pop Papa on the truck and then climb up yourself. We've wasted enough time here."

Felix helped Arno as gently as he could, murmuring nonsense, the way a parent would to a nervous child. He scrambled onto his own transport, ignoring the bruised and bloodied faces staring at him from the truck's slatted floor, and waved a hand to Kerstin.

She didn't look up.

The engines kicked into life; Kerstin lay as limp as a discarded doll.

Felix shouted—he shouted until his throat was raw and their building was no longer in sight.

She didn't look up.

CHAPTER FIVE

March 1943, Berlin

Has marriage lived up to your expectations?

For the year following Inge's wedding, that was the first question anyone seemed to ask. Well, not today, it hadn't. Of all the places she associated with wives, the last one she'd pictured was a classroom; that she was there as the teacher didn't help. Cookery, dressmaking, how to run a house: it didn't matter which topic the ever-hopeful administrator gave her, Inge was equally uninspiring in all of them.

Fifteen girls had been shunted from their factory benches to her BDM class this time, eager to be molded into good German wives. They were far more attentive than she'd ever been and expecting, until the lesson started, to learn from a shining example. What could Inge say? Marry a man who is clever and rich, hire the best cook, engage a good housekeeper? Her life was a foreign language.

Today's session had been disastrous, but at least it was done.

She gathered up her things, ignoring her chaotic workstation. *How to bake a nutritious pie and feed your family for next to nothing.* Foolproof, the administrator said, except Inge hadn't bothered to read the recipe, and the hungry family would have had to come to the table armed with pickaxes.

Not that it mattered; no one would complain. That elegant Frau Eichel would spare any of her valuable time was apparently enough.

Inge checked the corridors were empty before she slipped away: she had no intention of being volunteered for anything else.

There was no driver available to collect her. That would normally be a bore, but the skies were clear and, although it was only the first day of March and the ground still sparkled with frost, there was a sweetness in the air that promised spring and an end to the everlasting winter. Max wouldn't be home until late, if at all; nobody was waiting for her. Inge decided to make the best of things and walk to Alexanderplatz rather than catch a train back to her new home in Nikolassee from a closer station. The shops on the way might be empty for most people; nowhere was empty for her.

Has marriage lived up to your expectations? She still wasn't sure how to answer. She'd been a child when she'd married Max, barely fit to be a wife at all; she could hardly admit that. What she did know, and this seemed as unsayable as it was surprising, was that marriage was fun—something no one had mentioned it might be. Perhaps that's what she should tell the factory girls. Forget duty and country and being a modest little wife baking modest little pies. Forget sensible cotton and nice warm layers. Invest in scraps of lace scattered with rosebuds and marry for fun.

Inge carried on along the busy street, cheered by the thought of the administrator's scandalized face, conscious she was attracting glances. Envy and admiration, the usual mix. That was down to marriage too, or at least marriage to Max. He spoiled her. Other women could stumble around Berlin in cork soles and patchwork skirts—not Inge. "I want a wife who men admire, not a *hausfrau*." Her suitcase of clothes, all muddy colors and ill-fitting waists, had never reached their new hangers: Max had refused to give them house room. As for her lingerie: she still blushed at the memory of that unveiling. "None of it will do, not anymore. Take this." The *this* he handed her with such a flourish looked like nothing at all: a square of buff-colored card stamped with her name and his rank.

He'd smiled when she frowned at it. "Be gracious, sweetheart. Don't pout when you don't even know what the present is. That little card you're about to crumple is a passport to wonderland:

it lets you into the few shops left who understand how to dress a woman. Paquin. Schiaparelli. Whatever you fancy. We've conquered France, my dear: we may as well enjoy it."

She had. Her dresses and skirts and racks of blouses now commanded two full wardrobes; she stared into them each morning like a pirate admiring his treasure. Today she was cocooned in black cashmere and Persian lamb; tomorrow she might choose her Prussian blue velvet, or mulberry tweed, or order a brand-new outfit if the mood took her. She went to dances wrapped in gold lace and lemon silk, and as for her lingerie: unveiling that nowadays made her blush for very different reasons.

That was fun too: the bedroom. Inge grinned, she couldn't help it, and burst out laughing as the boy caught in its glow turned scarlet.

You are such a little innocent. Well, those days were done. Inge had been asleep and then there was Felix; now she was awake and there was Max.

Suddenly, for the first time in months, she failed to cancel one face out with the other and Inge lost her breath. She stopped so abruptly, a portly man had to swerve to avoid her. His fury bounced away.

Felix. Where had he come from? And why today? She had worked so hard to leave him behind. When she couldn't, he came back like a stab wound.

A woman paused to offer help, but Inge waved her away and gathered herself together. Because Max indulged her didn't mean he'd stopped watching. She walked faster, but the thoughts kept chasing. Felix was then, Max was now, and Max was real—that was all she needed to remember.

It didn't work. Everything about the two men was so different—that was what she should focus on. That didn't work either; it simply brought Felix back stronger. The way he drank her in, the way he had kissed her with an urgency that was overwhelming, that left her helpless. Max's touch, from the first, had been patient, a little restrained perhaps, although he would call it "instructive." *More like controlling.* Inge could hear Liesl almost as clearly as she could see Felix.

This was nonsense: Max had all the experience: it was right he set the pace. Liesl had no place in her life anymore and certainly no place butting into her thoughts.

Inge slowed down again. She had to stop this. Her life was perfect. Everything, from her beautiful clothes to her tasteful house to her handsome and charming husband, was perfect.

If Inge had one complaint, and she truly didn't want to have even one complaint, it was that life could be rather lonely. Max worked long hours and sometimes even slept at his workplace—not that he had any choice. The other BDM instructors kept her at arm's length—not that she blamed them, given how hopeless she was. The SS wives she mixed with were kind, but they were Max's age and treated her more like a daughter. Max's home (she still struggled to think of it as theirs) ran as well as it always had without her interference, as the housekeeper frequently reminded her. If Max didn't need her at a reception or a dinner, it was hard to find a place where she had a role, and even then her role was primarily as decoration.

What would it be like to have a different life? A smaller one, with a husband my own age who knows how to spin not waltz? The thought stopped her short again, brought her hand instinctively back to the bottom of her bag, to the space where the drawing was hidden.

This time, the man shouting as he scrambled for his spilled shopping was too angry to ignore. She had to snap out of this. It had grown darker while she was lost in thought and the streets were less familiar. Perhaps she should find a hotel and place a call to her father if Max wasn't around, have him send out a driver?

She was about to ask for directions when the air-raid siren shrieked, scattering the evening crowds like chickens. The first blast was swiftly followed by a second and a third, their howl tearing through her head until she couldn't make her legs move.

"This way. There's a shelter on the next corner." A stranger grabbed her arm and pulled, not slowing when she tripped. "It's not a practice. Listen."

The drone. There it was, in the gaps between the siren blasts. The steady thickening drone no one had heard for months, but no one could forget. Somewhere to the west, the swelling hum was met by the thump of anti-aircraft guns.

"Down here, quickly."

A yawning step into midair and Inge was in a twisting stairwell. It was horribly, totally dark. Their shelter at home was reached by a lift; it was fitted with electric lights and had a sparkling white bathroom. This was like falling into a cave. Inge groped for the wall and tried to find her footing. There was a candle burning at what she assumed to be the bottom; it was too black to see even a step ahead.

"Keep moving. There's more behind us. If they panic and push, we're all in serious trouble."

She scrambled, following the sound of voices. There was a maze of corridors, rooms opening off them. The space she toppled into was as poorly lit as the stairs.

"Over here." Someone else grabbing, pulling her onto a narrow bench.

Inge wriggled, trying to create a gap between herself and her neighbors, but the legs on either side remained firmly locked. As her eyes adjusted to the tiny pricks of candlelight, she realized there were about twenty people crammed around her. The smell was overwhelming: grubby clothes and sweat and a sharp chemical taint Inge couldn't bear to think about. There wasn't enough air to fill all the mouths.

Suddenly, there was a rumble from street level, a drawn-out rolling blast of thunder that rocked through the shelter. Someone screamed; someone started praying. Inge felt her insides turn to liquid and tried to get up to find a bathroom. The woman at her side wouldn't let her move.

"There's no toilet except a bucket and the last blast's likely tipped that over. Breathe and hold on. Have a cry; it'll help."

It did. Inge let the tears pour. From the sniffing around her, most of the others were doing the same.

"How long do we have to stay here?"

The woman shrugged. "Till they say it's safe. Go out before the all-clear and they'll shoot you for a looter."

Inge recoiled as she felt a hand run across the soft trim on her cuffs.

"Not your usual place, I imagine. Here, drink this. It will take the edge off your nerves and make life easier for the rest of us."

Someone laughed.

Inge took the bottle she was offered, wiped the top and took a swig. It was some sort of schnapps and so rough it set her eyes streaming. She took a second shot.

"Good girl. Not quite so fragile then."

Inge returned it but said no more than a thank-you. She was different and out of her depth and had no need to advertise the fact by falling into conversation.

Outside, the raid had begun to establish a pattern: heavy explosions that shook the shelter and pauses between them that gradually grew longer. As it became clear that Alexanderplatz was not the main target, the children quieted and the adults began to talk. Everyone but Inge had a story to swap, about shortages and petty regulations and snooping neighbors.

Inge stayed silent as the complaints rippled round, expanding in detail, staying good-natured. It was only when the word *Jew* was mentioned that the mood stiffened. It was a woman talking, her words so mixed with Berliner slang that a moment passed before Inge could follow them.

"I'm not sticking up for anyone, all I'm saying is that it doesn't seem right. Evicting families who've lived here all their lives and packing them off, goodness knows where, and then giving their homes to anyone who comes asking. I'd rather have Jews as neighbors than the criminals and communists who've swarmed in. At least the Jews kept themselves to themselves." There was a cough, a few heads turned away.

"There's Jews started working at the same factory as me." A man this time. "Something's not right with them. I've never seen people so thin, even with the shortages. They don't eat with us. They're not allowed to speak. If their production rates fall..." He paused. "One of the overseers said if that happens, they get shipped off to some camp in Poland no one ever comes back from. He's been fiddling the figures. If he gets caught, he'll pay for that."

"The trains never stop." Another woman picked up the thread. "I live near Anhalter and there must be two or three going out every night. What I don't understand is why they never take their luggage. There's always piles of cases lying about... and the black market around there? You should see the stuff people are hawking: fur coats, jewelry and the most beautiful candlesticks."

The shelter fell silent again. Inge waited for someone to correct the speakers. Father, or Max, would do it so well, better than she could, despite all the lessons she'd sat through. It wasn't just blood that was the problem with the Jews, although that was bad enough and a real threat to Germany if the races started mixing. It was also to do with the way they'd behaved in the previous war, refusing to fight and then profiting from the goods they sold. And how they had taken control of Germany's money.

"They've got a grip on us like a python. We need to slash through it." She'd heard Father holding forth at parties, praising Hitler's generosity in providing resettlement camps for Jews who were really no better than spies and defilers. He'd grown quite misty-eyed at the Führer's kindness.

If the camps were as good as Father said they were, no wonder the Jews didn't need to take anything with them. And she might not have read what Goebbels said about how using cheap Jewish labor would help Germany beat her enemies quicker—Max had explained that one to her—but didn't working people like these read newspapers all the time? They spent their whole lives in factories—surely they would understand the economics?

Inge waited for a reasonable voice to run through the arguments, but the concerns continued.

"It's the children you worry about." The first woman again. "The streets where we live in Mitte used to be full of them. Now there's none. They led the last lot out from a kindergarten, and I didn't see any adults. Where could so many children be going without their mothers?"

To new homes in more suitable locations. Inge wanted to say it, but a sudden image of motherless children turned the words hollow.

No one spoke again. The schnapps reappeared; someone produced a loaf of bread; someone else handed around chocolate. Inge waved it all on.

When the all-clear finally sounded, she slipped away, found a hotel and placed a call to Max, who was frantic. There were SS officers in the lounge with their wives, or not. One mention of Max's name and Inge could have joined them, waited for her car in company. Instead, she sat alone, nursing a brandy.

Nothing she had heard made any kind of sense. She knew the Jews were a problem that had to be dealt with. Everyone in her circle said it, and both Max and her father were adamant that no Jew had any place in the Führer's new Germany. They were being relocated and resettled. That made sense. But what about the workers who were too thin and sounded frightened? And the left-behind luggage? And what about the children taken from their mothers?

Inge ordered another brandy and waved an overfriendly officer away. She couldn't go blindly on, never asking questions. She was the wife of an SS Oberführer: she had responsibilities; she was an example. She had heard too many things tonight that she didn't understand. She needed to talk to Max.

"What do you think is happening, Inge?"

"I don't know. Relocations, resettlements; what you said. It's just…"

"It's just what?"

How could she put it into words while he sat there so poised and unreadable? When she didn't even know what *it* was?

"You're worried about workers who seem a bit thin and children who you think may have gone from somewhere to somewhere else without their mothers. It's all a bit vague. It's not what I expect from you. To be honest, it's the kind of deliberate, disquieting nonsense spread by the Reich's enemies, which no educated person would listen to. Do you really think your father would fill his factories with workers who are too sick to be there? Do you think that I—or any of the men we spend our evenings with—would send children anywhere unprotected?"

Inge looked away. *Why did he need to make her feel small?*

"Inge, I can't believe I have to ask you this, but have you lost faith in the Party, in what we are fighting for?"

"No. Of course I haven't." Inge twisted on the slippery sofa and wished she'd never started talking. She was exhausted. She'd barely slept in the two nights since the air raid: every time she closed her eyes, she heard the planes coming. To make it worse, Charlottenburg had been badly hit and she'd had to spend the entire morning trying to pacify her frightened and furious mother. Now she finally had an evening alone with Max and she'd chosen to bring up the Jews. She should have made him take her dancing. "I could never do that. Or think badly of you or Father. But the things I heard were detailed, Max, not vague, and they were unsettling. I don't know what to think."

"Well, that is different. You've heard things said that muddled you. You did the right thing coming to me to smooth it all out."

That smile of his, sometimes it was so smug she could scream. She blinked. It wasn't the first time that thought had popped up, but it was the first time she'd listened.

"Are you angry with me, Inge?"

How did he do that? Spool out her thoughts as if her head was full of ticker tape?

"I wouldn't blame you; I'm angry with myself. I should have sent a car, no matter how busy the day was. The thought of you caught up in that raid, of what might have happened. It's unbearable. And that you had to sit in that awful shelter with all kinds of rabble. You've had a terrible ordeal, my dear; it's no wonder you are confused."

No. Inge sat up straighter. He wasn't going to do that this time: wrap up her emotions to suit himself and package them away.

"I'm not confused, Max. I'm trying to understand. And I'm not accusing anyone or disagreeing with what I've been taught. You say the Jews need to be dealt with, fine. But those people didn't trust how you are going about it. They wouldn't come out and say it, but they think there's more to this than simply moving people."

His smile was still in place, but it had stiffened.

Inge hesitated. The easiest thing, the more sensible thing, would be to laugh her worries away and stop pushing him, but the voices in the shelter kept niggling. *Where could so many children be going without their mothers?*

Inge regrouped and softened her voice into a more placatory tone. "Them, Max, not me. They might be typical of what's being said in the city, they might not, but, even if it's only a few people who are starting to mutter, is that what you want? Rumor and mistrust when we should all be working together? I'm not doing so well at the BDM center, but I want to do better. I want to be a credit to you, and to myself, I suppose. I'm meant to be some kind of an example, showing girls like the ones who go into that shelter what being a good German means. Isn't it right then that I ask questions? So I can give the right answers?"

She'd surprised him. This time, his smile reached his eyes. "You are full of revelations today, Inge. I didn't realize you took your new position so seriously. Well, if that is what you want, to understand, then come and see how things are done. My office at Sachsenhausen is only an hour away. It's one of our best-run labor camps and the hospital there is as good as anything you will find in Berlin. Why not come and see how it's run?"

"Are you serious?" Inge sat forward. Max rarely discussed his work and she'd never heard him mention anywhere by name before. "You really want me to?"

"Of course. I hadn't mentioned it before, but I'm likely to be there soon on a permanent footing, so a visit would be perfectly fitting. Why don't I suggest a lunch party? The Commandant's chef is quite remarkable—French, I believe."

Inge nodded; she was too excited to speak. If she gave a good account of herself, maybe there would be more visits. Perhaps he would involve her in the important work he kept telling her he was doing. Perhaps he would find her a role to play that didn't involve making pies and teaching housecraft to girls far more skilled at such nonsense than she would ever be. Inge's imagination began to soar, flying her into Max's office, where she pictured herself managing his diary and answering his telephone with an elegance that would make his eyes shine. She was so excited, she clapped her hands.

Max started laughing. "Good, I'm glad you're so pleased. Let me make the arrangements. In the meantime, why don't you see about a new hat? Something to bring out those beautiful eyes and make the others jealous."

He got up, kissing the top of her head as he left. Inge barely registered it. *She was going to her husband's workplace.* Even Mother didn't do that. She leaned back into the sofa. Max had listened to her. Picking out a pretty hat was suddenly the last thing on Inge's mind.

Lunch was as remarkable as Max had promised, although Inge privately hoped she would never be presented with oysters or caviar again. She settled back into the Mercedes for the short ride from the Commandant's villa to the camp itself, gathering up all the satisfaction of a job well done. For once, homework had actually proved worthwhile. One call to Max's secretary, a lot of flattery plus the promise of a real silk scarf, and Inge had enough information on the day's guest list to make herself into an expert. Turning heads had been remarkably easy:

"Commandant Kaindl, I must congratulate you: every factory owner in Berlin is singing your praises for the way you've solved their labor problems..."

"Doctor Baumkötter, what an honor: a little bird tells me your research into ways of beating combat stress is groundbreaking..."

A nugget squirreled away for every officer and every wife, all of whom were paragons of motherhood and Party virtues and "an example to us all." By the time lunch was announced, the whole group was a little in love with darling Frau Eichel. When Max joined her in the car, he was beaming.

"How well you memorized all that. You are surprise after surprise, Inge. I shall have to keep on my toes."

She tucked her hand in his and basked in the admiration. There was one more surprise to come, but she could hug that a little longer; reveal it over dinner and candlelight. She let her other hand stray to her stomach as Max gazed out of the window. Twelve weeks, too soon to feel anything, but already her body seemed different. Her body and her moods swung on such a pendulum these days that she was amazed Max hadn't commented.

Perhaps that's why I'm so oversensitive. It made sense. In the bright light of an almost-spring afternoon, her behavior since the raid seemed rather foolish. Brooding on thoughts stirred up by uneducated, probably disloyal, strangers. Raising ridiculous doubts. Now that she had met Commandant Kaindl and Doctor Baumkötter—the camp's chief physician and Max's boss—she felt a little ashamed. Both men were clearly very proud of Sachsenhausen and the work they did there, as was Max.

As the car swept along the tree-lined street and turned through the stone gateway, Inge relaxed. That the main entrance was a simple white building rather than the forbidding portcullis she'd imagined simply reassured her further. Today was no day for mood swings: Max was proud of her; she was going to live up to that.

The Mercedes glided to a halt and Max helped her out onto the courtyard's spotless paving stones as a row of immaculately uniformed soldiers snapped to attention.

"This area has houses for the guards, the camp offices and a private hospital. Our men are well looked after; their hard work deserves it."

It looked like a neatly tended Berlin suburb. Barracks might be a more accurate description of the single-story buildings than houses, but Inge could see fresh paint on the doors and pretty checked curtains at the windows. There were flower beds already nodding with early daffodils, gardens surrounded by rustic fences and laid out with carved benches and tables. There was even a small pond complete with paddling ducks in front of the building that Max told her was Commandant Kaindl's headquarters. It was quite charming, far cozier than she expected.

She fell into step beside Max as the rest of the party gathered by the gatehouse where Kaindl was waiting, his bespectacled face as jovial as a favorite uncle.

The words *Arbeit Macht Frei*—"Work sets you free"—were coiled into the gates' ironwork. "To encourage incoming prisoners," Max whispered.

"Ladies, if you will indulge me. I have already said, perhaps I have already boasted"—Kaindl winked at the little ripple of laughter—"that Sachsenhausen is run on exemplary lines. It is, in fact, the model for all the other camps the Führer has established. But it is, nevertheless, a prison camp. Incidents happen; they are dealt with. You may see punishments; they may seem harsh. I do not need to remind you, as officers' wives, that nothing we do is more than is needed. Places like this exist, after all, to keep you, and Germany, free from those who look to despoil it. All I would ask is that if you find yourself close to a prisoner, you do not speak. None of them, of course, would dare to address you. Now, are there any questions? No? Then please, let me welcome you to my camp."

Kaindl was so delighted with himself, Inge fully expected a drumroll. He strode forward, waving for the gates to open with such an extravagant flourish she had to bite down the urge to giggle. A few steps through and into the wide expanse which, Max whispered, was the parade ground, and that urge fell away. It wasn't the long radiating lines of barracks that sobered her, although they were crammed in and dingy and there wasn't a flower in sight. It wasn't even the somewhat peculiar sight of men straggling around a long, semicircular running track, their bodies bent double under heavy packs. That was presumably one of the punishments the Commandant referred to and should be ignored. What caused her to break step was the gallows. Inge had never seen one outside a book, but there was no mistaking the stark, square frame and single knotted noose. It was impossible to come through the gates and not be drawn to it.

She turned to Max, who was speaking to one of his fellow officers and hadn't noticed her hesitation.

"How often does that have to..." She couldn't finish the sentence. Directly above her, fixed to a circular plate and high enough to be visible from anywhere in the camp, was a massive machine gun. Anyone standing on the parade ground would be positioned between the gun and the gallows as if they were slotted inside a macabre set of bookends. Her stomach lurched. "What kind of people are in here?" *Why on earth do you need such awful things so visible?* is what she wanted to ask, but she didn't dare.

Max frowned anyway. "The usual. Undesirables. Communists. And Jews, of course. Why?"

"I didn't expect the gallows and the gun, that's all."

Max raised an eyebrow. "It is a prison, as Kaindl told you. You're not going to be squeamish, are you?"

She didn't answer. One of the prisoners on the running track had reached the section closest to where their party stood. *I've never seen people so thin.* The voice from the shelter buzzed through her head as she watched the man stumbling. Thin wasn't the right word. Her maid Hannah had been thin; the people she saw on the streets of Berlin were thin. This man was desiccated. Inge held her breath as his jerky limbs moved like pistons. Despite the cool breeze, he was wearing a thin shirt with the sleeves so ragged, his arms jutted through. His bones were so close to the skin, his elbows looked likely to tear it. Bile rose in her throat. She clutched at Max's arm.

"What's wrong with that man? Is he ill?"

Max turned to see what she was staring at and sighed. "Is that what's upsetting you? This is getting silly. Some of them won't eat, Inge: they claim it's a protest. Don't look at him: any show of sympathy and he'll think that he's winning."

"A protest? That doesn't make sense..."

"Are you questioning me?"

Inge's attention was pulled back from the prisoner as Max seized her hand so hard she gasped. "Of course not, no. I'm sorry."

She kept her mouth shut after that warning, but his grip couldn't stop her thoughts spinning. *How can you come out with such nonsense and expect me to believe you? No one would willingly make themselves so frail.*

Kaindl was talking; she forced herself to listen and not look at the track.

"These blocks in front of you are the kitchens, those are the infirmary. You can see for yourselves our exercise area. It is quite an exceptional camp, ladies, believe me. Sturmbannführer Krueger even has his own troupe of artists, some of Berlin's finest, although that's a secret he won't be happy I shared!" Kaindl was clearly more amused with his exaggerated stage whisper than the stiff-faced officer standing next to him.

Inge tried to concentrate as he moved on to roll calls, but she couldn't keep her eyes from the skeleton-man, or the ones coming after him. What would Max say if she questioned him again: would he claim the whole camp was refusing to eat? Inge wiggled her bruised fingers and knew she wouldn't dare ask.

She couldn't concentrate and she couldn't hear properly. There was suddenly such a clattering and a clanging coming from the other side of the perimeter wall. She stood on her toes, straining to see, but nothing was visible except a heat haze shimmering above the rolls of barbed wire.

"It's the brickworks." Max in her ear again with his ready explanations. "About half the camp is employed there. We could visit that side of the site if you want, but it's not the cleanest place." He broke off as a young soldier approached with a folded note. "Wait here. Don't ask anyone else any questions."

Max hurried over to Kaindl, leaving Inge in the grip of a tightening headache. There was a dry dustiness in the air that parched her throat. All around the edge of the parade area, the broken bodies Inge was struggling to remember were human beings continued their crouching run. The relentless movement was making her dizzy. She gave up trying to find anything comfortable to look at and stared at the ground.

"Ladies!" Kaindl's sudden bark jolted her back to attention. "We are going to take our tour inside. A new group of inmates is about to arrive, and this area will doubtless fill up very quickly. Doctor Eichel has offered to take you into one of our excellent medical blocks while I attend to matters here. Please follow him and I shall return to you a little later."

Some of the other wives nudged each other and grinned behind their husbands' backs as Max stepped forward. Seeing Max admired—and knowing how much he enjoyed it, or why else would he cling to his striking black uniform when most had swapped to the far drabber gray—normally amused Inge, but she was still picking over the Commandant's words. The parade ground was huge: how many prisoners could it possibly take to fill it, and if, as Kaindl had said over lunch, the camp was already at capacity, how would they make space for these new ones?

"Frau Eichel? Could you follow your husband, please?" She had been too preoccupied to notice the officer hovering at her side or to see that Max was already loping away, the other women trotting after. The rest of their guard had fanned out around the wives, nudging them more speedily forward. *We must look like sheep. Or prisoners.* "Are you feeling unwell, madame? Forgive me, but you look rather pale."

Inge muttered something about a long day and let herself be guided toward the infirmary. A thud she presumed must be marching feet shook the air. The sound clashed with the brickwork's thumping in a discordant rhythm that made her head swim.

Inge entered the one-story barracks on shivery legs, hoping the building's interior would be quiet and soothing. Instead, the crisp white paint pricked at her eyes. She wondered if she should ask for water or a chair, but Max was already talking and the other officers had stayed outside, lining up in front of the long row of windows that stretched along the building. It would be unseemly to make a fuss; Max wouldn't thank her for it.

Inge moved away from the tightly knit group. No one paid any attention. She tugged off her hat, loosened the neck of her coat, and moved closer to one of the square-paned windows, conscious that her skin was clammy and her insides fluttering. The glass looked as cool and inviting as water. Inge leaned against the wall and rested her fingers against the panes. They shivered, rippling with the steadily approaching beat. Dust clouds eddied through the gates. Inge watched, mesmerized, as wave after wave of men flowed into the wide space outside, their feet bouncing in double time.

No one has a suitcase. The realization pushed her closer to the glass. Up above the parade ground, the machine gun began to move, roving over the forming ranks like a pointing finger. Her stomach twisted as if it was trying to keep pace.

"Line up! Don't leave spaces. Take off your hats." The windows were thin; she could hear the orders ringing, punctuated by screaming whistles and barking dogs. It looked like chaos, but there was an efficiency to the process that told how many times it had been done.

Kaindl was right: the parade ground filled quickly. The last groups to be herded through were pushed around the outside, closer to where Inge was watching.

It was the simplest movement that caught her eye, that pulled him out: a hand running through floppy brown hair, tossing it back. She had seen him do it when he danced, and in that first moment when he drew back from kissing her and gasped as if the world had changed...

"Felix?" The name was out before she could swallow it. *Why on earth are you here?*

"Madame, are you all right? Do you need something?" A young nurse appeared at her side.

Inge ignored her. Outside, Felix was suddenly looking right at her, his face sunbeam-bright.

"Hannah!"

Inge could have laughed. Who else would he call for?

The name rang out again, its notes floating over the brickwork's banging, and the demands of whistles and dogs. "Hannah!" The wrong name, but not the wrong girl.

Inge leaned into the glass. He was so close, a dozen paces away, if that. She pressed toward him. That smile. That look, as if he knew her down to her bones. How could she have thought she was done with him? The window trembled so hard, one push would break through it. His gaze held hers and the horrors all faded until it was no more than them: a boy and a girl catching each other's eye across a crowd and seeing their future.

"Felix."

His hand stretched out. She pressed against the glass, imagining the feel of his fingers, but then they were gone. Grabbed. His arm wrenched back. A stick raised, crashed down again. Why were they hurting him? What were they shouting?

"Felix!"

"Madame, please. Do I need to get someone?" The nurse fussed around her, her white veil flapping.

"Inge, is that you? What's the matter?"

Max. If he came over, if he started making connections to that day in the Tiergarten . . . Inge could see the gallows dancing. She had a minute, barely that. She whirled around, grabbed the nurse's hand.

"You have to help me. There's been a mistake. That man out there, the one they're hurting. He shouldn't be here. He's not a criminal—he's a good man, an artist. Look." She scrabbled for the drawing, thrust it at the startled girl. The lines had faded with her stroking, but its magic was still there. "One of the officers here, Krueger. He has artists working for him. Give him this. No, don't say you can't. His name is Felix, Felix Thalberg, and he shouldn't be here."

"Inge, what is happening?" The group around Max shifted. Inge felt the flutter as heads turned, as whispers and nudges disturbed the air.

The nurse was younger than Inge had first thought, and clearly terrified. Inge grabbed her hand and prayed the girl wouldn't realize Inge was equally as afraid as she was. "Krueger will be grateful for the information, trust me."

Inge glanced over her shoulder: the other wives were still thronging around Max, not yet ready to give him up. She pulled out her purse. "I have money, I can give you enough to set yourself up somewhere else. Use the drawing to bargain your way out and make a better life away from this miserable place." She forced the sketch and the money into the nurse's pocket. "Do what I say. Don't mention my name. I'll make your life far worse than anything here if you do. You can trust me on that as well."

There was a commotion behind her; Max was forcing his way through. Inge pushed the nurse away, refusing to think about how badly wrong this could go.

"Why are you making such a fuss? Are you ill?" Max was at her side, pulling her around, his face as white as the retreating nurse's.

"Yes." She didn't need to lie. Her head was whirling, her middle caught in a noose.

"She needs air. I'm taking her outside." Max steered Inge toward the door, waving away their craning audience. "What were you doing? Calling out like some common fishwife? Haven't I trained you better?"

She couldn't answer: the hand he had grabbed to take her outside still ached from its earlier bruising and now it throbbed so badly, she could barely think. Besides, she didn't know what Max had heard. *Although it surely can't have been the name. If he'd heard me call out Felix, he wouldn't have let that slip by.*

The parade ground was empty, but the air was thick with sweat and sour with a smell she now knew as fear. A crack pulled her head up. The gun was swiveling, like a telescope searching. She stumbled, saw dark patches on the gravel she prayed were shadows.

"Inge, pull yourself together." His grip was tight, his voice was tighter.

Inge didn't care. Pain crashed through her like a baton falling. She gathered it up and howled.

CHAPTER SIX

March 1943, Sachsenhausen KL

"Get down. Move. To the left. Move."

The orders were similar to the ones that had driven him in and out of Levetzowstraße, but there was a harsher staccato to the delivery. Felix scrambled from the truck into a melee of prisoners, soldiers and straining dogs.

"Form up. Into the station. Move."

There was no row of desks, no one asking for papers, no one checking lists. Cramped legs stumbled over the unfamiliar pace. A man to his left tripped and fell, was hauled to his feet and fell again. A shot rang out. Someone shouted, cursing the soldier. Another shot. Felix stopped looking. He jostled his way to the middle of the throng, keeping his head bent and his mind blank. If he thought about Arno trying to navigate this, he would be the next to fall. Trucks roared along the road on both sides, slamming on their brakes, dumping their cargo, roaring away. The air bubbled with burning rubber and scorched tar.

"To the left. Onto the platform. Move."

Felix didn't recognize the train station. There were no waiting rooms, no information boards, no signs that passengers ever came through. The platform was already five deep and there were more prisoners coming. If, by some miracle, Arno was here and not on the transports to Theresienstadt, he would be impossible to find without shouting; Felix was no longer such a fool he would risk that.

"Line up. Leave your cases and packages. Anything correctly labeled will follow. There will be food and water provided."

"It's true then: they do think we're stupid." The speaker was Felix's age, although taller and far stockier, with the kind of scars on his hands that hinted at furnaces and hot metal. "Look over there." The man nodded to the rows of windowless sheds edging the tracks. "Animal pens. Can't you smell the shit? This is a freight station, not a place where trains with dining cars stop."

"Silence!"

Felix inched away as best as he could. The air cracked behind him with the swoop of a whip; he could hear the deadening thump of batons landing across shoulders and backs. The soldiers were on edge, excitable, their adrenaline spilling into the dogs. Felix sank into himself and kept his gaze lowered. Below them, the tracks began to quiver. A few seconds later, a great plume of smoke spilled across the platform and the drawn-out shriek of a whistle announced an approaching train. He glanced up to see a great engine lumbering around the bend, black and belching, pulling a row of high-sided wagons.

"See? What did I tell you? They think we're no better than—"

The bullet hit; the man dropped. Felix felt a spray falling warm like spring rain across his cheek. He jammed his hands into his pockets. The wagons were in front of him now, great wooden crates with heavy double doors, each with one barbed-wire-covered rectangle placed high up and masquerading as a window. Cattle trucks.

The train squealed to a halt and the doors flew open, revealing cavernous spaces lined with straw. Soldiers jumped down; ramps appeared; the guards at the back started pushing. There was no need for shouting, but they did it anyway. Feet tripped on the uneven ramps; hands clutched out for help that wasn't coming. Someone stumbled; someone else tried to throw their case on board. The shooting was less precise now.

Felix leaped forward; there was nothing to be gained by hanging back. He ran up the ramp, found the farthest corner of the wagon and clung to it. More and more bodies poured in until there wasn't a hand's breadth between them. He wriggled against the rough slats, trying to find a space that wasn't full of shoulders and elbows and other men's sweat. It was no use.

The last stragglers jammed in; the heavy doors slammed. There was a teeth-grating scrape Felix assumed was the bolts being drawn and the train shuddered into life with a lurch that toppled the men one onto the other like falling dominoes. Heat rose through the floor as the pistons chugged into their rhythm, thickening the already dense air. Felix tried to breathe through his mouth, but the effort made him dizzy.

Someone spoke, their voice falsely bright. "At least we aren't going any farther than Sachsenhausen. What is that? An hour out of Berlin, two if this thing crawls? I heard that the trains going to Poland and Czechoslovakia take days."

Someone told the speaker to shut up.

Days? Felix tried to block the thought, but it kept on coming. How could Arno possibly stand this horror for days? *I should have chosen the bullet.* A short, sharp horror, but it would have been a merciful death, and maybe given him a chance to comfort his mother.

The train's rocking pushed up through his legs, turning him light-headed. Someone was asking for water, wondering about the food. Felix felt himself sway and closed his eyes. *I condemned Arno to this.* Except he hadn't—that bastard Eichel had. *"I can do what I like"*—the way he had said it wasn't a threat; it was a simple statement of fact. *"I can make you choose who dies first."* Another fact that Eichel had turned into a game. Felix gagged.

"Open your eyes!" The order barked at such close quarters made Felix jump and obey without thinking. "You've gone green. Throw up in here and you'll get pulled to pieces. Swallow."

Felix did as he was told again, but his stomach wouldn't steady. Maybe if he could get the pain out, he might master it.

"My father, he—"

"No. Put whatever that is away." More fierce words, more orders.

Felix opened his mouth, this time to roar, but the eyes staring at him held nothing but kindness. He swallowed again and the nausea eased.

"Good. It won't help to let it out, not now. Carry the rage with you. Let it keep you alive. This has to end someday: use it then."

Another swallow and Felix found he could take a deeper breath.

The man nodded. "Get through this. Get through whatever the next thing might be. Don't think wider or longer—live inside small steps and you might just survive."

Felix wanted to ask questions, to know what those steps might be, but the man looked away, his face so still, Felix wondered if he had imagined the words. Everyone around him had retreated into their own private world. Felix followed them into his. This time when he closed his eyes, he imagined windows opening onto beaches and sun-filled views. By the time the train finally slowed, living seemed a little more possible.

"Get out."

They were decanted down the ramps as fast as they had been loaded. Felix tried to stay close to the kind-eyed man, but he had whirled away into the crowds. There was a second train in a siding also disgorging passengers. This platform was even more packed than the one in Berlin, its air thickly wet with steam and hot with cinders. Voices rose in a babble: German and Polish and languages Felix couldn't recognize. People were calling out names, clutching each other, falling silent as they were pulled apart, as the inevitable shots rang out.

"Into line. Three at a time. March."

Felix stumbled forward as this station dissolved into the last like a film constantly looping. His legs were stinging with cramp and reluctant to pick up the pace of a march that was more like a run. The soldiers shoved them forward, herding them like cattle, pushing

them down neat tree-lined roads, past well-kept houses. Shutters
clattered closed; doors slammed shut; children were dragged in
from gardens. Felix stopped looking at anything but the cobbles
and the feet pounding in front of him. They ran along a street
bordered by a high wall and the close-packed trees of a forest and
turned through a gateway toward a low white building that could
have been the entrance to a country hospital or a well-to-do school.

A second pair of gates swung open. There were words twisted
into the metal, some message about work, but Felix was swept
through before he could decipher them. They poured through the
gap into what should have been a wide-open space but was now so
crammed with bodies, his group had to squeeze around the edges.
His lungs ached; his head swam. The air tasted like powder and
clogged up his nose. He could hear hammers falling, the ring of
metal on stone clashing with the whistles and the barking dogs and
the strange creaking from above him that sounded like the circles
a metal bird might make. Finally, the men in front of him slowed
and stopped and began to form into ranks in the last few feet of
space. Felix stumbled to a halt, his legs burning.

"Stand still. Take off your hats."

He no longer had a hat. What if they shot him because he no
longer had a hat? He put his hand up with the rest, pushed back his
sweat-filthy hair. No one shouted; no bullets flew. He drew a steadier
breath and raised his head, trying to get a sense of the place. As he
did so, the sun reappeared and bounced off a set of long windows
not far from where his group had landed. The glass looked clean
and inviting, somewhere comforting to look, but there was a line
of SS men drawn tight across it and Felix had no desire to make
eye contact. He dropped his gaze—at least he tried to. There was
a figure behind the nearest set of panes, looking straight at him. A
figure who moved in a sudden flash of blue, the hue of it so pure
it was as soothing to watch as the swell of the sea on a summer's
day. He knew that color; he'd carried it with him for months.

It's nothing. It's your mind playing tricks. A sensible conclusion, but he didn't believe it. He took a step closer, took a second. The blue became a coat. There was a mass of tumbling curls and then that face came into view, the one whose every kissed and caressed inch he knew better than his own. His Hannah, here, caught like him; calling out.

"Hannah!" She could see him—her face lit up like a Christmas morning. "Hannah!" *Please God she could hear him.* Her hands were splayed across the squares of the window as if she was pushing it. "Hannah!" Her mouth was moving; he could see his name on her lips. He reached out. For a moment, he could feel her, could smell the springtime in her hair. Surely the glass was too thin to withstand a pull like this?

"Hannah!" Felix stretched his fingers toward hers. There was a figure behind her, dressed in what looked like a nurse's white uniform. Suddenly, his arms were wrenched away so hard, his shoulders tore. And then a second shape appeared at Hannah's side, pulling her back from the window. A man in unmistakable black. Eichel. A man Felix knew in his heart as strongly as he would always know Hannah.

"Hey! Leave her alone!" But the soldiers were on him, raining blows, knocking him to the ground. "You don't understand. He has her!" The fist bursting his cheek filled his mouth with blood. "He has her!" But his words were all blurred, and no one was listening.

Felix did not expect to survive. He did not expect to be dragged into a barracks or have his head roughly shaved and his wounds roughly tended or to fall asleep so easily in the few inches of bunk someone rolled him onto. He expected to be shot.

"...Which you would have been on any other day. There were visitors here with weak stomachs, so executions were forbidden, and you get to live a little longer. You are a lucky man." The Kapo, who Felix now knew was in charge of the barracks and its meager medical supplies, laughed when he said that. So did the men struggling from the sardine-tight bunks, trying to find anything close to fitting in the piles of stained and patched uniforms being handed out.

Felix didn't laugh. Felix knew the Kapo was right: he was a lucky man. He was alive, Hannah was alive; both of them were finally in the same place. That it was Sachsenhausen didn't matter. *This has to end someday.* And when it did, they would be together. They had found each other. In the midst of all this turmoil, after all these months of searching, out of all the camps they could have been sent to, here they both were. What could that mean except they were meant to be together? *And there he was and so was I: right where I was meant to be.*

There were still hurdles. Felix did not know where the women were kept, or even if he could get to them. She was with Eichel and that was bad—even this giddy mood that gripped him couldn't paint that anything but bad—but there had to be a reason. Eichel had said he was a doctor. Felix was certain that the figure in white had been a nurse. Perhaps that barracks was a hospital block. Perhaps Hannah was sick; perhaps she was getting treatment? That made a sense he could cling to. And yes, it left hurdles, but hurdles didn't worry him: hurdles were for clearing.

Felix had so many questions. He tried to get the Kapo's attention, but the square-built man was shouting for silence.

"There is little time, so, new prisoners: listen. The guards will summon roll call at any moment, and if you are late or dressed wrong or breaking any other rule they choose to enforce, your stay here will be a short one. Put on the uniforms." He glared at Felix, who was still holding his striped jacket.

"Treat these like the best suit you ever owned but don't think about that suit: who you were before and what you had no longer matter. Do not lose your hat—it drives them crazy. If you have good shoes, keep them on. They may not care or notice. If they do, take the shoes off and pray to God you get a pair that fit as well as they did. Shoes are as important to your survival as bread. Learn that. And learn your camp number. The strip printed with that is on your bunk. Memorize it. Pin it below your triangle until you have time to stitch it. That is who you are now—your name is another thing that no longer matters. Stumble over your number or fail to answer it and the whole barracks pays. Do not be that man. At roll call you will be selected for your work detail. Do not argue. Do not say you have special skills or could do a better job elsewhere. You will be shot. If you are singled out for punishment, do what they say. If you are told to salute, squat and hold out your arms. Do not ask why—it is a game they have devised. Do anything different and you will be shot. Do not go near the gravel strip that runs along the electric fence—it is a death strip and you will be shot. Unless you are ordered to go there, because that is also a game. Then you must do it, and you will be shot." The Kapo's voice ground to a halt like a train out of steam.

A voice called from the back. "What about food?"

The Kapo blinked himself back. "Soup. Bread. One meal in the morning, one at night. Unless they choose to forget. There is never enough. You will never get used to it."

The barracks fell silent. Felix looked around: now was his chance.

"How do you find out who else is in here?"

The Kapo frowned. "Why would you want to know? The only people who matter to you, who might look out for you, are right here. Concentrate on keeping yourself alive—you'll have no energy for anyone else."

Felix nodded as if he agreed. The Kapo was clearly exhausted, but he could be made to understand if Felix explained it all carefully. "That's the thing. It isn't anyone. It's—"

He was cut short by a burst of whistles and the drum of running feet.

"Roll call." The Kapo was suddenly all energy, shooing the men out of the barracks at double-quick speed. "Get your hat on, check your number. I won't be punished for anyone's lateness."

The parade ground was filling fast, prisoners spilling out from the barracks and forming into rigid lines. Numbers flew through the air with frightening speed. Felix managed to concentrate long enough to catch his and throw the answer back, then he began to look around. The early-morning light was clear, but the striped and shapeless uniforms blurred all the bodies. No one else was looking up and the shaved heads turned everyone into the same unidentifiable gender. He rubbed at the patchy stubble covering his newly shorn skin and wondered if she would know him any better.

"Stand still." A hiss from his right, but it was too late. The eagle-eyed guards had already sensed movement. "Step forward."

"Do it. Or they'll beat us all."

Felix moved quickly out of the line and dropped his head again.

"Straighten yourself." The barrel of a gun poked cold under his chin, forcing it up. "You. Our little troublemaker from yesterday." The guard pulled the gun back and leveled it at Felix's chest. "Shouting, unable to stand still. You're very fond of attention."

They hadn't shot him yet. Felix had seen enough random killings to know how easily they could, or could not. *They do like a game.*

He took a deep breath. "I'm sorry. Yesterday, today, I couldn't help myself. There's this girl I've been searching for and I found out she's here. I even saw her. It's got me all distracted."

The guard stared, his gun suspended as if it was frozen. "A girl?"

Felix nodded. "A very beautiful one."

"What is this, *Romeo and Juliet*?" But he was laughing now, repeating Felix's words to the guards standing nearby. "Well, a love story in our own little camp. We are honored. So, tell me, Romeo, how far would you go to find your girl?"

Felix was no fool—he knew the odds were so stacked against him, no gambler would even call them odds. But they hadn't shot him, and they were still listening. Weak odds or not, he had to play on.

"As far as I have to. To the ends of the earth, if I must."

This time, the guard with the gun roared and the others started clapping. "A true lover's answer. All right, then, prove it. To the ends of the earth: I think we can do that."

A hand spun him around, stuck the gun in his back. Felix ran in the direction it shoved him as the day's selection started, groups peeling off in all directions. He was headed to the edge of the emptying parade ground, toward what looked like a running track. He could see a small group already huddled there, surrounded by guards, one or two of the prisoners taking up position as if they were about to enter a race.

"Boots off. Put these shoes on."

They were hardly shoes—they were pieces of thin rubber in the shape of soles, with material strips to fasten them. Felix had no idea why anyone would want to run wearing such ridiculous things, but he did as he was told.

"And this."

Felix staggered as a heavy pack dropped into his arms. It was both solid and shifting; he assumed it was sand. He pulled the straps up over his arms and felt his spine curve. *What kind of a race are they staging?*

"Now you're ready, so get set and go."

Felix stared at the track. It wasn't as straightforward as it had first looked. The lanes were laid out in narrow sections. Each one was covered with a different kind of material, gravel and cinders and broken stones, and none of those looked attractive to poorly shod feet. Felix had a creeping sensation he had misunderstood the challenge.

"What are you waiting for?" The guard, who was no longer laughing, eased his gun back out of his holster.

Felix maneuvered himself carefully onto the loose cinders, uncertain the thin rubber covering his feet could withstand anything harder.

The guard sighed. "Really? The easiest one? Is that what a man trying to win his sweetheart would do?"

Felix stepped across onto the gravel. The soles immediately turned as thin as paper.

The guard sighed again. "Romeo, oh Romeo, you are trying my patience. The harder you're tested, the more chance you have of winning her: isn't that how the best stories work?"

Felix looked down at the remaining section. His feet were already on fire from the sharp-edged gravel. He knew that the rubber soles would be ripped apart if he stepped on anything tougher. *It doesn't matter.* He took a deep breath. All that mattered was staying close by Hannah and staying alive, whatever hoops they made him jump through. Felix stepped onto the jagged lumps of broken stone and began to run.

The stones bit through his skin like knife points, until he was convinced he was running on his bare bones. The pain swallowed him, thickened around him.

On the first day, the rubber soles shredded into strips and his skin followed. On the second, the soles they gave him were tougher, but they were poorly molded and striped with ridges. Blisters bubbled and burst until his rubbed-raw feet felt like they were swimming in liquid. On the third day, the shoes they forced on top of the sores and the bruises were so solid, Felix could only think they were made from wood. Blisters formed on blisters and set into pain-filled crusts. He kept running. Blood soaked through the rags and dried into another agonizing layer. He wanted to cry, to scream, to howl out his pain like an animal. He kept running. He narrowed his blurring thoughts to a single point: *live inside small steps.* He took the words literally and ran and ran, promising himself she would be there after another ten paces, after another twenty. On the fourth day, he stumbled and his legs refused to help him recover. Felix hit the ground like a felled tree and waited to be shot.

"You amazed them. They'd never admit it, but you did." The hospital orderly, who also wore a prison uniform but sported a red triangle on his, soaked Felix's feet in ointment and wouldn't let him talk. "Your body needs every ounce of energy to heal. Whatever it is, ask me later."

Felix felt like he was floating.

"The shoe-testing track is the worst detail in the camp. Most people are lucky to manage two days, three is exceptional, and you managed four. You must have run a hundred kilometers. Please God you don't live to regret such stamina."

He was gone before Felix registered the threat. He was too tired to pick at it: his body was still running. He shifted on the sheets: they were so soft, he didn't care they were thick with stains. As he eased over, something on the table beside the bunk caught his eye. Paper, and a pencil. Without thinking, Felix picked them up and began sketching in the wide margins around the orderly's notes. A few sweeps and he had the bounce of her hair, a few more and he had her plump lower lip and the dark wing of her eyebrows.

"I can buy you an hour's rest, maybe two." The orderly was back, loaded with bandages. His hands were shaking so hard, half of them spilled. "Nadel is due this afternoon. He's heard about your escapades on the running track. This is all I need: some prisoner dumb enough to bring that madman to my ward. I'm not staying when he gets here; I'll find some excuse. He'll sweep up anyone who catches his eye or gets in his way—it won't matter to him who is the sick man and who is the orderly. Once you're in his hands, you're on your own. I'm not going down to his clinic with you."

Before Felix could ask what he meant and why this Nadel was so frightening, the orderly realized what Felix had done with the notes. "What are you doing? Defacing their records, are you insane? I was trying to be kind and you're determined to get us both punished?" He stopped as the door swung open and a stocky man in a grubby gray uniform barged in.

"Felix Thalberg?" The orderly stepped back from the bed. "Is this your work?" The guard thrust out a piece of paper and the image of Hannah danced into the room.

Felix sprang up, his pain forgotten. "Where did you get that?"

A blow knocked him back down again. "I ask the questions. Did you draw it?"

Felix nodded, unable to take his eyes from the faded sketch. He pushed the notes he had been drawing on across the sheet. "It's my Hannah. So is this."

The guard snatched the paper up, compared the two drawings. "You're an artist?"

"Yes, I suppose. Well, I'm really a printer."

The orderly coughed. "Forgive me, Oberscharführer Marock. This prisoner is scheduled for Nadel's clinic. He's due to be collected later."

A meaty hand grasped Felix's shoulder and dragged him out of the bed. The floor bit into his feet like wolves' teeth. "Not my problem. He's on Krueger's list now. An artist and a printer beats anything the needle-man wants him for." He threw a pair of shoes at Felix. "Put these on."

The pain as Felix stuffed his feet in made him dizzy. "Please. I don't mean to be rude, but that picture. How did you get it?"

The drawing disappeared inside Marock's sweaty hand. "Some officer-loving nurse after an easy route to promotion handed it over. What do you care? It's done its job."

"You have no idea, have you? What this nurse has done for you?" the orderly hissed, brushing Felix's hand away as he reached out for help to walk to the door. "Nadel is an animal; he's made a career out of pain. An hour in his clinic and you would have been screaming for an end. Another hour and you would have offered up your mother instead of you. And now he's coming and you won't be here for him to collect. Pray to God it isn't me who pays for that."

Felix wasn't really listening. The orderly was afraid, which he was sorry about, but this Nadel surely couldn't be as terrible as he sounded? Anyway, he couldn't think about that now. All he could think about was what Hannah had done. *She must have persuaded the nurse to help me, despite the danger that put her in.*

He had so many questions, but Marock's fists were curling. Besides, the answers no longer mattered. However she had done it, one thing was clear: Hannah Hüber must love him the way he loved her. In the midst of all this madness, she had risked herself and saved his life.

PART TWO

CHAPTER SEVEN

November 1944, Sachsenhausen KL

Felix's eyes ached. From when he woke to when he crawled back into sleep, the world was a blur of dots and waving lines; he even dreamed in patterns. If it wasn't for Sundays and their escape from light boxes and checking tables, Felix was convinced he would turn as blind as a mole.

Even then you would be luckier than most.

He put down his magnifying glass and rubbed his face, forgetting to check whether Oberscharführer Marock was watching. It was hard to stay as constantly alert as the work—and now the guards—demanded. Since the Allied landings in June, and with the German losses piling up on both fronts, Marock and Weber and the rest of the guards had snapped out of their lazy ways and grown jumpy. They were as likely to jolt a man back to work with a fired gun as an order.

Felix couldn't adjust to it: eighteen months ago, when he was bundled here from his hospital bunk, he thought that Barrack Eighteen, tucked away in a corner of the camp, was a sanctuary. Admittedly, Marock hadn't promised him that—*"Don't be fooled by what you see: you're as dead in there as the bastards out here. They've just given your corpse a holiday."*

Felix had been too disoriented to hear the warning. Or to ask why the barrack's windows, and those of the neighboring block, were whitewashed and swaddled with barbed wire and why guards patrolled around them.

Once the initial joy at being rescued had worn off, Felix became convinced it was a mistake. That the appearance of the drawing was some cruel joke. The whole way across the parade ground he was waiting to be called back or shot; by the time he reached this camp within a camp, he was too overwhelmed to ask a thing. Nothing was as he expected. Barrack Eighteen was pristine, cleaner than the hospital ward he had just left, and so comfortably heated that the men working at the mix of desks and machines were in their shirtsleeves. That everyone was warm and working and in their own defined space—not crammed into bunks, gray-faced and fretting—only served to confuse him further.

Felix could still remember stumbling in, stopping short, caught between the strangeness of his new surroundings and the dawning realization that there was a rhythm to the room that felt familiar. And a smell he knew, sweet and slightly woody, as if someone had distilled a forest. His nose had twitched like a rabbit's.

"You recognize it?" The prisoner Marock thrust him at, who introduced himself as Obler, clearly expected him to.

Felix did and he didn't. The hut, which was divided into sections, was like his old workplace at the newspaper offices in miniature. He could see what appeared to be a cutting area and a set of racks like those used for drying printed pages. Flatbed presses lined the back of the room and the walls were stacked floor-to-ceiling with cartons, the bottom ones slit open to reveal reams of paper.

"It looks, and smells, like a printing workshop . . . but what are you producing? Surely Sachsenhausen doesn't have a newspaper?"

Obler's laugh wasn't a pleasant one. "That would take a strong stomach to read. Try again."

There was a table nearby, its surface piled with tightly stacked bundles, the top ones covered with numbers and letters in an elaborately flowing script. Felix took a few halting steps toward it, wincing as pain shot daggers from his feet to his knees. Next to the bundles there was a light box and a magnifying glass. He scratched his head: the answer that made most sense seemed absurd.

"It looks like you're making money. Which would make you counterfeiters."

"Well done—that's exactly what we are." Obler took his arm and helped him farther into the room, toward a desk tilted like an architect's. "Kurzweil, it's the new one from the hospital, the drawing boy. Show him what you've got."

The man who looked up had the square-cut jaw and glossy mane of a film star. He nodded to Felix and fanned a sheaf of notes across the table. "Help yourself."

Felix picked up one of the white rectangles and ran his fingers over the black lettering. His English was schoolboy level, but he recognized the words *Bank of England* and the number *Five* and no one could mistake the seated Britannia. He turned it over. The paper felt thinner than a German note, but it was strong and it crackled when he folded it.

Kurzweil sat back and folded his arms. "Tell me what's wrong with it." His question, like Obler's, felt like an interview he couldn't afford to fail.

Felix sniffed at the note; he could almost smell the ink drying. It was a good copy, but it wasn't perfect, surely they knew that? If he overpraised it, he would sound like a fool; if he over-criticized, he could sound arrogant. He tried to steady his voice as he answered, sensing he would only get one try to make a good impression.

"Well . . . it's clearly a forgery. It's too fresh, not handled as often as a banknote in circulation. I imagine it has more processes to go through: anything in such good condition would be suspicious." He held the note closer to the ceiling light's bright bulb. "Whoever wrote the signature didn't press down consistently: it's thick in some places, thin in others. And someone's crossed the sevens. The English don't do that. If I had a magnifying glass, I could check it more closely. I presume there are patterns hidden in the image and the watermark on the original that make it hard to copy?" He stopped, wondering if he had overstepped. "I mean, I don't know. I'm guessing. I'm not an expert..."

Kurzweil took the note back and stared hard at Felix. "Well, that's a relief. I thought my job was gone. One in, one out: you know how the Nazis like a system."

"Take no notice of him; he thinks he's the camp comedian." Obler shook his head at Kurzweil, who shrugged. "And don't apologize for being confident. Your experience comes from photograph checking? That's good. You've an eye for detail—Krueger will be happy with that."

Felix, who was still trembling at Kurzweil's comment, looked around the room again. There must have been thousands of notes, all at different stages of preparation. "I can see what you are doing, but why are you doing it? Why forge foreign banknotes on so big a scale?"

Kurzweil placed the note back among the rest. "Because it keeps us alive."

"That doesn't make sense."

Kurzweil sighed. "Now he wants an answer that makes sense. Not my job. Our glorious leader Sturmbannführer Krueger will give you the spiel about our contribution to the war effort. Listen to him and watch out for Tweedledee and Tweedledum." He nodded toward Marock and a second SS guard slouching in the doorway. "They're not so good with words, but they can explain what the opposite to keeping alive is. You're still frowning. All right, Felix Thalberg with the photographer's eye, you must be a bright boy if you've got yourself this far, so why don't you tell me. What would you do with hundreds of thousands of fake English pounds?"

Felix's first thought was funding spies, but surely even Germany didn't run a network that big? He was struggling to think of any sensible reason and not wanting to admit it, when an image from an old newspaper he'd studied in school popped into his head. A man wheeling a barrow through the streets of Berlin filled to the brim with banknotes. His answer came out in a rush.

"I'd get them into their system. I don't know how, but I'd flood England's banks and shops with forgeries until their money was as worthless as ours was under the Weimar—when the prices went up every hour and bread could cost a million marks for a kilo. I'd crash their economy."

"Exactly." Kurzweil almost smiled. "Welcome to Krueger's band of merry men, a bunch of outlaws robbing the rich to make Germany richer. There's over a hundred of us now, spread between the two barracks, all working to the same end. First, we crack the pound and then they'll set us on the dollar. Once we can churn them both out, our beloved Führer will be able to buy whatever's left of the world once he's done smashing it. That's the bigger picture. Of course, now you know their secret, they'll have to kill you. Don't smile; I'm not joking. Which is why we forget the big picture and only care about the little one: if we get the work right, or not so right, it keeps us alive. You'll pick it up. You're here; you're not out there: in the end, that's all that matters."

He turned back to his work, leaving Felix bursting with questions nobody was interested in answering. Whenever he tried to ask anything, about the work, about the rest of the camp, about how he might find Hannah, he was met with the same answer Kurzweil had given him. *You're here. Be grateful you're not out there. Nothing else matters.*

He was grateful. To be spared the frenzied roll calls the counterfeiters could hear announced by barking dogs and whistles morning and night, and the haphazard executions that went with them. That he had a cot of his own, not a few begrudged inches of an already occupied bunk. That he had proper clothing and boots that fit and food enough to fill him. That there were soap and cigarettes and Sundays given over to cards and chess and the illusion that life was more than mere existence.

He was so grateful, he worked as hard as two men, until Obler not so politely told him to slow right down again. Within a month, he knew the language of the banknotes so fluently he could crack all their secrets, from the hidden dots to the off-center letters to the tiny breaks in their shading. He became Krueger's little treasure, his *Schatzi*. He buried himself in the work and stopped asking questions about why it mattered, but he couldn't forget the camp outside their tightly closed world, whatever advice he was given.

"We've all lost people, Thalberg. We could all go mad believing they're still out there. Leave her as a memory and be glad you have it. Young girls, especially lovely ones, don't get through this well."

Felix didn't argue with that, he dismissed it. If he was safe, Hannah was safe; that was how this played out. The drawing that had saved him had long disappeared. Their barracks was too isolated to get word in or out, but he wouldn't forget. So he picked up his pen and he started to write.

He was still writing eighteen months later, once a week and sometimes more; whenever he needed to talk to her. These letters weren't as long as the ones he trusted were still hidden in the alcove in Berlin. They were little scraps of things scribbled on leftover bits of paper and stuffed into his pockets for the day he knew Hannah would read them. No one cared what he was writing: plenty of the prisoners had developed a pastime to lift their days. Rozjen, who stood in as their doctor, made flocks of tiny folded birds. Cytrin, the head of engraving, sketched a gallery of portraits. Felix Thalberg wrote his secrets.

Felix told Hannah how much he loved her, how close to her he felt. He shared his hopes for a future that would find them together and his fears about the present they were trapped in. He wrote about the bombings that shook them awake all through the winter of 1943 and into 1944 as Berlin was pounded and hoped they hadn't scared her as much as they'd scared him. He told her how Pavel, who looked after the machines, had managed to tune their radio to frequencies where the news sounded less like Goebbels had written it. He wrote about Marock and the second guard Weber, and how their nerves were fraying as the Allies swept up through France and set Paris free and the Red Army punched its way from the east to meet them. He started each tightly folded square, *My Dearest Hannah*, and ended it with the kisses he longed to give her and the thanks he could barely put into words. But he didn't mention the things that kept him awake at night, which surely kept her sleepless too. The increasing chorus of gunfire that drifted over the camp. The gray powder that fell like grubby snowflakes through the mesh of their exercise yard and clung stickier than brick dust. The days when the camp stank like an abattoir. And he never mentioned seeing Eichel through the window, looming behind her. Or that his path had crossed with the doctor's again long after—during 1944's baking summer. There was only so much of life his little letters could bear.

"I don't have the skills or the medicine to treat this. His fever's too high and his chest is rattling. I'm sorry, but there's no choice: he has to go to the infirmary."

Felix lay on his cot, dimly aware of the argument sailing back and forth above his head. He didn't care where he went, he just wanted to get well. Sickness had swallowed him at the end of July, dousing him with shivers, burning him with fever. Two weeks later and it still clung. His bones ached as though every bit of him was broken and a cough rasped across his throat like sandpaper. He would have begged to go himself, and hang whatever the consequences they all seemed so scared of, but his lips were too cracked to speak. In the end, whatever the worries, Rozjen won.

"Send Marock with him to lay down the law. Krueger's not allowed to pull anyone else onto the counterfeiting team and he needs Thalberg's eye. The doctors and the orderlies have to treat him and they have to keep him away from the other prisoners so we get him back in one piece. They know the drill. Take him around the back of the infirmary block and move him in through the tunnel."

The next time Felix surfaced, he was being dragged out into the blistering heat, slung between Marock and Weber like a sack of cabbages. Sachsenhausen swung back around him. The gun trained across the parade ground, the black outline of the gallows that now played host to a field of knotted loops. The dull thud of hammers and shorter, sharper cracks he grew certain were gunfire. And there was something new. A dryness in the air that whispered its way like bitter smoke into his parched throat and stinging eyes. He flinched as a dog howled; his shoulders tore as the guards wrenched him down a short flight of steps.

He was in some kind of passageway, its walls sweating with damp. There were hunched shapes along the walls he didn't dare look at. When they pulled him up another set of stairs and into a tiny room, its startling whiteness made his eyes tighten. He hung swaying, too close to sweat-soaked armpits, as another argument broke out, unable to decipher anything except "Barrack Eighteen," and could have cried with joy when he was finally dropped, none too gently, onto a narrow metal-framed bed.

"You don't speak to anyone who's not an orderly or a doctor. Do you understand?" Marock's breath fell like rancid meat on his face. "If anyone gets near enough to ask—and there'll be hell to pay if they do—your job is sweeping the running track. Say nothing else. Give anyone but the orderlies your barrack number and God help you. Do you understand?"

Felix didn't, but saying yes would get rid of the stink, so he croaked out an answer and Marock stamped away.

"Keep still." Felix felt the sharp sting of a needle and then he was floating, his blood bubbling like a warm bath. He was asleep before the orderly finished telling him to count.

"Three days."

Felix blinked.

"You slept for three days and now you've woken up. I rarely get to tell anyone that. Open wide."

The orderly popped a thermometer in Felix's mouth and felt for his pulse. This man wore the same striped uniform and red triangle—which Felix now knew meant political prisoner—as the orderly who had saved him the previous year, but he was thinner and his eyes looked bruised. "Good. All back to normal. How do you feel?"

"Better. Like I could get up and get on with my work." It was true. Felix could feel energy in his bones for the first time in weeks.

"Excellent. I'll send a message to your lumpen guard. The quicker you're out of here, the better."

Felix frowned; there wasn't a trace of warmth in the man's voice.

"What? Did you think we wanted to keep you? Don't you get that all this takes effort? A private room; using up precious medicines to make you well; making sure no one discovers you. Why are you frowning? You can't think everyone gets treated like this? Perhaps I should let the other patients see you, with your fat cheeks and your shiny hair. That might wise you up a bit. Krueger struts around his kingdom and thinks he has his precious team all so well hidden. Well, we might not know what you do over there, but we know you are his *special Jews* who never get punished, who get to live on meat and good bread and lie around listening to the radio. That doesn't endear you to the rest of us—"

The corridor outside suddenly cracked with the slap of booted feet. The orderly broke off before Felix could reply. The man's gaunt face was ashen. "Get under the covers and don't move. Nadel's here sweeping the wards." That name again, said in the same clipped way.

Felix lay down, but he couldn't settle. "Did you say Nadel? The last time I was in here, before I was sent to Krueger, he was due to visit then. The orderly said I was on the doctor's list. He wasn't happy when Marock insisted on taking me away . . . What's the matter?"

"It's you? The crazy one from the track? The one who wouldn't stop running even when the guards thought his mind had gone? Of all the people to end up here again. You don't have a clue what you did, do you? I should hand you over myself."

Felix shook his head: there was so much loathing on this man's face, he didn't know how to answer.

"Nadel was coming that day, all right. He'd heard about you: the perfect specimen for his experiments. Who better to test stamina drugs on than the unstoppable man? Except you weren't here. So he took Bracht—the orderly that pig Marock overruled—to use in his trials instead. Him and all the other orderlies working on the corridor that day. Twelve good men in exchange for you. Please God whatever you're doing for Krueger is worth it."

Pray to God it isn't me who pays for that.

Felix thought he was going to be sick. "I didn't know! I couldn't. We're shut away. We don't know anything that happens in the rest of the camp. You have to believe me."

Whether he did or he didn't, it was too late. Feet rushed outside; doors slammed.

Felix shrank under the sheet, his heart hammering. "Are you going to give me to Nadel?"

"And risk Krueger having me shot for losing one of his precious workers? You're not worth it. There's plenty more choice for the good doctor to pick from—"

"Orderly, who is this prisoner? Why is he in here alone?"

That voice, those inflections. The last time Felix had heard it was outside his home, taunting Arno, ripping his family apart.

Whatever name they called him here, there was only one man this could be. Felix wanted to leap from the bed, grab any weapon he could and be done with him. And then he imagined the sport that would turn into. He lay as flat as he could and prayed that Krueger's orders could once again outrank this *Nadel's*.

The orderly, to Felix's relief, stood his ground. "He has Barrack Eighteen privileges, sir, as arranged by Sturmbannführer Krueger with the Commandant. He can't mix with the others. And he has a skin infection. It's nasty-looking and may be contagious. An examination could be risky."

There was a short pause and then Felix heard the laugh that was burned into his memory. "Such a privileged Jew he must be, getting to survive his infections. You can keep him. Or you can die if he does. A Jew's life more valuable than yours—how aggravating that must be." The voice dipped as if its owner was turning.

Felix risked one snatched look. Black uniform, dirty blond hair, a glimpse of high cheekbones. He sank back, soaked in sweat.

Eichel and his entourage moved off down the corridor, somebody calling out numbers as they went.

"Thank you."

No response.

"Will you tell me something?"

A shrug.

"Why do you call him Nadel? It's not his name."

The orderly continued sorting his papers. "It's a nickname: Doctor *Nadel*; Doctor Needle. Whatever concoction of drugs he's made up to test, whatever bit of his godforsaken victim's body he decides is his new playground, his experiments always involve a needle. He has his own set—apparently he fusses over them as if they were his children. They're all different sizes, some of them with points like bee stings, some ground down and blunted. That's what the rumors say anyway: it's not like anyone comes back to describe them."

The orderly did not invite further discussion. Felix spent his last hours in silence. He couldn't think about Bracht or about the others; he didn't know how to live with that burden. He couldn't think about needles or experiments or about Hannah standing at the window with Eichel behind her. About the risks she must have taken using the drawing.

Don't think wider or longer—live inside small steps.

He kept his mind blank by reciting nonsense: counting his numbers up and down in English, running through all of the colors in a paint palette. He couldn't think about anything real, not now, not here, or he would sink.

"Thalberg, wake up. Stop dreaming."

Felix jumped back into the present as Solly loomed over his desk.

"Those two don't need excuses to start cracking heads. At least try to look like you're working."

Unlike everyone else in the barracks, Solly had actually been a counterfeiter before the war and his sense of danger was far better developed. Felix realized he had been careless: he'd stopped work without checking where the guards were. Now Weber and Marock were prowling toward him, hands on their holsters. He quickly picked up a stash of notes and showed one to Solly as if they were discussing it.

The guards stopped but kept watching. Their tempers had been wasp-like all summer. Now that the war was dragging into another bitter winter, their resentment of the softly-softly way they were meant to police their prisoners had bloomed into hatred. Tension was high and not helped by the shortages that had finally reached even the counterfeiting block. Felix no longer crawled into his cot with anything like a full belly. There hadn't been soap for months and everyone was scratching. Cigarettes were earned, not freely distributed, and the guards were lashing out, drinking more.

Whenever they were drunk and snoring, Felix and the rest clustered around the radio, switching frequencies back and forth, trying to bring the outside world in. Despite what the official German stations spewed out about air raids pummeling London and the Allies turning on each other, it was clear that the tide of the war was washing away from Germany.

As reports worsened and the losses built past a point any sane person could believe were manageable, Krueger grew as edgy as the guards. Rather than bullying, he took refuge in ever more pompous blustering, lecturing the prisoners on his grand plans for hours at a time. "What Germany needs is a spectacular success to shift morale and I intend to deliver it." Krueger was done with failing: it was time to make good on two and a half years of promises and finally perfect his dollars and pounds. He would stand in the center of the room and deliver this pronouncement as if it was a spell to turn them all into Rumpelstiltskin, spinning paper into gold. Krueger's orders were simple: work quicker, work better. So were Marock's: "Do as he says. Whether it works or not, you're all going up the chimney." Everyone pretended not to hear the last part. It was Marock's new favorite saying, that and asking if anyone wanted a shower, which invariably sent Weber into peals of hysterical laughter. Everyone pretended to ignore that as well, although it sent the hairs on their arms crackling.

The counterfeiters' corner of the camp was meant to be sealed, but rumors seeped in and anyone, like Felix, who had been sent outside to the infirmary had smelled the bitter smoke and tasted the ash in the wind. They didn't know much, but what they could piece together from the whispers was bad enough. Something big was happening, something industrial. Coal trucks were arriving in greater numbers than ever, but even the hospital wing stayed cold. The chimneys on the other side of the perimeter wall shot flames out all day, although the brickworks supposedly responsible for the fires had never generated such a show before. There were rumors about gas, about "selections" that no one came back from. Felix tried to tune every bit of it out or the nightmares involving Hannah and fires and screaming burnt-up bodies swallowed him.

Whatever lay beyond the barracks, the men had no choice but to work harder: their shifts were raised to twelve hours a day. Despite their fears of getting caught idling, however—or, worse, deliberately causing delays—the counterfeiters didn't dare work better. Perfecting the notes meant the job would be done, which would make them expendable and bring the threatened chimneys closer. So, by silent agreement, they stalled where they could. Not too much—not so much it would raise notice.

Solly orchestrated little delays: the wrong paper ordered, the wrong inks. Little bits of damage here and there, usually to engraving plates and drying racks. Nothing big enough to risk stopping the presses completely and tipping Krueger's impatience over into fury and a search for scapegoats. Lengthening the tasks and making the reasons for failure too complex to unpick was goal enough. By October, Krueger was convinced the ongoing mistakes were caused by sabotage, but he couldn't prove it. The mistakes, therefore, continued.

Krueger went from pompous to paranoid. As his frustration had spilled out, Marock and Weber's increasing cruelty went unchecked. Stilled fingers were smashed under rifles, drooping heads were crashed onto tables. The weak and the tired could no longer be hidden, unless Solly's eagle eye got there first. Now, he made a great pantomime of taking the note from Felix and stretching it out between his spindly fingers, fussing about the lettering until the guards grew bored.

"Get caught slacking now and you'll pay," Solly whispered. "All this stalling can't last. Germany's cornered and if time's running out for Krueger, it's running out faster for us."

Weber and Marock moved on to another target as Solly continued to wave the note.

"You heard the broadcast last night, same as me. Belgium is liberated; Greece is lost; Poland is in uproar. The Allies are coming, this year or next, and the Nazis can't risk any trace of this operation falling into enemy hands. This or any other of the secrets Sachsenhausen's hiding. We're evidence, and no one leaves evidence. Which means we're under the guillotine, Thalberg, and the blade's dropping."

"How can you be so sure?" Felix handed him another note in case they were still under scrutiny.

Solly had always had a flair for the dramatic, but now his voice was flat and tired. "Because I spent the morning buried under requests for passports and identity papers. That team over there"—he nodded toward the farthest corner—"that's all they're working on. Fake papers for the high-ranking officers and their families—Italian, Swiss, Austrian. We're making them in every flavor. The rats are fleeing and I, for one, am not going down with this stinking ship." He dropped the notes and squeezed Felix's shoulder harder than he needed to.

"Which officers? What do you mean you're not going down? What are you going to do?"

But Solly had already moved on. Felix wondered about trying to see the fake passports, but that wasn't his section: sticking his nose in would draw attention. He would try Solly again later, ask about Eichel and whether he was one of the ones asking for documents. *The rats are fleeing.* Maybe they were, but surely Solly was wrong about the rest. Wasn't everyone in the camp evidence of some wrongdoing? They couldn't kill everyone. *They want us gone, every last drop of us.* Maybe they did, but wanting and doing were very different things.

There were tens of thousands of people in Sachsenhausen. It was preposterous to think even the SS would kill so many. Besides, how on earth could they do it? Shoot them all? And then where would they put the bodies? Sachsenhausen wasn't buried away in the middle of nowhere; it was in a town—it was barely an hour from Berlin.

He couldn't listen to this; he couldn't simply give up—he'd survived too much. And it wasn't only hopes of Hannah pushing him on. Kerstin was still out there somewhere, and, God willing, maybe Arno. His family would need him when all this was done. If he could imagine a future, then there was a future to be had.

The guards had finally gone outside. Felix could hear Marock revving up his motorbike, ready for his latest entertainment: spinning the wheels so furiously, gravel flew against the wooden walls like bullets and made everyone shake. There were some trimmings on the floor, strips from the edge of the notes but wide enough to take a few scribbled lines. Wide enough to say all that was needed.

Gravel ricocheted off the walls, followed by bursts of raucous laughter; Marock and his sidekick would be good for at least half an hour. Felix picked up the scraps and started to write.

My Dearest Hannah, it's your Felix. This madness is ending; everyone knows it. When it does, and the world comes right again, I'll be here, my love, waiting. I'll be here.

CHAPTER EIGHT

Was this what he wanted? Was this Inge *sophisticated* enough? Inge stared at the elegant creature reflected back in the mirror. The black column dress she would never have chosen did exactly what Madame Clara promised: the crepe's matte richness gave her skin a pearlescent glow and its clinging bias cut smoothed her body into sleek lines. The fan-shaped necklace and waterfall earrings accentuated her neck. The vivid pink turban, wrapped around her hair, framed her face into a heart. Her lips glistened; her eyes glittered beneath mascaraed wings. She had the air of an exotic and slightly predatory bird.

"No mistakes this year, Inge. I want a sophisticated wife, not an overwrought child. Everything must be different." Well, this costume was certainly that. She looked poised and polished and far older than twenty-one, which, she presumed, was rather the point. Inge watched her reflection slip on long silk gloves and a diamond-encrusted cuff.

"Don't let me down, not again." Max's parting shot as he left Inge to assemble herself for tonight's Christmas party, underlined by the sharp twist that had burned into her wrist like a rope mark and meant she wouldn't be able to remove her silk gloves. She twisted her head so the earrings flashed like little camera bulbs popping. *Don't let me down.* Maybe this new Inge could try saying that, instead of everyone else.

She leaned into the mirror and propped her chin on her palm.

"Don't let me down." She said it louder, her thickly lacquered lips snapping. It sounded good. She said it again, conjuring up Max's face, then her mother's and her father's. All the people who said it to her with as little thought as if they said hello or wished her good night. Was there anyone who hadn't issued her with that warning with its promise of disappointment already built in?

Felix.

She couldn't imagine those words in his mouth. His face swam in so quick, she reared back from the mirror as if it was electrified. The woman sitting there no longer looked elegant: she looked overpainted and overdressed, and cruel. Nothing like the spinning girl Felix made beautiful.

Inge gripped the side of the dressing table. She needed a brandy, but she didn't dare ring for one. If not a brandy, then some air: the room was so stuffy with the blinds jammed shut and the fire blazing.

Inge jumped up and crossed to the window, stopping again so abruptly, her heel snagged in the gown's flared train. She needed to push Felix away: how would looking through the window help? One thought of him caught on the next and the memories came piling back the way they always did, in a series of disjointed images. The parade ground filling; a hand raised to push back a shock of hair. Felix turning, a momentary burst of joy and then the guards, their batons raised. The nurse's white face, staring at her as if she were mad . . .

Inge sank onto the bed before her knees gave way. It would pass; it always passed. If she didn't fight, it would pass quicker. She held herself very still, moving her breathing from shallow to slow, the way she'd learned to do when, as Max put it, her emotions threatened to tip her into confusion. View it all calmly and it couldn't control her—that was the trick. Nearly two years on and parts of that day were still vivid, parts already lost or uncertain. She remembered Felix, every second of him. She remembered collapsing onto the gravel but waking in her own bed. She remembered a nurse who was all brisk efficiency and said little beyond "don't sit up" and "your husband will tell you." And she remembered Max finally coming and how he acted, although she would gladly forget that.

"Are you calmer? I've had to sedate you, more than once." His tone was clinical, not comforting.

"How long have I been here?"

"Almost a week. I couldn't leave you awake for any length of time: you were hysterical." There was such disdain in that word.

She'd steeled herself to ask, although she had already guessed. "What about the baby?"

Max had stayed at the foot of the bed. "You lost it, Inge. Perhaps if you had asked for help sooner, or stayed calmer, things might have been different. As it was, there was nothing to be done. I still struggle to comprehend how you could have had such a reaction to the arrival of prisoners and to the disciplining of them. Events that you were warned might happen. It was embarrassing. It was disappointing. You let me down, Inge. You lost my child." Not one word of pity. It was as if she had lost the baby through deliberate willfulness. He was shaping her again and she couldn't permit it. If she took the blame for this, where would it end?

"That's not how it happened."

He ignored her. "There's something else I hope you can finally shed light on. Hauptsturmführer Wegner's wife mentioned to me, and to others unfortunately, that a disturbance in the yard that day was linked somehow to you. That the prisoner at the heart of it looked at the window, at you, or so she says, and then he shouted. That, even more inexplicably, you shouted back. She was quite definite, even under questioning. I am at a loss, Inge. Can you help me understand?"

Menace dripped through his tone, but she wouldn't let it touch her. *He didn't know. If he did* ... Inge forced herself upright. Whatever the nurse had decided to do, she hadn't told Max. That bought a little courage.

"No. That is wrong. This whole retelling is wrong." Her voice was shaking, but she forced herself to calm it and continue. "I called out, of course I did. For you, Max! I was afraid: I knew something was wrong with the baby. What else would I do faced with that but call for my husband? As for what a prisoner was doing, what would I care about that? Why would I take any notice, particularly when, as you said, we were warned they were coming? I called for you, Max, and I begged a nurse for help. You dragged me away. You dragged me outside. We are either both to blame for what happened, or neither of us is."

His face tightened; his hand curled, but something flickered in his eyes that Inge decided was doubt. She leaped on it before he could fight back and found him an absolution.

"It strikes me that this troublemaking is less about some stranger trying to catch *my* attention and more about that woman trying to catch yours. The way the wives flock around you, is that such a surprise?"

He sat back. She could almost see him preen. "Perhaps you are right. It is certainly a more palatable explanation. The transports that day were all Jews. The accusation that you might be interested in—or disturbed by—the fate of a Jew is unworthy of us both. I will speak to her husband. Her behavior is his concern, as yours is mine. You acted poorly, my dear, but perhaps I have been harder on you than you deserve."

He reached for her hand; she let him take it. "You must rest. Whoever that man was, he will be dead soon enough. Apparently he had some value which spared him the rope, but that doesn't matter. Troublemakers like him never last."

Inge remained still while he kissed her cheek and smiled when he promised to return to check on her once his work that day was concluded. She stayed silent until she heard the car doors slam and the tires crunch across the gravel, and then she started to laugh. She laughed so hard, the nurse came running back with a sedative. Inge waved her away. She had saved him. She had played the most danger-ous game she had ever played and she had won. But *who* had she saved? Could Felix—kind, gentle Felix—really be a Jew? Everything she had been taught about them was his very opposite.

I don't care. The thought bubbled through her warm as brandy. *I don't care. He can be what he wants to be, as long as he's Felix and alive.*

When Max returned, she was properly sleeping; when he came back again the next day, she was pretending. She avoided him for days. But she couldn't face the darkness that sank over her once that first elation was gone. Felix was alive but in the worst of places. Her baby was lost and she had wanted it so badly. And Max was still here, and she didn't want him at all.

How could she, after he had been so uncaring, so eager to blame her over the baby? And after she had let Felix back into a heart she knew she had been fooling by keeping him out? Whatever this marriage to Max had been, whether it was about status or the chance to play at being an adult or simply what she had been expected to do, it wasn't fun anymore and it wasn't love. Not in the way Inge now knew that she wanted.

Two weeks slipped by. She couldn't find the energy to leave the bed and nothing the kitchens conjured up could tempt her appetite. His patience clearly waning, Max prescribed a rest cure in the forests and lakes of the Spreewald. Inge was so desperate to be away from him, even his insistence that Grete travel with her seemed bearable.

Sitting on the bed of this new house Max had put her in, while she avoided going downstairs to join her husband and play the good wife, Inge wished she had fought Max for any companion but Grete on that trip. She wrapped her hands around her stomach, cradling its new softness. Finally, another pregnancy to announce—how that would delight her mother.

Grete had managed some semblance of sympathy for the first week they'd spent together, but then she was done. *"You've ducked your responsibilities long enough. You need to get pregnant again and you can't do that hiding here."* Back to the same old Grete before the trip had barely started, focused on duty, never mind the cost.

The thick pine forests and picturesque villages of the Spreewald had felt centuries away from the war's reach: in her kinder moments, Inge had wondered if that was why Grete hated it. With Eric fighting on the Western Front and Gunther on the Eastern and no word of either for weeks, Grete had seemed to take the area's otherworldliness as a personal insult. Inge, on the other hand, had sunk into its sweet air and slow pace and, eventually, waking each morning grew easier. She could not forget or understand. She would not turn Felix into the monster her world said he was; she could not make peace with the baby's loss. All she could do was cling to the hope that Felix had found a space he could survive in.

Grete had had no more patience with her daughter's halting recovery than she did with the sleepy countryside—"How long do you plan to drag this out? This doing nothing? You are the wife of an important SS officer and yet you act as if you haven't an interest in anything outside your own head. Stop indulging yourself. Stop letting everyone down."

If only I'd bitten my tongue and let that complaint wash over me with all the rest. Perhaps I could be somewhere very different than this hateful house.

It was too late to wish for that now, or even to imagine she could have held her tongue through her mother's goading. So many weeks alone with Grete had rubbed her temper raw.

"Who is this everyone you're always so quick to parade? Who am I letting down this time? Do you mean Max? He's certainly disappointed, although I doubt he's missed me. Or is it Father? Didn't he get everything he wanted when I married? I doubt he's bothered about me either and, if he's fool enough to miss your company, I imagine he has plenty of other options. Or is it you? Poor Frau Ackermann, saddled with a daughter unable to meet her Fatherland baby quota. That must be it: what a failure you must feel."

The outburst had earned Inge a bruised cheek and a flurry of packing that had finally pushed her to an apology.

"Mother, I'm sorry. I'm not ready to go back to Berlin, but I understand if you are. I could easily engage a different companion. Max said that I should take as long here as I need."

"Except I doubt he meant months. You lost a child, Inge. It's a pity, but there it is: plenty of women miscarry and move on. And if you think your father has *plenty of options,* perhaps it's also time to consider Max. There's *plenty* of women who would gladly step into your shoes. Is that what you want?"

Inge's face must have betrayed her; at least that time she had been quick enough to avoid Grete's slap.

"You stupid little fool. Whatever fantasies are in your head, you can stop them right now. Your marriage holds up a lot of lives. You're going back to it."

She'd stalked away then and refused to see Inge that night or until the car drew up the following morning.

"Get in." Grete had climbed into the Opel convertible, ignoring Inge's protests, insisted that the roof be snapped shut despite the cheery morning and closed her eyes the moment the engine started. Inge had sat as far away from her mother as she could, hugging her misery as the tree line disappeared and the roads filled up with troop convoys. What should have been a simple journey stretched into hours: they were forced on and off the roads by the overloaded trucks most of the way to Berlin.

And all that time she never thought to tell me... Neither did Max, who could have written or called or sent a message when he and Mother arranged my return. What was I to either of them except a package for delivery?

Inge got up from the bed, ignoring her glittering reflection, and moved to the window. She didn't need to open the blind: she knew the view. Across the snow-swept gardens, across the high wall and there it was, no distance away: Sachsenhausen, spreading its shadows through her days.

Inge pushed her palms against the blind until her knuckles turned as white as they had in the car when it had turned the wrong way and Grete had answered her questions as if she had no right to ask.

"Stop fussing. You're aren't going back to Nikolassee. You have a new home that is far better situated for Max's work."

Inge's body had grown cold from the inside out. "This home... it's not... at the camp?"

Grete had ignored her.

"Mother, please. I can't live at Sachsenhausen; I won't." Images had fallen around her like photographs falling. The gun, the gallows, the gaunt and starving man. Felix shouting, Felix on the ground. "I'm not ready. I still need quiet. Let me come back with you. Tell the driver there's been a change of plan." She had tried to tap on the partition, but Grete's hand was too fast.

"What is wrong with you? Your husband works there. Half your father's workforce comes from there. The workforce, by the way, that keeps us all rich. The house Max has arranged is so grand it's almost palatial. Why isn't that good enough for you?"

The pressure on Inge's wrist had tightened as her mother pulled her around. "It's true, isn't it? That's why you won't go back there. The Wegner bitch said you knew one of the prisoners. Is that it? Did that little whore Liesl lead you so far astray? What was he, some communist from Wedding? Tell me, Inge, is it true: is one of those degenerates someone you know?"

Is it true? Inge spread her fingers across the blind; the cloth was thick and yet she could still feel the cold seeping through. Please God the prisoners weren't still out there, lined up on the parade ground, trying to stand still despite the dark and the thickening snow. She knew how long the roll calls lasted. In the early days living here, when she could still face the garden, she used to hear the shouts to line up. She would shake at the barking and gunfire, her nerves straining through the long wait for the call to dismiss.

Is it true?

What if she'd said yes? What if she'd thrown herself on Grete's mercy, confessed everything she knew and everything she didn't and begged for help?

She would have said I was threatening everyone's future. Or mad. Or both and had me locked away. Like Max would, if he knew the truth.

Like he'd already threatened. So no, it wasn't true. She had lied, denied Felix's existence again. So many lies, so many secrets; she was full of them.

Inge's hand moved back to her stomach. How could anything good grow out of this?

"Why are you still in here?"

The door had opened so quietly, she hadn't heard it. Max, dressed in a black evening suit perfectly cut to flatter his broad shoulders and narrow waist. His beauty could still take her breath away; she no longer took any pleasure in that.

"Our guests are starting to arrive."

"I'll be down in a minute." He raised an eyebrow. Inge switched on her smile. "I'm sorry. I was running through the names again, recalling what I needed to know. I want to get the details right."

"Good." He came closer. "Turn around." She did as he asked, moving in the slow way he liked when he was checking an outfit. "Clara has done very well. Just one thing." He drifted his hand over the bare skin at her neckline, ran his fingers over her collarbone and up to her cheek and teased a curl or two out from under the turban. She shivered; he smiled. "Now you are perfect."

His hand crept around the nape of her neck and tilted her head until their mouths were almost touching. "No mistakes tonight, Inge. No repeat of last year. Why?"

"Because we are all being watched, all the time, and measured. Since the attempt on the Führer's life, all of us—officers and their wives—have to work harder to prove our loyalty." She repeated the lesson he had taught her, word for word.

"Good girl." His hand moved from her neck into the open back of her gown. She tensed, waiting for the pinch or the too-hard pressure of thumb burrowing against skin and knew that he felt her reaction. That he got as much pleasure from that as the mark he could leave. "The world is moving fast, Inge. You don't want to get left behind, do you?"

She shook her head. She had no idea what he meant, but it didn't matter: knowing the right answer was all that counted.

"Excellent. It's so much easier when you remember what's best." His mouth moved closer; her lips opened. He smiled again as he left. "Downstairs soon, my dear. It would be a bore to have to come looking."

Inge groped back to the bed, heart hammering. Everything he did felt part threat and part game and, whatever he did, it shook the ground around her. Almost three years married: she never described it as fun anymore. What had he said? *You don't want to get left behind.* What if she did?

Noise drifted up from the hallway, chattering voices she had no interest in hearing. What if she could live a different life, without Max's watching, without her mother's scolding? The woman staring back from the mirror could do that.

And she's not you. You had your chance and you weren't brave enough to take it.

The clothes, the makeup, it was all gilding. She was pregnant, this time with a child she didn't want no matter how hard she tried. Outside this life, she knew no one, had nothing.

Loneliness hit Inge like a blow. How had this happened? How had she become so shut away? Spending her days following Grete to her endless committees, following Max to receptions where she was expected to stand like a doll. Not even the make-believe BDM teaching to call her own anymore. Not a single friend. How easily she had thrown Liesl away; how she longed for such a simple friendship now. Except it wasn't simple anymore; nothing was. Music—dull, boring, stuffy music—drifted up the stairs.

Inge closed her eyes, overwhelmed by memories of last Christmas and Liesl. Where, once again, all the trouble began...

Once the idea had taken root, it had been impossible to dislodge: it was Father who could help her find out if Felix was still alive. Three months in the new home that clung to the side of Sachsenhausen like a tick on a dog and Inge knew it was finally try or go mad. There was nowhere she could escape the camp. If she looked out of her bedroom window, the first thing she saw was the wire-topped wall and the watchtowers. She stopped looking. If she left the house, she could hear the hammers and the roll calls, the barking and the bullets. She stopped leaving the house, unless Max or her mother forced her. She moved around the house like a shadow, flinching at noise, picking at her food, while Max grew increasingly impatient.

"All that time recuperating and you're back where you started. Men in my position can't afford neurotic wives, Inge. Pull yourself together."

Except Inge couldn't, not until she knew if the good thing she had done had been canceled out by her cowardice in the face of her mother's suspicions. She couldn't march into the camp and ask. She couldn't turn to Max. The only option open was Father. She persuaded herself he could do it easily, if he wanted. There must be lists of everyone in the camp: all Father had to do was ask for Felix as one of his workers and then she would have her answer. What could be simpler? What was that silly little rhyme he used to sing? *No one can wrap me 'round their finger like Inge!* Please God she could still do it.

The idea was one thing; crafting the reason was harder: she could hardly announce she was looking for a Jew. She gnawed over it for days until she realized that Grete had unwittingly provided an answer. *A communist from Wedding.* That's what she would tell Father. Felix was in the camp accused of being a communist, but he wasn't, of course: he was an innocent caught up in his family's nonsense. The more Inge thought about it, the better it became: communists were working men, so he was perfect for a factory line. That was a good start and then, on another sleepless night, she built the plan even stronger. Felix wouldn't be just some boy Inge knew; he would be a dear friend of Liesl's. How could Father ignore that? He didn't know they never spoke anymore.

There were pitfalls, Inge couldn't deny that, but she was prepared for them. Father might decide to speak to Liesl; he might use the request as an excuse to see her. If that happened, Inge would agree that he should, while carefully making it clear that Liesl didn't know, that Inge couldn't bear to tell her. That, in fact, telling Liesl her friend was caught up in Sachsenhausen would be cruel, especially if the boy couldn't be found. Father surely wouldn't insist if he risked being cruel.

As to how Inge knew, that was easier. She had seen Felix's name on a list in Max's office. And, of course, she should never have looked—in fact Max probably shouldn't have left it there; bringing it up would cause embarrassment or annoyance and Father wouldn't want that. Father still held Max on a pedestal. She'd thought of everything and, besides, if Father was true to form, he wouldn't pay much attention anyway. He'd always been happier to grant her demands than "listen to her prattling."

There were some risks she couldn't control. Father might tell Max, rather than indulge a wife keeping a secret. And Inge had no idea how the prisoners were recorded: if Felix had *Jew* entered against his name, then she would be in trouble. But dangerous or not, Inge had no choice. Besides, she'd gambled once and not been caught—perhaps her luck would hold? If Felix was alive, she could help him; if he was dead, she could mourn him. What she couldn't do was carry on living next to the camp, pretending to forget.

She waited until the week before Christmas when Max seemed particularly distracted and then jumped in with all the confidence she could muster.

"I'd like to go to Spandau today, to visit Father."

Max looked up from his coffee, his frown already forming.

"I know you're worried about the bombing, but the clouds are heavy enough to stop the planes and, if I take a car, I will be back long before dark. It's easier to visit him at the factory rather than at home now they've moved back out to Wannsee."

"You mean you've seen as much as you can take of your mother." At least he was smiling.

Inge buttered a slice of toast before answering. The more normally she acted, the more responsive he would be. "You've caught me. She's even more difficult than usual at the moment, all the complaining about having to *winter at the summer house* because of the bombs. The things she would do if she could get her hands on the British pilots, I swear the Führer should recruit her."

Max laughed. Inge took a bite of the toast and forced herself to swallow. "It would do me good to see him. It's been an awfully long time."

"We have the Globke reception tonight. You know how important that is."

"And I will be back well before we need to leave." She took another bite. "So, what do you think: can I have a car?"

He put his coffee down and began gathering up his papers. "I'd rather you weren't in the city at the moment, that's true, but how can I refuse when I've been encouraging you to do more outside the house? You won't be able to let him know you're coming, though, you realize that? The phone lines are badly disrupted."

Inge had no intention of calling at all, but she pretended just the right amount of concern for Max to decide there was nothing to worry about and the car was there within the half hour.

The clouds over Berlin were too heavy to be simply the heralds of bitter December weather. They were thick and oily, as if someone had painted the sky with tar. Inge stared at them as the Mercedes battled along the cracked and potholed roads. There wasn't a bird to be seen.

"It's better gray than blue." Heinz, Max's personal driver, had seen her watching. "It's the bombs and the flak that make the sky all dirty and streaked like that. It's a mess, but it's safer than the sun cracking through and bringing the bastards back."

"I didn't think it would be so bleak." Inge hadn't seen Berlin since the latest relentless wave of air raids had begun in November. This campaign was far worse than the strikes in the early months of the year that had left her shivering in the communal bunker. Although the little town of Oranienburg where the camp was situated remained untouched, they could hear the relentless pounding night after night as Charlottenburg and Wilmersdorf and Wedding were smashed to shells. The radio gave away little, but Max had told her how the zoo had been hit and the animals burned, leaving nothing but a crazed elephant and some terrified monkeys and the rumor of wolves on the loose. And how the first planes that flew over marked out a square with their bombs and then the next wave filled it, like children doing a jigsaw from the outside in. When he told her about the crush at the bunker in Kreuzberg and the people stuck half in and half out who died, she had to tell him to stop.

Even all that hadn't prepared her. Berlin's bustle was gone and its beauty. There was no sign anywhere that Christmas was coming. The few remaining trees were shriveled and charred; the snow was filthy with ash. There were buildings split open to the air, their tattered carpets and curtains flapping like the sails on broken galleons. The few people she could see were bent over, scuttling, turned in on themselves like hedgehogs avoiding attack. Berlin was drab and downcast and heartbreaking.

Inge closed the window blinds and didn't open them again until the Mercedes swept through the double gates adorned with her family name. It had barely pulled to a stop when a reception committee came running.

"Fräulein Ackermann— Forgive me—I mean Frau Eichel. How delightful. Is your father expecting you?"

Inge skipped past the two bespectacled men fighting to open the building's ornately carved front doors. "No. I'm here to surprise him."

She was in a wide reception area, its blue carpet and cream walls dominated by a sparkling pyramid of cylinders in all shapes and sizes.

She waved at a receptionist whose lipstick had sunk into the creases around her pursed mouth. "If you're phoning him, please don't. Let's not spoil it."

From the flustered glances, she guessed his office was up the stairs; she sprang over the gold-stamped carpet far quicker than her guides could match her. As she reached the first landing, a door flew open and Karl emerged, clearly alerted despite her request. His tie was loose and his face pink and sweating.

"Inge. I thought I heard your voice. What on earth are you doing here?" His welcome was not as warm as she'd hoped.

"I came to see you, of course! It's been months, Papa; far too long." There was a wide window facing her, the view looking out across long hangars and low wooden sheds. "And to see the factory. Do you realize I've never been? I thought it might be fun."

Karl shuffled, rubbing his hands. Inge had never seen him look so uncertain. As he stepped back to close the door left ajar behind him, Inge caught a glimpse of a cherry-red dress and a tumble of bright hair.

"Who's in there?"

"No one. My secretary."

But Inge was already past him and into the office. The blond head turned, all smiles. Inge stumbled to a halt. It was Liesl, lounging in a chair at the side of the mahogany desk, looking perfectly at home. Inge didn't know whether to burst out laughing or scream. Of all the things she had prepared for, to be caught out like this. *Plenty of other options.* She should have known who he would choose.

Karl ran in, waved Liesl to get up; Liesl ignored him. They both began to speak, Liesl far more calmly. Inge raised a hand before either could fabricate a story.

"Don't. I'm not a child or a fool. How long?"

Liesl plucked a cigarette from the silver-edged box on the desk. Inge couldn't miss the heavy gold bangle or ruby-set ring; she wasn't meant to. Grete had a set almost the same that she never wore.

"Does it matter?" Liesl waited for Karl to offer her a light. "Would you be happier if I said one month or twelve?" She smiled at Karl and patted his hand with such casual familiarity, Inge had her answer. "I've missed you, Inge. Now that you know how things are, perhaps we can pick up again."

Karl's face bloomed an even deeper pink. Inge sat down, waiting for him to take some semblance of charge. He spluttered into a tone she imagined he thought was a stern one. "Perhaps it would be best if you were to leave now, Fräulein Hüber. Let me have some time alone with my daughter."

Liesl pouted; Inge watched Karl's resolve collapse.

"I'll make it up to you, I promise. Something pretty."

No one can wrap me 'round their finger like Inge. That was clearly no longer true, if it ever had been.

Inge stared out of the window, ignoring Liesl's goodbyes. Her plan was already sunk and she had no idea how to refloat it.

Karl closed the door and blundered around her like a flame-drunk moth. "Inge, I'm sorry—truly I am." He sounded like a schoolboy. "You know how things stand with your mother. She can be so cold—you know that. I was never her choice. You can't—"

"No." Inge stood up and faced him. They were almost the same height; she'd never noticed that before. "You don't make me party to this." He was still blushing, still perspiring. He looked fat and very foolish. "But Liesl, of all people? What are you, thirty years older? She'll make an idiot of you." She shook her head as he blustered. "I won't discuss this with you. I won't tell Mother, but I won't discuss it."

Relief flooded his face. Inge watched him with a glimmer of hope. *A secret shared for a secret kept.*

"But I've come all this way because I wanted to see you, so why don't you give me a tour?"

Karl beamed. "A splendid idea." He led her down the stairs, gathering flunkeys up and his position back as the swelling entourage hurried through the reception area toward the huge factory doors. "I think you will be very impressed with your father, my dear. Now we have the labor problems sorted, our production rates are excelling anything we've ever achieved. Max was such a help with that, and with all the contacts he's pushed my way. Your father is one of the Wehrmacht's leading and most reliable suppliers of bullets and shells—even the Führer says so."

On and on he went. Inge wasn't listening; she was too busy trying to reframe her plan. A few steps inside the doors, however, and her attention was caught.

"See, look how shocked you are! Isn't it wonderful?" Karl flung out his arms as if to embrace it all. Inge stopped, mesmerized by the scale of the production shed, which looked big enough to swallow most of their street.

"I didn't expect it to be so huge."

Karl bounced away; Inge trotted after. He was unstoppable, reeling out statistics, pointing at turbines, stopping to admire a towering cutting machine here, to pat a pile of shell casings there. He revolved as quickly as the barrages of motors and spindles whirling around him. The noise was hypnotic, a swirl of stamping and grinding, and so was the movement. Not merely the machines, but the people clustered around them. Pulling at levers, pressing at buttons, picking through the heaps of glistening cylinders and spheres in a thousand tiny coordinated movements as if man and machine were connected. Inge was captivated by the minutely choreographed patterns, the relentless swoop and fall reminding her of the great flocks of birds she had watched dancing through the skies in the Spreewald. And then she looked closer, separated bodies from metal. Striped uniforms, gaunt faces, blank eyes. This wasn't the Spreewald with its peaceful beauty; this was Sachsenhausen's misery drawn in a different shape.

"How many people work here?"

"Two thousand." Karl's chest puffed with the number. "We house them all in purpose-built barracks and feed them from our own kitchens."

With what? Air? Inge tried to hold an even tone. "And all of them come from Sachsenhausen?"

Karl led her on through the ranks of machinery. Inge tried to pick out the faces she passed, but they blurred into a dingy mass of stubble and sharpened bones. "They do. Ukrainians, Poles, Czechs. As many as we want and always plenty more to replace the ones that wear out. I wish we could maintain the machines as easily."

If any of the men heard or understood their boss's delight in them, they didn't show it. No one lifted their head; no one paused. Inge glanced up at the high walkways circling the factory floor: armed guards patrolled them—of course they did. Her father was still talking about ratios and food costs. She cut across him, too sick with it all to play games anymore.

"Do you ever select the people you want?"

Karl's laugh bounced around the machinery. "What an odd question. Why would I select them? All that matters is numbers.

I put in my quota and, with the amounts available, I don't even need to worry about quality. In this business that in itself is worth a fortune. Inge, are you all right? You are as white as a sheet. Clausson, some brandy for my daughter. It's too much for you in here, too hot and noisy. Let me get you back to the waiting area."

Inge accepted the brandy and didn't argue when Karl hurried her back into her car. As he waved goodbye, his shoulders finally relaxed. She kept the blinds and her eyes closed all the winding way back to Berlin. She had made the kind of plans a child would make. *Can you find my friend for me; I don't know where he's gone?* How could she be so stupid? *"They don't have names here."* Or flesh on their bones or hope, if their eyes were anything to go by. It was nearly ten months since she'd seen Felix fall to the ground. She'd bought him some kind of reprieve, but he was still in Sachsenhausen. What if he was in the same dreadful state as the men who worked here?

And then she remembered the stick figures crawling along the running track and her heart lurched. What if he was reduced to something far worse?

By the time they'd arrived back at the house, the light was fading and specks fell from the sky, although the air didn't feel cold enough for snow.

"Maybe this will keep the planes away." Heinz shrugged as he opened the door. "This weather, I mean. Even the British won't fly through a snowstorm."

He got back in the car and said nothing beyond a muttered good night. Inge was so tightly wound she considered reporting his rudeness, but the thought of the explanations and the inevitable punishment a complaint would entail stopped her. Besides, there was something odd about the snow. It was only falling on the side of the house nearest the camp and it had a burnt, charcoal taint, not the nose-tingling freshness she would have expected.

Inge took off her glove and caught a few flakes. They were dark gray, and gritty where they should have been white. Even now, a year on, when Inge was so used to the sight she had trained herself to ignore it, she could still remember the prickle that ran across her neck as the grubby little things sat on her palm and refused to melt.

That night she had drunk two large brandies in quick succession while she got ready for the reception and far too much champagne when they arrived. The alcohol was meant to block out the day; it didn't help. As it didn't help when she asked Max, far more loudly than she realized, what all the savings from not feeding the prisoners were spent on and why the camp was making its own snow and what happened to all the machine-people who broke and couldn't work anymore.

He had been furious—not that he showed it. He had taken her home in silence, led her upstairs in silence. Locked the bedroom door. The first blow came so fast she didn't see his hand move; by the third, she simply wanted it done. He was quick and efficient and he knew where to hit her. She thought he might kill her; the bruising on her body took weeks to fade. He didn't do it again; he didn't need to, or not on that level. He waited a few days. He watched her duck and try to hide it when he came close. He let the fear sink in. And then Max sat her down and explained very carefully about the special facilities wives who couldn't deal with the world were sent to when they pushed their husbands too far. When he wondered if she could perhaps do better in the future, Inge agreed without hesitation that she definitely could.

That was twelve months ago—Christmas 1943. She'd been on her best behavior ever since. She had to be. Felix was out there and in need—and who knew that but her? She had to keep going, but it was so hard to keep up the pretense. So, if a drink or two, now and again, helped blot out the world, she took them more discreetly. Max wouldn't forgive her another mistake. Of all the things she had pushed away in the last year, she'd hung on to that.

The music was louder now and it was a while since the last car door slammed. *It would be a bore to have to come looking.* Well, she couldn't have that. Max hated to be bored; she had learned that lesson well enough not to need a repeat.

Inge got up and gathered herself together with one final look in the mirror. *Another night of being perfect; how many more thousands to go?*

CHAPTER NINE

February 1945, Sachsenhausen KL

Don't stop, don't look, don't ask. Felix woke every day to the echo of Kerstin's warning. The year had changed and brought nothing good. Heads bent when the shift began and did not come back up voluntarily. No one chattered. The guards kept the radio tuned to martial-sounding music and no one asked to turn it to the news. "We're still working; they still need us." Someone said that every night and they all went through the motions of nodding.

One part might be true, but Felix wasn't so sure about the other: yes, the counterfeiting continued, but whether it needed them all anymore seemed increasingly debatable. Punishments were swift; people disappeared. Johannes complained that the longer shifts made his vision blur and his work rate less efficient; Johannes was taken outside. Pavel's shaky hand knocked ink all over a freshly minted stack of bills; Pavel was taken outside. Neither man ever came back. The exercise yard became a place no one willingly walked: snow was easy to clear; bloodstains and the ash that now fell as steadily as the snowflakes proved more stubborn.

"Now isn't the time to slow your efforts, my friends, not with success so close." Krueger said it every morning and part of that was also true: they were so near to perfecting the dollar, even Solly couldn't pretend they still struggled. As for slowing down, the days of risking that were done. The more necessary for their survival delaying the counterfeiting task became, the more impossible it was; they were too closely watched. Solly's belief that the end was coming grew more certain with each tightly wound week.

"Haven't any of you noticed? Krueger's not looking for millions anymore; he'd be happy with a couple of perfect handfuls. This isn't about breaking England or America; they've given up on that. We're working to fill the officers' pockets with the bribes that will pay their passages out of Germany before the Allies arrive. Mark my words, in another few weeks there'll be nobody left but the guards who are too stupid to leave. God help us then."

Felix ignored him as much as anyone could. Then Krueger swept up the faked passports and identity papers—and the two unfortunates still applying the final touches—so no one could pretend Solly was wrong. The rats really were leaving. All Felix's fantasies of revenge, of the gates opening and liberation coming and him handing Eichel over to answer for everything the bastard had done, or killing him himself, were no more than that. Another set of dreams to help him survive. Whether Eichel was already gone or not, he had no way of knowing. No one was sent to the hospital anymore: the only medicine nowadays was a bullet. Felix lay awake at night imagining he could hear a car pulling away, imagining Eichel and his pampered wife snug in the back, praying a bomb would hit it. Not directly but close enough to guarantee a slow death. It was poor compensation for the denouncing he'd planned, but at least there would be pain.

All through January the counterfeiters had stumbled on, retreating from each other, turning in on themselves. Felix moved from task to task without thinking, focusing on the processes and the product; on the things he could understand. After Albrecht was caught with a handful of notes in his pocket and executed in front of them, Felix stopped writing his letters and concentrated instead on how to keep them safe. Losing them would make the days impossible. He spent the few quiet moments he could snatch not scribbling but unpicking the lining of his jacket and sewing the tightly folded cotton-wrapped squares inside. If Solly was right and this ship was going down, Felix was not about to invite his own murder with an ill-timed crackle of paper.

In the end, the call to pack up came without warning and perfectly calmly, during the shift change on another unremarkable February morning. There was no shouting: the machines simply stopped running. The silence took them all by surprise. Since Christmas the presses had been running twenty-four hours a day, seven days a week. Felix went to sleep and woke and worked inside the whirring of the gears and plates. It filled his ears so full, sometimes he only knew when bombs were falling from the way the ground shook. Now there was silence, and such a stillness no one knew what to do.

When the doors opened and the guards poured in, everyone cowered, expecting bullets, and dropped to the floor like boulders tumbling.

"Gentlemen, gentlemen, what are you doing? Do you think we are brutes?" Krueger's face wore an affable smile, but his hands were twitching. "We turned off the machines because we are relocating. What else would you think? That's better. Now my workers look less like whipped dogs."

Krueger moved farther into the room. His hair lacked its normally meticulous grooming, and Felix could see a muscle jumping at the corner of his left eye. "This is the most important job I've entrusted you with. Everything must be dismantled and packed ready for a journey. You have four days to complete the preparations—a substantial allocation—but you must remember that care, not speed, is the watchword. Everything you take apart has to be reassembled and be ready to function straight away. Any damage, any mistakes, will cause delays. Delays will benefit no one. Am I clear? Good, then off you go. With delicacy, my friends—with great delicacy."

With the machines hushed, other sounds crept in. The gunfire rattling like hail across the camp, the bombs dropping relentlessly across Berlin, were all noises they expected. What unnerved everyone was a deeper chorus, a steady rumble the older men said was heavy guns, artillery; the sound of the enemy coming.

After that, no one spoke. They broke the machines into their jigsaw parts, nestled them into straw-stuffed crates and tried to ignore the rifles now openly trained on every movement they made. When the generators flickered and ran short of power and it became too dark to work, no one slept. They lay awake listening to the night's new music, wondering if the next morning's crates would be shaped to fit people.

On the morning of the second day, the machine convoy left, but there were still the notes to be dealt with. They crammed those into waterproof cases sealed with metal straps and hauled them onto the next convoy. Then there was only the cleaning left. Felix mopped with the others, sweeping every trace of the operation away, and all he could think about were Solly's words: *We're evidence, and no one leaves behind evidence.* When the third convoy appeared, and this time it was the men who were hustled on board, Felix wasn't the only one to weep.

The tarpaulin came down quickly over the truck, but Felix managed to lean out, to see if other inmates were being rounded up. To see if he could catch one impossible glimpse of her before Weber knocked him away. He wished he hadn't looked. The parade ground was full of corpses, bodies cut down to skeletons with desiccated arms and legs and shoulders and chests carved into hollows like over-mined quarries. Except they weren't corpses. They were moving. Shuffling in lines, some toward the wall where the chimneys still flared, some surrounded by screaming guards and heading toward the gates. They could have been any sex; they could have been any age. They had long slipped past being human.

Felix huddled back down as they bounced along a road surface that quickly changed from smooth to cobbled as the trucks approached the town. He didn't look out again; for the first time since Felix had watched Hannah run away in the Tiergarten, he didn't want to see her. He couldn't bear to attach her face to any of those broken bodies.

In what felt both like no time at all and a lifetime, the streets narrowed, the trucks pulled to a stop and the silent men were forced out. They were back at the station where the nightmare had begun. After the confines of the camp, the sudden rush of space was overwhelming. The air was so clean, Felix almost choked on it. It took him a few moments before he knew the thin and lilting sound in his ears was birdsong. That the green dot he could see wasn't an ink spot or a watermark but an early spring bud unfurling.

He went to pick up the first crate to put it on the train and found his hands were shaking. For the first time since Eichel had come knocking, Felix believed he might live. Not hoped, or wished for, or fooled himself, but believed. He worked faster than anyone, filled with a new energy that made the guards clap and laugh. When the platform was finally clear and there was nothing left facing the counterfeiters but the guards and their guns, Felix didn't panic; he knew it wasn't over.

When the order came to climb onto the train, he nodded. When he was handed a cloth-wrapped packet of bread, he nodded again. The food wasn't much, not for the four-day journey they were told was coming, but it was food and its giving proved they had value. There was water in the wagon, wooden benches and blankets, room to move and air to breathe. It was all as it should be. *We are not cattle, we are men; we are needed.* He had no clue where they were going, but they were going with their machines. There was still a job to be done; perhaps, with the bombing so close, that job simply needed a safer location. He would survive this. He was out in the world, and the world was welcoming. And he was away from Sachsenhausen's horrors, so the worst was surely done...

The euphoria lasted almost the entire journey. It took hours to reach Berlin, well over six by Felix's rough calculation, which made him wonder how long a four-day journey could actually last. The train crawled, stopping without warning, idling and restarting while men ran along the lines shouting about broken signals and damaged rails. But it lumbered on and, with every mile that stretched away from Sachsenhausen, the men's faces grew less pinched. Eventually, they came into the city itself. Felix jumped to his feet and pressed his face against the narrow window, trying to spot some place he knew.

He smelled Berlin before he saw it. A charred charcoal stickiness hung in the air like hearths died down and left to molder. The air was wrong and so was the light. Even though it was afternoon and the February day was mild, the sky was as ashen as the smell and there was a scorched dustiness to the wind blowing through the chinks in the wagon's sides.

Felix stood on his toes as Berlin's central districts came into view. He had never hunted: he couldn't bear the thought of being so close to the kill. *This must be what it's like when a stag falls: when its beauty is split open and gutted.* The stations they passed through were too smashed to have names. There were lakes of rubble where streets should be, dust clouds clinging like mushrooms popping up in a plowed field. Felix looked for the landmarks that might fix him, but the buildings still standing were needle-thin columns, pushing up through the rocky floor like stalagmites. Single walls or the hollow points of a corner formed the skyline, not houses; rooms were ripped like cardboard, staircases dangling. There was nothing solid, nothing to hang on to. The city lay smashed and torn open, its skeleton exposed to the washed-out sky.

Felix groped back to the bench long before the train shuddered to a halt. His face was wet. *Home.* Two years holding on to the shape of it, to the hope of it, despite the warning messages left by the broadcasts and the bombs. Two years holding on to the dream of an open door and Kerstin's smile. Two years believing in a girl waiting to be found and a city still alive and saving a place for him. And now Berlin was broken, and what if the worst had barely begun?

CHAPTER TEN

February 1945, Sachsenhausen SS Estate

The old year crawled gray and bitter into the new. Bombs pounded Berlin night and day and continued to shake the ground as far as Sachsenhausen. Inge rarely went out; Max wouldn't allow it unless she was inescapably with him. When he was away, which was most of the time, the doors were locked and the servants were deaf to her. The roads were impassable or congested with troops, and the city itself—or so Max said—crawled with drunks and deserters and refugees. Thousands of people with nothing to their names, pouring into a city with nothing to offer.

Inge gave up any thought of traveling; reliable phone lines were a thing of the past, even if she had anyone she wanted to call. She had no desire to speak to Karl, and Grete was beyond her reach. Since the news of Eric's death arrived in the week after Christmas, and the news of Gunther's barely a fortnight after, Grete had retreated into the once-despised seclusion of the Wannsee house. Whatever comfort Grete wanted, she did not want it from Inge and she had no interest at all in her daughter's grief for her brothers.

Max was absent more than he was at home, spending his days, and increasingly his nights, at the camp. He claimed an impossibly mounting patient list and blamed the relentless winter and typhoid and the chronic shortages for that. Inge knew he was lying. Sachsenhausen was thick with gunfire, and the snow that wasn't snow kept falling. Whatever the prisoners were getting, Inge doubted it was medical treatment.

"*The world is moving fast.*" No, it was disintegrating and whatever Max was up to was surely part of that. *Whatever Max was up to.* She doubted he'd answer honestly if she asked. Max toed the Party line so tight these days, it was as if he lived in the sight of some imaginary audience. He let nothing go. When she tossed aside *Das Reich* because "who seriously believes Goebbels's claim that Germany is strong and the Allies are exhausted, when the sky is yellow with sulfur and Berlin's heart is broken?" he had taken her to task as if the Führer's entire cabinet had joined them for breakfast. The following day, he'd lined up the staff and read them the article she had dismissed, praising its unwavering call to arms and emphasizing Goebbels's boast about the German people *loving the truth* as if the servants were children. Inge knew he was giving a performance—what she couldn't fathom was why.

Believing Max was impossible; believing the newspapers was impossible. Inge turned instead to the radio to unpick the gathering storm. Not to the authorized channels, with their rallying cries and rallying music, but, now that she was so often left to her own devices, to the illicit German-language broadcasts pumped out by the BBC. Despite the Party's attempts to jam the frequencies, the BBC German Service remained easy to find for anyone with the patience and opportunity to turn the dial. Although she was alone when she listened, Inge was still careful. She locked the sitting-room door and retuned the set when she was done. She kept the volume low and huddled as close to the set as a front-line general awaiting disaster. Which the radio told her, without any shadow of a doubt, was coming.

A million men lost on the Eastern Front. Factories from the Ruhr to Berlin without coal or steel or fuel of any kind to make or move what the beleaguered Wehrmacht needed. The Allies fanned out along the edges of German soil from Belgium to Switzerland. The railways broken, the suicide rate rising and the Soviets drawing unstoppably closer. As January wore out, Inge barely moved from the speaker's side. If anyone had asked her what outcome she wanted for the war, she wouldn't have known how to answer. She couldn't be German and want Germany to lose, but she wasn't sure she understood what being German meant anymore. She didn't know what losing the war might mean for the camps and the prisoners, though she was in little doubt what Germany winning would mean for them. In the end, all she wanted was news. She sat with her ear pressed to the wire casing, waiting for the drumroll, for London to be calling, hypnotized by the perfectly accented voices reading the names of captured prisoners and the lists of battles lost and won. She listened so late some nights she forgot to sleep.

When she woke in her chair as dawn was breaking on the first day of February and heard banging, her first thought was that the muffled sound was the sleepless camp or the distant bombs. It was only when she turned the crackling radio off that she realized the steady thump was the rise and fall of footsteps from the floor above.

"Max?"

She eased herself out of the sitting room and crept up the stairs. It was too early for the kitchen girls to emerge from their basement and all the other staff lived in the annex.

"Max?"

She inched along the landing toward a strip of falling light. Max's bedroom door was open. His suitcase lay half packed on the bed next to his brown leather briefcase.

"I didn't hear you come home."

Max was wearing his gray uniform, not his black. He didn't turn as she entered.

"What are you doing?"

He continued to cross from the chest of drawers to the case and back in a methodical way. He wasn't in any obvious hurry, but there was a stealthy urgency to his movements that reminded her of a lion she had once seen pacing in its cage.

"Your broadcasts are done then?"

Sweat suddenly pooled in her collar.

"Don't bother finding an excuse. I don't care that you listen. At least you know the state of things." He carried on folding his shirts, rolling up his ties. She could see files in his briefcase and the slim canvas pouch he never went anywhere without.

"Where are you going?"

"Away. Before the window to do it closes."

Inge lowered herself into an armchair. His answer and his preparations were too calm for this to be a sudden decision.

"Were you going to tell me?" He finally looked up. "Or take me?"

"Do you know, at one point I was. I got everything ready as we were instructed, the papers and the passports, on the basis that I would. You've been a lot easier to handle these last few months, and, when all's said and done, you're still an Ackermann and the one remaining heir. But now..."

She waited for him to complete the sentence. He went back to his packing. Dear God, was it really going to be this simple? Was this finally the end of them?

She took a breath, kept her voice level. "But now what?"

He shrugged. "Now I'm not. I can move easier on my own and there's always the risk you'll turn unpredictable again. It's not worth it. Don't worry yourself—you'll be as safe as anyone can be. Your father has made provisions to safeguard his interests. He'll keep going pretty well once all this is done. Go to him, stay out of Berlin and ride it out."

Ride it out? With the Red Army barely fifty miles away and all the horror stories they trailed with them? The depth of his indifference was staggering, even by Max's standards.

Inge could see he was nearly finished, patting the layers of clothes flat, collecting up his hairbrush and shaving set. She had no desire to change his mind, but she needed a clearer picture than the one he was painting if she was going to survive.

"Why are you leaving now? The war's not lost."

He snapped the case shut. "It will be soon. The army will fight to their last breath, as the Führer has ordered. He won't surrender; he's pledged to die first. This war won't end in dishonor like the last, but there won't be a victory. Tomorrow there will be an order passed forbidding officers to leave their posts. There are exceptions, for people like me whose work continues to be needed, but there's no guarantee that will be honored in the field. So I am leaving now, before the order goes through and some fool wants me to provide an explanation I've no interest in giving."

It had been a performance then, reading Goebbels's boasts out from the newspaper, throwing the household off the scent.

She got up, took a step toward the door. "That's good then, that they still need you. Even this close to the end."

He didn't bother to conceal his contempt. "I'm a doctor, Inge. Of course they need me. My work has more value than you could imagine."

My work. She watched his methodical movements and closed face. In a place like Sachsenhausen with its gallows and its guns and its emaciated men, what did *doctor* actually mean? She paused in the doorway. She should slip away, let him leave and be thankful, but this might be her last chance to understand what she had spent so long living next to. What Felix had lived under.

"What really goes on in there, Max? Will other people see its value?"

His shoulders stiffened. "What a ridiculous thing to ask. And who do you mean by *other people*? If you mean Germans, the only ones who matter, then yes. They will understand that everything I have done is for our country's good."

Be quiet, Inge—just let him go. Max had grown very still, but something inside Inge had loosened and couldn't stop.

"No, I don't mean them. I mean the Allies. The soldiers who are coming. There've been rumors. About camps the Russians found in Poland. Terrible rumors. No one is using the word *good* about them."

"Be quiet."

"I'm always quiet—you won't let me be anything else. But if it's ending, if you're going, why shouldn't I ask? There's been talk, on the radio, about what the Russian soldiers found. Stories about ovens and bodies and people so starved there was nothing between their skin and their bones. Like the prisoners here at Sachsenhausen. The English won't say if any of it is true: they don't trust the Russians any more than we do. But you could tell me. If you wanted."

"I said, be quiet. Who the hell do you think you are to question me? I'm still your husband. I'm still in charge here." He rushed at her, so quickly that Inge instinctively coiled her arms around her middle. His hand dropped. "What are you hiding?"

Before she could think up an answer, he'd grabbed her, cupped her stomach, run his fingers over her breasts.

"I thought it was me keeping secrets." She winced as he snared her wrist. "Well. This changes everything."

"No. It needn't." His grip tightened as Inge panicked. Why hadn't she seized her chance when it sat there? She swallowed hard: if there was anything recoverable here, it needed logic, not emotion; he'd never responded to that. "I was going to tell you. I was waiting till I knew it was safe. But surely a baby is all the more reason for me to stay? I'll do what you said, I promise. I'll go to the Wannsee house. Once the war is done with, you can come back and find me."

He didn't answer. Instead, he pulled her through the adjoining door into her bedroom so fast she stumbled and cracked her knee on the bedpost.

"And abandon my child? Get packing. Clothes for a journey, nothing fancy, and stow your jewelry carefully; it might prove useful. Hurry up."

He already had another case opened, dresses and blouses pulled out of the wardrobe and heaped onto the bed.

"Max, stop . . ." Her voice shook from the pain in her knee. "This isn't a good idea. It would be dangerous for me to travel; you must see that. After what happened before."

She thought she could reason with him; she had forgotten who he was, how fast he could move. He wrenched her arm behind her back, slapping his hand over her mouth before she could scream at the pain.

"Shut up or I'll snap it. What happened before was your fault, no matter how you tried to twist it. I should never have let you get away with that. Or believed your lies about the boy. I don't know what you did, but you did something that day. He disappeared and so did that nurse—don't tell me that was a coincidence. It was only your father's pleading that made me keep you then. After all I've put up with, you owe me an heir. This time, I'll be watching and you won't be so careless. Put this on." He grabbed a plain wool suit and flung it at her. "For the first stage, you can pass as my secretary. Traveling with a wife could look suspicious. After that, well, it's up to you: stay pregnant and you stay safe. I won't keep telling you, Inge. Hurry up!"

He let go of her but didn't back away. Inge's arm throbbed, but she didn't dare rub it. She peeled off her dress as best she could and struggled into the too-tight skirt, fastening the dark green jacket over the waistband's gap. There were so many threats spinning around her, she didn't know which way to turn. She couldn't risk another attack: the baby meant he wouldn't hit her body, but she doubted he still had any qualms about her face. The only thing that might work on him was pointing out what a hindrance she would be.

"Max, please. I'll slow you down; in my condition, it's inevitable."

Her case was full. He picked it up and threw a heavy tweed coat around her shoulders.

"That's a chance I'm prepared to take. I'm not leaving my child. You, unfortunately, come with it. Now, you either walk to the car or I'll knock you out and carry you—it's your choice."

Inge could hear a car approaching; the sweep of its headlights flashed through the gap at the bottom of the blind.

"Good. Heinz is on time. The earlier we're on the road, the less chance of hitting any problems. I've been called to another hospital; that's why we are traveling. You'd better remember that." He pushed her through the bedrooms, collecting his bags as they went, grabbing a pile of papers from a drawer, hurrying her down the stairs and out into the pink-tinged morning before she could protest any further. The wind bit at her fingers and face. She tried to stop, to make a play of fussing at her shoelace, but Max pushed her into the car and closed the partition between them and the driver. "If we have to stop and anyone asks questions, don't you dare speak. I won't have you ruining this."

"Where are we going?" The car sped away. "I haven't said goodbye to anyone."

She twisted around, so desperate for a glimpse of the camp, she wondered for one crazy moment if she could ask Max to drive there first. Ask him if there was anything he might have forgotten that required a stop at his office. She would promise to sit in the car; she would promise not to move. She would do anything if it would get her closer one last time to where Felix was. Even to breathe the same air would be enough.

The car accelerated while she was trying to form the right question. Max picked up his briefcase and began checking through the thickly packed folders.

"Max, where are we going?"

He barely looked up. He carried on working through the closely typed pages as calmly as if they sat at the breakfast table. "Why does it matter? You're going where I say."

CHAPTER ELEVEN

March to June 1945

The train sat in Berlin long enough for Krueger to inspect his stock and for the guards to roll in a second water barrel. There was no more food. Krueger no longer looked at their faces when he counted them or wasted time on pleasantries.

By the time the train shunted out again, some of the men had eaten one slice of bread, some had eaten two. Felix kept his packet unopened; as the train lumbered on at the same slow pace, he kept the packet concealed. No one had any idea where they were going. The train twisted and turned, creeping along lines reduced to a single track, skirting around cities where the stations were all shattered, rarely stopping for more than the time it took to take on water or fuel.

On the fourth day, they passed a place so pulverized it made Berlin seem untouched. The wind seeping into the wagon stank of melting tar and rotting meat. Heinrich, the paper expert, said the city was his hometown of Dresden; he threw up when he saw its fire-blackened corpse. The city's name meant little to Felix beyond the comfort that they were still somewhere in Germany.

Now when the train halted, no one opened the doors, even when the men begged for relief. Felix clung to his place by the window, pushing back into it when he was forced to move and use the slop bucket. A couple of blankets had been sacrificed to make a screen around that, but the flapping material could do nothing to mask the stench.

On and on the journey went, the promised four days stretching to six. Felix hoarded his bread, nibbling a quarter of a slice over the course of a day, sipping at his half cup of water as delicately as a bird. Maintaining the discipline gave him something to focus on.

On the seventh day, the signboards they all watched for, hoping to pick out some recognizable place, switched from German to Polish. That stopped the complaints about hunger and thirst. Poland. *"They get shipped off to some camp no one ever comes back from."*

Felix stared through the iron bars at the unfamiliar language, wondering if one of the string of letters unraveled into Theresienstadt. German cities, Polish cities: they were all broken up the same.

The four days stretched to eight. By the twelfth, Andras and Maté, two of the oldest engravers, were so silent and shrunken and waxen-looking, no one was sure if they were alive or dead. Then the train came to a sudden stop and they toppled and stayed toppled and the question was answered.

Felix counted fourteen days before the train finally shuddered to a halt long enough to suggest a final resting place. At the first sound of running feet, he was up, rubbing life back into his cramped legs, determined, despite his light head, to be ready for whatever orders came.

"Get out. Get moving. Line up."

The standard pattern, although this time there was shoving, not shooting, to bolster the words. The men spilled out of the wagons and huddled shivering on the narrow platform. The early-morning light was weak, the sun still a whisper in the silvery sky. Felix couldn't see a sign. He couldn't see Krueger either, or Marock, but Weber was there, instructing the waiting guards with a lot of shouting.

When the order came to march out, Felix burrowed into the center of the three-man-wide column. Some of the others were looking around, drawing attention, hope of escape too clear on their faces. Even if he had the courage, it wasn't the time: they were too closely guarded and the march was a fast one, short and quick and up a steep hill. Felix was dizzy by the time they reached the high walls.

"Mauthausen." The man to his right, Isaak, squinted up at the sign. "That's an Austrian name. I think it's by Linz or Vienna."

Vienna? How could they be near Vienna when they were surely still in Poland? Vienna was six hundred kilometers at least from Berlin.

Isaak caught Felix's arm as he stumbled. "It makes sense. It's all lakes and mountains around here, a good place if you've got things needing hiding."

The guards were yelling again, herding the column into a huge square, a parade ground surrounded by thick stone walls punctuated by archways as evenly spaced as cathedral cloisters. It was as packed as Felix remembered his first days at Sachsenhausen. He could hear hammers ringing against stone just the same as there, and yet it wasn't like Sachsenhausen at all.

Felix choked back a sob. He knew he was thin and he knew he was starving, but he was a picture of health compared to the wretches around him. The camp was crowded, the parade ground already packed with people, when their column arrived. Despite the lingering frost, half the prisoners already crammed in—the ones he now realized were being led away—were naked and so gaunt he was convinced he could hear their bones rustling against their bruised and filthy skin.

Is every prisoner they've taken reduced to this? Dead before they've killed them? How can so much hatred exist? He could feel himself slipping, overwhelmed by a realization that the terror the Nazis had unleashed was on a scale beyond his imagining.

"Felix, stop looking. This is past anyone's understanding so don't try. Stay with me and stay close." Isaak linked his arm with Felix; made Felix do the same to the man on his left. "If we get separated and mixed up with the rest, there's no hope for us."

Two men in SS uniforms were arguing with Weber. Felix could hear Krueger's name, could see Weber gesticulating. He looked down, focused on breathing through his mouth. The air was as ripe as a farmyard. He began to wish he'd run at the station and taken his chances, but whatever Weber was saying, it must have held weight. Their group was suddenly moving again, carved back out from the rest of the yard.

"Block Twenty. No talking. Move."

Felix ran with the rest, away from the main lines of barracks and into a long hut that backed directly onto a slab-like wall. They were clearly going to be held apart at Mauthausen as they had been at Sachsenhausen, but there, as outside, the resemblance stopped. There were no cots, just damp mattresses blooming with mold. There was no washing block and the walls were rusty with bloodstains and peppered with bullet holes. Felix didn't care: the crates were there, set in long lines along the center of the musty room. As long as the crates were there, they were still needed.

The men fell into an exhausted sleep that night, the thinly covered straw as good as feather beds after the train. The following days took on a rhythm that was half inside the life of the camp and half out. There was separate accommodation but no separate roll call. The counterfeiters were trooped out with the rest, given their numbers and expected to be as fast as anyone with their replies.

At least we kept our clothes. The other inmates were scarecrows, their coverings more holes than cloth. Every day, bigger and bigger groups were stripped and sent away.

Despite Isaak's advice, Felix couldn't learn not to look as the bodies shuffled away, heads down, hope long gone. He couldn't stop wincing at the all-pervading smell of fires that never damped, or rinse the smoke's acrid taste from his mouth. He couldn't close his ears to the whisperings about the game the guards played at the top of the quarry where those fit enough to work were sent, a game that sent prisoners plunging into the freezing rock-filled waters below. He couldn't block it out. He was afraid that if he managed that, if the horror faded into a background he could live against, his own humanity would die. So he saw and he heard and he bore witness and all that he could do to stop himself going mad was to retreat further and further into himself.

Every day, he stood exactly where he was directed. He listened for his number, shouted his answer, marched back and buried himself in the machinery's needs. He was alive. He was one of the fortunate ones whom fate had left standing. There was no rhyme or reason to that. He wasn't unique. Everyone in this camp and all the others could have a Hannah, a dream they believed in; everyone could get lucky. Luck could run out. He set himself, therefore, a simple set of rules. He was still alive—as long as he did his work and drank the watery soup they slopped at him, and didn't think and didn't dream, the longer, perhaps, he would stay that way.

Three weeks passed. The presses were ready. They went to roll call, they came back. Felix invented work, adjusting and polishing, anything to keep busy. And then, finally, Krueger came, fixed them with his affable smile and told them to take it all apart again.

With delicacy, my friends—with great delicacy.

Felix waited for the last part of the order. Krueger walked away and didn't look back.

What was unsaid said it all: whatever this operation had been, beyond lunacy or vanity, beyond a life raft for an unfeasibly lucky few, it was finished.

Escape. It was all Felix could think about. From the moment they were marched back down the hill to the station, he was on the alert, ears pricked like a gundog.

He had lost track of the days, but he guessed spring had moved well into April from the new warmth in the mornings and the blossom tangling the hedgerows. He had no way of knowing how the war was progressing, but the speed of this dismantling was an answer of sorts. The machinery would never be used again: they'd broken it apart with hammers.

None of the counterfeiters felt safe anymore. Isaak wasn't the only one whispering about secret places: they had all heard the rumors about mountain tunnels supposedly full of new weapons that should or would still win the war. Tunnels where all kinds of things could be buried. And of other camps hidden away and filled with constantly burning ovens.

When they arrived at the station this time, the waiting train had no wagons, no seats, no water. The hundred or so of the original troop of counterfeiters from Sachsenhausen still surviving were crammed into two open freight cars, as tightly stacked as the cases of notes they'd not long resealed. Whatever value they once had was clearly used up.

Felix worked his way to a corner, to a place he could jump from, but this train moved too quickly and the sides were too high. On an ordinary day, the landscape they traveled through would be breathtaking. Fairy-tale houses dotting flower-filled meadows that nestled beneath snow-covered peaks. Felix saw nothing but fields stretching out without a trace of cover and tiny settlements where no stranger could blend in. He longed for a city, no matter how ruined. The camp they were finally dumped at was a fortress, a brooding lump of granite without visible barracks and with entrances leading not inside but under the ground.

Go down there and you'll never come up. Felix no longer cared whether running risked a bullet: no one was going to bury him alive. He unloaded the crates as directed and waited for the first order to carry their contents underground. It didn't come.

No orders came beyond *unload; lie down; be quiet.* For three days, the men did nothing but sit and sleep in the open air and watch the guards, who were no longer really watching them. There were new rumors to chew over: the guards were overheard discussing a lake, no more than a mile away and deep enough to hide a train. There was no food beyond dried-out heels of bread, but there was water from a nearby stream and there was rest and the air was as fresh as the breeze on a mountain. Felix felt the first signs of strength creeping back.

On the fourth day, just as the men began to hope they might have been forgotten, a truck arrived, then a second. They loaded up the crates again; no one told them to take any care. Then a third truck came and thirty men were randomly pulled out and loaded on. *This is it.*

Felix kept to the edges of the group, head thrust inside his jacket, hands wedged against the seams concealing his talisman letters.

The next morning one truck came back, another thirty men were loaded on and this time two of the guards were also called up. The three who were left shouted and shook their fists; the driver shrugged. By evening, another one of the guards was gone. *This is it.*

He couldn't take another camp, another step closer to that final selection. He wasn't risking a lake or a firing squad. His luck, the gift Hannah's sketch had brought him, wasn't just running out—it was down to the last drop. *I can't waste it. I can't sit here knowing death is coming and just let it come, not after the risk she took.*

Felix held on to his shredding nerves until darkness fell, until he saw the first shadowy shape peel off. Then another man went, rolling through the grass like a discarded ball. The guards didn't see or didn't care—they were too busy drinking.

Felix knew that wouldn't last. He had seen how drunken guards behaved; he doubted Marock and Weber's behavior in the last months at Sachsenhausen had been unique. Out here, with no one to care or notice, killing would become a sport. His body was slick with sweat, his mouth was sour; he didn't trust his legs would hold him as far as the forest, but his choices were diminishing.

He moved suddenly, keeping as close to the ground as he could, scuttling like a wood louse ready to curl up. A dozen meters became a mile. He was sure the trees were moving backward, taunting him.

One goal, that was all he needed.

Get to the tree line and you'll be safe.

He muttered it as he went, focusing on small steps the same as he had done a lifetime ago on the running track. If he could reach the forest, nothing else mattered. After that he would get up and he would run and let the guards shoot him if they could.

He reached the first line of trunks and he didn't stop. He ran and he ran until the trees enveloped him, until he tumbled into a tangle of roots and sleep claimed him.

The next morning and the next, he plunged on, with no idea where he was heading. It was so dark under the forest canopy the days began to merge. He kept to forests when he could, clung to reed-edged rivers when the trees cleared.

Once he realized no one was chasing him, Felix slowed down. At first, the spaces were so big after the camps' confinement they frightened him, turning him small and vulnerable. Then he let his hands linger for a moment as they cupped water that was crystal clear not brackish. When he sat down, he spread his fingers through the springy moss and turned his head up to the sun and breathed in air so fresh he could taste the green. He realized there was beauty in the world again and he wept with the hope of it.

He grew light-headed, happy to lie on a riverbank and watch the clouds play. It took him a day of doing that before he understood that he was starving, closer to death than he had been when he escaped. That made him move.

He stopped caring what he put in his mouth. He ate mushrooms, he robbed birds' nests and ate anything he could tear from the bushes that looked vaguely edible, keeping going even when his stomach gave out. He slept less and did that with more care, curled up in tree trunks or marshy hollows. He waded through water when his stink overwhelmed him, desperate to be clean and human again.

He heard gunfire. Some nights the ground rumbled so deeply, he dreamed herds of elephants were charging. He kept going. He had no idea whether he was running toward Germany or Switzerland or Italy. He didn't care. He was alive.

On the seventh day—or maybe the sixth or the eighth; the world was beginning to blur—he stumbled onto the edge of a town. The few houses he could see were pockmarked, but smoke of the right sort floated from the chimneys. The river ran clean, not dotted with bodies, and the air smelled of sap and not like a slaughterhouse. He crept around the side of an empty station and found a battered signboard: *Wels.* He had no idea what town or even what country that meant. He was still looking for clues when he heard the shout. Instinctively, he hunched over, ready to roll for cover.

The shout came again. He didn't know the words, but there was a twang to the accent he recognized from his long-ago records and the radio. Surely it was American?

Felix straightened up and turned slowly around.

The soldier coming toward him wasn't pointing a gun or screaming orders. He was smiling and waving what Felix guessed was a bar of chocolate.

He must think I'm a child. Felix looked at his ripped and muddy clothes, at the bruised and bony knees and skinny calves poking through the tatters. He ran a hand through his straggling hair and wondered what on earth his dirt-engrained face must look like.

The soldier kept grinning, kept waving the chocolate bar; began making a strange clucking noise he must have thought was enticing.

Felix felt a sudden prickle in his nose, a catch in his throat. For the first time in far too many years, he began to laugh.

At first, his defenses were dismantled by the sweet rush of the chocolate. Then he remembered who he was in this redrawn world and he panicked. A soldier, after all, was a soldier. Felix began to sidle away. When the man put out a hand to stop him, he reared back.

"I want to help." It took the soldier three tries before Felix understood what he meant. "You don't have to come if you don't want to." He stood by the jeep with the door open, keeping his distance, treating Felix with as much care as he would a skittish horse.

I can't carry on alone. Felix forced himself to focus on unpicking the man's words, trying to tell if their meaning differed from the tone they were offered in. He scanned the man's face, looking for flaws like he would with a picture, and couldn't see anything there but pity.

Slowly, stumbling over the language, Felix managed to recover enough English to make it understood that he had come from a camp.

The soldier's smile fell; he turned white. When his next words were "I'm sorry," Felix finally felt safe enough to climb into the jeep.

They drove to a base, which bustled more than most of the towns Felix had passed by. It was dense with tents and filled with Americans sporting snappy names like Bob and Brad and the whitest teeth he had ever seen. The first soldier handed him on to another. He quickly drew a crowd, all jabbering and eager to help him, or so he hoped. When they led him to a shower room, however, the whispers the counterfeiters had shrunk from at Sachsenhausen whirled back and Felix fell to his knees, shaking with terror at how these soldiers had tricked him.

Then the watching men quieted, helped him up, turned the hot water on and off and let him go in and out until he remembered how to breathe. After that, no one hurried or crowded him at all. When so much dirt had washed away he felt lighter by years, they took him to a dining room and sat him in front of a plate piled with food Felix had forgotten existed. Stew so thick it coated his spoon, potatoes cooked to a silken creaminess and bread so soft his swollen gums nestled into it like a pillow.

They made him eat slowly; they tried not to stare. Finally, they took him to a bed with sheets so clean he was almost afraid to touch them and left him to sob and sleep and wake up without wondering if that morning would be his last.

It was only then the soldiers told him it was done, that Germany had surrendered, that the war was finished. Felix refused to believe it until someone brought a stack of newspapers whose stark headlines needed no translation: *It's Over. Victory. Hitler Dead.* He didn't know what to think, what this end the Americans called victory, but which he knew on some level as defeat, actually meant.

The soldiers kept telling him he was safe. He drank their beer and wondered what they wanted from him. *Nothing* seemed to be the answer, except the chance to do something good in the midst of a misery these bright-eyed boys clearly understood no better than he did.

A week went by and then another. The soldiers separated out from a uniformed pack into men who talked about books and films and girlfriends, and those who wanted to tell him about the cities and countryside they came from, not the battles they had fought.

Felix listened to descriptions of wheat fields in Kansas and bayous in Louisiana and arguments over baseball so impassioned he thought fights would break out. He was asked over and over what Germany was really like, by boys who were a generation or two away from being German themselves, who had surnames that would have guaranteed them a warm welcome in happier times. Who had no more idea why they were meant to be enemies than he did.

He worked on his English; he ate whatever they gave him. He still didn't feel safe. He had no money and no papers; he had nothing except the bits of clothes they'd found for him and his rolled-up scraps of paper. And a plan: to get back to Berlin as quickly as possible. When he announced that intention, his new friends told him he was crazy.

"It's not the greatest idea, bud. The Russians got in there first. Street-to-street fighting is what we heard and not a woman left safe. They've got a lot of revenge to take. Why don't you stay with us a while longer? We can find you work: HQ's crying out for translators. It's good you want to get home; it's what we're all desperate for, but give us a chance to sort out the last pockets of trouble, give you something worth going home for."

They tried to persuade him and didn't stop until Felix admitted it was a long-lost girl he was going back for, and to find his missing mother. Then the mood changed.

Photographs appeared from wallets, a much-thumbed gallery of wives and girlfriends and mothers. All missed as much as Felix longed for Kerstin and Hannah, all spoken of as the "one good thing" that kept their men going, whose arms would one day soon wipe away the horrors of war. Nobody thought Felix's plan was a wise choice, but nobody argued anymore.

A haversack appeared stuffed with spare trousers and shirts, a baggy brown jacket that hung from his shoulders and enough candy to start him up in the confectionary business. They held a thing they called a *whip-round,* which resulted in a wallet fat with dollars and Reichsmarks that was dismissed as "nothing much; forget about it." There were more good wishes than he could count and there was a ride, first as far as Regensburg, then the promise of another to Nuremburg. "After that, you're on your own: our detail doesn't go any farther. But there's trains moving from there, or should be by now; it'll get you closer."

It did, although the journey was so bleak, Felix wondered if he'd made the wrong decision. The roads in all directions were crammed with washed-out people, pushing carts and strollers, lugging bundles and hollow-eyed children. Everyone, even the babies, looked old. When the troop trucks and the tanks approached, the straggling groups stepped into the ditches at the sides of the road and waited, in silence, as if they expected to be shot or rounded up and would obey whatever was ordered without question. Their desolation was unbearable.

Reaching Regensburg should have been a relief—the town was at least standing and running with some semblance of order. Within a day of their arrival, however, it was so jammed with refugees that Felix didn't dare leave his driver's side until another was found, for fear of being swallowed up.

The farther north his journey took him, the worse the horror grew. Corpses scattered the roadsides, crumpled where they fell, with no one to clear a grave or offer a prayer. As for Nuremburg, it was decimated, barely a building left that wasn't a shell.

"It was where your guy started it all—whole place had to pay," his driver informed him, without bothering to ask what Felix might think.

Your guy. Felix sat in silence, wondering if any German would ever be allowed to give an honest answer to that.

The station he was finally dropped at was mobbed. Trains limped in and out through the shattered yards, passengers hanging out of the windows and off the sides. It took Felix three attempts to reach the platform: every time he got close, his stomach heaved. When he did get there, the first train went through without him: he was so busy trying to find out where to buy a ticket and where to stand that the carriages were swamped before he could get near them.

When the next one came, hours later, Felix was ready to take on this new Germany where people pushed and no one paid and hanging back meant losing. He was prepared for the journey to take far longer than it should. What he wasn't prepared for was the fear it plunged him into. Or the way his skin crawled as elbows and shoulders pressed into his shrinking body. Or the growing, overwhelming certainty that the train was taking him away, never to come back.

When they finally crawled into Potsdam to be informed that the last thirty kilometers of track into Berlin were impassable, Felix could have cheered. As everyone dismounted furious and grumbling, he found the road he needed and set off at a pace sure to pull him away from the crowds. He was done with groups, with being herded.

He found a small farm on the edge of the Wannsee, swapped some of his dollars for apples and bread and a piece of chicken the size of his thumb. He chose paths that skirted the lake and kept clear of the roads. When he reached Nikolassee and the Grunewald, he plunged into the forest with a sense of relief. He walked each day until he was worn through and slept where he dropped.

On the third day, he realized he was in the once-familiar streets of Wilmersdorf and Charlottenburg. There was nothing he knew. The roads wound beneath mounds of fallen masonry and broken brick so high it felt as if he was circling the moat of some great fallen castle. Sometimes, for an hour or more, he saw no one, passed no habitable houses. Then, as he drew closer to the center, more people emerged, only to vanish again so quickly he thought he was hallucinating. It was a long time before he realized the shadowy figures weren't disappearing but retreating underground. Then he looked more closely and saw lights glint through basements, saw families huddled like cave dwellers in candlelit cellars. Life in Berlin had turned on its head.

There was no pattern to the destruction. He crossed into one street and there were shops open, curtains fluttering at still-intact windows and men walking down the pavement in smart silver-gray hats. He crossed into the next and the houses were split open and the ragged children playing in the burnt-out chassis of a car ran when they saw him. He rarely saw a woman.

That night, Felix swapped his dollars for a bed in the only house that didn't slam its door in his face. The room was tucked in an attic whose roof was so broken it was mostly sky and he woke in the night to find rats creeping around him. His first lodging back in Berlin and it was meaner than a Sachsenhausen barracks; the impossible, inescapable reality of that kept him awake until dawn.

By the time he got to his old neighborhood of Wedding, he was exhausted, disoriented. He asked for directions and got a shrug or a vague wave. No one was interested in strangers; no one was interested in anything. In the end, he walked the length of his street and back before it took on any shape he knew. A weed-choked pile of rubble finally offered up the memory of a park. A tangled mess of metal unknotted itself into railings. The house itself proved as hard to find, until he stopped looking for three stories and focused on one. When it finally materialized, he didn't know what to do. What spell could he cast to make Kerstin still here? To have Arno appear in the hallway behind her, rubbing his glasses and smiling his shy smile?

Felix climbed over to the door, stopped, walked away; went back and knocked three times as if that number might magic life back into this wasteland. His hope vanished as quickly as a dandelion clock. The face staring back was hard-worn and sour.

"Don't know her. Never heard of her. Whoever the place belonged to before, it's mine now."

Every angle Felix tried, the man batted it back until he pulled a handful of dollars from his pocket.

"What did you say her name was? Thalberg? Maybe I remember someone. A good-looking woman, with reddish hair? Maybe I saw her. She can't have been much, though: this flat was seized, reallocated. What was she, a communist? Don't tell me she was a Jew. If she was, she'll be long gone, and good riddance. If that's the type you're looking for, you can clear off too." The door slammed before Felix could explain or throw a punch or get his breath back.

He stumbled away to a corner with cleaner air. If this was how the end of the war played out, what hope could the future hold? He sat out of sight, trying to collect himself. This, finding his home, was as far as his plan went; he hadn't thought a moment further. He waited, not knowing what else to do. Eventually, as the sky started to dip toward dusk, the man emerged, head low, hat rammed on.

Felix stayed in the shadows until there wasn't even the suggestion of a footstep and then he moved. One hard shove and the door gave. Inside was no better than out. The walls were covered with cobweb cracks, the paint peeling in scab-like flakes. All Kerstin's things were gone; the furniture he could see was no better than junk. Quickly, one eye to the open door, he crossed to the alcove. A swift kick and the brickwork gave way. The tin was still there. Felix grabbed it, shook it until he heard the letters rattle and stuffed it inside his jacket. He rifled through the bedroom and the kitchen, peering under the sagging bed, throwing open the tilting wardrobe, the drawers of the one remaining cupboard. Nothing. All traces of Kerstin and Arno—and Felix himself—had vanished. He wanted to cry. He wanted to sit on the floor and sob like a baby and roar for his mother. Instead, he fell out of the ruin of his family and he walked.

He had no ideas left; he had nowhere to go. There was nothing for him in Wedding, or in Wilmersdorf. He had no idea where the American soldiers were now even if he could face the journey south again.

This is just one step back. You stayed alive. You made it to Berlin. You don't know Kerstin's dead. It's another search, but you'd be searching for Hannah anyway.

He tried to believe any of that was true, but *you're alone and you've nothing* had a louder voice. He kept walking, as if his stride could outstrip his fear. When he looked up, startled by the unfamiliar peal of a bicycle bell, he realized he was in the wide streets surrounding the Tiergarten. He picked up his pace, clutching at the tin of letters as if to conjure up a genie. Except the magic was as dead here as everywhere else. What should have been a sea of trees was a burned and blasted wreck, littered with blackened stumps that rose from the scorched earth like rotten fingers and crumbling graying ghosts where white statues had once stood.

Felix finally stopped. He sank to his knees and he wept, great tearing cries as if he would retch up his heart. Nobody passing by broke step. He wept for Arno and Kerstin and Hannah and himself. He wept for Berlin, and he kept on weeping until his body was as hollow as the city. Then he walked on, the dirt still clinging to his knees, until he found a bar, where he pulled out the last of his dollars. The barman poured him a brandy and kept on pouring.

"Hey, buddy, you doing okay?"

These soldiers were older and their uniforms were smarter than the boys Felix had spent his days with, but their smiles were as welcoming. Loneliness slammed into Felix so hard that leaving the warmth of the base suddenly seemed his most stupid decision. He raised his glass in a salute and was more relieved than he could admit when they waved him over.

Names were swapped, brief battle histories were shared, although nobody wanted to dwell on those. Nobody pressed Felix to tell his story beyond the barest facts. "Anyone who's survived has seen too much—no need to rake it over if you don't want to" was said with the same kindness he'd heard at the base. Someone ordered another bottle.

After a while, as his edges softened, Felix asked them what they were doing in Berlin, now the fighting was done. Most of the answer was lost somewhere in a jumble of letters and acronyms he assumed were company names or administrative departments, but one thing stood out and he made them repeat it.

"This ain't no ordinary war. There's been crimes committed here like you wouldn't believe. It's our job to collect the evidence."

Felix put his glass down and straightened up. He waited until everyone was quiet, until they were looking at him. "That's what they called us in the camp: evidence, something to be got rid of. They did a very good job."

"Which camp?" It was the first direct question Felix had been asked.

"Sachsenhausen, for two years. Then, briefly, Mauthausen."

"Two years? None of us thought that was possible." The officer paused. "A few of us have been to those places. Hell isn't a big enough word. An hour inside and I swear I lost all my faith in the world. How could you survive that for two years?"

"Because I was lucky."

"Lucky?" The men around him shook their heads; one rubbed his eyes.

"There's no other word." Slowly, and very deliberately, knowing that they would listen and they would care, and needing the burden of all he had witnessed to be shared so that it would inch off his tired shoulders, Felix Thalberg began to talk.

CHAPTER TWELVE

March to September 1945

Why does it matter? You're going where I say.

His tone had been one of utter indifference. Inge sat perfectly still as the Mercedes pulled away. She had to stay calm, focus on where they were going. If she knew the route, perhaps she could find a place to escape. Max had said the window of time was closing. Surely any corridor they could run down was closing too?

The BBC broadcasts had spelled out the war's progress: the Allies were advancing west through France and Belgium and up from the southern tip of Italy; the Red Army was swarming through eastern Prussia. The two prongs had Germany caught like a mouse between pouncing cats and the final bite was a matter of when, not if. To make matters worse, there were rumors of more heavy bombing raids to come across the Rhine and the Ruhr. Inge couldn't imagine a place they could go that wasn't under some kind of siege.

She knew the car had turned south, taking them through the cobbled streets of a still-sleeping Oranienburg. Now there were flashes of green that suggested they were driving through countryside, not into the city. At a guess, that meant they were skirting Berlin to the west, on the far side of the river Havel. That route would make sense. The roads in that direction were less likely to be bomb-damaged or used for troop movements. They were also roads that ran easily back to Berlin. All she needed was one chance.

She tried. When they reached the edge of a sprawling forest, she begged for a break, complaining of an aching bladder. Max was one step ahead of her.

"Go with her."

Heinz marched her to the tree line and stood guard while her face burned.

"At least have the manners to turn your back."

She managed quite a sprint before Heinz's fingers grabbed hold of her hair and dragged her to her knees.

"Hold her still."

Max aimed the blow well. It hit the side of her head and rattled through her cheekbones.

"I know how to do this, Inge. It won't harm the child, but it will hurt you. Don't test me."

She would rather try to bolt from the car when it was moving than go through that humiliation again.

By nine o'clock, she judged they were past Berlin and its suburbs and coming toward what looked like Potsdam. Inge could see wide, well-swept streets and domed buildings glinting in the early-morning sun. And lanes far too narrow for a car to speed down, where surely she could outrun Heinz's bulk? It was another chance; she couldn't let it slip away without trying. She adopted the most pleading tone she could manage.

"My legs are awfully cramped. Could we stop for a while? Let me stretch them?"

Max ignored her. She wriggled and groaned; he ordered Heinz to go faster. Nobody stopped them, even though a checkpoint had been set up across the main square. One look at the sleek Mercedes and the unmistakable uniform in the back and they were waved through with a sharp salute. The moment to run was gone, if it had ever existed. Inge forced herself not to look back.

The car continued south, turning to the west. The roads began to fill. Trucks bulging with tired-looking troops competed for space with armored cars whose wheels looked more suited to tractors. Heinz kept up a steady pace, holding back when he needed to, gestured to go first more often than not when the car's SS and Party insignia were spotted. When refugees spilled in front of them with their bundles and their handcarts, he barely gave them time to scatter. As the roads became more pothole than surface, their progress slowed, but the ragged crowds looked too hungrily at the car to make Inge want to get out of it. Eventually, she fell into a jostled sleep and woke up exhausted in a square full of pink and yellow and cream gabled buildings. She thought she was hallucinating.

"Where are we?" The car turned up a narrow winding road lined with elegant houses set inside tree-screened gardens, Max directing Heinz toward a set of eagle-topped gateposts.

"Wittenberg."

Inge knew the name, something to do with Martin Luther; another history lesson she hadn't paid attention to. What she was sure of, however—her geography having improved considerably thanks to her addiction to the radio—was that this meant their direction likely lay toward Leipzig or Frankfurt. Neither of which was surely any safer than Berlin...

The car purred through the driveway and came to a stop by a set of steps where a woman was waiting. Her perfectly curled hair and cobalt blue dress made Inge feel faded and lumpy. Whoever she was, she greeted Max with a kiss and Inge with a cool nod. Max didn't introduce her. When she showed them to their room, the woman kept her arm firmly through Max's.

"You must be tired, my dear. I'll send a supper tray. Max and I haven't seen each other for years. We've a lot to catch up on."

Inge let them go without comment. Max didn't come to bed that night, or at least not to hers. When she came in to breakfast after a sleepless night spent with her head full of road maps, neither he nor their hostess paid her any attention.

"Helge is an old friend, from Vienna."

Inge stared out of the car window as they drove away and thought it best to say nothing.

After that, the journey's pattern quickly established itself, a chain of "old friends" passing them from one charming, still-well-run house to the next. Sometimes it was a woman full of smiles and not-so-secret glances. Sometimes it was a man claiming himself as a fellow student or colleague at some place Inge didn't recognize but stored away. Max clearly had an extensive network and a life with far more in it than the one he barely shared with her. Whoever they were, they were all older, they were all staunch Party members and, taking their cue from Max, they paid no attention to Inge.

She was happy to stay in the shadows. Their belief in themselves and the rightness of their cause was unbreakable; their optimism in the face of the coming defeat unfathomable. Max behaved as blithely as their hosts: acting as if no one knew or cared that the war's front was barely a matter of weeks away, as if this was some delightful holiday they were all engaged in. Inge watched them in silence, memorizing faces, soaking up the name-dropping and the gossip that seemed to be their lifeblood. Not to impress Max and be a good wife anymore. Not to be the parrot she now realized she had been, learning without thinking, without understanding. To know her enemy.

She and Max moved like trains on separate tracks. He stowed his bags in the same rooms but never came to her bed. He stayed silent in the car. He didn't need to repeat his threats. Inge had stopped thinking about running—she knew the moment for that had outpaced her. Her pregnancy was becoming obvious and awkward. Five months in and she was sure she could feel butterfly stirrings. She didn't mention that to Max. She tried not to think about the baby at all beyond getting it born. And then . . . The next step was hazy, but the goal was clear: to get away.

He'll never let you go: not with the baby. That thought pushed in every day. *I could leave the baby behind* pushed in too, but she wasn't ready for that one yet. At least she had stopped frantically praying to lose it. After Max had dragged her into the car, for those first few dumbstruck days, that was all she had done. This baby glued Max to her. She wanted it gone and hadn't felt more than a flicker of guilt at wishing it. Then she had caught Max watching her the way he did when her thoughts showed on her face and had barely been able to stop a shiver when he asked how her health was.

Stay pregnant and you stay safe. He meant it. He would kill her if she miscarried again. Not in some dramatic fit of passion, but clinically and efficiently, like a farmer dispatching a cow that had gone past its value. Max would kill her and Heinz would bury her and she would become nothing more than another casualty of war. That hadn't made her want the baby, but wishing it dead was too dangerous. And, now it had flickered into life, it was too cruel. Whether she could risk staying with it, once it was born, was another question entirely.

The journey crawled along the back roads and high roads that ran past Leipzig and Bayreuth and the outskirts of Frankfurt. Inge had guessed where they were going, although she didn't mention that either: Baden-Baden, far down in the south and the site of Max's family home. It was a logical destination. There were fewer reports of air raids in that region, or had been when she last heard, and, unless things had changed dramatically, it was the French who were advancing that way. Max loathed the Soviets, and the English and Americans unnerved him, but he had nothing but contempt for the French. They, as he frequently commented, "would sell their souls to stay alive and have no notion of honor." If he had to live under an occupation for any length, Inge doubted Max would feel threatened by the French.

The thought of Baden-Baden and the Eichels brought the only comfort on the journey. Inge barely knew them, but she remembered Brigitte as a motherly sort who would no doubt be thrilled to become a grandmother. There were worse places to get her strength back.

And then they arrived in Karlsruhe and Inge realized nowhere was safe, nowhere had gone untouched. The scale of destruction was worse than the journey had lulled her—and, from the shock on Max's face, him—into expecting. He watched the broken streets pass by with a twisted mouth and spent longer huddling with Heinz that evening than with his hostess.

This time when Inge appeared at breakfast, Max was dressed not in his uniform but in an unremarkable tweed suit of the kind a family doctor might wear. And he had cut and tamed his wavy hair into a far more nondescript style. All that did was sharpen his cheekbones. Max was transformed as much as Max could be and Heinz was gone. In place of the Mercedes, their belongings were neatly stowed into a blue Opel Olympia, a squat and ordinary-looking thing with patches of rust on the fender. When Max climbed into the driving seat, Inge struggled to suppress a smile: she was so used to him being treated like royalty, it was a relief to see him in an everyday setting doing everyday things. It diminished him into more manageable proportions.

"How interesting that you are entertained. I am thinking of our child's safety, like I always do, yet you appear to think this is a game. I hoped pregnancy might help you grow up."

She kept her head down and her mouth shut for the rest of the way, although her palm itched to slap him.

Baden-Baden, to her relief, was intact and the Eichel house, a stunning three-story French confection with a façade tricked out in narrow columns and plasterwork heavy with fruit and vines, was a haven.

One mention of Inge's pregnancy and Brigitte became a whirlwind of comfort. Suddenly, there was a lavender-scented bath, thick towels and a torte studded with hazelnuts and real cream whipped up from a kitchen Inge could happily have spent the night in. She let herself be mothered in a way that was as new as it was delightful and sank into the soft pillows, luxuriating in the fact that there wasn't a sound from outside beyond a barn owl.

A baby could be born here, could be safe here. For the first time in the two weeks since Max had snatched her away, Inge fell into a dreamless, soothing sleep.

The view from the bedroom was postcard-perfect; it was a joy to throw back these curtains.

Inge unlatched the window and leaned out into air that was crisp and apple-sweet. The colors were as bold as a child's picture book: dark red roofs, bright blue sky, deep green forests. She ran a brush through her hair and dressed quickly, wrapping herself in layers against the mid-February chill.

Breakfast first—sleep had sharpened her appetite—and then out to explore. A walk and some time on her own to think and face what was coming with the birth and what might be possible after. A clock chimed along the hall: it was nine thirty, much later than she realized.

Inge ran down the stairs, rehearsing her apologies. As she reached the marble-floored hallway, an elderly maid laden with plates tripped out of the breakfast room. Voices drifted through the open door.

"I hadn't intended to bring her, no, but once I knew she was pregnant, what else could I do? She doesn't know a thing and I'll keep it that way."

Inge stopped, the skin on her arms prickling as Max continued.

"If there's one thing I've learned about Inge, it's that the less she knows, the easier she is to lead. Tell her too much and she turns skittish, sees monsters. Managing her has always been a chore."

That he could speak so unkindly was no surprise; what had Inge clutching for the doorjamb was Brigitte's response.

"This is our fault, Max. I'm so sorry. We pushed for the match, thinking she was young and malleable enough to make a good Party wife. Instead, we saddled you with a liability. Well, who knows what will happen when it comes to childbirth? She is a very little thing…"

Inge's clammy fingers pressed feathery patterns into the paint.

"As long as the child is safe, and the Eichel and Ackermann fortunes with it, what happens to her doesn't matter."

That indifference again—it was more frightening than fury.

"Given her past behavior, if she does come through the birth, it will likely make her unstable. That will give me an excuse to be rid of her. However it turns out, the eventual outcome will be the same: there's no long-term place in this for her."

Inge stuffed her hand in her mouth to keep from crying out.

"Karl has been making arrangements?" Gustav Eichel shared his son's efficient way of speaking. "The money is moving?"

"It has been for months, since the restrictions on investments outside Germany were eased; the odd bribe here and there has got the wheels turning. He has more than enough to rebuild and, with what is waiting for me, so have I. Everything should be in place when we eventually arrive."

"And you aren't concerned they might join the war?"

Inge leaned in closer, her bitten knuckles as raw as her nerves. Who was *they*? And why and where was money moving?

Someone got up from the table: part of Max's answer was lost in the scrape of a chair.

"Even if they do, it doesn't change anything. It's still the best place. There is a receptive government and work there I'm needed for until Germany's future is settled."

Where was this *best place*?

Inge turned at the sound of footsteps. It was the maid coming back, frowning as she saw Inge hovering in the doorway. Inge raised a finger to her lips and slipped back up the stairs.

When Brigitte came in, as Inge expected she would, she was back under the covers. Brigitte, also as Inge expected, was all motherly concern.

"You're resting. That's excellent, just what you need. Why don't you stay here and I'll have a tray sent up? And then, if the day grows a little warmer, we could go for a stroll in the gardens. How would that suit?"

Inge managed a smile and a nod; she didn't trust her voice. She also managed not to flinch when Brigitte patted her cheek.

"That's a good girl. Now go back to sleep. We'll take care of you."

She wanted to bolt, but then she heard the click of the key in the door. For one mad moment, she imagined the window, a rope knotted from sheets. Except she was three floors up and couldn't climb or tie knots or do anything useful. Besides, where would she go? A pregnant woman in a town her husband's family all but owned?

Inge's thoughts scrabbled and slid. Who else wasn't fighting yet but might be? Where on earth were they going? Could it be Switzerland or Austria? Both were easily reached, and yet how could either country be considering joining the war when Switzerland was neutral and Austria conquered? Her head throbbed, reeling from what had been said and the callousness so easily dripped through it. From trying to determine where the biggest threat lay.

She curled up and wrapped her hands around her curving stomach, pressing until she felt the butterfly flutters. They were stronger than a week ago. There was no leaving the child here—Max and the Eichels weren't fit to be anywhere near a baby.

Inge rolled over and stared out of the window at the cloudless sky. Where Max was taking her didn't matter. What mattered was staying well and bringing this baby safely into the world. And then getting them both away. Back to Berlin, to what she knew; where she had found happiness once and would find it again.

A good girl. If that's what this needed, that's what she'd be. She'd had enough practice. Inge would go home and start again. Surely even Grete would take her side when she understood how dangerous Max really was?

That part of the plan was for later. All she had to do now was play Max's game. And win.

Three days after their arrival in Baden-Baden, Max announced they were leaving. Inge had never been happier to leave a place, but it took all her strength to get back into the Opel. It was one thing to gather her courage alone in a bedroom; it was harder to hold it sitting next to the threat.

Max paid her no more attention on this drive than the last. In the end, their final destination wasn't Switzerland or Austria, although they drove through both and Inge could have settled for either. Like the Spreewald, both countries seemed to be living in a far kinder century. The long and winding drive took them along blossom-edged lanes, past chalet-style houses that belonged in a storybook and lakes that shimmered impossibly blue.

They crossed the Swiss border, and then the Austrian, with new passports at both and rustling envelopes that stopped questions. Inge found it hard to match what she saw with what she thought she knew. The last time she had properly heard any news of the war, the Russians had been sweeping through East Prussia with their sights set firmly on Austria.

When she mentioned that, carefully, without sounding as if she was questioning their route, Max smiled his patient smile and explained she hadn't understood how big the country was. The Russian Front was nearly seven hundred kilometers from the sleepy little villages they sheltered in and had less practical meaning than the change of the seasons or the pull of the moon.

Inge buried her fury at his condescending tone in imagining a life in one of the geranium-decked houses, the baby growing fat on milk and cheese, crawling through the clover-sweet meadows. Then they crossed the Brenner Pass, so high in the mountains the air tingled like ice, and Inge realized their road was leading to Italy. The urge to wrestle open the locked door and run almost overwhelmed her. Italy wasn't a country considering joining the conflict—it was completely embroiled in it. Half the country had surrendered to the Allies; half was still ruled by that clown Mussolini. How could a place on the brink of civil war be any safer than Berlin?

They crossed the Pass with the papers and envelopes still working their magic and finally arrived in Milan in an April that was already stickily warm. Inge tried to memorize every detail, but the battle to stay alert was beginning to defeat her. Long weeks on the road, changing houses almost every night, holding herself quiet and compliant day after day, had left her worn out and dull. The pregnancy sat heavy. Inge was swollen and cumbersome, unable to believe she would grow bigger; unnerved by thoughts of a birth around which Brigitte flew like a bad fairy. She swallowed her fears, the word *unstable* echoing through her mind. She smiled when Max asked her how she felt and kept smiling, even when he examined her so intimately she wanted to scream.

They edged through Milan, through streets as dust-choked and broken as anywhere in Berlin. The city was in splinters. What must once have been beautiful galleries and elegant churches were crushed as if a giant had gone wandering.

How is this safer? Inge sat choked with the rage of him bringing her here, chewing on it until she was so full of anger she thought she would vomit. She sat in bloated misery as the car twisted and turned through blocked roads and detours and men in red scarves leered and shouted obscenities. By the time they turned into a quiet street away from the center and through the gates of a building that was thankfully intact, even Max's knuckles were white. This time, the woman who came to greet them was a nun; Inge could have cried with relief. She was not religious, and she had no time for Catholics, but there was a comfortable air about the nun's placidly plump face and pristine habit that made Inge want to curl up and be petted.

"This is where I leave you."

Hope must have flared in her eyes.

"Oh, Inge, you do give yourself away. It's not for good; I'll be checking on you until the baby comes."

Whether Milan was dangerous or not, the relief of being in one place and without him ran through her like an injection of oxygen. He unloaded her bags and he was gone.

Inge stood in the courtyard, watching the car disappear. Maybe the war would catch up with him; maybe he would be caught or killed. She didn't care which, as long as it stopped him returning. Maybe this was the place she would finally build an escape from.

She stood there, wishing for good luck harder than a child blowing out candles, until the nun caught at her arm. She led Inge inside, chirruping away in her indecipherable language. The building was dimly lit, haunted by white-garbed women whose hands talked as much as their mouths. Inge was taken to a spartan whitewashed room that was more restful than any of the overstuffed houses she had bounced through. There was a garden to walk in, cheery with flowers and humming with tiny birds whose wings fluttered so fast they were almost invisible.

For a week there was no sign of Max. Inge slept, ate simple food with the whispering nuns and let her body expand to meet the baby. She could make no sense of anything they said to her. She heard the word *Partigiani* a lot, usually coupled with *Resistenza*, and couldn't tell if it frightened the nuns or pleased them.

One morning, early and without warning, Max reappeared. He was a little thinner, dressed in rough clothes that made him look even more handsome. He barely acknowledged Inge but spoke to the nuns in an Italian whose fluency astonished her. Whatever they answered, it made him happy enough to go.

As April closed and May beckoned, the nuns came to her room, flapping like a herd of spooked sheep, and insisted she look at the newssheet they thrust at her. The photographs it carried were bizarre, terrible things: bodies strung upside down from lampposts, crowds punching the air. When they made her understand it was Mussolini, Inge knew the end of the war could only be a matter of days.

The next sheet they brought had a headline that needed no translating: *Hitler è Morto*. It was done: what German would go on fighting after that?

Inge watched as the nuns hugged, lit candles, flocked to their chapel. She went back to her room, cradling her swollen stomach, not knowing whether to celebrate the end of a conflict that had cost so much or weep for the losses endured and the reprisals sure to come.

Her country was defeated, her brothers were dead; goodness knows what her husband had done. Felix was lost—she couldn't put his name next to *dead;* she had to have some hope, no matter how absurd, to cling to. Inside its safe little world, the baby kicked and rolled. Singing floated through the corridors. Inge had no one to give thanks for, no one to pray for. The only prayer she could think of was that Max would never come back, that some harm would befall him. She doubted there was a god who would listen to that.

"Why won't you help me? I don't understand. Whatever you're saying, I don't understand."

Why wouldn't they do something? Couldn't they see how much it hurt? As if nuns knew any more than she did about having a baby.

Nothing worked. Inge had tried lying down and tried walking around. She had yelled and she had bitten her lip, which the nuns clearly preferred. She was still in agony. Why had no one warned her? All the pictures commemorating childbirth painted things so very differently: a doting father gazing adoringly at a radiant mother, a beaming baby staring up at her as if she were a goddess. Where in those was this mess of blood and leaking liquids and animal smells more suited to a farmyard?

Whatever she did, the nuns screeched like parrots, pointing and jabbing as if that made their monstrous language any easier to decipher. In the end, Inge stopped pacing and crawled back into bed because her shaking legs could no longer support her. She was so cold. The too-bright sun streamed incessantly through the window, but Inge's limbs felt like ice and her teeth chattered as if they were dancing.

Maybe it'll be me who dies. All that hoping it would be the baby, or Max. Maybe this is my punishment.

Her body cracked open, clamped shut, each wave of pain hitting her harder than the last. *"She is a very little thing."* This agony was Brigitte's doing, a curse to get Max his heir and the *liability* gone.

As the next contraction lifted her up, that fate seemed like a blessing. Her body was splitting. Inge screamed and screamed louder. Someone was shouting, someone was holding her hard against the bed. The pain was red and black and everywhere. And then it stopped. It spat her out and fell away in a great slithering rush.

"Bambino! Il bambino è qui!"

There was a new noise in the room, a cry as sharp and high as a cat squalling. Cool hands pulled her up, wrapped a thick blanket around her shoulders, thrust a blood-smeared bundle into her arms.

"Un figlio. Tu hai un figlio. Boy! Boy!"

She had a son. Max would be pleased.

The bundle wriggled, tiny fists flying and framing the scrunched-apple face. Inge stared at the tight-shut eyes, the wide-open mouth. What was she meant to do next? She was exhausted, her head ached as if someone had punched it and her lower body was consumed with fire. She lay rigid as the baby squirmed, its mouth shivering, its little head butting into her battered body as if it was searching.

One of the nuns pointed to a painting on the wall: a Madonna feeding her child. Inge stared in horror as the nun nodded, as the others beamed and pointed the same. Was she really meant to do such a thing? She tried to imagine Grete feeding her or her brothers in such an intimate way—it was unthinkable. Why had no one ever told her the mechanics of this?

The baby resumed its high-pitched wail; the nuns frowned and pointed more emphatically at the picture. Mortified, refusing to meet anyone's eyes, Inge rolled down her nightdress as discreetly as she could and squashed her son to her chest. All it did was make him angry. She tried again; it made him worse. By nightfall, the baby was howling and Inge was howling and no one could get a wink of sleep.

Another miserable hour passed and then, as Inge reached the point of despair, another woman appeared. She was gray-haired and dressed in black and had a body composed of circles. Without a word, she picked up the miserable baby in one meaty hand and grabbed Inge's swollen breast with the other, pulling them both so forcefully into place, Inge was stunned by the speed of it. The baby gasped and started to suck. The minute he moved and began to grumble, the still-silent midwife shifted him efficiently from one side to the other. Gradually, he turned from red to pink, dropped away from Inge's aching chest and fell into a deep, unmoving sleep.

The baby settled, the midwife hustled Inge out of the bed and into a bath and a clean gown. By the time Max arrived, all traces of the birth were wiped away and Inge was as calm as she needed to be.

"A son. You did well. He is exactly what I wanted."

Inge watched Max settle the baby into the crook of his arm with an ease she couldn't yet imagine possessing. He looked like a man well used to holding babies, although she wasn't aware he had ever been around them. Max was being so gentle, clearly delighted with his son; a sob caught in her throat. He looked so handsome and the baby was so peaceful. All the ingredients were in place for the perfect family portrait, if love and truth weren't needed in the mix.

"I thought we could call him Gunther Eric, for my brothers..."

The Max she knew snapped back in charge. "Absolutely not. I'm not saddling him with sentimentality. We will call him Wolfgang—Wolf for short. A brave name for a brave boy."

The baby began to snuffle. Inge stretched out her arms. After all, the name didn't really matter, as long as her baby was well. "He's hungry. Let me take him."

Max raised an eyebrow. "You're feeding him yourself?"

She nodded, presuming he would leave.

"You said he was hungry. Why would you keep him waiting?"

Face burning, Inge slipped the gown off her shoulder and brought the baby up to suckle.

Max watched impassively, as if she was a patient undergoing a test. "You are managing well. I suppose it will make things easier. You can have another two weeks in the convent—that should be ample."

Inge shifted the baby, wincing at the strength of his tug. "Ample for what? We surely aren't going to stay in Milan? You haven't taken a house here? The nuns are so on edge...I thought the city was in chaos?"

The flicker of anger brought back the old Max. "Of course we're not. Do you think I have so little care for my son? Milan isn't safe for anyone, especially Germans. The partisans have rounded up and shot thousands of our countrymen. It is anarchy. No decent country would tolerate it. We were never staying in Italy—even you must have realized that."

Another hidden move. She was so tired of it all. "Then why come here in the first place?"

His face tightened; the baby began to fuss. She shifted Wolf onto her shoulder and kissed his soft head. Wolf molded into her, heavy with sleep. It wasn't hard to love him. Inge had worried it might be, after the miserable months of the pregnancy and the shock of the birth. She had worried she might need to put up a pretense around Max, making a show of a bond with the baby to keep herself safe. But loving her son wasn't difficult at all—it was as easy as breathing.

After that first dreadful few hours, he had proved to be the sunniest baby; Inge was convinced, despite the nuns' shaking heads, that he was already smiling. The thought of taking him out into a world where bodies were still falling made her want to weep for them both. Except weeping was exactly what Max would expect.

She tried a softer voice. "He's so tiny, Max, and two weeks is nothing. Surely it would be dangerous to travel so soon?"

Max reached out and stroked the baby's cheek; the movement brought his fingers too close to Inge's face. "He's what makes it safe. The Italians are sentimental about children and mothers, especially pretty young mothers. No one will question us. Family and the Church—they would die for them both. We have that covered." His fingers trailed across the hair that tumbled onto her shoulder. She sat very still.

"Then at least tell me where we're going?"

It was a waste of breath. He left, as he always did, without answering.

This time, however, he didn't stay away. He came early in the mornings when she was still sleeping. She would wake and find him whispering to Wolf by the window. Once, as the sunlight danced around father and son, she forgot, for a moment, what their marriage was. Then he turned, saw her watching and cradled Wolf with such ownership, she could hate him again.

At the end of the promised two weeks, he came before even Wolf was up, told her to pack and led her to a car where a priest sat waiting. Inge hesitated. She knew Max had no time for religion and especially not for Catholics, but now he moved in a world where nuns and priests were his normal companions. He hurried her into the car, offering nothing about their companion beyond a cursory introduction.

"This is Father Petranovic. He will accompany us." Neither of them said to where.

Inge held tight to the baby as Milan's crowded streets gave way to vine-studded hillsides and shady chestnut trees and rivers running deep despite the fierce July sun.

They were still going south. Inge could no more unpick this journey than the one that had brought them to Italy. The farther south they went, surely the stronger the Allied presence would be—how could that be any less of a danger than trigger-happy partisans?

Max drove in silence, the priest nodding beside him. Wolf fell quickly asleep, lulled by the motion. Inge grew increasingly anxious. The baby was a sticky weight and there was an unpleasantly spicy odor clinging around the priest's dark robes.

They had been driving for hours and any attempt she had made to start a conversation that might throw up some answers went unheard. Eventually, she opened a window to try to sweeten the air; there was a hint of salt in the wind she had never smelled in a city.

"Max, why can I smell the sea?"

It was Petranovic who turned and answered, in a heavily accented German. "Because we are coming to the coast, to Genoa. Where you will stay for a week or two, depending on the speed of our arrangements and where, Frau Eichel, it is most important that you speak to no one. I hope we can rely on you." His gaze was uncomfortably direct. "Genoa is a mongrel of a city, filled with the type of people you should not be bothered with, Jews and the like. I have arranged comfortable lodgings; you will have no need to go out." His tone was so level, it was a moment before Inge realized that was an order.

"You said for a week or two. After Genoa, where next?"

Max's back stiffened. He might hate her questioning, but perhaps a priest would feel more compelled to tell the truth.

Petranovic's smile was as bland as his voice. "Home, Frau Eichel. Where you will be welcomed and surrounded by people like yourselves. A good life waiting, as your husband's hard work deserves." He turned his back on her again and began whispering to Max.

Inge stared out of the window as the blue curve of the coast came into view. What would a priest in Italy know about Max's work? And *home*? That was the wrong word to choose. That meant Germany. For a moment, she wondered if they were going to turn back around, if all this traveling was some complicated ruse to keep Max out of the way until the war's end was settled. That, however, was illogical—and nothing Max ever did was illogical.

They were going downhill, through winding roads to a port still bustling with ships despite the extensive bomb damage all along the harbor. *Ships*: such an obvious clue and yet she never managed to make sense of it, despite all the maps she'd pored over to follow the fighting. Perhaps that was the problem: she had spent so long obsessing over Europe, she had never considered a wider world.

Later, when Inge stood on the deck, her mouth sour with rage, watching the land disappear through eyes that were red and raw, she wondered whether she was, in fact, the fool Max took her for. Two weeks they had kept her shut away in Genoa. She should have tried harder to get out, found some excuse to take the measure of the world around her, but Petranovic was immovable, untrickable, and there wasn't a thing in the shuttered house that offered a clue. They were in the car, bags packed, before Max showed her the last set of passports, the papers signed in Rome and stamped with permission to leave and permission to sail. Papers it must have taken months to arrange, since before they left Berlin. She had shaken her head, unable to believe him.

"You can't do this. I won't go."

"Then stay. I'll engage a nurse for Wolf. It's your choice."

Except it wasn't. *I am meant to go back.* She had made herself a promise, a bargain: *Be a good girl and you get to start again.* As if she had something to bargain with, as if she had an ounce of control. From the day they left Oranienburg to the day they sailed, Max had known their destination. *You're going where I say.* Except he never had said. He had kept it a secret; she had let him. She had fallen into line like a sleepwalker, like a child. Like she had done since the day she was handed to him. She really was a fool. She had thought she could learn Max so easily; that she could get the upper hand. And now here she was: not going home, going instead to Argentina. She had been a good girl and where had it got her? Sailing to a country she had barely heard of. Sailing away from everything she knew and everything her heart still dreamed of.

He had won this time, presenting her with a choice that wasn't a choice. But he didn't hold all the cards. As the coastline vanished and the sea spread gray and thick around her, Inge hugged that thought. She was a mother now; she had someone else to fight for, someone who mattered more than her. She would store away every detail. She would learn Max better than he knew himself and, one day, whatever the cost, she would beat him.

PART THREE

CHAPTER THIRTEEN

October 1947 to July 1948, Berlin

I don't know the exact date they marched us out of Sachsen-hausen on the death march. There hadn't been snow for a while and there were green shoots in the forest, so I think it was toward the end of April. I do remember the last day in the camp, because everything was different. There weren't so many of us left by then; a lot of the barracks were empty, including the ones rumor said the money-makers were kept in. When the shout came for roll call, the block leaders left the sick in their bunks and gave the rest of us a blanket each and a chunk of bread. Some people gobbled theirs at once. I held on to mine; that could have been what saved me.

The guards lined us all up together, men and women; not that you could see a difference. There were still thousands of us. They forced us into a column with guards along the length and dogs snapping front and back. The pace was brutal and the crack of bullets never-ending. Anyone who lagged behind was shot. After a while, no one tried to help their neighbors or looked anywhere but straight ahead. It rained endlessly.

We marched for days through villages where no one gave us a glance. No one had any idea where we were going, although there were rumors: that we would be driven off cliffs and into the sea, or crowded onto boats that would be pushed out and sunk. At night, they herded us into sodden forests, made us sleep on the ground with nothing to lie on. I rationed my bread out crumb by crumb. After it was gone, I made sure to curl up by a bush or a tree, anywhere that might have buds to suck or bark to gnaw. So many of us died and were left where we fell. We shed bodies along those roads thicker than a dog sheds fleas.

The death march. Felix shuddered. He had no idea these had happened, out of Sachsenhausen or from the other camps, until the first bodies were found and the testimonies started tumbling in. They were well named: forced marches of sick and starved prisoners with the only intention to kill them. Clearing out the camps before the Allies could liberate them, obliterating the evidence. Sixty thousand people marched out of Auschwitz alone; fifteen thousand of them dead and abandoned along the way. Even in the Reich's dying days, the Nazis kept on killing.

"Thalberg, for goodness' sake, man. It's after ten. How many nights is that this week? You need to go home."

Home. Such a throwaway word and scented in Kramer's memory, no doubt, with Coca-Cola and apple pie.

Felix put down the pages whose close-packed script had worn out his eyes and tried not to grind his teeth. Not that Kramer would notice his irritation.

It had been two years since Felix had poured out his story and started working for the Americans. First as an interpreter, next as a clerk with the International Military Tribunal, one of the hundreds of German speakers collating evidence for the Nuremburg trials. Now he was employed by CROWCASS—the Central Registry of War Criminals and Security Suspects. In that time, he had had good bosses and indifferent bosses and, more often than not, exhausted bosses, but Kramer was the first one who was arrogant, who believed his every utterance fell on grateful ears.

Felix, like the rest of the Germans who worked with him, freely acknowledged that he didn't always understand his American colleagues. Some days, he was entertained by them; some days, he was mystified; on occasion, he was exasperated. They were a good-hearted people, he knew that, horrified by what their own boys, and Germany, had been through. They were also apparently coated in an unshakable confidence and a bottomless optimism as hard as the shells on their candy. *Pep.* That was their word and the quality they admired and what they were desperate to instill into Germany's pinch-faced and starving people to get them back on their tired feet. It was a laudable ambition, but sometimes Felix longed for a less enthusiastic approach.

The new recruits were the worst, the ones who arrived fresh out of training with big ideas, who hadn't seen the suffering. The ones who dragged treasured family heirlooms back from the burgeoning black market delighted at their "bargains" or were thrilled by bomb-battered streets and referred to them as "local color." Most of them were brought swiftly into line and turned shamefaced by their more experienced officers.

Those older men called Felix in and got him to paint a picture of what it meant to live through five years of war and ten years of fear. To explain that the broken spirits and hopelessness the new men could not fathom was a result of war's misery, not an innate element of the German character. The only one who had sat through the lecture and hadn't blushed and softened was Kramer. He was uninterested in Germany's past and thought it had no bearing on the country's future. He would have annexed the whole country if he could. Most of his compatriots gave him a wide berth. Felix worked too closely with the man to avoid him so had learned to bite his tongue and count his blessings instead.

The blessings were not inconsiderable. Working for Uncle Sam meant he had a salary and a serviceable room in a city where the majority counted their wealth in cigarettes and still lived out their lives in dust-choked cellars. It gave him access to a canteen stuffed with recognizable meat and real cheese and the exotic delight that was peanut butter, while civilian stomachs gnawed at rations too meager to fill them and growled as loud as they had in the war. For rewards like that, Felix had learned to smile past a lot of ignorance. Now, he looked up from his work to where Kramer was hovering and fixed on a rueful grin.

"You got me, I'm sorry. I had no idea of the time."

Kramer shook his head in what Felix assumed he thought was a fatherly fashion. He was the latest in a series of officers assigned to try to manage the chaos that was CROWCASS; the team was already running a book on how long he would last. Since Felix's reassignment, he had watched each new face arrive, all eager and filled with purpose. And he had watched them stumble out again within a matter of months, defeated by the Herculean task of filtering good Germans from bad with a script that constantly changed.

Felix couldn't blame them. The war had woven a tapestry of horror across Germany that few of its own citizens were willing to unpick, never mind outsiders. More and more people were turning their backs on any mention of the war's inhumanities, preferring to look forward than to look each other in the eyes and wonder. Some days, Felix wished he could do the same. Then he would sit at his desk and turn over another sprawling story or another grainy photograph whose halting words and stark images brought his own war back and knew he couldn't leave it alone. This question of who did what and why, and where that left his country now, haunted him. And so he sat, night after night, while the building emptied, because this job—this increasingly thankless job—of sifting through the voices still clamoring to be heard was not one to be slotted into office hours. Or so he told himself. Better believe that than dwell on thoughts of *home*.

Now he waved at the documents scattered over his desk and acted surprised to still be here, not with the intention of stopping, but in the hope that Kramer would leave him alone.

"I'm staying too late, you're right. It's the trial that's all—there's barely two weeks before it starts and I've still got all this testimony to catalog. I can't risk missing even the smallest bit of evidence. Once that's done, I'll slow down, I promise."

Kramer's placid face didn't alter, but his tone shifted from bonhomie to a sympathy Felix's thin skin decided was patronizing.

"I doubt that very much, Felix. I've been watching you: you never stop. As for this, leave it—it will keep. I'm sorry, but that's not a request. The Soviets don't want it and they won't use it. It doesn't matter what we dig up: Sachsenhausen is in their sector, not ours, which means this trial is theirs, not ours, and all they care about is how the thousands of Soviet prisoners who died there were treated. What happened to the Jews is of no interest to them."

Kramer silenced Felix's protest. "Whatever you think of me, I'm not defending their stance, but it's out of our hands. We are neutral observers here, nothing more; given the way relations between us and the Soviets have deteriorated, that's more than we expected. If we start interfering or pushing a different agenda, we won't be allowed in the courtroom at all."

He coughed and shuffled his feet. "I gather you were there, at the camp. That's a terrible thing, but, as much as I hate to say it, Felix, in this instance you have to put your experiences aside. You asked to attend the trial, I've agreed, but the colonel has reservations. I've assured him you can remain professional. I'm not wrong, am I? You're not going to do anything with this stuff that might embarrass us?"

Kramer could be no older than his early thirties, but generations of family wealth and privilege sat fat beneath his skin, giving him the pompous air of a far older man. If Felix had been feeling charitable, he might have recognized the truth in Kramer's advice and ignored his unfortunate manner. He was, however, too tired, too burdened by the weight of all the testimonies, to try that. He could, almost, ignore the blunt stupidity of *stuff* but *professional* was a step too far. If Kramer meant by that could he trust Felix to bury his feelings, then no, he was not wrong: Felix had been doing that half his life.

He stared at the pile of pages he had painstakingly collected and was less than halfway through reading. Kramer could lecture him on the political reality as long as he liked, but he would never understand. The Sachsenhausen trial did not belong to the Soviets. It belonged to him, and to all the inmates like Isaak, stuck in a Displaced Persons' Camp miles from home, who had reopened their wounds to contribute their testimonies. It belonged to the people who had died, and the people who had survived and needed to find a reason for what they were told was their good fortune.

Everything he had done in the past two years had been a preparation for this, for Sachsenhausen's reckoning; for the day he would bring the camp into the light...and find the pieces needed to convict Eichel. What did sectors and zones and some politically motivated division of Berlin have to do with that?

Kramer was still waiting. Felix picked carefully around his reply.

"I do understand the Soviet position, and how delicate ours is. I appreciate that the accounts here are from Jewish prisoners, but the thing is, by the end, they were no longer segregated from the Russian ones. Given that I've read most of these anyway, it wouldn't hurt to cross-check them against the names of the accused, to see if anything might be relevant. If I could see the final list of those standing trial, a link might jump out."

"I really shouldn't." Kramer's hand tightened on his briefcase. He had the list then.

Felix tried not to sound too eager. "If the Russians got wind that we had information about their people and didn't disclose it..." He let the sentence hang.

Kramer sighed, but he opened the case, flicked through the contents and handed over a single typed sheet. "A quick look, that's all. You can't copy it out. They are insanely sensitive about any information leaking."

Felix scanned the page up and down. Kaindl the commandant; Baumkötter the doctor; Brennscheidt, who directed the shoe-testing track; Sakowski, the prisoner forced to play hangman. A handful of record-keepers and guards. Sixteen names and not one of them Eichel's.

His control cracked. "How can there be so few? There were thousands of us held prisoner there. What's the latest estimate for Sachsenhausen? Two hundred thousand men and women held between its opening in '36 and the liberation in '45. Over half of those shot or gassed or starved to death. No one knows how many were lost on the death march alone—we're still looking for the bodies. A hundred thousand people killed. That took more doing than sixteen men."

Kramer retrieved the list before Felix shredded it. "Sixteen is more than anyone thought the Soviets would prosecute. Come on, man, don't pretend you don't know how they work. As soon as they discharged their obligations at Nuremburg, they made their position clear: all responsibility for all atrocities belongs with the officer classes and the elite, with Hitler and his inner circle. They won't count ordinary men, who claim to have done no more than follow orders, as criminals."

And neither will anyone else, although the world, it seems, is choked with ordinary men.

"No. Square up all you like, but I'm not going to debate you." Kramer's voice had hardened, Felix forced himself to listen. "I thought you could do better than this. When I arrived here in August, the first person I heard about was the unshakable Felix Thalberg: the German survivor who could do the work of three men. From everything that was said, I expected to meet a veteran, but what are you, twenty-four? And yet you can get people to open up in a way that eludes generals twice your age and your eye for detail on photographs most of us can't even stomach is remarkable. You have skills, Felix, that could take you a long way, but you're not a team player. I've been here nearly two months and I've barely seen you speak to anyone. You keep too much to yourself—you're obsessed. I watched you checking that list: you were looking for someone specific; you blew up because you couldn't find him. You can't do that. You might be a German and an ex-prisoner, but that has no bearing here. The war is done with and, like it or not, our task has one aim: to get the best outcomes for those who were hurt and those who did the hurting so Germany can heal itself and move forward. Revenge has no part in it. You can't make it personal, Felix. Do that and you're no use to us. You're probably no use to yourself."

Kramer finished his sermon with no sense at all of the insults laced through it. Felix stared at him, at his straight-across shoulders and his corn-fed face, at his stance plumped up with the confidence of a man who had never been tested. He couldn't trust himself to speak.

Kramer closed his briefcase with a snap. "You're a good man, Thalberg, but you need to let things go. Now, get home with you— let's have you fresh for tomorrow."

Felix sat very still as the lieutenant bounced away. *You can't make it personal.* He stared at the piled-up pages running thick with loss and misery and fear, with pleas for a voice, for justice, for someone to care. How many had he collected since he first started this work? Tracking down people whose lives were still broken, pulling words from those who could barely shape the nightmare that had swallowed them and would never comprehend it.

A tear rolled fat and slow down his cheek. *You can't make it personal.* He remembered the turned-away faces, at his old printing works, at Oranienburg, at Levetzowstraße and Rosenstraße and on all the streets he once thought he was part of. He remembered the stars and the colored cards; the frightened mothers and sleep-deprived children and the tired old men, all of them marked out like cattle. And he remembered the photographs. The first one, paper-clipped into one of the hundreds of folders collected for the trials. A black-and-white square that had made him retch until he was hollow. And the fiftieth and the hundredth and all the rest seen and still to come. The only way he could approach them was as part of a quest: he trawled through the endless images then, as he did now, desperate to find any trace of Kerstin or Arno or Hannah, equally desperate that he would not. Bodies tangled, stripped of their dignity and their humanity, reduced to matchstick bones and tissue-stretched skin.

You can't make it personal. The refrain danced ugly and grinning through his aching head. It was people who died and people who killed them: what could be more personal than that?

They know how to put on a show.

Pankow City Hall, the venue for the Sachsenhausen trial, had, like everywhere else in Mitte, seen its share of bombs. The clock face was missing and the tower was badly damaged. The Soviets, however, had made certain none of the visitors swarming into their sector would dwell on the scars. Its fire-red bricks glowed, scrubbed clean of the dust that still tarnished most of Berlin. The intact windows had been polished crystal clear and the damaged ones covered with fluttering banners.

A painting of the Soviet leader Stalin crowned the whole spec-tacle, draped from the highest balconies to the top of the doorway on a scale even Hitler would have envied. The Americans had been determined to mask their annoyance at the display, laugh-ing loudly from the trial's first morning at "Uncle Joe's" bristling mustache and equally bristling medals. Felix watched the banners wave, their hammers and sickles neatly aligned, and felt the stir of uncomfortable echoes.

The reception was just as carefully staged inside as out. Soldiers stood stiffly to attention along the marble-floored hallway. Photographs of grim-faced grandees lined the walls, their uniforms so thick with decorations, Felix wondered how many unseen hands it had taken to prop the men up.

"Pity the poor Berliners stuck in this sector. Not a view to be had for miles except these jowly old horrors." Kramer repeated his observation every time he had an audience, beaming at his own wit.

In the immediate aftermath of the war, Berlin had been divided by the Allies into four administrative sectors, one each controlled by the French, the English, the Americans and the Russians. Kramer's joke was a play on a popular saying about the spoils of war grabbed in the partitioning that Felix had never found the slightest bit funny. *The French got the wine, the Russians got the food, the British got the people and America got the views.* The Americans chanted the refrain like a boast, but Felix had no idea why. Partition may have brought the wealthy boroughs of Zehlendorf and Schöneburg under United States control, but what was the use of pretty streets and stucco-covered mansions when the Soviets controlled the access to the east with its wheat fields and coal?

He kept the thought quiet, as he kept all his thoughts about the division of Berlin quiet. His city, and his country, were conquered places. The hordes of foreign troops and foreign administrators that reality brought with it did not sit well with Berlin's citizens, who were expected to be grateful for the help they got while still being treated as the enemy.

There was nothing to be done, however, except get on with a daily life that was tottering, on the surface at least, back to normal. Power was on more than it was off. Trains and trams were running, even if timetables were more of a hope than a certainty. Food remained everybody's biggest worry. Rationing was brutal, based on a calorie count that left the city's people lean and hungry and with no reserves. The prospect of another winter as bitter as the one that closed 1945 was a frightening one. Few Berliners had the surplus energy to worry over the ramifications of partition or to concern themselves with the deepening strains between the Soviets and the Allies. On a day-to-day basis, which was as far as the majority could manage, who was in charge of where carried little practical significance.

Since his return to Berlin, Felix had kept away from the French sector in the city's north: the only neighborhood he knew there was Wedding and that was a place he would never revisit. As for the rest, apart from the banners and the Cyrillic street signs in the Soviet sector, he could barely tell from the look of a place if he was in Russian- or American- or British-run Berlin. Whether he wandered through Mitte or Charlottenburg or Kreuzberg, there were still teams of women clearing the rubble and dozens of potholes needing to be patched. Tram stops, train stations and churches still sported their boards covered in fading photographs and washed-out names. Every street corner played host to its black market, where crowds huddled around half-opened briefcases and bartered with the cigarettes that held more value than coin.

By the trial's third morning, Felix had stopped looking at the streets. His mind was already in the courtroom, wondering whose testimony would form the day's focus. Whether it would be Kaindl on the stand, peering over his round glasses like a stuffy librarian. Or Sakowski, with his too-pale face and fluttering hands. Or Baum-kötter, who stared into the distance and never met anyone's eye.

The drive, with all its checkpoints and diversions, became an irritation. As soon as the convoy reached the hall, Felix was out, scurrying to join the melee of observers, interpreters and reporters pushing to get inside. He would wiggle as close to the front as he could and sit with his pencil poised, ready to take copious notes, his attention moving back and forth between the judges' bench and the dock like a man intent on a particularly taut tennis final. Unlike a championship match, however, there was no drama to these proceedings. Questions were put directly and answered in the same way.

"What kind of exterminations were committed?"

"Until 1943, prisoners were killed by shooting or hanging."

"Did you change anything in these procedures?"

"In March 1943, I introduced gas chambers for mass extermination. It was a more efficient and humane way."

No remorse was asked or offered. The whole thing was conducted as clinically as a postmortem.

For seven days, Felix sat and watched and listened for Eichel's name. It didn't come. He wasn't worried: there were weeks, perhaps months, of evidence still to hear.

And then, on the eighth morning, the mood shifted. Only two of the four judges took their seats. No one positioned microphones in front of the dock. The area normally packed with clerks was virtually empty and there were no paperwork towers. Most of the observers stopped unpacking their pens and sat back.

"Should be a short morning—whole thing done by lunch, hopefully."

The statement was so absurd, Felix whipped around to challenge it, but the courtroom was being called to order and the moment was lost. First one judge and then the other began to deliver what were clearly closing statements; neither spoke for long. Felix sat in mounting disbelief, staring at the interpreter's mouth as if reading her lips would provide a different set of words to the ones his ears were rejecting.

"What's happening? Why have they moved to summation so quickly?" He tugged at his neighbor's arm, not realizing how loud his voice had risen until Kramer leaned forward and looked along the packed row.

The man he disturbed, who wore a British Army uniform, shrugged. "Because they're about to bring in the verdicts."

Felix wondered if he hadn't made his concern clear and framed his next sentence in carefully modulated English. "But there's hardly been any witnesses and barely any written testimony. How can a trial like this be done in a week?"

The officer frowned. "How long did you expect it to last? The Soviets have been clear all along this wouldn't be spun out like one of ours. Thank God, I say. How long did Nuremburg last, eleven months? No one has the appetite for that anymore."

Felix dropped his voice, trying to appear calm, although his heart was racing. "But they've barely covered anything that was done at the camp, except in terms of numbers. Nothing of the real horrors that were suffered there."

His neighbor shifted. "Do we need more of that? Look, I don't know who you are or what your experience is, but you must have realized this is a bit of a show. If Sachsenhausen hadn't dealt so badly with the Soviet prisoners, I doubt they would have bothered at all. They'll do things properly—there'll be a recess now, not immediate verdicts, but the outcome was always going to be the same: life for Kaindl and anyone directly involved in administering camp directives, shorter sentences for the rest."

"Imprisonment? That's it?" Felix's voice was rising again. If the British officer could have moved, he clearly would have.

"What were you expecting? Executions? Who wants any more of those? It's not as if we could get Hitler and his henchmen onto the gallows, the ones who should have paid. Besides, the Soviets don't apply the death penalty in peacetime, 'for humanitarian reasons,' as they put it. It's a bit rich, them taking the moral high ground after the way they ravaged Berlin, but that's how it is. And isn't that the way of things everywhere now? Short memories making the best rebuilding blocks and all that?"

"That can't be right! That's madness!"

But the clerk had called the recess and the officer was already up, pushing his way through the clearing courtroom with a very determined step.

Felix got slowly to his feet, ignoring Kramer's waving. He'd noticed some kind of courtyard through the narrow windows; a packet of cigarettes bought him access to it. There was frost in the air, the last day of October feeling more like December. The shock of it was a welcome relief after the overheated courtroom. Felix headed for the farthest corner. There were no benches—they had gone for melting long ago—but there were enough statues still standing whose plinths offered a perch. Felix sank onto the stone, hands cupped around his cigarette for warmth. *Eighteen years old and you still can't remember a scarf.* The memory hit him like a punch.

"Drink this."

A silver hip flask appeared in front of him, its open top rich with the sweet woodiness of bourbon. He grabbed it, swallowed a mouthful; swallowed another.

"Good. Whatever the ill, this is pretty good medicine. Provided you don't drown in it."

The decidedly American voice was as rich as the drink and had a kindness running through it, although not too much, not more than was needed.

Felix sensed he could look up and his wet face wouldn't attract comment. When he did, the woman watching him took the flask back, wiped the mouth and stowed it back inside her oversized coat. She wore a fitted olive uniform beneath that and a tilted cap that was struggling to confine a tangle of dark curls. She was small-boned, but nothing about her suggested fragile, as nothing suggested the word "girl." Her cheeks were tinged with pink and her long-lashed eyes sat somewhere between green and blue. When she smiled, which she did as soon as Felix glanced up at her, he forgot how cold the day was.

"See, it's working already." She grinned wider and stuck out her hand. "Captain Kitty Johnson, Women's Army Corps, and also one of CROWCASS's beleaguered pen-pushers, based in the office two doors from you. You look surprised. Is that because of my rank? If I was to tell you that I can say *How are you today?* in three languages, which is three more than most Americans can speak, would that explain my meteoric rise? Or is your surprise because we work so close and you've never noticed me before?" She winked, so unexpectedly that Felix burst out laughing. It wasn't until a good deal later that he realized that was exactly her aim.

"Felix Thalberg." He shook her waiting hand. It was surprisingly soft.

"I know." She sat down beside him and suddenly his hand was curled inside hers. It was an intimacy he normally would have shied from. "The man who collects stories and sees photographs with an X-ray eye. I know who you are, but what I don't know is why you scuttled from the courtroom like a rabbit scenting a wolf pack. Why don't you tell me? I talk a good talk, but I listen pretty well too." As she spoke, she leaned in closer. A scent whispered from her that was nothing like the cheap rose perfume so popular among the girls in Berlin. Kitty smelled of the last notes of incense lingering in a church, of autumn fruit and trees after rain. There was a complexity to the perfume that sat at odds with her direct manner. The combination loosened his tongue.

"This trial's finished too fast and will be forgotten as quickly. They're not going to pay—Kaindl and the rest of them—not how they should. And who are these sixteen anyway but the tip of an iceberg no one will go looking for once this is wrapped up? Trials are meant to be for the victims, but no one here cares. It's a sham."

Her response was not the soothing set of platitudes he expected. "Who did you lose?"

No one had ever asked him, or not so directly. He tried to stop them, but the tears, and the words, tumbled.

"My father, Arno. He was taken to Theresienstadt in 1943 and I can't find a trace of him beyond the record that he was sent. And my mother, Kerstin. When I got back to Berlin, there was nothing left of her. I don't know if she got sick or was taken or what happened at all. It's like she never lived. The other prisoners, the men I survived Sachsenhausen with, I've tried to find them, but they've vanished. Or I track them to a Displaced Persons' Camp and go back a week later and they've gone again with no forwarding address. It's like the whole world won't stop moving. And my home, and my city, for whatever they once meant and..." He stumbled. "And I lost..." He stopped. How to put the impossibility of Hannah into words? What could he say? *I lost hope, a dream; the belief in something bigger?* He fell into a silence he expected Kitty to fill with sympathy. Once again, she confounded him.

"Before all that, who were you?"

He stared at her. Did she think there was only one answer?

"A printer."

Kitty waited.

A Jew to everyone except the Jews. A useless son. The luckiest unluckiest man in the world. What did she want to hear? "I was an apprentice. I wanted to be an artist. It's hard now to imagine that." *Or to explain the truth: that my drawing days are done because every time I pick up a pencil, all it does is pour out ghosts.*

Kitty squeezed his hand. "So much loss, it's terrible. And to think about that multiplied across Germany and all the countries that were conquered is unimaginable. Even saying it sounds meaningless. You're angry with the way the trial has been run, I get that. But help me understand this better: is it revenge you're after? Would the deaths of these men, or the ones that got away, really make up for all you've suffered?"

He jerked away, but she held him.

"I'm not criticizing—it's what most people would want. If you tell me their executions will bring you peace and make living with the loss easier, I'll believe you. I promise."

Of course it would. Felix opened his mouth to snap out the words, but there was something about her measured manner that stifled his quick answer. *The hangings have to keep going until they catch up with Eichel*: that was more truthful, but the weight of the explanation made it unsayable. As did the possibility of how this curious woman might answer. *How many will it take to get to him? And how will all these killings be different from those that went before?* He could imagine her saying it; he didn't want to hear it. He took refuge in anger instead.

"Don't you get it? They weren't even sorry. They presided over murder and the worst kinds of torture in that camp. There were things done you couldn't imagine, that Kaindl and Baumkötter knew all about. Yet there wasn't a moment of remorse for their victims, not even a hint of it."

"Why would there be?" This time, Kitty needed both hands to hold him. "They aren't sorry, Felix: if there's anything you have to face, it's that. They never will be. I interpreted at the Nuremburg trial, and at the Dachau one. Those men, like the ones here, did what they did in the service of a cause that runs as deep in them as a religion. You could parade the dead in front of them until the end of time and their thinking wouldn't shift. Look for revenge if you want it, but don't go looking for remorse. You'll never find that."

"Then what about fairness? What about justice?" He was shouting. Other observers had bribed their way out of the court and into the fresh air. They turned, nudging each other; he barely noticed. "The figures for the murdered rise every day. No one counts in thousands anymore—they've moved on to millions. All those deaths on one side and what's on the other? Ten hanged after Nuremburg, a handful of executions ordered at the trials since, but none carried out and the Soviets banning the death penalty on 'humanitarian' grounds. Where is the balance? You've sat through the trials; you seem to know who the Nazis are. You're quick enough with your questions, so why don't you tell me what needs to be done to make the loss *easier*."

His voice was so shrill, his face so close to hers, he thought she would leave. That she didn't, that her tone stayed as steady as when she had offered him the flask, was one of the reasons he fell in love with her, or convinced himself he had.

"Because I *don't* know. I *do* know what revenge looks like, and it looks like more of the same. I don't know what justice is. Unless it lies in keeping the memory of what was done alive so that it never happens again. Whether hangings will do that, or prison sentences, or never letting a story go unheard, I don't know. And I don't know who the Nazis were—no one does. If ever there was a missing piece to the puzzle, there it is: eight million people joined the National Socialist Party and not one of them, apparently, still lives in Germany. Everyone is baffled by what Hitler did, and how he got the power to do it. Or they are resentful we're asking if we scratch too hard, which is why we've stopped scratching. But then I'm not German—I didn't live through this, so the confusion might make more sense to you than it does to me."

The *Jungvolk* and the *Hitlerjugend*, becoming a *Flakhelfer*. *Whatever you had to join to melt in with the masses.* Kerstin, doing what she thought was right.

Felix looked away; Kitty continued as if he had answered.

"Exactly. People followed what Hitler demanded. They must have had their reasons; please God they didn't all just want to kill Jews. But how are we supposed to know? All the tests we've brought in to try to separate the good ones from the bad: we may as well go back to ducking stools. You've seen the *Fragebogen* forms. Everyone in CROWCASS knows they're a joke. They were meant to be a simple check to see who was suitable to hold public office. Except the questions are useless and, even if they weren't, we can't process them all. There are millions of completed ones boxed up and never read, did you know that? Do you know how many people all across Germany that leaves still holding the positions they've always held? In the police, in local government, in schools? Of course it doesn't matter, though, because none of them were Nazis."

She paused, but he had nothing to say in his country's defense.

"If we can't work out who is fit to process housing permits, how are we meant to work out who were the murderers?"

Everything she said was true. The same discussions had filled every office he'd worked in since the war ended. Where did responsibility lie? Was a teacher forced to teach the Nazi curriculum a frightened civil servant or a Nazi? Was the priest who told his parishioners to follow Hitler's laws trying to save them or a Nazi? Were the ones who knew and never asked, the ones who turned away, monsters too? Round and round the conversations went. He'd never joined in; most of the Germans employed alongside him hadn't either. What could he say? Felix wanted the world in black and white and it wouldn't shift from gray.

As if Kitty sensed it, she slipped an arm around his waist and kept it there until he took a steadier breath. Her body was warm, her hold on him definite.

"Felix, none of that means you shouldn't search for justice. It just means it will be harder to find. People are tired of being blamed. If the Soviets continue down their separate path and start building harder divisions between East and West, maybe there won't be an appetite for blaming at all. No one hates a communist more than an American: we'll forgive the Germans a lot to get them on our side with that."

There was a shout, a bustle that put out cigarettes and emptied the courtyard.

"The verdicts must be in." Kitty released her grip. "We don't need to go back. We know what will happen. We could find a bar, put the world to rest the way we'd like it."

When he hesitated, she raised a hand to his cheek.

"I've watched you, Felix Thalberg, all hunched over your papers and your pictures, poring over the past. A little step into the future might not be the worst thing."

Except it might lose me the past.

He stared into her eyes, which were so free of shadows, and knew that he wanted to kiss her, that a bar would lead to a bed. He could sense that whatever this was that was circling around them would be more than a transient thing.

Kitty held out her hand. Her smile said that she was certain he could take the step she wanted.

But I don't know if I can or I should . . .

A bed with Kitty was one Felix suspected he could stay in for more than an hour, for more than a night. Even the thought of that felt like a betrayal.

What if I see Hannah when I look down at Kitty? What if she comes back?

She always had before. Every girl he had turned to for comfort had ended up as the wrong face on the pillow. None of them had mattered that much, but Kitty was different. She would demand—she would deserve—better.

"Felix?" She was still smiling, despite his hesitation.

He was so tired of searching. So lonely. He couldn't stop hoping, but was it wrong to start living?

He took Kitty's hand, stood up. Perhaps she might be the one to rescue his heart and fill it back up again. He smiled at her and watched her face light up.

Perhaps.

The wedding was a small one, the guests mostly awkwardly smiling colleagues, neither side having any family to fill out the ceremony. There was a short reception with sparkling wine that was too sweet and a thickly iced cake, sent by Kitty's parents, which was too dry. There was no religious ceremony to follow the civil one: Kitty had no interest and Felix had left any care for religion long behind. When he told her that he felt no more connection to being Jewish now than he did when the label was stuck to him, she pronounced that as a good thing.

"It makes your work less personal—people will believe it more."

Felix didn't agree with that any more than he had agreed when Kramer had said it: nothing felt any less personal and he didn't care how people listened, as long as they did. And anyway, the problem was not that he felt no connection to being Jewish: he didn't dare think about it—he was too afraid of his own blood. She would think he was crazy if he admitted that.

In the six months they had been together, Felix had decided life was easiest if he absorbed Kitty's certainties as his own. She talked about a settled future, about having a home and children, as if these things were a given. There was a comfort in that, in the belief that life could be solid; he didn't share it, but he wanted to.

Kitty brought shape with her. She spoke as if marriage was a step they would have got to anyway, that the threat of her rotation away from Germany simply pulled the decision quicker into the present. When she spoke about the war and its atrocities, it was couched in work, not emotions. He found it simpler when he was around her to do the same. If he wanted to talk about the camp or his family—something he rarely did—and could find the words to do it, she would listen. She never dug beyond what he chose to tell. If he couldn't find the words and retreated, she let him sit quiet until she judged he'd done that long enough.

"You need to live more in the moment, the way I do."

He'd smiled at that like the idea was a new one: he wasn't sure *don't think wider or longer—live inside small steps* was quite what she meant.

As for his secrets—his locked desk drawer where the tin of letters lived, the stumbling halt he would come to in the middle of a memory—she left them alone. Kitty constructed their life and made it comfortable for him to live in; Felix let her. Even sex was straightforward. She enjoyed it, she expected to enjoy it and, if he slipped away from her sometimes, she pulled him firmly back to her kisses and to her body. The words *I love you* came as naturally to her as breathing. When she said them, Felix said them back and he meant them, although he knew his was a love based too much on need.

He couldn't tell her: the longer they lived together, and the more enmeshed he became in this life she thought he was as equally involved in, the less honest he could be. He would lie awake after sex, wishing he could love this funny, clever, determined woman the way she deserved, wondering how his heart could feel at once so heavy and so hollow.

Kitty, he made sure, never saw it. She held him and kissed him as if he was whole, and Felix acted his part, waiting for the day when she would make it come true.

CHAPTER FOURTEEN

December 1950, Buenos Aires

His nightmares were all her fault. Inge clutched at Wolf, her heart racing as she tried to soothe his screams. His little body was rigid, his fists playing a drumroll on her chest.

"Want Daddy. Want Daddy!" *Of course he did.*

"Hush, sweetheart, hush." The nanny was so much more efficient at this, but Inge couldn't let her in: whatever Wolf said would be repeated straight to Max. "It's a dream, nothing more."

Except it wasn't. The horrors stalking Wolf's restless sleep were all too real. How could she have been so stupid? Four years faithfully locking the scrapbook away and all it took was one night of forgetting for her inquisitive, into-everything son to find it. No wonder he couldn't sleep—its images still made *her* feel sick. That hadn't changed from the first photograph—a grainy muddle of a thing that jumped from the paper one unsuspecting morning in 1946 and made her retch. The next day, the papers carried more and the day after that they carried a flood, each image so much clearer than the last. She couldn't leave them alone, couldn't stop thinking about them. Max had been furious they were printed at all and banned every newspaper from the house with the exception of *Der Weg*—the Party beauty parade Inge never opened.

"Propaganda and insults. A smear campaign by our enemies and not to be tolerated anywhere near my child. Infants are easily frightened and they hold those memories."

Inge had nodded; the thought of Wolf seeing anything so terrible horrified her as much as it did Max, but the pictures and articles that she'd torn out and hidden before he could dump them wouldn't let her go. She pored over them as forensically as a scientist. The sightless staring faces. The multiplying list of camps. The stories about slave labor and experiments, about mass executions, that now switched from rumor to fact. The names in stark headlines whom she knew as real people, recorded in trials and executions and suicides and men who had slipped away and gone missing. The gaps in Max's life were filling like a storm-drenched river.

Inge became a collector. Whether she was picking at pastries at the Confetería Ideal or flinching through dress fittings in Calle Florida's overheated salons, her only interest was in the papers her hosts could supply. That the ones she gathered were in Spanish made no difference: names and photographs needed no translating. Soon, her handbag was crammed so full with torn-out bits of paper, she bought a memo book to store her secrets in. By the time the first trials were concluded and their verdicts reported, her Spanish had limped from words into sentences. *Nuremburg, Auschwitz, the Judges' Trial, the Doctors'*. Inge squirreled away every account she could find. The Sachsenhausen piece she carried around unread for a week, unable to move beyond the names listed in its opening. Kaindl, Baumkötter, a handful of men she'd never encountered; not a mention of Eichel. When she finally labored through it, the smell of the camp stuck so thick in her throat she couldn't swallow properly for days.

"How many prisoners were exterminated while you were commander?"

"More than 42,000."

"And how many prisoners died by starvation during this period?"

"I think 8,000."

All of it painstakingly pasted into her book. Four years of images and verdicts and stark portraits of men sentenced to death or, increasingly, acquitted or handed sentences too light for their crimes. Four years looking for Max's name, fearing she would find Felix lurking in one of those desperate creatures. Some days, her vigil felt like a penance. Some days, it felt like a memorial. There were days she wished she had never begun. There were others when she hated herself for the blinkers she had worn through the war, through most of her marriage. She hated Max more than ever. She had vowed to learn him, but every new piece of the puzzle made the task more repellent. How could she look at him, or any of the believers they lived among, and not see ovens and clipboards and numbers far too high to possibly mean people?

Inge knew she should leave—she longed to—but without money of her own and with a child to take care of, the how was beyond her. All she could do was gather every scrap of information until a plan could reveal itself and try to act normally in the meanwhile around a husband who sickened her.

She withdrew; she drank a little more than she should on the days that were darkest. She convinced herself it would all be worth it to keep her child safe. Except she hadn't even managed that. She had damaged him and it made her heart tear.

Wolf's sobs were growing louder, building dangerously close to convulsions.

"Inge, what's going on?" The front door slammed. Inge flinched: she hadn't heard it open over Wolf's crying.

"Wolf, sweetheart, please. You'll upset Daddy. You have to stop."

Max's voice bounced up from the hall. "Inge, what's happening?"

There was a pause she didn't know how to fill and then the shake of footsteps crashing up the stairs.

"Why is he screaming? Why haven't you calmed him?"

Max pushed her from the bed, pulling Wolf out of her ineffectual arms. He covered the child's damp hair with kisses, cradling him as if he was made out of air. Wolf's body loosened, his flailing fists uncurled. "What is it, little man? Where are the monsters?"

A sniff and a gulp and then out poured the words Inge dreaded. "In Mama's book. They're nasty, Daddy. All broken. They're coming to eat me." Wolf's voice rose in another thin wail.

Max hoisted the boy onto his shoulder, rubbing his back like he used to when Wolf was a fussy baby. It worked now as it had then.

He does it so much better than me, or so he'd have me believe.

"What book, Wolf? Tell me and I can make it go away. What book does Mama have?"

Wolf's words fell with a five-year-old's logic. "The sticky one. With the twig men. Their mouths are wide open and they have twisty-up claws. They're really thin, like the thinnest thing you've ever seen. That's why they want to eat me."

Max's hand whipped out and caught Inge by the wrist. "Get it."

"Max, I'm not sure that's—" She winced as his nails tore into her skin.

Wolf nestled into his father like a seed in a pod.

Inge got up, moving as if she was underwater. She went into her bedroom, to the drawer she should have nailed shut. She didn't try to think of an explanation—there was no point.

When she handed the book to Max, he kept Wolf's eyes shielded. He turned slowly through the thickly pasted pages. When he got to Kaindl in his round glasses, he dropped the book to the floor.

"Mama is a silly." Max moved Wolf gently onto his knee, keeping the boy's face focused on his. "I don't know why she didn't tell you the truth and stop all this upset. The pictures are made up, Wolf. They're from a film, not a nice one, and goodness knows why Mama keeps them, but it's just a film, like they show in the theaters in town. The things you saw aren't real people—they're plastic, like the dummies in shop windows. That's why they can bend into all those funny shapes. Do you understand?"

Wolf nodded, his thumb finding its way to his mouth.

Max rubbed the boy's nose and pretended to steal it. Wolf grinned. "There now, that's better. Mama's naughty, isn't she?

Keeping things in the house that could frighten you. Perhaps we need to send her to Mama School."

Wolf burst out laughing. He began repeating "Mama's going to Mama School" in the singsong voice he was learning with his nursery rhymes. Inge blinked back her tears and tried to join in the laughter. At least it made a change from Max's favorite *Silly Mama*; she'd heard more than enough of that. Parroting Max's words was a game to Wolf—Inge knew that. Her boy was as sweet and loving, when she could get him alone, as he had been as a baby. His hand never left hers when they walked in the gardens. Only last week when she was reading him his favorite, *Snow White*, Wolf had held the cover up to her face and told Inge, quite solemnly, that it was she who was the fairest of them all.

Inge shivered as she caught Max smiling at her refusal to cry: it might be a meaningless game to her boy, but it was no such thing to Max.

"Wolf, my darling, I'm so sorry." She put out a hand to stroke his head, but he reared away, butting into Max's side, clearly still shaken by the book and more comforted by Max's clever response to it than her panicked efforts.

Tell him to come to me. Max would laugh if she said it. The older Wolf grew, the more Max swooped in, correcting her; making her nervous around her own child—"You're too strict"; "You're too soft—you're smothering him"; "Can't you see he needs you? You're meant to be his mother: can't you trust your instincts?" As if, after so many years of his questioning, she had anything left of those.

Perhaps if she had been better able to cope when they had finally arrived in Argentina, things would have gone differently and she could have stamped herself more firmly on Wolf, but the shock of the transition kept felling her. Buenos Aires' vivid colors after Berlin's war-torn gray were overwhelming. Add to that the heat and the language, the unimaginable distance she had come and the sleep-draining, emotion-twisting shock of a new baby, and Inge felt like she was drowning. She had kept herself moving, kept herself stable; focused what energy she could muster totally on Wolf. Max told her every day it wasn't enough, that she had to do better. That she was damaging Wolf with her constant exhaustion, that the baby would sense she didn't love him enough and be marked by it. She knew it wasn't true... but then Max would quiet the baby quicker than she could, or Wolf, because he saw his father less, would choose Max's waiting arms over hers and Max would push at her trust in their bond.

I love you just as much as he does. I'd die for you. She stared at her son's turned-away face as if she could make the words spill from her head into his. The little boy was growing heavy with sleep. If Max hadn't been here, Inge knew Wolf would have folded happily into her arms, twisting her hair around his fingers as he drifted to sleep. Now she couldn't get near him. It was Max who lowered him carefully under the covers. When he started fretting again, it was Max who reached out for him. Inge retreated into silence as Max picked up the book.

"All right, little man, time for some magic. I'm going to make this horrid old thing disappear." He got up and went over to the fireplace. The grate was empty: it was December but as hot outside as July should be and still light although it was close to eight o'clock.

Five years in Argentina and Inge was still topsy-turvy with the seasons and had never quite mastered the time difference between Buenos Aires and Berlin. On the increasingly rare occasions she telephoned her parents, they were at dinner or at some event she was supposed to remember or, worse, they were sleeping. If they did answer, they were so irritated by the multiple operators and crackling connection, they could barely feign any interest at all. "Max told us that already" greeted everything she said.

Now Max lit a match and dropped the book into the hearth, pushing it with his foot until the spark caught.

"There. The fire will eat the nasties up until there's nothing left but ash. The best thing all around, wouldn't you say, Mama dear?"

Inge stared into the grate. The pages blackened, crisping and crackling as the flames bit deeper.

Max waited until Wolf's eyes were closed and the fire little more than a glow, then he grabbed Inge's arm and dragged her into the hall.

"You stupid bitch. What were you trying to do?" Her back was flat against the wall, his weight an inch away.

"Nothing. I'm sorry; I'm so sorry. He wasn't meant to find it." His mouth was so close she could taste his cigar.

"Why would you keep a thing like that?" His hand was on her shoulder, barely a touch, but it kept her there. "Do you like the pictures? Is that it? Do they excite you?"

He laughed when she stiffened.

"Oh, Inge, there's so little sport in you. So, what is it? Are you looking for someone? Do you sift through the names and think you might find me? Or is it your little Jewish friend from the camp that you're after? Do you think his corpse might still be handsome?"

His mocking tone was more frightening than anger. She blinked as hard as she could to stop the tears falling. Not that crying would stop him. Nothing stopped Max, not even a new country: his star had been rising since they stepped off the boat. They had been welcomed like royalty. There were no immigration formalities, although the rest of the passengers were led into long lines. There was a Cadillac waiting and a house in the affluent suburb of Recoleta, even bigger than the one she had left in Germany.

It was his particular medical talents, or so Max said, that had propelled him straight into the Argentinian president's inner circle and a directorial role in Perón's newly created National Ethnic Institute. Inge had filed that name away until she could unpick it: it was pointless to ask Max what his new role involved. Or, in the initial months at least, to find one of her own.

They had a nanny for the daytime and a nanny for the night. Neither reported to her. On the weekends, the only person Wolf wanted was his daddy—his daddy made increasingly sure of that. Once she stopped feeding the baby and Max began wondering aloud what her function actually was, then Inge had pulled herself together. She hosted dinners, began attending receptions; put her capacity to memorize people to work. She made herself useful, she made herself charming; she kept her eyes and ears open. And, despite every effort, she knew no more now than she had then. Buenos Aires' business with her husband was as closely guarded as the camp's had been.

Max leaned in closer, his fingers curling. She had to focus. What had he said: her *little Jewish friend*? Why would he ask about that? What response could he possibly want?

His hand cupped her chin, the grip a fraction from a caress. "I can almost hear the wheels grinding. Stop it, Inge. Stop trying to work out what I might want to hear. It's as exhausting as this charm offensive you think will keep you safe. I don't care, for the Jew or for any of your nonsense. It was a drawing, wasn't it?" He laughed as her head jerked back into the wall. "I got to the bottom of it in the end—I always do. That silly little nurse didn't get away far enough. Well, you bought him a bit of time, but you didn't save him: Krueger's little band of pampered Jews was destroyed in the end, just like they all were. All you did was put off his death; perhaps you made it harder. That's something to think about."

He pulled back abruptly, adjusting his cuffs, checking his watch, leaving her gasping. "Obsessing over lies and misinformation, tying yourself in knots about things you don't have the intelligence to grasp. It's pathetic. Keep your secrets, for what they're worth. I have no interest in what you think, Inge, I truly don't, but I won't have you feeding nonsense to my son. He'll learn what he needs when the time is right. He'll learn his country's history from me and he'll know to be proud of it. Germany's done with feeling sorry—don't you get that? I doubt the pictures you drool over are even published there anymore. Do you honestly think decent Germans are digging over the past? They know the good we did. They know the Party cleaned up the country and plenty are still grateful, inside Germany and out. If you don't believe me, look how well we are treated here." He paused.

Inge wasn't stupid enough to think he wanted her opinion. The quieter she was, the quicker his lesson would go.

"If you are going to base everything you believe on the papers, you need to read them properly, my dear. Take the men they've appointed to Germany's new government. If you could see your blank face. You have no idea, have you? Look up Globke the next time you go digging: don't you remember him, the man who drafted the race laws? You liked his Christmas parties well enough. If you hadn't been searching for all the wrong names, you might have seen his again. Globke advised on who should be given the key appointments when the German Federal Republic was set up last year. Why? Because he knew the right kind of men to pick. What is that, if not a message? The clock is turning back. Don't you think we prepared for this? It's why so many of us got out: so we could carry on our work and, when the time comes—which it will—take it back to Germany."

Inge stayed perfectly still. Whether Max was right or whether he was deluded, her innocent child would play no part in this reborn National Socialist future.

He took another step back. "And there go the wheels again. I can read you, Inge, remember? You can't hide your thoughts—you never could. Wolf is my boy, not yours. He knows that better than you. If you weren't here, he wouldn't notice. You'd do well to remember that. You only stay because I let you. That will wear thin soon enough." He brushed a speck of dust from his cream linen suit and looked at his watch. "Tonight's reception is too important to waste any more time on this. You have half an hour before the car comes. Change that dress—the neckline belongs on a nun."

He turned and headed toward his bedroom. Inge unpeeled herself from the wall.

Felix... I saved him. That rang louder than the truth in *Max wants you gone* and the lie that was *Wolf doesn't care.* Shock shivered through her body. *I saved him, but what if it was only for something worse?* No. She couldn't think like that or the sky would cave in. Others had survived, why not him? Besides, if Max had proof, he would have gloried in it.

A wisp of smoke from the burning book wandered through the door. Inge smelled ovens and gagged. She needed something to calm her.

Max suddenly paused, as if her thoughts had danced down the hallway and tugged at him.

"The brandy is locked up. Don't go looking for it. And no drinks at the party either. I'll let the waiting staff know. I've no patience left for anything else tonight—don't be stupid enough to think I have."

Inge crouched by the wall until his door clicked shut.

The limousine sped along the gently darkening roads that wound from Recoleta to the presidential palace—the Casa Rosada. There was a slight breeze, just enough to lift the fronds of the palm trees and set them rippling. Inge watched the leaves dance. There was a calmness in their movements, a soothing rhythm quite alien to every other aspect of life in Buenos Aires. The city was perpetually spinning: as soon as Inge caught any kind of hold on it, it slipped out of her grasp again. Everything about the place was so alive, it made her feel dowdy. No matter how many layers of silk or armfuls of jewelry she cloaked herself in, it was as if Berlin's dust still clung.

The people—the men as much as the women—were as sleek and highly strung as the horses they all worshipped, and impossible to read, no matter how well she spoke their language. The streets they made their theater were constantly changing. Every spare patch of land bloomed with scaffolding and rising structures, each competing to be the tallest or the smartest or simply to hold the most people. Each street was different from the rest; sometimes each building was different from the rest. Delicate Spanish arches rose on one corner; Greek pillars dominated the other. Curving walls carved all over with flowers billowed down one side of an avenue; solid cut squares and rectangles marched up the other. It was dizzying—there was no plan to it. The new clamored to be heard as loudly as the old and Buenos Aires shuffled up and made room for it all.

Even the streets spanned different centuries. From the back of the car, Inge could see Daimlers and donkey carts, motorbikes and bicycles, trams and open-topped carriages pulled by tightly reined horses, all bustling down a road as wide as a river. Everything was too changeable to be any comfort. Buenos Aires never stood still and it never slept.

When Inge was driven away, early and alone, from the formal receptions Max always remained at, the city's nightclubs were just beginning to open. She would wind down the window, craning to hear the sultry music, which the orchestras she danced to never played, spilling out across the packed and laughing streets. No one Max mixed her with would go to such places, or so they always insisted.

"Do you really want to spend your whole night dancing poker-stiff waltzes with men twice your age?" The memory flew back so loud, Inge started and had to blame the stupidity of a too-close cyclist for her sharply drawn breath.

Max was watching her, fingers tapping the seat. She doubted he would touch her tonight; she would make her behavior so perfect he wouldn't be tempted. She'd grown very good at that. He hadn't hit her since Wolf was a baby and she'd questioned his treatment for a particularly exhausting bout of colic. Why do anything when the threat of a blow was enough, when words made such good weapons?

That silly little nurse didn't get away far enough. She couldn't think about that either. There were so many layers to this man she crept her days around and they all harbored dangers that once could have submerged her. *Not now.* Not now that she was watching him back.

Inge sat the rest of the journey with her hands folded, her mind deliberately empty. By the time the palace swung into sight, her breathing was slow, her face perfectly held.

The Casa Rosada dominated the sprawling Plaza de Mayo, its rose-pink bricks glowing in the sunset. It was decked out for a show. Blue-and-white-striped banners fluttered between the sparkling windows, each one centered as perfectly as the soldiers lining the red-carpeted steps. The balcony President Perón treated as his personal stage was swathed so thickly in fabric rosettes, it looked like a flower basket. Vivid paintings of Perón and his wife, Eva, guarded the doorway, their smooth, smiling faces twenty feet high. As the limousine pulled up, Inge could see the banners repeated round and round the square. Such pageantry: it was little wonder Max could refer so easily to this city as home.

Servants hovered at the entrance to the towering hallway, collecting wraps, offering champagne. Inge clutched her sour tonic water as the usual pathway opened to welcome Max in. Everything was as stage-managed inside as it was out. The men were trussed up and flattened in immaculately cut evening suits; only Perón wore his uniform, so startlingly white he was as unmistakable as a diamond dropped in a coal seam. The perfectly polished women wore satins and silks in rainbow colors, their suntanned backs and shoulders bare, their beckoning arms accentuated by tightly buttoned gloves. They were, for the most part, considerably younger than the men they draped themselves around.

Eva Perón—Inge could never think of her as Evita; the affectionate diminutive sat better with those who had never met the First Lady—like her husband, also wore white, a dazzling column that rippled down the blue carpet. She stood in her usual position at the top of the staircase, where the huge chandeliers set her skin glowing and everyone had to walk up to meet her with hands and faces lifted.

Inge was in no hurry to claim her welcome. The first time she and Max had attended a presidential reception, she had been dazzled by Eva. She was no more than a few years older than Inge and the age gap between the newly married president and his wife was even wider than hers with Max. When Inge blurted out to Max that she hoped they would have enough in common to become friends, her husband had laughed so loudly heads turned.

"Oh, Inge, that is priceless. Friends, the two of you? Tell me, because my imagination fails me, how that is going to work? The spoiled little princess and the girl who dragged herself out of the gutter into the presidential bed: what a heartwarming story that would be, worthy of a cheap novel. And what sage advice will Frau Eichel offer Señora Perón? The woman who can bring a crowd of thousands to silence and has Argentina eating out of her hand? I truly cannot wait to hear it."

By the time Max had finished, Inge could barely stammer her own name and Eva had looked straight over her head.

Tonight, she was no different, although Inge was no longer in awe. Eva kissed Max on both cheeks, squeezed his hand, demanded "as many dances as will make the rest of the room jealous" and barely nodded in Inge's direction.

"It isn't the most comfortable place, is it, standing in the shadow of the beloved? Even I have had to learn that one, my dear."

Inge held her hand steady as the president lingered over her gloved fingers and waited for him to raise his eyes out of the bodice of her halter-neck dress. Every man she met at these receptions was the same, considering themselves perfectly at liberty to comment and touch as if she was a piece of fruit arranged on a platter. Every party danced to the same theme. The men overstepping, the women batting attention away or inviting it in, measuring every engagement for the value to be had; treating every new face as a rival. She really needed a friend, someone who saw her as more than just a conduit to Max, someone to gossip with and pull these people back to a manageable size. *Liesl would revel in this.* Inge closed her eyes against another rush of memories. It was a moment before she realized a hush had fallen.

"Señora Eichel, perhaps you did not hear my invitation?" Perón had not moved on. His hand was still outstretched, his smile stiffening. "To accompany me in to dinner? Were you not aware of tonight's arrangements?"

She was, but she had forgotten in the fuss with Wolf. *I will lead in Eva; you are to accompany him. It's an honor, a recognition of my work. Don't make a fool of me.*

Max was turning, his mouth disappearing into a hard line.

Inge recovered herself quickly and turned her lie into a flirtation. "Forgive me, Señor Presidente. You must think I have no manners. I was trying to imagine you left in the shadows and the idea was so impossible, it quite distracted me."

Perón beamed. There was a little ripple of relieved applause.

Max turned away again. Inge took the heavily braided sleeve with a little curtsey that had Perón pronouncing her a delight and allowed herself to be led in to dinner.

The next two hours passed with a deadening slowness. Max's table was filled with laughter. The president dominated theirs with meaningless pronouncements that strained Inge's powers of concentration. The waiters had been well briefed and served her nothing but water. The women at her table interpreted that as the first hint of a pregnancy and she was happy not to argue; at least it had the benefit of stilling Perón's wandering hands. By the time the dancing began, the president had moved on to more willing prey and Inge had the beginnings of a headache. She looked around for Max, hoping to plead herself an exit, but he was nowhere to be seen.

Under the excuse of finding a restroom, Inge wandered out of the ballroom, in search of fresh air. Billowing curtains at the end of the hallway and a glimpse of fairy lights promised a garden. Quickening her pace, she slipped outside. The air was sweet and clean, the heavy honey musk of jacaranda blossoms undercut with a tang of salt from the sea. The space was a courtyard rather than a garden, laid out in neatly swept squares, each marked by a filigreed bench set beneath squat palm trees. Inge crossed to the nearest one, slipped off her shoes and stretched out. The fairy lights danced through the palm fronds like stars caught underwater. Her eyelids were heavy; she had barely slept since Wolf's nightmares began. Her head lolled.

"There is important work for you here. Work you are better suited to than selling farm equipment."

Inge stiffened, her senses at once awake and alert. It was Max, whispering and clearly with no wish to be overheard. She pulled her legs up into the shadows.

"What we are doing at the Institute builds on everything we did for the Reich. Perón has the same aims for Argentina that the Führer had for Germany and all the support, and money, that he needs."

"He doesn't carry himself as if he does—giving speeches about the importance of the people. The wife is even worse." Inge did not recognize the second voice. It carried none of the more lilting inflections she and Max had picked up from being surrounded so much by Spanish, suggesting this man was more newly arrived.

Max laughed. "Propaganda, all of it, a sop to a nervous world. Surely I don't need to explain that to you. Yes, Perón has a vision for Argentina that rests on the people, but he means the right kind. That is why he needs us: to eradicate the elements in the way of his ideal. Why wouldn't you want to be part of that?"

There was a pause, some indistinct murmuring and the flare of a match. Inge wriggled forward, the better to hear the second man's quieter voice.

"I want to continue our work as much as you. The genetic strides I made were just beginning to bear fruit. But there is a bigger price on my head than yours. You kept yourself better below the radar; my work fell into squeamish hands and my methods, well, let us say they are recognizable. You can tell me Perón is welcoming and Germany's new government will come around, but what about the Jews, or the Israelis, or whatever name they choose to go by now? They are gaining support; they are growing louder."

"Which is why our work is essential. Think about it at least. He's asked for you. It's why he helped you come here, same as me."

Whatever the man's response, Inge couldn't hear it. Other guests, overheated from the dancing, had spilled into the courtyard, their chatter as loud as a flock of parakeets. As she waited, craning to hear what might come next, Max stepped out of the huddle of palm trees that had been sheltering him.

"We should join the others; everyone is eager to meet you."

Inge shuffled along the bench. Max's companion was hard to see in the flickering light, but his profile was sharply cut and his thick hair unmistakable. She leaned farther forward and had to bite down on a scream. Josef Mengele. The doctor who had gathered such horrific stories around him he had become a monster in the eyes of the world overnight. What on earth was he doing in Buenos Aires, and why was he closeted with Max?

As Inge tried to get a better look, the two men moved away and were immediately pounced on by an adoring crowd. She stared after them, only snapping back when she realized that Max was bowing and clearly offering his goodbyes. She pulled on her shoes, almost breaking the straps, and crept around the side of the building toward another open door. She couldn't be found in the garden: if Max thought she was spying on him, his fists would fly. She made it into the ballroom with seconds to spare. When Max arrived, she was sitting quietly, waiting to be collected. He led her to the car without any interest in her evening and closed his eyes once the door shut.

Eradicate. Ideal. The right kind of people. Inge stared out into the dark, desperate not to lose one thread of the overheard conversation. She could have pulled all those words from the trial reports. *There is a bigger price on my head than yours.* She knew people were looking for Mengele. There was a man working out of Austria whose name had appeared in more than one report. Simon Wiesenthal, that was it. And there were lawyers too, in Germany, although she couldn't recall the firm she'd seen quoted.

If people were looking for Mengele, could they also be looking for Max? Inge glanced over at him. He was asleep, his face as carefree as it always was. He was so handsome, his good looks highlighted by the suntan he had acquired in Argentina. And he was so loving with Wolf, always patient, always enamored by everything the child did. But underneath? *He is a nightmare as bad as any that frighten my baby.* Inge gazed at the shadowy palm trees that no longer soothed her. She needed a new notebook, one that no one would stumble on. She needed to remember everything.

They passed the whole journey in silence. When they got back to the house, Max went straight up the stairs. She followed him into Wolf's room. The boy was sleeping peacefully, spread out like a starfish. Ignoring Max's muttered order "not to disturb him"—which he uttered as if that was Inge's sole intention—she settled in the rocking chair to think and watch over her son, just as she had when he was a baby and as she still loved to do. A few hours a night with no one around to take over, when Wolf smiled when he half woke and saw her sitting close by him; when he still felt truly hers.

What if I can't protect him? The thought jolted her out of the sleep she had not meant to fall into. *What if Max has plans for Wolf in this new world of his and I can't protect my boy?*

Inge roused quickly, pulling at her wrap, groping for her watch. Three o'clock. No wonder she was cold. Wolf was still sleeping, his beloved bear with its chewed ear and mismatched eyes pinned beneath his outstretched arm.

I have to get him out of here. She was halfway to the bed, ready to bundle him up, before she caught hold of herself. This was madness. What could snatching him possibly achieve? Wolf would shout, Max would come; goodness knows what would happen to her then. *There are special facilities for wives who cannot cope.*

Inge slumped back down. She had to leave Max. She should have done it long ago, but it could not be a haphazard, panic-driven thing. It needed planning and careful thought. It needed money. Inge stared at her hands, at the diamonds twinkling on her fingers, circling her wrists. There was money there, but Max knew every piece in her jewelry box: if she didn't rotate them, he noticed.

Wolf stirred in his sleep, pulled his bear closer. *Max is wrong: Wolf would know if I wasn't here.* He was so much Max's son, but sometimes she caught a flash of Gunther or Eric in the curve of his cheek, the tip of his nose.

Father. The thought caught her bright as a moonbeam. She'd gone to him for help before and failed. This time, she would think things through better, devise a simpler idea with less space for mistakes. Inge sat forward, her mind sharpening. Perhaps if she said she wanted the money for Max, a nest egg to help her plan a surprise; a trip perhaps for their tenth anniversary. That should do it: a special surprise for Max would surely appeal to Father and there would be no need to overdo the importance of secrecy.

She was shivering again and her shoulders were stiff from the chair's hard back. She should go to bed, get some sleep. Tomorrow morning she would start drafting a letter: that would be a far better way to approach Father than a disjointed telephone call.

Inge blew Wolf a kiss, Max's warning not to disturb him still ringing in her ears, and crept out into the thickly carpeted hall. The house was silent. No one would stir until six at the earliest. Bed and sleep and a clear head in the morning.

Inge turned toward her room, but another voice was nagging. *You would do better with a brandy. Just one, to take the edge off.* She hesitated. Max had said it was locked up, but there would be a bottle in his study, where he wouldn't expect her to go. Or if not brandy, whisky. Or if not his study, then the kitchen would surely yield up something. She really did need to sleep, but her mind was whirling.

She inched down the stairs, keeping to the edges where the boards wouldn't creak. Max's study was the closest. She pressed gently on the handle and eased the door open. Inside, the room smelled of leather and tobacco. Inge rarely came in during the day, finding its dark walls and heavy furniture oppressive. Now she crossed the room quickly—there was no need to put on a light—heading for the nook where the decanters and glasses sat waiting. One measure, the glass carefully rinsed in the little bathroom tucked into the alcove and then the drinks and the tray perfectly repositioned. She would order it replenished in the morning. No one would know.

She poured the drink, swallowed it in a gulp. One more, then sleep would be certain. She poured the second measure a little larger, sipped it more slowly. She was so tired from the upset with Wolf, from the night's revelations. She should sit down. Not on the sofa or on the armchairs: the cushions there were placed with mathematical precision. Inge slipped instead into the seat at Max's desk, taking care not to touch the blotter or pens. She took another sip. It felt rather powerful to sit at the huge desk, papers at the ready for whatever orders she fancied giving. She ran her fingers up and down the tightly closed drawers, wiggling the curling brass handles. Except for the bottom one, they all opened smoothly. Taking another sip, Inge pulled the locked drawer a little harder. It wouldn't budge.

Keep your secrets, for what they're worth. What might Max's secrets be worth? She tugged at the handle. Enough to get away? *This is stupid. This is dangerous. Even if you found anything, what could you do? You should go to bed before this gets any worse.* It was a good thought, but not one two glasses of brandy cared much for.

Inge pulled the other drawers open, searching for a key. It was in the middle one, tucked behind a boxed set of pencils. Inge marked its position, lifted it out, fitted it into the lock. The drawer opened as easily as the others. She left the key in place in case she needed to move quickly, although she knew no explanation would survive this discovery. There were two objects inside: a slim roll of canvas secured with loosely caught ties that Inge recognized and a leather-bound book.

She took the pouch out first and unwound it, after checking the knots to make sure she could copy them. As it fell open, she snatched her hand back. A set of loops ran across the middle, each holding a needle. There were half a dozen of them, in different sizes, all gleaming like new, some with tips as fine as a bee sting, some squatter and blunter.

She tied the roll back up and took out the book. It was a beautiful thing, maroon with gold embossing; there was no author or title. *Perhaps it's a diary.*

Later, when Inge closed the cover, sick and shaking, part of her wished she had listened to the nagging voice urging her not to open it. With two large drinks inside her, however, curiosity had won. The handwriting inside was copperplate neat. She skimmed over the table of contents with its lists of drawings and diagrams and turned to the first page. A graph covered most of that, its frame drawn under a neatly ruled headline.

Vienna 1939–1941. Am Spiegelgrund Clinic Euthanasia Program: Numbers of Exterminations by Age and Month.

Inge read the title and then she read it again. She traced her finger over the red-inked line, matching its spikes and dips against the numbers at the side, then got up, still clutching the book, and poured another drink.

Three thirty. Two and a half hours before the house woke up.

Slowly and very deliberately, Inge turned over the pages and began to read.

CHAPTER FIFTEEN

May 1953, Berlin

Felix walked along Platanenallee, slowing his pace to peer up at gates and down driveways. It should have been easy to find the Ackermann house, but there was no logic left in the street. Platanenallee, like much of Charlottenburg, still wore the scars of the bombs that had battered Berlin's western suburbs. Some of the double-fronted villas that dominated the road before the war were still intact, but they were scattered: following what should have been a simple numbering pattern had turned into a guessing game.

I should have asked Kitty how to find it. She knew the area better than him—some of her colleagues had taken over properties here. He hadn't asked; he knew he couldn't: whatever excuse he came up with for his interest in the house, she would know he was hiding something. *She already does.* That was an alleyway he couldn't go down.

He pushed on, peering more closely at the buildings. The surviving properties were separated by weed-choked lots, or the remains of half-collapsed homes that clung like drunks around crumbling chimney stacks. There were signs, here and there, of repairs being made, or planned at least. Felix could see patched-up stucco work, repainted windows, new layers of plaster; piles of waiting bricks and scaffolding poles. What had been attempted, however, was shoddy: the colors were mismatched and blotchy, the plaster already peeling. The work left the street looking not strengthened but vulnerable, like an old woman or a child half dressed and then abandoned. That there was nothing remarkable in this saddened him almost as much as the damage.

Eight years on from the war's end and wide stretches of West Berlin were filled, as they had been then, with broken, struggling streets. The city was choked with buildings unsure if they were going up or coming down. Or speckled with the box-like structures shaped without a single softening feature that had appeared all over the city and looked to Felix like a virulent rash. Elegance was being eaten away, function apparently everything in this re-forming Berlin. Columns and archways and anything put back on too grand a scale was mistrusted. It was as if no one had a plan for the city except to erase its past.

Spirits deflating, Felix continued his quest, skirting the tree stumps that tore cracks in the pavements. The plane trees the area was named for were gone. He assumed they had been chopped up for firewood, if not in the war, then during the Soviet blockade of 1948 and 1949, which had cut Berlin off from food and coal and which, with an irony that escaped no one, had finally been relieved by Allied airdrops. The new decade's great replanting program, which was meant to spread new shoots from the decimated Tiergarten across the city, had clearly faltered here.

Felix stopped and doubled back as the houses began to peter out. Finally, after he had slowed to a snail's pace, he found it: number 1730. The sign was so discreetly placed against the high wall, he'd walked straight past it. Pushing the gates open with a sharp click, Felix entered a driveway that curved away, rendering the house, at first, invisible. When it did come into view, he could have laughed. The building was untouched. Or perfectly remade. There wasn't a mark on the cream façade or a break in the roof or a crack across a single window.

Why am I surprised? Everything he had learned about Karl Ackermann confirmed one thing: the man had the survival instincts of a cockroach. No factory complex the size of his, supplying arms to the Wehrmacht on the scale he managed, could have prospered the way Ackermann's did by honest methods—without taking full advantage of the Reich's bottomless well of slave labor. Or without contacts in some very high places. Yet Ackermann had emerged from all his wartime dealings with nothing stuck to him except the cover-all label "Fellow Traveler." Responsible for what he did and yet not responsible, simply another hapless industrialist caught in the Führer's sticky web. *I had to use their labor. I had to supply their demands or my family would have suffered. None of it was of my making. None of it was my choice.* Felix had read Ackermann's testimony with its pity-me pleas and couldn't tell it apart from a dozen others. He had been interviewed once in 1946, served with a fine that was barely a day's takings, and never been called to account since. Now that the Allies needed his flourishing factories to bolster their backs against the Soviets, Felix—and no doubt Ackermann—knew he would never be bothered again. Eichel had chosen his father-in-law well.

Carry the rage with you. Felix made his way along the driveway, aware that he was clutching his briefcase to his chest like a shield. It would make a very flimsy one—his file on Eichel barely merited its own folder. All the years looking and the doctor remained as elusive as he had been in the camp. Sachsenhausen's records were destroyed or vanished into Soviet hands. Felix had questioned the few survivors he could find, but their accounts of Eichel's dealings in the infirmary were as intangible as his own.

He had found one listing in the records for the Am Spiegelgrund Clinic in Austria—the center that specialized in the killing of sick and mentally disabled children. From what Felix could piece together of the man's timeline, Eichel had spent two years as a resident doctor there before the war, before he married Inge Ackermann. From February 1945 onward, there was nothing at all: Eichel had disappeared as completely as his victims. Now the only link left was through the Ackermann family, and Felix had little hope of that. Karl Ackermann was as hard to pin down as his son-in-law. He had refused Felix's calls and ignored his letters. When Felix visited the factory headquarters in Spandau, he hadn't made it past the fiercely manned reception desk.

As for the daughter, Inge, all Felix could uncover of her was a photograph of a little girl presenting a posy of edelweiss to Hitler. The caption included her name, but the tiny figure with its braids and smock and turned-away face could have been anyone.

So now here he was, at the house, clutching at his very last lead and staring at the polished door, with no plan beyond talking his way through it. His knock, which was supposed to sound authoritative, rang out too loud across the quiet afternoon. Even to his ears it sounded accusatory.

"Can I help you?" The tightly drawn woman dressed in a plainly cut dress guarded the door rather than opened it. Felix smiled. She continued to examine him.

"I was hoping Herr Ackermann might be at home." She waited. "I don't need very much of his time."

"You are?"

"Felix Thalberg. I'm a lawyer with Bruckhaus and Gottlieb."

That was a mistake. The woman stepped back.

"Herr Ackermann is not here. If you had an appointment, you would be aware of that."

"Perhaps Frau Ackermann, then? It's a family matter. I could discuss it with either." He sounded like the worst kind of salesman; it was little surprise the door slammed.

"Don't take it personally—no one gets past." A man had emerged around the side of the building, pushing a loaded wheelbarrow. He was softer-looking than the housekeeper, but his graying hair and lined face put them at a similar age. "My wife." He shrugged. "She's protective of the family, that's all. Especially of Frau Ackermann: the war was hard on her."

Felix did his best to look sympathetic. "Is it true both of her sons were killed?"

The gardener nodded. "Within weeks of each other. A dreadful thing for any mother. It broke her heart, and his of course. It's hard not to have sons to leave all this to."

Felix forced himself to wait while the man took out a cigarette. "But they have a daughter left, don't they?"

"They do, but it's not the same. Although there's a grandson now, which helps a little. Not that they've ever seen him—not with the journey being such a long one."

Felix should have waited. "A long one? Why? Where are they? Is she still with the husband?"

He was too eager. His words tipped out so quickly, the man blew out the match he'd just struck.

"What's that to you? I didn't catch your business. What do you want here?" The gardener's body had straightened, his shoulders squared up.

"A family matter, to do with the house. And inheritance…" Felix trailed off as the man took a step forward.

"If I were you, I'd have gone by now." There was no trace of the earlier softness.

Felix went down the driveway far quicker than he came up it. He didn't stop moving until he was clear of the narrow suburban streets and into the wide expanse of the Spandauer Chaussee—the great sweep of a road that stretched from Spandau across to the edges of Charlottenburg. His heart was thumping, his blood surging through his body like a freight train. Eichel was alive—he must be. Surely the gardener would not have reacted like that if he were dead or would have said something if Inge was a widow.

Felix sank onto a half-finished wall and pulled out his own cigarettes. His hands were shaking so much, it took him two attempts to light one. *Eichel was alive.* Even if he was a long way away, that news was a start. No, it was a huge leap forward. Finally, a lead that led somewhere.

Felix took a long draw on the cigarette and watched the steady flow of cars pouring in and out of the city. He let his mind wander back through maps and folders, pulling up the route he had always half known. *For his set of Italian passports, Dr. Eichel ordered that we use the name Ago.* Isaak's testimony had suggested it was at least Eichel's intention to head toward Italy. That had always made sense: the Eichel family home in Baden-Baden would have offered a refuge, even in the last days of the war, and easy enough access to Austria and Switzerland and on into Italy to make the risk of going there worth taking.

Felix had already tried to investigate that link, but Italian records were in even worse shape than German ones. With his resources limited to writing to a war-crimes office in Rome, no doubt as short-staffed as CROWCASS, Felix had made no headway; his letters had gone unanswered. Besides, even if Italy had been part of the journey, Felix had never believed it was the final destination, not with the depths of anti-Fascist feeling that erupted there in the war's dying days. And now, if the journey could be described as *such a long one*, he was sure of it. There was only one logical route onward from Italy and that was along the escape lines set up before the war's end, with no little help from the Catholic Church, although the Vatican denied it. Eichel had run, as so many of them had, into the welcoming arms of South America.

Felix stubbed out his cigarette. It wasn't the complete answer, not yet. South America, in reality, could mean Chile or Brazil, Paraguay or Argentina; the web of possible hideouts was a wide one. That didn't matter. He jumped up, grinning so broadly a woman stepped off the pavement to avoid him, and set off back to the office. The pin wasn't firmly stuck in the map yet, but it was getting much closer.

*

It was late when he arrived home, long past eleven. The apartment was in darkness, the bedroom door shut. There was no sign of Kitty. In their early days together, she would have waited up. He would have done the same if she worked late—both of them eager to share the day. That habit had got lost somewhere along the slowing route of their marriage. He hadn't mentioned it; if she noticed, she didn't say.

Felix made his way to the small kitchen, pulled out bread, salami, a jar of mustard, and began assembling a sandwich. By the time it was made, his appetite was gone. He finally knew where Eichel was and it changed nothing. All the euphoria of the discovery had drained away, leaving him dried out and bone-weary. *What a sight I must have been, bouncing into the office like a child who'd triumphed at a treasure hunt.*

"I've found him. He's alive! I've found him!" Felix slumped at the kitchen table, cringing at the memory.

Levi, the Gottlieb half of the legal practice Felix had joined when he completed his law degree, had come running at his shout. So had Lena, the firm's motherly secretary, and Daniel, the other junior.

"Eichel. The doctor from Sachsenhausen who carried out the endurance experiments and sent my father to Theresienstadt. He's in South America—I'm sure of it."

It took less than a minute for their faces to switch from eager interest to the muted sympathy he detested.

"That's good, Felix. That's really good. You've got an answer at least. South America, eh? Not such a surprise then. We could stretch to a phone call or two if you want to try to get a bit closer. If you know who to speak to." At least Levi had waved away Lena and Daniel and spared him that much embarrassment.

"No. I mean, thank you, but that's no use. Don't you see? I need to go in person. I thought I could start in Argentina. There are flights now, out of Frankfurt, so I'd be away no more than a few weeks. It's a real lead, Levi—a good one."

Levi didn't answer. Felix had looked up from the papers he was sorting through.

"Don't you believe me?"

"Of course I do. That's not the point. Think about it, Felix: even if we had the money to send you, which we don't, what would you do when you got there? Run around the streets of Buenos Aires asking where President Perón keeps his Nazis? You'd end up with a bullet. If it's true that Eichel is in South America, then he could be anywhere. You'd be better off approaching one of the military agencies, or that Wiesenthal guy who's kicking up a fuss in Austria. Even then, you need to be realistic. If no one can find Mengele, or Eichmann, with all the information on them that exists, your Eichel won't be high on anyone's list." Levi had put an arm around Felix's shoulders and didn't react when he flinched. "If I could do more, I would—you know that. No one understands this burden you carry better than me. But there's limits, Felix. I'm sorry."

It was kindly said, but there was no room for arguing. Levi had left shortly after, with a fatherly "get yourself home now" they both knew Felix would ignore. He'd sat on at his desk in the darkening office without a clue what to do. He couldn't find fault with Levi. None of the other firms Felix had applied to when he had graduated had wanted anything to do with concentration-camp cases. Levi, who had crawled out of Auschwitz and left behind his whole family, had understood at their first meeting what had driven Felix toward the law.

Now he gave Felix one day a week to work with survivors and comb through suspect lists, even though the chances of a winnable case were as good as nonexistent. Felix knew how much his obsession stretched resources; how much it potentially threatened the firm's credibility. The world had moved on, as Kitty said it would. Chasing fugitive war criminals had slipped out of official hands and become the province of anger-driven amateurs. No one with any real power was looking, even for those whose escape routes, and crimes, had long been suspected. Josef Mengele, whose medical experiments were so widely reported he had turned into an Angel of Death bogeyman. Adolf Eichmann, who had expertly organized the mechanics of extermination. Both of them were believed to be in Argentina, living quite openly, if rumors were true. In his darker moments, Felix was beginning to think that, even with an address and a line of pointing fingers, nothing would be done about either of them. *So why did I expect anything different for Eichel, whose name barely registers?*

At CROWCASS and in his first year of studying, despite all the brick walls he ran into, Felix had held some hope that justice would grind in the right direction. Until politics ran past him. After they showed their hand with the Blockade, the threat to the West from the Soviets had grown bigger than any threat from long-vanished Nazis. Germans were no longer to be regarded as untrustworthy: they were to be wooed. The foundation of the German Federal Republic in 1949, which united the French and British and American sectors across Germany, had reset the country's clock and blanketed over the war's atrocities. *Short memories* weren't just the *best rebuilding blocks*: as the Red Menace loomed, they were the only ones permitted. *Schlussstrich*—"the final ending," the backslapping politicians called it, or Year Zero. Whatever the label, the outcome was the same: the past was bundled up and buried. The final war trial was concluded, the last executions rushed through before the new government's founding; there was even talk of an amnesty.

"They've overturned the death sentence on the guard Herta Ehlert for her crimes at Auschwitz and they're likely going to let her out. She's turned into a model prisoner apparently." Kitty had brought that news home barely a week ago.

When Felix had railed at the injustice, never mind the irony, Kitty had met his anger in her usual matter-of-fact way.

"This will keep happening, Felix, the farther away we get. It goes deeper than forgetting: people don't want to believe. Never mind Ehlert. What about Herta Oberheuser, who's already free? The crimes she was accused of can't be fitted into a civilized society and it's easier to close eyes and ears than try to make sense of them. No one wants to face the horrors anymore."

She was right, but in that moment, he hated her for it. *The farther away we get.* It had only been eight years. If that wasn't long enough to mend the war's visible scars, how could anyone have expected its deeper wounds to be healed, or even recognized?

Of course no one wanted to face the horrors. The injuries inflicted and then deliberately infected; the operations without anesthetic; the monitored and agonizing injections. Oberheuser's crimes were terrible things. That she hadn't been some insane lone wolf, that every camp had an Oberheuser or a Mengele or an Eichel, and no one knew how many hundreds more carrying out their orders, passed beyond understanding. *Which is why we have to keep asking, keep looking—keep facing the horrors that humans can do. Without that we're simply waiting for the next set of uniforms to unleash the next twisted crusade.* Felix thought it and said none of it.

He and Kitty lived their lives in separate worlds. He was obsessed with the mess left by the old war; her post at the new American Mission to Berlin had her obsessed with the threat of a new one. What Germany had done wasn't the problem anymore—what Russia might do was. The fear of communism sneaking into the West through Russia's foothold in Berlin sucked all the air up. It had made Felix into a dinosaur and turned his monsters into myths no one thought were worth hunting. Which Kitty never said, but that he assumed, from the depths of her silences and the despairing way she sometimes looked at him, she thought.

The salami's spicy smell had grown too strong for the small room, sickening his stomach. Felix got up and swept the sandwich into the bin. He should go to bed. Tomorrow, with a clearer head, he might be able to find a more persuasive strategy to sway Levi. Argentina was out of reach, but not Austria. Perhaps he could suggest a trip to meet with Wiesenthal, the Nazi hunter, once he'd done some digging on him and got the mettle of the man. It was the start of a plan; perhaps he would sleep.

Felix began to open the bedroom door. And then he hesitated. Kitty wasn't always the deep sleeper she liked him to think and he was so worn out he didn't trust his defenses. If he disturbed her, he would end up telling her about Eichel: it was too much to keep in. She knew the name and some at least of what Eichel had cost him. She would listen, she would be sympathetic, but, ultimately, Kitty would agree with Levi. She would point out the sense in Levi's advice, wait for Felix to nod and assume the matter was done. He couldn't bear her managing, not tonight. The half telling, then swallowing his emotions while she told him how to feel. He needed to pour out his fears and frustrations without picking over his words and policing them against Kitty's reactions.

He eased the bedroom door shut again and went instead to the small sitting room, which opened out from the kitchen. Taking out his key ring, he unlocked the bottom drawer of the bureau that served as a desk. *It's nothing but a few bits and pieces that belonged to my mother, things I can't bear to look at.* Kitty had asked him about it once, in the first days of their marriage, and accepted his explanation without comment. That she hadn't pushed any further had been a source of both relief and resentment. *If she truly loved me, she wouldn't let me have locked drawers and secrets.* As he pulled it open this time, he remembered how clearly her lack of interest had hurt. Now he plucked out the tin and took it to the table, completely forgetting what Kitty did or didn't feel.

There were so many letters crammed into it. He took them out gently, separating them into piles. The oldest ones, dating from almost ten years ago, were starting to yellow and felt worryingly brittle. He would need to find new envelopes for them. Some of the scraps he had carried from Sachsenhausen were so battered, he had copied them out onto larger sheets of paper. He had not been able to part with the originals, a superstition that made as little sense, he knew, as the rest of it.

He put aside the older letters, whose contents he knew almost by heart, and turned to the newest batch. They were ordered by date: 1949 for the first of them, a week ago for the last. Four years since he had begun writing again and hadn't been able to stop. *Because Kitty couldn't save me.* That was his excuse the first time, and the one it suited him to stick to.

The letters had grown longer with the years; each one penned in the middle of the night in a script that was sometimes neat and sometimes scrawled. They were all different. Some were outpourings about Kerstin and Arno, and the numbness that went with their loss. Some were descriptions of the nightmares that still plagued him, the ones in which he watched himself marching skeleton-like into the flames. Others, the ones where the words flew across the page without a thought for sentences, were cries for help to make sense of a world he could not trust would hold steady.

If he stood back, he recognized the collection as a diary, but, when he'd started again, he'd framed the writing as letters because that was what he knew. The familiarity in their form was a comfort; crafting them was a release. Some mornings, all that got him out of bed and into the day was knowing that the night and the writing was coming.

Now he sat at the table and let the silence settle around him. A breath or two and he wasn't in the apartment anymore. He wasn't a married man, close to thirty, trailing years of loss. He began his preparations, always carried out in the same order: selecting a clean sheet of paper, smoothing it out, setting it square on the blotter, picking up a proper pen, not the new ballpoints Kitty liked to use, filling it with dark blue ink, wiping the nib on a scrap of chamois leather.

Another breath and there he was: young, trusting, whole. He began to write. They might all be different, but the start was the same.

My dearest Hannah, it's your Felix…

*

It was a sob that woke him. A shuddering intake of breath falling into a groan. Felix came to as groggily as if he'd been drinking, confused by the sound and by the daylight streaming through curtains he could have sworn were closed.

"Who is she?"

He struggled to sit up, his arms and legs pinned by the blanket he had pulled with himself onto the sofa. He remembered finishing the letter. He remembered settling into the cushions, worn out, for a nap that should have lasted no more than an hour. Now somehow it was morning and there was Kitty, sitting on the floor, cross-legged and childlike in her pale blue robe. The contents of the tin lay scattered around her like a snowfall.

"It's not what you think."

"How would you know what I think?" Her unaccustomed snarl trapped him on the sofa.

He cast around for a better defense, but his head was full of air.

"I asked you a question: who is she?"

"She's nobody."

It was the wrong answer. Kitty tore into the letters like a tiger at a kill.

"Nobody? Is that the best you can do? Every letter starts 'My dearest Hannah' and tells her you're her Felix, but she's nobody? And then, worse than that, the things you write. They're quite something, these feelings you've poured onto someone so unimportant. 'Every morning I run through the roll call and see all their faces, begging me for help, and I can't do a thing. The guilt runs through me like acid.'" She tossed that one aside, moved on to the next. "This one's poetry. 'They've gone, my love, my parents and too many more, vanished like dust in the wind and my heart is ground to powder.' Oh, and this one, this one really jumped out. 'You were the only light: if you are lost, how do I stop the darkness?' You wrote all that to *nobody*?"

The word beat on his skull like a hammer.

When Kitty looked up, her face was slick with tears. "You've never said anything like that, not even a fraction of it, to me."

The ache was worse than the anger. Felix slid to the floor. He reached for her hand, desperate to make some kind of a bridge between them.

She shoved him away so hard he fell backward. "Don't you dare touch me. I heard you last night, hovering outside the bedroom. I waited and I hoped and I hated myself for being such a fool to think you might actually come in. So, do you know what I did? Oh, the stupidity. I came to you. And what did I find? My husband sleeping like a baby and his heart all over these pages." She crumpled the letter still in her hand. Felix flinched and couldn't hide it. "Seriously? Tell me who she is, or I swear I will burn them."

He answered too quickly, his one thought to stop her. "A girl. Someone I knew a long time ago, in the early years of the war when we were both very young. Before things turned sour."

"So not *nobody* then."

Felix stayed silent, hugging his knees.

"No. You don't get to do what you always do." Kitty's voice was so hard, it forced his head up. "Don't give me that blank stare. You're hoping I'll shut up now and not ask anything else. Or take what little you've given me and shape it into an explanation we'll both pretend we can live with. Not this time. Oh, how well I know you. Although that's not your story, is it?" She scrabbled at the letters, plucking out one Felix could see had become creased and smeared. He tried not to look at it. "How did you put it? 'Kitty doesn't love me like she says she does. If she did, she would know what I needed—she wouldn't let me keep secrets.' The oldest, most pathetic excuse: *my wife doesn't understand me.* You bastard. Tell me who she is." Kitty was trembling so hard, the letters around her knees started fluttering.

Felix bit down the urge to gather them up before she hurt them any more. How many had she read?

He spoke carefully this time, picking around what she might already have discovered. "Her full name is Hannah Hüber. I don't know much about her, I really don't. She was Jewish, I'm certain of that, and I think she was from Mitte. I met her in a dance hall. And I lost her."

"And went looking for her."

Felix nodded.

"And never found her."

They were statements not questions: he said nothing, unsure what Kitty wanted.

Her shoulders slumped. "Do you think I mind that? That you wrote to some girl when everything was starting to go mad? When your father was sick or when you were taken to Sachsenhausen? You've kept them all; they were never sent. In some of them you thank her for saving you. I get it: she was some kind of a beacon. 'If I survive, you will survive.' You wrote it more than once and it makes sense that you clung to that feeling: the hope of good coming out of the misery. It would take a very hard heart not to understand that. Is that what you think I have, Felix: a hard heart?"

This was calm Kitty, reasonable Kitty. If he could keep hold of this Kitty, everything could surely be put right.

"No, Kitty, of course not. I didn't tell you about her because I didn't want to dredge it up. It was all so long ago."

The way she looked at him, as if she was empty. "Except it wasn't, was it?"

I'll admit to her that I'm still looking. That I know it's foolish, that Hannah's most likely dead or thinks that I am. That nothing will come of it, but I can't help myself. Maybe that will placate her. Get me my letters back.

He began to speak, but she cut across him.

"Don't, Felix, please. I know that you're still searching for her. I always knew there was someone else besides Arno and Kerstin, who was lost like them and never found, who was threatened by

Eichel. I don't know what you hope to find of her now—I doubt you do either—but the searching doesn't matter. And the old letters don't matter. I'm not upset by any of that."

The old letters. He was a step behind her.

When she gestured to the pile nearest her feet, he finally understood.

"It's these. The ones I read out from. The eloquent, honest, burning accounts of everything you've been feeling since I've known you. Those are where the hurt is. You hid them so carefully. You must have known what they'd do to me."

She paused, searching his face. The look she gave him stripped off his skin.

"You never even considered it—1949, 1950, on and on through our marriage and more of them with every year, and you never considered what that meant to me; to us."

Now he could feel her pain, see it spreading like a sickness.

"Why, Felix? I was here. Your wife. I would have coped with anything you gave me—I longed to. Why did you pour it all out for her and none of it for me? Why—" The word broke on a sob far bigger than it.

Felix hugged his legs tight. Nothing would do here but the truth, and he had no idea how to tell it. This was meant to be his pain, not Kitty's. And it wasn't a pain that he had ever dared drag before into the light.

"I couldn't." He groped for the words, fearing every one of them would land like a rockfall. "There's such a need for revenge in me, Kitty. So much rage to get even, with nowhere to go. It scares me to go near it. I hide it and I hide from it, but there's days when I think it's all I am."

He could feel himself slipping, stumbling like a man used to living in a city forced to crawl across a desert. Maybe if he turned the spotlight off himself and onto her, he would make it through.

"You saw something different in me, Kitty, something better. Beyond names and labels and what I'd been; beyond this hollow thing I'd become. You loved me. I thought if I could love you back, I'd turn into that man. But I got stuck."

She was watching him so closely he felt like a specimen.

He took a deep breath and tried for an honesty he had never attempted before.

"I messed up. I should have told you. I wanted you to help me. I truly hoped you would dig under the surface and find me a way out. But you didn't and, in the end, I couldn't talk to you. That's why I wrote the letters."

"That's part of it. I think you believe it might be all of it."

Kitty's response wasn't what he wanted. He wanted forgiveness and sympathy, not the bone-deep weariness filling her voice.

"I'm trying to give you the truth. Is honesty so pointless?" He sounded like a child; he hated that she heard that, that she responded to that.

"Don't fall back on that get-out, Felix, please. I know what honesty cost you in the past, I know how you learned to work around it. But that was then. I'm scared you don't know what honesty is anymore. Don't defend yourself again—I can't bear it. I'm not trying to be your enemy and I won't let you be mine. The first bit was the truth—I accept that. You've been burying your anger, your need for revenge, whatever you want to call it, since you were a child, from what I can see. But the rest? You wanted me to help you? You wanted me to dig? That's nonsense, another story to hide behind. You pushed me away so hard when I tried, it was like laying a siege. This is not my doing, Felix. You chose this. You chose to write letters to a woman who isn't here, rather than risk laying yourself bare to the one who is."

There was nothing she said that he could argue with. Her understanding of him, and the waste of that, tore at his heart. She was right: he had never let her know there was anything to find. *I was a coward* was what he should have said as soon as Kitty stopped speaking, but she started again before he got up the nerve.

"What is the point of living like this? You hoard your ghosts and all you do with their memory is insult it. They died, Felix, when they still had lives to live. And here's you: walking around cut off from the world and acting as if you've joined them."

"You have no idea."

Except she did. She was too bright not to. *I married her because I was lonely and broken and thought she might save me and I never gave her a chance.* He curled his nails into his knees and gulped the pain in. He should have reached out and told her all that. He waited a second too long again and he didn't. Kitty flew.

"Don't I? Why? Because I didn't live through it? Because I didn't suffer enough? Because I'm an American and my country wasn't ripped apart like yours, so I don't have the imagination to look through the pictures and see the people?"

"Yes!" It rushed out in a roar he knew was fury at himself, but she didn't. "You don't know a thing. You don't know what it's like to have your life reset by rules you can't understand and then have it ripped away from you. To be treated as inhuman. To live constantly in fear. You look at us and you think you would have done so much better. You wouldn't have been broken, or beaten, or controlled, oh no: you save the world; you don't get crushed by it. You think you can write the future and every bit of it will be safe and certain—"

"I don't think any of that. Felix, how can you look at me and think I could be so arrogant and stupid?"

Her anguish pulled him back. "But you must. You plan. You imagine your children and honestly believe they will live happily ever after because you say that's how it will be. How can you think like that, Kitty?" He was panting so hard every word was an effort. "You talk about us having a baby—you're always pushing for it.

Instead of asking all these questions, why don't you tell me how in hell that would work? Do you imagine a fireside and me telling family stories? You think a kid would survive that? Or thank me for passing on my bloodline? A baby. What an idea. You playing mommy while I can't keep even you safe." He stopped. He realized he was crying. If he had looked up properly, he would have realized so was she. His voice and his anger fell away. "Is that it, Kitty? Am I done? Is that enough honesty for one day?"

"It's a good start. You're talking. I believe you. I wish we'd talked like this months ago."

"If that's what you wanted, why didn't you try?" He didn't mean it as an accusation; he didn't know how it came out as one.

"Because you would never let me."

And here we are again, back on the opposite sides of a gulf too wide to step over. One accusing, then the other, the same fight constantly circling.

Kitty was still talking. "But if you'd thrown me the tiniest line, I would have tried."

He had never heard her voice so hopeless. When he looked up, all he could see in her eyes was love.

"Kitty, what have I done?" He would have reached for her then, but she curled away.

"There were so many walls, Felix, too many: I said it was like a siege and I meant it. I knew you were suffering, that the war hadn't left you. Don't you see? I thought if I made you a safe world, you would start to trust me and the real talking would come. I thought I was doing it right, taking it slow. I listened when you could speak and tried to untangle your emotions when you couldn't. I tried to help you find ways to make the past bearable and you resented me for it. You wanted me to put the right words in your mouth and then you loathed me for doing it. You wanted me to be everything. It was impossible; it was exhausting. All I did was fail tests you never wanted me to pass. You drank me up, Felix, and gave nothing back, and all the time your walls went higher. I should have left, but I loved you. I love you. And yes, I wanted a child. I never knew why you didn't. You never told me. I thought a baby might fill in the silences, give us a bond. I thought you might fall in love with it and there might be some of that love left over for me."

Her honesty was brutal; the gulf between them was heartbreaking, filled with broken hopes and shadows from the past that he hadn't let her love near.

But I could. This hole we've dug can't be too wide to get over, if we can bare our souls like this. The thought of what could be pushed Felix onto his feet.

"You love me. You just said it. If that's true, then it's not too late. We could try for a baby. I could try harder. We could make it work better."

There were words missing. Kitty smiled the saddest smile and he saw, with a horrible clarity, that it was too late to say them.

"But it's not about who I love, is it? And what about these?" She nodded to the letters he had completely forgotten. "You betrayed me."

He could answer that. He grabbed her hand; it was lifeless. "No. I didn't. You must see it's not like that. Hannah was a dream. What was it you said? She was a beacon. What I felt wasn't real—how could it have been? And she's not real, she's not here. You are. I was stupid, Kitty, and I'm desperately sorry. But it's not a betrayal."

She slipped her hand away, wiped her eyes. There was a deliberateness about her movements that frightened him.

"Kitty, please. I'm so very, very sorry."

"I know you are."

She got up, shaking the letters away. Calm Kitty was back, realistic Kitty. He wished that she wasn't.

"But you don't understand. I wish Hannah was here. Then you could get her out of your system, or not. The harm is already done, Felix, far more than if you had found her and slept with her and left it at that. You gave, you go on giving, all the best of you, all the truth of you, to Hannah. There's nothing left for me. That's the betrayal, Felix. That's the worst kind." Her words were as measured and even as a tolling bell. He would have begged, but she had already left him.

"What will you do?"

"Nothing dramatic. We've neither of us a need for that. I will go to a friend now, apply for a temporary assignment in a little while, or visit the States. Put a little space between you and me."

She paused. Even later, sitting alone with the letters still scattered about him, Felix failed to understand that there had been a moment when he could have tried to make her stay. When he could have gathered all his mistakes up and offered them to her, let her burn them or shred them, whatever was needed. When he could have told her the whole tangled story of Hannah and used the voice Kitty had found in his letters, the one that took his feelings and laid them out without hesitation. A moment when he should have done something, anything, to buy himself an extra hour with this woman who knew him like nobody could. And loved him despite it. It was years before he understood that and how much Kitty had longed for him to try.

"I don't want you to go." He managed that much at least, but it was too soft, too late; the bedroom door had already closed.

When Kitty stepped out again, she was neatly tidied up, her tears smoothed away, her smart suit like armor. He tried again, his voice louder this time.

"I don't want you to go."

But the front door had shut and he was sitting alone on the paper-strewn floor. His words were gone, used up. All he could do was sob at the mess he was left with, a mess that was nobody's making but his own.

CHAPTER SIXTEEN

September to December 1955,
Bariloche and Buenos Aires

The little town nestled into the curve between the Andean foothills and the lake was the most immaculate place Inge had ever seen. They had made the final leg of the journey through heavy snow, but the streets in Bariloche were swept and salted. The blinds fringing the prettily arranged shopfronts were an identical shade of forest green. Not one perfectly arranged flower in the hotel lobby was wilting, although Inge could have melted from the log fire's heat, and the carpets looked as if they had been newly laid. Inge expected to be grabbed and polished if she stood still too long.

"Isn't it remarkable?" Max had beamed as proudly as if he had staged it all. Inge had never heard of the place until Max announced they were taking a trip there, but his knowledge of the Argentinian ski resort was encyclopedic. As the driver negotiated the hilly roads, Max enthused over the soaring mountains and the crystal-clear lake and praised the architecture of the neatly spaced wooden and white chalet-style houses with an enthusiasm Inge found both bizarre and overbearing. Wolf was as excited as his father: twisting and turning, clapping and pointing, until Inge protested he would get carsick and was dismissed as a spoilsport. She had retreated into silence, unnerved by the taverns and chocolate shops that felt so out of place.

"It's as if someone scooped up Bavaria and dumped it here."

The overeager hotel manager took that as a compliment. Inge felt no more comfortable in the lobby with its hunting trophies and antique maps than she had in the car. A day's drive had whisked her out of Argentina and back in time. The little girl by the desk, holding tightly to her mother's hand, wore braids and a smocked dress Inge could have plucked from her own childhood. The little boys in their tan shirts and dark brown shorts, racing cars in front of the fire, could have been Gunther and Eric. Echo piled on echo. When Max bundled them out again, the cathedral they passed could have been transported from the Rhine. Children in crisp white shirts and black neckerchiefs ran around a playground, jumping and rolling in an ordered program of exercises and whooping with enthusiasm despite the biting cold. By the time she had gone in and out of enough shops to realize that no one was speaking Spanish, Inge was completely disoriented.

"What on earth is this place? Some kind of German amusement park?"

Heads turned. Max snarled her away from a *bierkeller*'s gaudy poster. "What is the matter with you? Isn't it nice to see and hear our language everywhere? Do you know how insulting you sound? Germans have been settling in Argentina for over 100 years. You can see how cut off it is. Is it such a surprise that old ways linger?"

He shook his head at Wolf and raised an eyebrow. Wolf immediately mimicked him: they had perfected *Silly Mama* to a gesture. He was lying. Nothing here was lingering—it was under cultivation.

Inge plastered on a smile. As Wolf ran from window to window, exclaiming over the chocolate-covered marzipan and the delicately iced gingerbread, she was careful to compliment the eye-catching displays.

Six weeks into a far longer stay than she expected and that uneasy first impression had not changed. Inge, however, had been careful to praise Bariloche since her first clumsily handled day, even at these dinners that made her stomach turn. *See what I've learned?* If Max wanted to believe she finally knew her place, she would let him. *I can read you, Inge: you can't hide your thoughts.* Well, not anymore he couldn't, or she wouldn't still be walking.

"Madame? Red or white?"

From the nudges at the table, it was obvious this wasn't the waiter's first time of asking.

Concentrate. Don't let him start looking for problems. Inge made a play of jumping and a joke out of her distraction before Max could swoop.

"Forgive me. My head was on the slopes. Today's lesson went so well, I might finally move up a class tomorrow. I might even catch up with Wolf and stop embarrassing the poor darling."

The perfect answer in this ski-obsessed company; better still, the perfect mother's answer. Her dinner companions laughed, offered over-gallant compliments and turned away again.

Inge covered her glass with her hand and requested iced water. She didn't look at the bottles being offered. Did she want red or white? She wanted both. And brandy, and whisky, and anything else the bar could bring. She always wanted, but she wouldn't listen to that voice anymore. Inge hadn't had a drink since December 1950. Not a single one since she'd replaced the leather book in its drawer and washed out her glass with shaking hands, although that night, and every night since if she was honest, she could have drunk a cellar full.

Conversation washed around the table. It had little need of her. Max had picked up her mention of Wolf and was holding court. Inge watched him, so tuned to his mannerisms she could have written him a script. The way he cocked his head, the self-deprecating smile he assumed as he apologized, oh so charmingly, for sharing another anecdote about his talented boy. She watched the women leaning in, the men repeating Max's witticisms and growing a little taller in the retelling. Max was forty-eight now and, although he had filled out a little, he was every bit as handsome as he had been at thirty, and no doubt at twenty. He had the face of a man who'd lived an easy life, who sat perfectly comfortable in his skin.

Inge clutched her bag beneath the table, pressing her fingertips hard against its metal trim. *You're safe in this room, Dr. Eichel, but what would decent people say if they knew the real you?* A bowl of soup she wouldn't taste appeared in front of her. Decent people were still looking for answers. She would do a good job of recounting him when the time came; she would be just as entertaining a storyteller. She'd had years to pick over the details. Inge lifted her spoon and turned to the overstuffed man on her left. He paid her no attention. *Might it be interesting to practice that now?*

Max has always been so good with children. Especially the ones who are poorly. The ones whose limbs don't work, or eyes, or brains. The ones who might grow up just able enough to pollute all the pure ones. Honestly, he was a marvel with them. So quick with the needle they were gone without crying. Perhaps he's mentioned it?

That would be a good tone: measured, not at all savage.

Inge blew on her soup as her neighbor continued to ignore her. She turned instead to the man on her right.

He moved on from children quite quickly, of course. I suppose there weren't so many once Mengele cornered the market. Is he here, by the way? Have you met him? I have, such a pleasure, although he seems rather reluctant to go back to medicine. Endurance testing, in case you're wondering: that's where Max took his talents. A wonder with a needle there as well. Cocaine, amphetamines, oxycodone—I think I said that one right. Into cut-open veins, into the heart; he's nothing if not imaginative. Forgive me, I'm prattling. What did you do, by the way? In the war, I mean. What was your preferred method of killing, your trademark as it were?

This one caught her looking and gave her a smile and a name she doubted was his real one. His swastika pin winked from his tie. Max looked over, checking. She caught up with the real conversation until he was bored watching. *I can read you, Inge.* Heaven help her if he could.

Venison replaced the soup. The table kept laughing. Inge cut into her meat, agreed that the potatoes were impossibly crispy, that the gravy was seasoned just right. As if she cared. All these good National Socialists and their obedient wives, flocking to Bariloche like it was a shrine. Hanging on Max's every word. Inge knew that if she said what she was actually thinking, they would call her a traitor—or they would call her mad. Speaking out anywhere was a passport to danger; speak out here and they would line up to commit her.

But if you stay silent, you might as well be one of them.

Inge smiled at the plump woman in rapture over the carrots, imagining the scream if she threw the steaming bowl in her face.

I am not like these people. Their silence is nothing like mine.

They fawned over Max because they shared his beliefs. They didn't hate him, or fear him. They weren't stuck in his trap. That night years ago, in his study, the night she had forced her way through the pages of his hideous book, her first instinct had been to scream, her second to run. To grab Wolf and put so much distance between her and Max, no one would ever find them. She'd fled to her room, started pulling out clothes, gathering up her jewelry, and then she'd picked up her purse and reality had dawned. She knew everything and it changed nothing. She still had no money, no means of escape. She had sat, paralyzed, on the bed until the sun came up and brought her maid. All the times she thought she was trapped, she hadn't understood anything.

That morning, she had pleaded a headache. When Max came in and laid his hand on her forehead, she had vomited so hard, he'd left her alone. "Obviously Wolf can't come anywhere near you." His parting shot had her out of the bed. *Wolf is my boy, not yours.* If she fell apart, Max would make that come true.

With no other idea what to do, Inge had reverted to her original plan: she wrote to her father. Six weeks she calculated for one letter to go out, for one to come back. Six weeks to keep her mouth shut, to play the good wife; to stay away from the drink that was calling so loudly and keep a clear head. Six weeks, not even two months. If it meant getting Wolf out from under Max's influence, it was a pact she could keep. And then the letter came.

> *Schatzi, how sweet of you to plan a treat like that, but you must understand why I could never underwrite it. Whatever the reason, a secret is a secret and that is a thing with no place between a husband and wife.*

The hypocrisy of it was almost amusing. Inge had nearly reached for the brandy again, but the need for control overtook the need for a drink. A job, of any sort, was unthinkable: all that was open to her was selling her belongings or stealing. She'd slipped away to the jewelry stores along the Avenida Belgrano, all her least-worn pieces stuffed into her purse. If Max noticed anything was missing, she would blame the maids.

It had been a wasted journey. Her Spanish was good, but her accent was unmistakable: no one would buy "without your husband's permission."

Ignoring the housekeeper's pursed-lipped irritation, she'd requested a list of the household expenses, scouring through them for any pockets she could pick. Every bill was paid on account. Six weeks stretched into six months spent grubbing for pennies like a street urchin. By the end of the year, the truth was unavoidable: Inge had less money as a wife than she had frittered away as a child. And so she had stayed; noting everything, saying nothing. Promising herself her moment would come.

The gravy-stained plate disappeared from her place setting as smoothly as if conjurors, not waiters, circled the tables. A slice of Sacher torte appeared, its shiny chocolate surface piped round with cream. Inge picked up another spoon. The trick was to do everything normally. Eat the right amounts, exercise as much as expected, play with Wolf as often as he would let her. Attend receptions and host parties with equal amounts of grace. Be quiet, but not too quiet. Never draw Max's attention. Never let anything he did escape hers. *Keep my head and keep my son.*

Dessert done, coffee followed, the liquid cocooned dark and fragrant in a tiny swastika-embossed cup. Inge sipped it slowly and sat back from the conversation, letting her gaze drift around the banner-draped room, across the too-familiar portrait with its bunch of edelweiss beneath. She watched them—the men listed in neat columns in the thin notebooks she kept now, which were easier hidden than a journal, tucked inside never-worn sweaters and skirts. The ones she knew were guilty; the ones she suspected. Sharp-nosed Priebke, who ran Bariloche's German school, and the craggy-faced Reinhardt Kopps, who fancied himself a charmer but who made Inge's skin crawl.

Argentina was crawling with men who appeared and disappeared inside Max's circle, inside her house, like a succession of ghosts. Or stayed and made themselves far too welcome. Mengele, who was Max's colleague now, who sat in her sitting room praising Wolf's cleverness like a genial uncle. Adolf Eichmann, the narrow-mouthed man who preferred to be called Klement, who talked about the cars he worked on as if they had been his lifelong career. They all had secrets. Inge collected their conversations and scoured the newspapers, determined to uncover them. The number of articles printed was dwindling, but what they said was more focused, naming key suspects and, increasingly, looking toward Argentina as their most likely hideout. People were combing the clues and searching: Wiesenthal's name still appeared and that firm of lawyers in Berlin—Bruckhaus and Gottlieb. No governments were looking yet, but perhaps that would come. These men had secrets and they had enemies; Max's name might not be listed, but his crimes were.

All it took was one mistake, or one person brave enough to act, and the carefully crafted life he had built would come tumbling down.

Inge sipped her coffee, imagining her hand stretching out and the feel of that push.

Wolf was exhausted, which meant Inge was exhausted. The morning had started well enough, with the two of them throwing snowballs until they were both sick with laughter, but then Wolf had insisted on skiing run after run, refusing to listen when Inge told him to stop. In the end, her patience snapped. She bundled him into the car; he threw a tantrum better suited to a four- than a ten-year-old, full of complaints about her she knew Max would collude in. Max spoiled Wolf; he indulged the child's every whim. There was nothing Inge could do about it. When she tried, she was the spoilsport. *As Max, no doubt, intends me to be.*

Their stay in Bariloche had run on too long. Inge wasn't unhappy that they had left Buenos Aires: President Perón's grip on power was loosening and the city was restless. The air strikes by his opponents on the Plaza de Mayo in June had terrified everyone. When Max had suggested a holiday away from the city, she was happy to go. But they had arrived in August, it was now past the middle of September and there was no sign of a return date, or none that Max would share. Wolf needed to be in his lessons, in his routine. When Inge had pointed this out, after one too many late nights had resulted in a particularly fraught morning, Max had dismissed her concerns with his usual portion of blame.

"Wolf is unsettled because you are unsettled. Manage yourself and you'll manage him better."

Inge had gritted her teeth, rather than pointing out how unfair that was. How it was him, not her, who was behaving out of character: avoiding the office that was normally his life; taking long phone calls early in the morning and late at night and snapping at anyone who interrupted.

Now, as she once again dragged an overstimulated and arguing child out of the car, she was ready to risk Max's anger. He could stay in Bariloche until the last snow melted, if that was what he chose: she was taking her son back to Buenos Aires.

"Go with Nanny, sweetheart. You need a nap. If you're a good boy, and calm down, there might be hot chocolate later."

"I'm not listening to you. I want my daddy!"

His regular cry, but this time it bounced off her.

Something was wrong. The reception desk was deserted, the normally buzzing lobby empty.

"Take him upstairs." Inge hurried the nanny away, ignoring Wolf's furious protests.

The doors to the formal lounge were closed—another first. Her neck prickling, Inge slipped into the large bay-windowed room. It was both too crowded and too quiet. Small groups gathered in huddled knots, their whispered conversations so low she couldn't make them out. More people were packed around the television set, their bodies blocking the screen.

Please God it isn't war again.

Her fear was not without good reason. Inge had watched the division of Germany, and Berlin, and the Americans and Soviets squaring up to use her country as a weapon, with as much dismay as Max. She hated this new term "Cold War" and refused to use it: whatever label the politicians hid behind, war was war and war meant suffering. When Stalin had died in 1953, all Max's circle had hoped to see an end to the barriers separating the Soviet-backed eastern sectors of Berlin, now adrift in the new East Germany, from the western.

However, Nikita Khrushchev, the new Soviet First Secretary, appeared to have as little tolerance for the ongoing Allied presence in the city as his predecessor. The divisions were threatening to become as physical as they were ideological.

Inge moved closer to the television, convinced that she was about to see her hometown in flames again. She could see little beyond flickering images, but whatever was happening, the backdrop to the story wasn't Germany.

"What is it? What's going on?"

"There's been a revolution. The military has seized power. Perón is out—run off to Paraguay, from all accounts." The reply, thrown over a shoulder, was so matter-of-fact, Inge thought she must have misheard it.

"What do you mean he's out? I don't understand. Has there been fighting? Is it still going on?"

This time, the man who had answered turned around. She didn't recognize him.

"It's a revolution—of course there's been fighting." He was looking at her as if she was an idiot. "Buenos Aires is in an uproar. We'll be lucky if the whole country doesn't tip into civil war. Don't you live in the city?" As if to mirror the strangeness of the day, this man spoke in Spanish without any hint of a German accent.

Inge flushed. "Of course I do."

"Then why are you asking? Why are you surprised? Maybe you should go back to the hairdresser's and let hubby explain it." He turned his back before she could answer.

Why would I look surprised? Because I didn't believe it was coming. I thought Perón would crush this year's rumbling unrest like he crushed all the others.

Inge waited for someone to reprimand the man for his rudeness, but no one was interested. The mood in the room was verging on hostile, arguments breaking out, voices rising. Inge's stomach lurched. Civil war: that was unthinkable—that had no boundaries.

She had a sudden flashback to Milan, the city tearing itself apart in jeering crowds; Mussolini swinging from the lamppost like a lump of slaughtered meat. She wanted to tap the rude man on the shoulder, tell him she wasn't the fool he thought she was.

Tell him she knew Perón's grip on the country had grown shaky, that his popularity had begun fading three years ago with Eva's death, except that wasn't a memory Inge wanted to be replaying.

The glamourous, unstoppable Eva Perón dead from cancer at thirty-three. *The age I am now.* Inge had filed past the open coffin with the rest of the mourners, sickened that anyone so young could be in it. She had been tormented for weeks afterward with nightmares in which it was her head lying on the silken pillow while Wolf strode by the casket without looking in. So, yes, she had known, but now he was out and Buenos Aires was fighting.

Inge groped for a chair, felled by the thought of another city in ruins, more death and destruction.

"Frau Eichel, please. Come, sit. You are pale." Priebke was at her elbow. He steered her toward a corner table where Max was sitting, drinking coffee and chatting with his usual cronies. He looked so at ease, Inge wondered if he had heard what was happening. "Would you like a drink?"

She shook her head.

"Then a cake perhaps; they have some wonderful fruit tarts today, or a savory maybe?"

Why is he using that soothing voice and offering me treats as if I'm a child?

"Order something, Inge." There was nothing soothing about Max's manner. He waved a waiter over; asked for hot chocolate when she didn't respond quickly enough. He waited until the boy had trotted away before addressing her again. "It is important to remain calm, do you understand? Not to attract any undue attention. An event has occurred—we are neither upset nor worried by it. That is all you need to remember."

Not at ease then—managing things.

A mug appeared, heaped with cream. Inge took a sip: the drink was too sweet, thick and sickly. Max was watching. She took another mouthful; decided to test the water.

"You *knew* how serious it was. That this time Perón could fall."

Max's fingers knotted. The other men at the table stiffened. "That's what all the phone calls were about. And why we are still here in Bariloche, long past when we should have gone home."

Kopps reached for her hand. It took all her energy not to recoil.

"Frau Eichel, a little more care, please. *Knew* about an event of this type is not the word we would choose. It could imply involvement, do you see? Which is nonsense, but one never knows who is listening. Or prior knowledge that wasn't used to offer a warning. That, too, has its difficulties. Shall we agree instead that your husband, and the rest of this group who I hope you count as your friends, were aware of the possibility of the current unpleasantness. As were so many others. Could we agree to that?"

Kopps looked at Max, who nodded. *They're not as sure of themselves as they're pretending. Perhaps this new regime is a little choosier about who it harbors.*

Inge withdrew her hand and picked up her cup. Her suspicions had been right: this wasn't a simple holiday. This was Max removing himself again from a potentially dangerous situation and forming new networks for reasons she wasn't privy to. She stirred the cream into the chocolate. There were risks—there were always risks—but there was an opportunity too, if she chose her words carefully.

"Forgive me, Herr Kopps. I will, of course, be more aware of what I say." She turned to Max; adopted a tone she hoped would give away nothing. "There's still fighting in Buenos Aires—I heard someone discussing it. Do you think it's safe to go back?"

"Would you prefer not to?" Max scooped up the last cherry tart from the sticky plate he hadn't offered her. "Would you rather stay in Bariloche?" He put the question reasonably enough, but she knew better than to trust it. Staying in this place would be a life sentence, but she couldn't let Max suspect that.

She shrugged. "If you think that is best, then, of course. But I wondered if there might not be an alternative." She paused. He neither stopped nor encouraged her. "If Buenos Aires is dangerous, perhaps it is time to consider somewhere safer. Perhaps we should think about returning to Germany."

There was a smack as Priebke put his cup down too hard on the glass table.

Max leaned forward. There was a glint in his eyes Inge wished wasn't there.

"That's an interesting suggestion. Is it a plan you've been considering? For a while, maybe?"

Priebke put his hand on Max's arm. Max brushed it away.

"Is that what you want: to be away from this life I have made you, to be *safer*?"

He knows. Inge sat perfectly still. The idea was ridiculous. If Max had any inkling of what she knew, any suspicion that she had gone through his private things, he would have made her pay long ago. Not because of what she had read—Inge imagined the book with all its meticulous records was kept as a treasure, not hidden because he was ashamed of it. No, she would pay because she had dared to dig into his life and then stored away her new knowledge. Inge had learned long ago that Max would rather she kept her body private than her mind. That she could conceal her thoughts from him: that was where the danger lay.

She sat up straighter. He didn't know, but he didn't trust her, despite all her efforts to wear the right face.

"You're so agreeable these days, my dear. You never take issue with anything. Isn't it awfully tiring? If it was anyone else but you, I'd wonder what the aim was." He'd said that over a year ago and the memory of both the words and the amused, slightly contemptuous tone still made her shiver. Now, she decided to answer as if there was no depth to the question.

"Well, isn't *to be safe* what we both want for Wolf? And isn't that more likely in Germany than in a country about to tip into chaos?

The war at home is long forgotten. You told me that. And you've always said your work would be valuable there again one day."

Max sat back, said nothing. Inge leaped on.

"If life in Buenos Aires is going to become challenging, wouldn't it be easier to go back to what we know? You've done well here, but you're not one of them. Whoever takes over from Perón might not value you so highly."

She had overstepped. Max got up, brushing down his jacket as if he brushed her away.

"What do you know about how I am valued? I have served Argentina every bit as loyally as I served Germany. Once the immediate nonsense has died down, of course we will go back to Buenos Aires. The new regime will welcome me as gladly as the old. The only thing *challenging* in this is you."

The room was stirring, emptying out as people went in search of telephones and more immediate information.

"I'm going to see Wolf. I want to hear about his day. Let us hope he had a good one."

He left, followed by the other men, who no longer had any interest in Inge. She let them go. There would be a summons soon, more accounts of her inadequacies to be settled; another reckoning.

She ordered a coffee, a slice of strudel. Let Max have his victory—she would celebrate her own, no matter how small it was. Not Berlin; she had done a poor job of that, but at least Buenos Aires. Not Bariloche and no hope of escaping. At this moment, even a revolution was preferable to that.

Max was wrong. The new regime did not welcome him. In the immediate aftermath of the coup, they took no interest in him or any of his cronies at all. After a week of encouraging reports and no arrests among the men he knew, Max finally declared it was time to return.

Inge felt increasingly sick as the car approached the city. Despite all the promises, she expected to see broken buildings, tanks and dead bodies. Instead, the streets were filled with smiling people and the shops were all open and business as usual. Max was visibly impressed.

"It's a clever tactic. Demonize Perón, blame him for all the vice and corruption, absolve everyone else. Just think how much effort the Allies could have saved themselves if they'd done the same in Germany."

He assumed Inge agreed; she gave him no reason not to. No reprisals, the slate wiped clean and everyone welcomed in the country's new future. It was an ideal Inge wasn't convinced would hold. Max might not understand how long resentment could simmer, but she did. The city's celebratory mood was hollow—chests had puffed up on an intake of breath. It was the impact of the exhale that worried her.

October came in sunny and stayed that way. Wolf returned to school and a sunnier mood; Max returned to his office at the National Ethnic Institute. Life went on, with the promise that it would go on getting better. Except Max spent less time at his job than closeted in his study, his temper was frayed and the phone rang at odd hours. The more he was in the house, the more Inge contrived to be out of it. Hair appointments, dress fittings, afternoon teas for committees that bored her. She didn't care where she went as long as she was guaranteed gossip.

"All this digging for scandal. They've widened the net, you know. Cabinet ministers, congressmen, civil servants: no one can think themselves safe from arrest anymore. Soon it will be an offense to even mention the name Perón."

Buenos Aires was drowning in rumor. Inge gathered them all up and tried to square their affronted anxieties with the optimistic headlines in the city's newspaper *Clarín*. The task was impossible. The city's calm was starting to crack. As November arrived and the temperature kept rising, Inge could hear its breath letting go.

"They've shut the Institute." Max slammed the front door so hard the chandelier rattled. "Just like that. No warning. No recognition of the work we've done or still have to do. Perón started it, so that's reason enough to end it. They're short-sighted fools, the lot of them."

He stormed into his study before Inge could ask what else might be coming. The next morning's news delivered the answers.

The coup's leader was gone, replaced by another loud voice in a uniform. Anyone with links to the Perónist government was out of office; Perón and his followers were all declared traitors. Tolerance and forgiveness were done.

For the first week, Inge kept Wolf at home, fearful fighting would break out again. He did not take kindly to it. Max rarely left his study; the phone never stopped ringing. The news was full of arrests and pledges of more coming. Inge kept waiting for the knock on the door. She became addicted to the radio again and the television. The information available could have been scripted by Goebbels.

"We're leaving." Max made the announcement in the middle of a dinner during which all the previous conversation had centered on Wolf.

"When?" Timing was the least of Inge's concerns, but she needed time to marshal her thoughts. They ate dinner with Wolf most nights since Max had curtailed his social engagements. He'd been on edge through every one of them, but he'd given no indication he was considering a move.

"In three weeks or so. By Christmas at the latest. I don't like the way this administration is going."

Three weeks. If that timescale was possible, this move was planned out. As she steeled herself to ask the next question, Inge caught a smile flashing between father and son. She put her cutlery down and patted her lips with a napkin. Better if he thought there was no urgency to her asking.

"Have you decided where we are going?" *Have you given any thought to my suggestion?*

Max grinned. Her hand itched to pick the knife back up. "Why don't you tell Mama, Wolf? You've been such a good boy to keep our little secret."

So Wolf was the adult now and she was the child, kept out of all the decision making no matter how well she behaved. Inge watched Wolf erupt with excitement and wondered how much of her son was hers anymore.

"Bariloche! We're going to live in Bariloche!" He banged his spoon over and over on the table as Max laughed. "And I'm going to the German school. And I'm going to be a champion skier. And then I'm going to be a doctor just like Daddy!"

Inge reached for her water glass and prayed she wouldn't be sick.

"Aren't you pleased, Inge? When we were there, you didn't seem averse to the idea. And look how excited Wolf is. There are so many opportunities for him there, mixing with the right kind of people. Hasn't it all worked out rather well?"

Wolf was singing *we're going to Bariloche* and beating time on the table with his spoon. The noise drilled into Inge's head.

"Go to your room, Wolf. You're being silly."

He took no notice. Max gave him a second spoon to bang and continued to address her in a tone coated in so much disappointment, Inge knew he was playing with her.

"To be honest, I thought you'd be a little more grateful. The problem is that life in Buenos Aires is starting to become, as you put it: *challenging.* Weren't you clever to think that it might? But have I let that worry me? No. Wolf's school is arranged. My position as Head of Research at the Anthropological Institute is arranged. I've been busier than you could ever imagine and yet I've still made time to set you up with a lovely house. As I always do. I thought you would at least thank me for taking such good care of us."

Inge swallowed more water. She couldn't afford to rile him. If he took them there, she would never get Wolf out.

"I'm sorry. You're right. You've done everything that's needed. It's just that Bariloche is a little cut off. I've never lived anywhere but cities before."

Max ruffled Wolf's hair. "Why does it matter if it's cut off? It's not like you ever go anywhere."

It was an opening, barely a chink, but Inge grabbed it. "I want to go home." She blurted it out so loudly even Wolf quieted. Max raised an eyebrow. "For Christmas. That's all I meant." She had no plan for this, but plans had hardly gone well before and he hadn't said no yet. Inge blundered on. "Father is getting old and Wolf has never met him. Once we move to Bariloche, traveling will be harder to arrange. Maybe, before we get settled there, this would be the right time for a trip. Father would love it—I know he would. He would thank you." She was gabbling. She forced herself to stop.

Max turned to Wolf. "What about you? Would you like to visit your grandfather?"

Wolf shrugged. "Will he give me a present?"

Inge pounced. "Of course he will—lots and lots. And you will love Berlin. There's a zoo and lakes to go boating on, or more likely skating, as it will be very cold. And Christmas in Berlin is so special, Wolf, so pretty with all the lights and…" She ran out of steam as her last memories of the city crashed into the picture she was trying too hard to paint.

Wolf shifted on his cushions. "Will you come, Daddy?"

Max sighed. "That may prove a little more difficult."

Inge kept her eyes on Wolf in case Max noticed her relief. Wolf's lip began to tremble.

"Let's talk about it later, little man, just you and me. Now, it's time for bed. Run up the stairs and I'll come and read you a story."

Wolf scrambled away, singing his Bariloche song. Max got up to follow him. Inge froze. If she let Max go with the idea half-finished, he might dismiss it. If she pushed too hard, he might as easily refuse. Images of Bariloche flew back like birds circling. The banners, the swastika pins, the edelweiss. Kopps and Priebke and all the other shadowy men who would no doubt be flocking out of Buenos Aires with the same hideout in mind. *This is it. This is my last chance to get us away from him.*

"Max."

He stopped. She let his gaze wander over her—weighing; judging. *I'm going to be a doctor, just like Daddy.* All the years hunting for a gap she could wriggle through, she could not let this one close.

"Going home: it wasn't a whim. Or a reaction to us leaving. It would mean a lot to see my parents again. To have them meet Wolf."

He carried on watching her. The muscles in her face felt like they were about to jump into spasm.

"And seeing Germany would be good for him, don't you think?" Still, no reaction. "So that he knows where he came from, and properly understands his heritage. Maybe I could take him to visit your parents too. I am sure there's lots they'd want to share with him."

Whatever Max was thinking, she couldn't read it: she was paying so much attention to how she presented her argument, she forgot to think about how he heard it. It took her a month to realize her mistake, but by then, she was on the plane and it was far too late to change anything. All the times she'd held her tongue, all the practice she'd had staying silent, and then, when it mattered the most, she forgot. She filled in the silences.

"And you would do that, Inge? You would explain about the world he comes from? You would help him understand the real Germany?"

"Of course. Whatever you want." Wolf was shouting for his daddy. "He worships you so much, sometimes I think there's no space for me. Let me have this time with him, Max, please. Before he gets too old to need a mother." She sounded like a child begging. She didn't care. If it got Wolf away from whatever warped future Max was building, she would get on her knees and promise him anything. "Can I do it? Can I make the arrangements?"

Wolf's shouts grew louder.

Max nodded. "Of course. Arrange whatever you want."

Wolf's cry broke across Inge's tumbling thanks. "Daddy, where are you?"

"Coming, Wolf."

Overwhelmed by relief and the delighted shock of his so-easy agreement, Inge closed her eyes and missed Max's smile.

"Be a good boy now. Daddy has something to tell you."

With their belongings packed up, the house felt like a stranger. Inge wandered through the shadowy rooms and could barely remember how they had looked. The furniture Max had dismissed as not worth the cost of moving hunkered under draped white dust sheets. Packing cases lined up across the bare floors in neat rows.

It looks like a cemetery. Inge's nerves were on edge. She had spent the last four weeks counting the days, expecting the trip to Berlin to be derailed on a whim, the same way she suspected Max had granted it. Now there was only one night left and its hours stretched endlessly. She had given up trying to sleep, given in instead to her need to check and recheck every last inch of the arrangements. Everything was, of course, as it should be. Her suitcase still waited in the hall, Wolf's smaller one beside it. The tickets were still safe in her handbag, the travel papers stamped for exiting Argentina and entering Germany ready in their wallet.

The sight of them didn't settle her. Despite the endless check-lists, she couldn't shake the feeling there was something she had missed. Wolf's favorite books and toys were in his case where, at Max's cajoling, he had eventually put them. Her notebooks were safely stowed away, in a pocket she had cut into the lining. All her good jewelry was wrapped in her underwear and hidden, only costume pieces packed into the trunk destined for Bariloche. She had separated the precious stones from the paste with shaking hands, half expecting Max to open the jewelry box and check through its contents.

Max, however, had shown no interest at all in her preparations. Perhaps that was what was niggling: his lack of involvement. Inge wasn't even sure if he had contacted his parents. Not that she had any intention of asking or repeating her ill-thought-out suggestion. It would be a cold day in hell before Brigitte got anywhere near her child.

Inge opened her handbag again. Tickets, documents; she even had money—not much, but it felt like a fortune. Max had handed her the wallet, together with a small handful of Deutsche Marks for Wolf, suggesting he buy a gift for his grandmother. He'd taken them but shown little interest.

Perhaps that was what was bothering her: not Max, but Wolf. Every time she'd tried to talk about their holiday, as she carefully called it, he'd shrugged her away unless Max told him to listen. Even tonight, at bedtime, he hadn't behaved as if the morning would bring anything special.

He's scared of leaving Max, that's all. It's completely natural and Max plays up to that. Heaven forbid he be the less popular parent.

She went back into the hall where the suitcases nestled. This was a new beginning, for both of them. Wolf didn't understand—how could he? The first days of separation from Max, maybe the first weeks, would be difficult, but she could manage that. All she had to do was show Wolf how much she loved him and prove how happy their life in Berlin would be. He would soon realize she was all that he needed.

Moonlight splashed across the polished floor, shining into Max's study. The last part of her preparations, the one she had been waiting all day for. Checking the stairs for the umpteenth time, Inge slid through the open door. This room was as bare as the others. The desk was gone and the high-backed chair. The bookshelves had been emptied into a packing case, which stood open in the middle of the floor, waiting for the last few volumes. There was a second case next to that one, its lid closed, but not secured.

Inge paused, listening. The house was as quiet as if it had already let them go. She lifted the second trunk's lid. There they were: Max's things, packed up and ready to move into the next phase of his charmed life. The contents of his desk were arranged neatly inside: files, photographs, loosely bound papers all set inside their drawers. His tidiness was a gift.

Working with one eye to the door, Inge sifted through them until she had it. The maroon-covered book. Max's secrets. She had asked herself years ago what they were worth and now she knew. Nothing in Argentina, but in Germany they could be a shield; if she played them right, they could be a weapon. Max would come after her, Inge had no illusions about that. Once he realized she had no intention of returning—more importantly, that she had no intention of Wolf returning, God alone knew what he would be capable of.

She had no idea how wide his connections stretched. She had no idea whether her father would protect her, although she suspected not. But this book...Max could claim all he liked that Germany no longer cared about the crimes done in its name, but Inge didn't believe it. Someone would care—the lawyers or the Austrian; she just had to find them. She would reveal Max, and all his cronies she'd so carefully recorded. The world would know the truth. And so would Wolf. He would give up his father then.

Inge ran her fingers over the embossed leather. It was warm, as if the horrors it contained were still living. There was a risk in stealing it, but not enough to dissuade her. Their flight was early; the morning would be busy—Max would be highly unlikely to be bothered with the trunks in his last hours with Wolf. And once they were on the plane, once he knew, what would it matter? The book was neither particularly heavy nor particularly large; she could slip it in her suitcase and no one lifting it would be able to tell any change in the weight.

Her senses on fire, Inge ran back into the hall. The catches on her case cracked like gunfire in the stillness. Nobody came. She pulled out a heavy sweater, a thick skirt: things that would blur the book's outlines, just in case.

One more night and all this is done.

Sleep was impossible. Inge sat down on the stairs in the darkness to wait.

"He's fussing over another toy to take. Go to the car. I'll have the cases sent out and bring him down directly."

Inge hovered in the hall, her stomach flipping. Wolf had refused to come out of his room for breakfast, had refused to see her at all. Max, of course, had refused to tackle Wolf's bad behavior.

"It's to be expected, Inge. He's never been away before, from home or from me. Once he gets on the plane, the excitement of flying will take over."

Inge knew Max was right, but that didn't settle her. No sleep and too much coffee had her light-headed and chewed up with anxiety. With every delay, she imagined Max wandering into his study; she wasn't a good enough actress to bluff her way through that.

Max went up the stairs; Inge waited at the bottom. Wolf's door opened and closed; she thought she heard laughter. That was surely a good sign, although no doubt the tantrums would start as soon as he got in the car. *I'll have to learn to manage them, that's all. Other mothers must do it. And at least no one will interfere when I try.* She wanted to see him come down for herself, but Max would be annoyed if her found her still fussing and that wouldn't help Wolf's volatile mood.

She went out to the Mercedes and made herself as comfortable as her bitten nerves would allow. The partition separating the passenger seats from Karl, Max's taciturn driver, was closed. Before Inge had time to tap on it and extract a good morning, Max appeared around the side of the car. He knocked on the hood, his habitual signal for the engine to start running, and climbed in beside her. The door clicked shut.

"He's not still being silly, is he?" Inge sighed. "We can't afford to waste any more time. He needs to grow out of these moods, Max—he's too big for them."

The car was moving.

"Max? What is Karl doing? Why is he pulling away?"

The car was at the end of the short driveway and nosing out into the side street.

"Stop him! He must have thought Wolf had got in as well."

She twisted around, dreading the sight of Wolf screaming, thinking himself abandoned. There was nobody there.

As the car picked up speed, the house slipped out of sight. "Max, please, this is crazy! Get Karl to stop."

She leaped toward the closed partition, but Max yanked her back.

"Sit still. Do you want to cause an accident?"

What was wrong with him? Did he not understand what was happening? "No. Listen. There's been a dreadful mistake." And then Inge stopped and saw how calm he was and realized the only mistake all along had been hers. She fell back against the seat, the breath punched from her body. "He was never coming, was he?" Her voice sounded old, decimated.

Max loosened his jacket, removed his hat and gazed out of the window as the Mercedes sped through the patchy early-morning traffic on the Avenida Santa Fe.

"How did I not see that?"

"Because I promised him all manner of treats if he played along. It became a very entertaining game."

His complete lack of emotion took away Inge's words beyond "But why?"

Then he turned. He looked like he might laugh. "Why? Are you seriously asking? All right, if that's how you want to play it. Because this little holiday to see the wonders of Berlin was never a holiday, was it? It was some childish scheme to whisk Wolf away from his big bad daddy. Bless you, Inge: you're as transparent as water, even when you're so sure you're not."

Her heart was beating so fast, it filled up her chest, every thump threatened to choke her. So many questions crowded her head; she narrowed in on the easiest. "Then what are we doing now? Where are we going?"

Max frowned. "I swear, the effort of managing you is exhausting; I'll be glad to be done with it. To the airport. You wanted to go home to Germany, so you're going home to Germany."

"No!" She jumped for the door. He grabbed her again. Inge tried to break free, but his grip was so strong she thought her arm might be breaking. "I'm not going anywhere without Wolf!"

"Sit still, you little fool." His hand was in her hair, pulling her tight against the seat. "The door is locked, so there's no point in battling for it. What were you going to do? Jump out at speed? Have me push you? Don't think I haven't considered it, but the mess would be a bore." The pain was enough to force her into stillness and Max loosened his grip. "That's better."

"I mean it, Max. I'm not going anywhere without my son."

He straightened his jacket and wiped his hands on his hand-kerchief before he answered.

"No, Inge. You're not going anywhere *with* him. The sooner you accept that, the easier this will be. Your demand to go home slotted the last piece of my move perfectly into place. You aren't part of the plan. I don't need you. Wolf doesn't need you."

It wasn't even said with anger. Inge fought her urge to scream. If he could be calm, she could be calm. *Except he can do it because he holds all the cards.* She fought that away too.

"That's not true. Wolf is still a little boy. He needs a mother—"

Max's tone didn't change. "He doesn't need one like you. You're an embarrassment. As gauche as you were ten years ago, but now with an added layer of hypocrisy. I had to bring you to Buenos Aires; I don't need to drag you anywhere else. Or burden Wolf. It's time to let go, Inge. You know it's what you want."

The car was accelerating now, the lakes on the edges of the city flashing past. Another twenty minutes and they would be at the airport. She couldn't fight him, but she couldn't let him win. She would have got to her knees if there was room in the car.

"It's not. It's really not." The tears were coming so thick her voice choked. "I'm sorry I've failed you, truly I am, but I'm still Wolf's mother. I can't let go of him any more than you could." She reached for his arm, but he knocked her away. "Don't do this, Max, please. Don't take my boy." If she had to spend the rest of her life subservient to this man in order to stay with her son, she would do it. "Whatever you want. I'll do better, try harder. Don't take him from me, I'm begging you."

She caught Karl's eye in the mirror as Max pulled his coat from her scrabbling fingers. Karl must have known the plan—he must have been able to see what was happening, but his face was completely expressionless. Max, however, was no longer calm: she could feel his anger burning the air.

"Stop embarrassing us both. You can't do anything differently. I wouldn't want you even if you could. You're a parasite, do you know that? All these years living in the houses I provide, spending the money I provide and turning a blind eye to anything you didn't want to know. And then you see a few photos, read some badly written nonsense and everything about me, and your life, sickens you? That takes some nerve. You hide behind your bland little smile and your meaningless small talk, but I've watched you. In Buenos Aires, in Bariloche: staring at good men and their perfectly decent wives as if they were shit on your shoe. I won't have it near me anymore, and I won't have it near Wolf. And don't pretend that you have a bond with him that matches mine. You have no idea how special he is, how special his future could be. You're a stain and you need removing."

The force of his contempt smacked into her like the blows he used to throw.

I've never been a step ahead of him, not even once.

Inge knew there was nothing she could say that he wouldn't smash down. She was no more to him than a faulty item for returning. She doubted he would even care about the theft of his book. All the creeping around, all the care she had taken to play the good girl: she might as well have fought back from the beginning. *There's no long-term place for her.* Something snapped inside her, like a trap springing open.

"How can you do this?" His shoulders stiffened. "I don't mean take Wolf away or hurt me. You can clearly do that without a thought. No. How can you claim to love a child so much when—" She paused—some things were still so hard to pull into the light.

"When what?" He was looking at her now, his face unreadable.

Whatever I say doesn't matter anymore—it might as well be the truth.

"When you killed so many other children with such ease."

There was a flicker of surprise, but no shock, no guilt.

"Where? At Sachsenhausen? There weren't any children there."

Inge shook her head. "No. In Austria, at the Spiegelgrund Clinic. Where you worked before we were married."

"How did you know?" She was going to tell him, the consequences couldn't be any worse, but he waved her away with a dismissive flick. "Actually, don't bother. I don't care. The secrets you keep. Perhaps I underestimated you after all. What has Austria to do with Wolf?"

He genuinely didn't seem to see a connection.

Inge rubbed her eyes; her head ached. "You murdered children. How could you do that and say you love your son?"

To her horror, Max laughed.

"Oh, Inge, you silly girl. You think I did what I did out of hatred. You do—it's all over your face. Why would I hate defenseless children? Here is the hypocrisy: you pass judgment and yet what did you think all the lessons you sat through on racial hygiene actually meant? You didn't think, did you? You never do. They were suffering. All the little ones who came to me at the clinic were in pain, or incapable. Not one of them had the hope of a productive life. What I did was a kindness. I saved them." His voice was as soft as when he read stories to Wolf.

"No." He was still smiling. "Don't sweeten this. You were a monster. You still are."

Max shook his head. "Such a meaningless word. Which paper did you learn it from? A monster, really? A husband who always provided lavishly for his wife. A father who loves his son and would do anything for him. A doctor working as hard as he can to make the society he believes in the best it can be. Where is the monster in that?"

They were on the approach road to the airport—she could see the glass-fronted terminal building coming into view. He had her defeated, but she wouldn't let go.

"How can you talk about Wolf and your work in the same breath? How can you talk about love?"

"Because I understand what it is. Far better than you. I always treated my patients with the utmost care, at Sachsenhausen, and at

Spiegelgrund. Every adult I worked with at the camp knew exactly what to expect: I explained each step with care, so there would be no shocks for them to deal with. As for the children in the clinic, I held them till it was done, every last one of them. What is love if not that, Inge? Doing what you must with gentleness, for a greater good? Everything I have done has made me the father I am. You should be proud. Instead, you act as if my work is some shameful, dirty little secret. It was never anything of the sort."

There wasn't enough air; she was going to be sick. Inge reached for the handle to crank open the window, but the car had already come to a stop.

"Good, we are here. Now, this is what is going to happen. You will get out; Karl will give you your bag. What comes next is that you go to Germany, like you wanted, and make a life of your own, or fall back on your father if you can't. I don't care either way. But be very clear: if you stay in Buenos Aires or anywhere in Argentina, and try to get close to Wolf, then I will have you killed."

The car door opened. Inge stayed where she was. *He may as well kill me now—I've nothing left to lose.* "And what if I refuse to go? What if I scream so loudly the whole airport comes running? What if I tell the world that you're stealing my son?"

Max looked at his watch. "Well, that is also a choice. Do it if you want. It won't help. Creating a fuss will simply prove you are unstable; it will make my case for me. And who would argue, given how you've behaved? Running away from your husband and abandoning your son, screaming in public when you're caught out, like a hysteric. What is that if not unstable? And then there's the drinking of course."

Inge stared at him. "I haven't had a drink in years."

"Oh, but you long to—everyone's seen it. The way you can't even look at a bottle of wine. The burden I can just about contain in public, but not at home. The pity that will pour at the thought of a child in such a dreadful situation, the exhausted father trying to protect him. You'll be lucky to get out of wherever they put you before you go gray. Especially if there's no one to sign the release." He smiled as patiently as a teacher waiting for a pupil to grasp the complexities of a new subject. "Now, I have things to do before Wolf and I leave and poor Karl is still waiting. Come on, Inge: what will it be?"

She got out of the car. Karl handed her the suitcase. Max stayed where he was and never looked around.

This is a mistake. Or his way of scaring me into line. He'll come back in a minute; he'll give me a second chance.

The Mercedes accelerated and sped out of sight.

Inge stayed where she was. *I have two tickets. The airline will help me when they see I have two tickets.*

"Madame?" A porter was at her side, his hand out waiting. "Señor Eichel said you would be traveling alone today and that you had been unwell. Everything is ready for you."

Inge didn't know whether to laugh or cry: Max really had outsmarted her at every turn.

Not knowing what else to do, Inge followed the porter into the terminal and out onto the tarmac. And then she stopped, one last hope suddenly leaping.

Wolf will want to come. Max might not care about me, but Wolf won't want to play the game anymore when he realizes what it means. He loves me. He'll make Max bring him here.

She stood still. She waited until the porter insisted politely that she move. No one came.

The porter handed her on to a stewardess, who fluttered around her, all movie-star glamour. The plane was half empty, the seat next to hers vacant. Its emptiness was unbearable. Inge sat down, trying not to look at it for fear she would scream.

I will have you killed. She didn't doubt him for a moment. She surrendered her coat; accepted the magazines she was handed. She was so cold. There was pain coming, she knew that. Her body was tensed and ready, waiting like a patient after surgery for the drugs to wear off and the nerve ends to start screaming. *When they do, they'll never stop.*

She closed her eyes as the engines roared and the plane shuddered into life. When she opened them again, Buenos Aires and her baby had disappeared beneath a blanket of cloud.

"Madame? Can I bring you anything?" The stewardess was back, all bright eyes and brilliant smile. "A drink perhaps?"

There were so many voices in Inge's head, but only one she could hear. *If I let the hurt in, it will kill me quicker than Max could.*

She nodded. "A brandy, if you have it. A large one. And bring me another as soon as that's done."

PART FOUR

CHAPTER SEVENTEEN

April 1956, Berlin

I have built a life.

The pleasure in that was as fresh as the pale green paint on the kitchen walls. Five months ago, when she had stumbled, blurred and bleary, onto Frankfurt's snowy tarmac, she had been unable to imagine any life at all. Now she had her own front door and the beginnings of a new place in the world. Inge blew on her coffee and smoothed an invisible wrinkle out of the cherry-printed tablecloth.

The distance between those humiliation-filled days and these stretched out like an ocean, but she wasn't sorry her memories were hazy. She had no recollection of getting off the plane or any clue about who had organized the taxi she found herself in. The mechanics of continuing the journey from Frankfurt to Berlin had been beyond her brandy-muddled abilities. Wherever it was meant to take her, she had demanded a hotel instead. Had fallen into its bar and would have fallen into some stranger's bed without the intervention of a red-faced hotel manager. Somewhere in the midst of black coffee and a rambling story, he had extracted a phone number. And locked her in her room. She remembered the light in the morning when he let her out: it had grated her eyes like sandpaper. "There is a car, madame. Your father sent it." Inge had been too dry-mouthed to argue.

The drive to Berlin had lasted an agonizing six hours. If it hadn't been for the bottle procured from a waiter when the manager was distracted, Inge would never have managed even half of it. She had done a lot of shouting, she knew that, once she realized they were headed to her parents' house. She wouldn't be delivered anywhere in silence anymore.

As soon as they reached Berlin's suburbs, she told the driver she would get out and walk. She had been very clear, or at least very loud. He took no notice. When the car finally swept into the Ackermann drive, she had clambered out in a temper that was quickly swallowed by confusion. Given the pounding Charlottenburg took, some trace of the war should have been visible. Instead, the house was as white as a wedding cake, its gleaming windows twinkling.

"How is it still so pretty?" Her first words, falling over each other. She'd tried them again, but the effort of staying upright on the neatly swept gravel had needed all her attention.

"Inge." That voice. Even the memory dragged across her like nails. That night it had made her body shake as if bombs were still falling.

She had tottered forward, convinced by the brandy or a trick of the light that her mother's arms were outstretched.

"Max has taken my baby!" A howl, but it hadn't moved Grete. "He's stolen my boy." What a sight she must have made. Her legs had given way. She had fallen to her knees, fingers clawing at the close-packed stones as if Wolf might be buried there.

"Bring her in." Strong hands had lifted her. A man's, rough and calloused.

Afterward, Grete told her that she wouldn't stop yelling and couldn't make sense of the simplest direction. Inge had no memory of that. She had no certain memory of anything that happened in the next few days, beyond a nurse and a needle and a darkness that ran on and on. She must have tried to speak: she remembered Grete hushing her. And her father coming and hovering by the bed: whether he spoke at all, Inge had no idea.

Finally, after what her mother told her was four days of little beyond babbling, there was a morning when she woke rather than surfaced, when she felt hungry not sick, and the light from the window was no longer a threat. Everything was as clear as a bell after that.

"Good. You have some color." Grete had stood at a distance from the bed, her foot tapping, while Inge hauled herself up. "Downstairs today, outside tomorrow. A few more days' rest and then an end to this nonsense. There is a clean dress laid out on the chair. I'll leave you to bathe and see you in the drawing room. Don't take hours about it."

Inge had lain weightless in the bubble-filled tub, the steam loosening her chest. Without the brandy, the pain that was Wolf roared back, his loss tightening around her like a bruise. She dressed and moved slowly downstairs, her legs still skittish. The house was quiet, with none of the bustle of servants or visitors Inge associated with it. Grete sat straight-backed in her lemon-colored audience chamber, presiding over a pot of coffee and an untouched plate of pastries. Inge had eyed them hungrily, wondering how many she could eat before her mother's eyebrows raised. As soon as she had sat down, Grete gestured to a sheaf of papers spread out on the glass-topped table.

"I have contacted a number of agencies with a view to hiring you a companion. I thought you might wish to look at the replies."

Inge had barely given them a glance. "Why do I need a companion?"

"Because the journey is a long one and traveling alone is clearly not something you do well."

Inge had looked up from her half-eaten slice of plum torte. "What journey?"

Grete sighed. "Back to Buenos Aires, of course. To your husband and your child."

The idea was so absurd, Inge had laughed. "I'm not going back. Besides, Max isn't in Buenos Aires. He's taken Wolf to some godforsaken mountain village and forbidden me to follow.

He's threatened to have me killed if I try. So it's not me who'll be traveling, it's Wolf: I'm bringing him to Berlin, where he'll be safe. I hoped you might help me."

Another sigh. "Max warned us you would be like this. He explained the problems you've caused with your fantasies and your drinking."

Inge had clung to the chair's slippery brocade. "What do you mean?"

"When he called, a week ago, he said you had run away with your head full of nonsense. That you had abandoned Wolf. That you have, let us call it, a *fondness* for brandy. He was mortified; so was your father. The shame of it, Inge. On all of us."

How is he always one step ahead of me with everyone? Inge had stared at her mother's flint-cut face and refused to panic.

"That was very clever of him, setting his stall out first. I didn't run, Mother: he forced me to go. And I didn't abandon my son. How could I? And I don't drink, not anymore. That was a foolishness a long time ago."

Grete's stony expression didn't flicker. "You don't drink? So what explains your behavior the night you arrived? Or did we imagine the sorry sight and the smell of you?"

Inge had flushed. "That was a mistake. The first drink I've had in years. I was desperate."

Grete had sniffed. "Desperate? What do you know about desperate? Did he buy you another house you didn't want to live in? You're spoiled, Inge. I blame your father. You've never grown up." That steely tone, the way Grete used it to shut her voice down. The only way to tackle it was to stay patient.

"This is nothing to do with houses, or me. This is about what kind of man Max is, about the kind of man he intends Wolf to be."

"You mean a good German? Like your brothers?" Grete had turned to the photographs that dominated the room. Gunther and

Eric in their uniforms, their images placed side by side in silver frames threaded with black, a vase filled with silk edelweiss placed between them. The tableau gave the room the air of a shrine; Inge had refused to look.

"No, Mother. Not like my brothers. Not like any soldier who died an honorable death. Something worse—Max is worse. The things he did went far beyond anything done by decent men."

Grete was already shaking her head.

Inge had continued, refusing to tolerate another defense. "You don't know him. Not like I do. Your precious son-in-law is another Mengele. He's evil. He's not fit to be anywhere near a child."

"That is enough." Inge half expected Grete to lash out, but her hands had stayed tightly clasped. "Max is right: you are deluded. You have put him through hell, Inge. It cannot go on. If you won't listen to me, perhaps he is right and a doctor is our only hope."

A weight fell across Inge she realized was sadness, not surprise. There was nothing to appeal to here, not a hint of softness, not a drop of motherly affection. Nothing had changed, or ever would.

"Why are you always like this? So cold? I'm your daughter yet you would rather think badly of me than a man you barely know beyond a uniform and a pile of contracts. Why? What did I ever do? I don't understand how you can call yourself a mother and have so little love in you."

There was another photograph on the sideboard—Grete as a young bride, soft-skinned and beautiful. But not smiling: Inge had never noticed that before.

"Unless you'd used it all up before I even got here. Father once said he wasn't your choice. Is that it? Was there someone else you couldn't have, and we all had to suffer for it? Is that why you were so hard on me before I married Max, because I had a chance of the happiness that was snatched away from you?"

Grete's mouth was hanging open, her face gray. For a moment, there was a crack in the façade, a flash of pain that twisted her lips and closed her eyes. Before Inge could grab at it and force a connection, Grete's twisted pride had snapped back and she rallied.

"How dare you? You have no grounds to reproach me. I never abandoned you, never humiliated you. I have been the best wife, the best mother. Your brothers knew it. If you and your father didn't, that was because you were weak, not me. You have no idea what sacrifice means. I wasn't *hard* on you, Inge: I saved you from yourself. I made you do your duty then; I will make you do it now. You are a wife and a mother. That is it. That is all your value."

She's like a rat, fangs bared when she's cornered. All her life, Inge had been waiting for the moment of understanding that would lead to the close bond she craved. She had hoped it might come when they were both mothers, but all that had done was crack their divide further. If she really harbored any fantasies, this hope of a mother-and-daughter reconciliation was surely it. Inge had looked at her mother's face, all eaten up with bitterness and rage, and knew there were better battles to fight.

She'd got up. The sunlight shone on Grete's face, illuminating its wrinkles and age spots. "That's strange. I thought my value was a monetary one. Isn't that how you and Father, and Max, have always seen me? Well, that's done. I hoped for your help. I didn't expect it. I'm not a wife; Max has decided that. But I am a mother and, somehow, I'm going to get my son back. I'm staying here, in Berlin, and you can make whatever story of that you want for anyone who cares. I'll get an apartment and a job, and I'll do it on my own. No, don't say anything: whatever new failure you think I'll make, I don't have to hear it. This is my life, and it will be Wolf's. It's not in your control anymore."

Sitting now, sipping coffee in a kitchen her own money paid for, Inge remembered the shock on her mother's face. The open-mouthed silence that quickly gave way to rage and dire warnings. Inge had walked away. She had gone to a hotel, handing over the last of Max's money with the last scrap of the day's confidence. The need for a drink had screamed so loud that not listening to it was her proudest achievement.

It had taken almost two months to put everything she now had in place; some of the days had felt like months on their own. She had sold her jewelry. This time, no one raised an eyebrow when she tipped her emeralds and sapphires across the counter. The price she got wasn't a fair one, but it covered the first week's rent on an apartment whose landlord had no more interest in her than the jeweler. Berlin was full of women whose families had splintered, who had to make their own way without husbands to draw on. Her carefully laid-out story was too common to comment on.

An apartment secured, the next step was a job. That gave Inge sleepless nights as her hopeless BDM days rushed back to haunt her. Berlin proved kinder there too. The fashion industry was booming and, as Inge artlessly pointed out in the first shop on the Kurfürstendamm she plucked up the courage to enter, "I might not know much, but, after so many years as a clotheshorse, I do know fashion." One delighted customer who didn't know that lilac chiffon would bring out the blue in her eyes, or "how darling" Juliet caps could be, and Inge had a job before she'd barely started asking. It was frivolous and it was fun and her commissions were soaring; while she found her new feet, she could let that be enough.

The broken city Inge had fled was reforging itself with an all-sweeping appetite for the new. Inge embraced it, although she couldn't entirely shake off the past. The afternoon she walked past Hella's Ballhaus, not recognizing at first its fairy-light-wrapped garden, brought her to a gasping halt. The evening she caught sight of Liesl, wrapped in fur and strolling on the arm of a far older man, drove her home shaking. She avoided the Tiergarten. A glimpse of a brown-haired man pushing back his hair had more than once reduced her to tears. For the first time, Inge was grateful she and Felix had had so few meetings: at least the city wasn't soaked with their footsteps. She couldn't shake the past, but she could sidestep it.

There were too many crumbling houses dotting the leafy streets of her childhood. She moved instead into one of the modern apartment blocks springing up all over the city, delighted by its clean lines and plain frontage. She reveled in the circle skirts and ponytails, the loose jackets and quiffs that jostled dull suits and prim hats off the pavements. She ignored old faces and smiled at young ones and tuned the décor of her apartment to the same gum-chewing, American-talking frequency. She hunted out the right pieces for this new life with forensic care, preferring to keep the space sparse than be invaded by anything that held the weight of history or the dubious pedigree of previous owners. She kept her work colleagues at arm's length—close enough for cinema visits, but not to unpick her story. And she took nothing from the Ackermanns but their name: Grete's parting "you've let us down—you always do" was the permission Inge needed to finally walk away.

I have built a life. She wrapped herself in that thought every morning, clinging to it like a blanket while she cried for Wolf. When she wrote to him, as she did twice and sometimes three times a week, addressing her letters to the German school, she told him the same thing. *I've built a life. For myself, and for you, my darling boy: always for you.* He never replied. Inge doubted he ever saw the letters, although she held tight to the hope that one day he would.

In the meantime, she had a far more dangerous ghost to exorcise than shadow-spotted streets. She had found the lawyers, Bruckhaus and Gottlieb. She had been to their office, files in hand. She had intended to go in, to spill the whole story. Until the reality of entering the quiet building, of giving her name and telling her story while secretaries and office staff whispered and nudged and wondered how much she was still hiding, dropped her hand from the bell. She had hovered, hoping the door would open, that a smile might sweep her inside. Instead, the lurking so-hard-to-lose fear that someone might be watching had wriggled back in.

In the end, she had telephoned—a gabble of a call that left her feeling foolish—and arranged a meeting in a café. Neutral ground, only one person to judge her. Somewhere she could easily walk away from when the telling was done.

CHAPTER EIGHTEEN

April 1956, Berlin

Bruckhaus and Gottlieb. By the end of the year, when Otto Gottlieb finally retired, it would be Bruckhaus and Thalberg. Felix had a life far beyond anything he could have imagined when he stumbled back from the war to Berlin.

"It's come early. Thirty-three is young to be a partner, but no one deserves it more. That the firm has grown is down to you." Levi had already had the new sign made. "I thought you might want some time to get used to it. Your name, Felix: stamped onto something to be proud of. Another ghost settled."

He had left Felix blinking, staring at the gleaming metal, remembering cardboard squares and the indignity of numbers. The next day, he had blushed more than his colleagues knew he could when Levi poured champagne and raised a glass "to the hardest-working lawyer in Berlin. Who might, when his name goes up, throttle back enough to let the rest of us breathe."

Felix had laughed along with the rest and made sure, for that night at least, he was the first to leave.

Another ghost settled. That phrase came back to him as he leafed through the messages waiting on his desk—an envelope in Kitty's neat hand uppermost among them. Levi hadn't said it lightly: the firm's offices in Joachimstaler Straße were new, but the area they were in hummed with old memories. The street ran from Hardenbergplatz to the once-again thriving shops and restaurants of the Kurfürstendamm. For the first days after the relocation,

Felix had walked with Kerstin all around him and thought he was going to break. On the third morning, he caught sight of a green hat bobbing through the crowd and chased after its owner. Levi had emerged from Zoo Station to find him clinging to a wall, face wet with tears, legs shaking.

"Don't fight it, Felix. Let her back in."

Felix had thrown Levi's arm from his shoulders and called him callous; Levi had refused to take offense.

"You have to trust me. I know your parents' loss is so total it can feel like they never existed, but they're here, on the streets. You have to learn to walk with them, or Berlin will never be yours again." He had gripped Felix's arm, steering him across the square as if he was an invalid. "You told me Kerstin worked near here, that this is where you used to meet. So, tell me now, what did you do, you and your mother, just the two of you? That was no one else's; that made you both happy? Come on, there must have been something." It was easier to answer than battle Levi's persistence.

"There was a game we played when we walked home from our shifts together."

"Good man, that's a start. I know it hurts, but you need to remember the happy days, not just the pain, or you insult their memories."

His words were such an echo of Kitty's, Felix's knees buckled. Rage bubbled through him, but there was nothing to fight against: Levi's face and his voice were filled with compassion. It was at that moment, as Felix stood paralyzed in the middle of his past, that he realized Kitty's intentions had been exactly the same. He'd started to shake again.

Levi's voice had dropped to a steadying murmur. "Keep walking. Tell me about your game."

As soon as Felix groped around the first words, he could hear Kerstin's laughter. "We would go the long way home, along the Kurfürstendamm. Do you remember the ridiculous displays at the start of the war? All the shops piled high with faked goods and everyone pretending we could buy them? We used to go window shopping, laughing at the painted handbags and the colored-water perfume and imagining what we would choose if money was no object and the items were real."

"Excellent." They had reached the office, but Levi wouldn't let him in. "Go and do it now. Play your game and keep on playing it until you can carry her comfortably."

He had left Felix on the pavement, feeling foolish. He had marched sullenly off toward the Kurfürstendamm and stomped past the first refurbished department stores and chandelier-hung fashion houses as if he wore blinkers. Then he had caught sight of a young couple admiring a dining set, and a girl and her mother nudging each other outside a bridal shop. They were enjoying themselves. Just as he and Kerstin had enjoyed themselves. Felix had stopped. He'd crooked his elbow as if his mother was holding it. The traffic didn't come to a halt; the crowds didn't melt. The day bustled on as busy as ever, but Felix had felt his chest expand. He'd wandered on at a more leisurely pace, pausing where he fancied, letting giggling conversations loop around in his head. When he had returned to the office, Levi had smiled and Felix had smiled and nothing more was needed. Now he meandered along the Kurfürstendamm once a week with Kerstin tucked in beside him.

Pushing the other papers aside, Felix opened Kitty's message. The first page was a note. It was short and to the point, but there was an excitement underlying the sentences that prickled his neck.

> *This is newly in—I thought you should see it. If the case goes to trial, which the feeling is that it will, it could signal a shift in the mood concerning war crimes. You've seen the talk in the papers about a new investigative unit: if a trial leads to a successful prosecution, this could be the push needed*

to set it up. This one has captured the public's imagination, Felix. It could be the missing piece.

Kerstin's ghost settled, others surfacing.

Felix unclipped and scanned the attached report, slowing down as he realized why Kitty had sent it. The outlined case was an unusual one, the crimes detailed in it uncovered purely by chance. Bernhard Schweder, the head of a refugee camp, had been fired and had filed a complaint against his dismissal. A local paper had reported it, accompanied by a photograph. Not a matter of much interest, except one of the paper's readers had seen Schweder before: heading up a Gestapo unit responsible for massacring Jews in Lithuania. The story had collected other witnesses and snowballed: the alleged murder roll now stood at over five thousand.

As he read through the allegations, Felix's pulse quickened. This wasn't another set of vague charges aimed at men who were missing. Schweder was in custody in Germany; he could be placed at the scene of multiple crimes; families were clamoring for justice. And the story was still spreading, picked up by one paper and passed on to another, moving from the back pages to the front.

A shift in mood: Felix had almost given up hope. Press attention in absconded Nazis had dwindled to next to nothing. Wiesenthal's Documentation Center in Linz had closed. His one day a week combing for cases had faded to one day a month. His lead on Eichel had petered out on the coastline of South America. The only person in the last two years who had asked him if he was still hunting was Kitty.

Felix put the report down. *Kitty*. Another lost face resurfacing. That dreadful morning when she had uncovered his secret still turned his stomach. Felix had dragged himself to work, not knowing what else to do, and come home to empty closets. There was a note on the table with her friend's address, but nothing more. He hadn't acted on it.

I threw her away. It had taken him far too long to understand that and Kitty's "you could have found me; I wished you had" broke his heart all over again.

I didn't know that, Kitty, not then. I'd never found anyone before, no matter how much I searched. All I knew was loss.

It had taken him even longer to understand that, and Kitty had been gone from his life for nearly two years before he had a chance to explain it.

In the immediate aftermath of her leaving, he couldn't have explained anything at all. He moved through the world like a machine, working every hour Levi would let him and plenty Levi argued furiously against. In the end, after a year in which Felix shrank to a shadow, Levi threatened him with dismissal, not a partnership, unless he started to rebuild some kind of life. Felix tried. He went on dates helpful colleagues arranged, but he had fallen so far from the art of conversation, he was barely fit company. Then, in the summer of 1955, he heard through a client that Kitty was back, based once more at the Mission. He picked up the phone a dozen times. He never got as far as dialing. In the end, he went to her, which, as Levi said, was the least he could do. He sat on the steps of the Clayallee compound, watching the polished faces that could have stepped out of CROWCASS, smoking cigarette after cigarette until she finally appeared.

"I went to the States, and then on temporary assignment to Paris. I thought it might be time to try Germany again."

The same direct Kitty. Except she was not the same. Her thirties sat on her as prettily as her twenties had done, but there was a new poise about her, a polish reflected in her crisply cut dress and neatly curled hair.

"You look lovely." He didn't know where else to begin. He sounded gauche.

"You look like Felix." She sounded so unsurprised, he'd laughed. She was right, his uniform was unchanged: white shirt, dark suit, loose tie and hair that flopped irrespective of fashion. No doubt there was an ink stain somewhere on his fingers. "I wondered if you might come. Why did you?"

"To make things right."

Kitty had raised an eyebrow. "That sounds simple. Do you think it will be?"

He could have lost his courage right there, but she'd moved her hand and the wedding ring she was still wearing flashed.

"No. I think it will be anything but. I'd like to try, though. To talk, to see where that takes us."

She didn't make it easy; he didn't want her to: old patterns were the last place he wanted to go. She wouldn't supply him with his words anymore or untangle him when he stumbled. She wouldn't discuss the time they had been apart. She measured him against a standard he was desperate to meet; after a few months when he wore everything that he was plain on his sleeve, he began to believe she would let him. Coffees became drinks, became dinners. Weekends brought long walks reclaiming the city. He told her every scrap about Hannah, what he understood and what he didn't, and offered Kitty the letters. She wouldn't take them. When she finally accepted he had never written another, days extended on into nights. *I love you.* This time he was the one who said it. *Me too.* He could see in her smile that the real words were coming, that the chance to rebuild their home and their life together would follow.

A telephone rang along the hall, pulling Felix out of his daydream. He put Kitty's note and the report in his desk drawer, already imagining the conversations and encouragement they would lead to. Now, however, he was hungry and in need of fresh air. Leaving his jacket on the peg, Felix grabbed his wallet and was about to go out into the sunshine when his office door opened.

"You're leaving—never mind. I can give this to Levi." Hilde, his briskly efficient secretary, was frowning, which was unusual enough to make Felix pause.

"What is it?"

"A telephone call. Some woman who talked so fast I could barely make her out. She has some information she wants to hand over."

"Did she make an appointment?"

Hilde shook her head. "Not exactly. She wants to meet in Café Lotti and she wants to meet now, which is ridiculous. I should have said it wasn't possible, but she sounded... I don't know. Like she would have lost her nerve if I questioned her. Maybe it's best left. If it's that important, she'll call again and I'll arrange things properly."

"And leave a damsel in distress on such a lovely day?" Felix winked. Hilde pursed her lips, but he could see her eyes twinkle. "I'll go and see what the drama is. I don't suppose she gave a name or a description?"

"Nothing." Hilde turned to go and then stopped. "Although she had a slight lilt in her voice that suggested she might be Italian or Spanish?"

Felix grinned. "A dark-eyed señorita? Maybe I won't come back at all."

He ducked past her scolding and out into the street. It was a perfect Berlin spring day: bright blue sky, clouds like pillows, temperature warm enough to loosen ties and unbutton blouses and set strangers smiling. It was the kind of frivolous day that demanded chocolate cake and cream-topped coffee.

Felix set off at a stride toward the Kurfürstendamm and Café Lotti. He pushed open the door into the velvet-draped, vanilla-scented room, thinking how like the old Café Kranzler it was and how much Kerstin would have loved it.

There was a black-haired woman sitting alone in a table by the window, clearly waiting for someone. He smiled at the waiter and was about to ask to be taken to her table when something caught his eye. A flash of blue. It pinned him to the spot.

A tumble of sunshine-colored curls. He gasped for air, certain she would look up and be someone else entirely.

And then she did, and there she was. Hannah Hüber. In a Prussian blue dress, in a Berlin café, with her hair all gold in the sun and smelling, he knew, of springtime.

CHAPTER NINETEEN

April 1956, Berlin

"Hannah?"

He didn't know a face could drain so quickly of its color.

"Drink this." He grabbed a glass of water from a passing tray—thrust it toward her. She emptied it without taking her eyes from him. "Hannah: it is you?" It was the most stupid question, but her silence unnerved him. His knees began to tremble, although not as badly as her hands. He sat down, not trusting she would ask him.

"Can I get you something, sir?"

He no longer wanted anything except for the waiter to go. "No. I mean . . . coffee. And a piece of chocolate cake. And a brandy. Perhaps you'd better make that two."

"No!" The slap of the word was a shock, but at least she had spoken. "Just water for me. Nothing else."

She looked so terrified, Felix half expected her to bolt. He moved his chair a fraction as if he might block her escape. All the words poured into letters played through his head and now here she was and he didn't know how to start.

"You survived." It came out with no thought for the impact. Her eyes widened. "I'm sorry—I put that badly." All the people she could have lost, all the things she could have seen, and here he was, blundering in like an elephant. "It's just the last time I saw you. In the camp. I was so afraid. I wanted to believe you'd got through it, but that place was so awful, it seemed too much to hope for. Especially after I realized the danger you'd put yourself in, getting the drawing to the guards."

"The drawing...you knew it was me?" Her voice was so beautiful, even more musical than he remembered it.

He smiled. To his delight she smiled back at him. Shyly at first and then with a warmth that turned her back into the dancing girl from the Ballhaus. "Who else could it have been? The bravery of it still amazes me. Especially with him standing behind you."

"With who?" The smile vanished so fast, he wondered if he had imagined it.

The way she was staring. Felix had imagined so many reactions when he found her, but never this white-faced fear.

"The doctor. Eichel. The one the orderlies called Nadel and were terrified of. He was right by you, at the window."

She started to cough so hard the waiter came running.

Felix took the water jug; waved him away. "Christ, what's wrong with me? I shouldn't have brought up his name. You must have been as scared of him as everyone else. The man was a monster. I still can't believe you got away."

Now she was crying. Slow-running tears that trickled down her cheeks without her seeming to notice; her misery tore at him.

"Hannah, please. Whatever he did to you, it's done; it's over. You've nothing to be afraid of anymore." Such a stupid thing to say: some memories stuck stronger than glue. She was staring at him like she didn't believe he was real.

"I thought the drawing might have made things worse. I heard all Krueger's men were killed and the deaths they endured were terrible. I couldn't bear the thought that I'd caused you more suffering..." She stopped; bit her lip.

Felix wanted to take her hand, but he didn't yet dare. "How do you even know about the printers?"

She retreated back into her chair, her hands twisting.

"It doesn't matter. You got me safely into his unit and we were well-treated there, almost until the end. They transported us to Mauthausen, which meant we escaped the death march. They did mean to kill us all, I'm sure of that, but I ran and I got away. You saved my life, Hannah. How can I ever repay you for that?"

She shook her head. She seemed to want to say something, but the words wouldn't come.

He picked up his fork, but eating was beyond him.

Without thinking, he laughed. "Look at me with my untouched plate. Could you have imagined that in the camp, when we were always so hungry? When I got out, I was no bigger than a stick man."

Her water glass spilled. "Don't say that—don't. I saw the pictures from the camps. I scoured them for your face. If I'd known how you were being treated..." She began scrabbling for her bag.

Something in what she said didn't make sense, but he wasn't interested in picking at it. All that mattered was making her stay. "Hannah, I'm a fool—forgive me." If she ran one more time, he didn't think he could bear it. "Treading over your memories like this. I'm so used to talking to survivors, sometimes I forget what a shock reliving those experiences can be. I'll take more care, I promise. But, please, don't go: not again."

When she put down her bag, Felix thought he would cry.

"What do you mean, you talk to survivors?"

This was steadier ground. Perhaps if he shifted the conversation into the present, it might settle her.

"It's my job, or it was. After I made it back to Berlin, I became a translator. I worked on the Nuremburg trials, collating evidence. Then I moved to CROWCASS—the Central Registry of War Criminals and Security Suspects. We were trying to identify Nazi war criminals, or at least set up guidelines for what that might mean."

"And do you still do that? Identify...Nazis?" She could barely say the word, but then neither could he, even after all the practice he had had.

Felix took a sip of his brandy as an excuse to look at her properly. She was even more beautiful than he remembered. Whatever horrors she had endured had left no visible scars. Her skin was as sun-kissed as her hair and her eyes had lost none of their brilliance.

"Not in the same way. CROWCASS closed down. There's not been much appetite here for digging up old crimes—everyone is far more concerned with rooting out communists."

A look flashed across her face he could have sworn was disappointment. Felix sat forward. Perhaps Hannah had scores of her own to settle.

"But things are changing. I'm a lawyer now and there's this case come up, an ex-Gestapo officer arrested here in Germany with too much blood on his hands to ignore. He's likely to go to trial. Even a year ago I wouldn't have believed that would happen."

Hannah's hands had stilled. She pulled out a packet of cigarettes. Felix scrabbled for his lighter, but she was too quick for him.

"Would you work on a case like that?"

"If I could. It's the reason I trained. I've never been able to find anything winnable, though, and I know I've pushed my partners' patience trying. So I work too hard on other cases to compensate and try their patience with that. That's why I'm here today. I was supposed to meet a new client. It was all very mysterious, but I doubt it was interesting." He glanced over at the window table, but it was empty. "Whatever was worrying her, she seems to have gone. Are you all right?" The cigarette had dropped from Hannah's fingers and already charred a small hole in the white linen cloth. She ignored it.

"You were meant to meet someone here?" He nodded. "Do you still want to catch Nazis? If that's what this new client wanted, would you have helped them?"

"Of course."

"Even ones who aren't in Germany? Who got away? Would you go after them?" There was an odd light in her eyes that suggested it wasn't a casual inquiry.

Felix decided to risk Eichel's name again. "I'd like to. I've tried, but it's been impossible so far. If that changes, then yes. I think Eichel, for one, might be in South America. I'd give up a lot to get him back."

Hannah lit up another cigarette. Her hand was shaking so much the tip danced like a firefly.

"Why him? Because of the camp?"

"Yes, and because he caused my father's death, and my mother's. And I thought he'd caused yours. And he killed a good man who was trying to help me, never mind all the hundreds I never knew. I've been hunting him. I got close. I know he went to South America by following his wife's family, but I couldn't get any nearer than that."

She was bone-white again. Ash from her cigarette showered the tablecloth.

"You found his wife?"

"No. She went with him, probably to Argentina. I assume she's still there. But this is too much—it's enough raking over the past. I'm frightening you. Oh, Hannah, if you knew all the times I've imagined this, all the speeches I've prepared." Suddenly, the years were tumbling out in a rush his tongue could barely keep up with. "Do you know how hard I fell when I met you? It was as if all the lights in the world had come on. You took my heart the first time I kissed you and I've never got it back. When you disappeared, at the Tiergarten, I thought I'd go mad. All I wanted was to find you, but then my father got sick and everything unraveled. And after the war I searched and searched, but there wasn't a trace of you. I wrote you so many letters—" Her eyes widened as she hung on his words.

"You wrote to me?"

Felix blushed. "I couldn't stop. I wrote them at work, at Sachsenhausen, for years after the war ended. Even when I..." He didn't know how to finish the sentence. He knew he should tell her about Kitty, but there wasn't room at this table.

Hannah smiled again, a tentative shadow of a thing, but it still made his heart soar.

"Where on earth did you send letters in wartime?" Her face lit up at the idea's absurdity. She was so close to a laugh, Felix could feel it hovering like a collector senses a rare butterfly.

"I didn't. I couldn't. I still have them, kept in an old tin for when I found you." He stopped. They stared at each other. "For when I found you. What happened to you, Hannah? Where have you been?"

The spell broke. Her face closed so quickly it was as if the blackout was back. He could feel her pulling away, loosening the ties he knew had just wrapped back around them.

"Away, Felix, just away; there's nothing else I can tell you."

As he had been expecting since he sat down, she was on her feet, her body tensed. "I wanted this as much as you, believe me, but no good can come from it." She was crying again, the tears falling so quickly they splashed like raindrops onto her blouse. "I can't do this. I've never wanted anything more in the world, but I can't do this. Keep your dreams, Felix. They'll make you far happier than I ever could."

He jumped up: this piece of history was not going to repeat itself. "Hannah, don't. Whatever happened to you back then doesn't matter to me. But if you leave again, if I lose you again, I'm done for."

He reached out. Her hand was in his. It was as if their skin remembered. Their fingers laced; her touch was like silk. The café disappeared. Felix pulled Hannah into his arms and he kissed her. Her mouth was like syrup, her scent full of apples. He dissolved through her edges and swore he'd come home. There were whistles and cheers, somebody tutting.

Felix surfaced, his body fizzing. There was nothing in his head but this moment, but Hannah. He grabbed her hand and, together, they ran.

*

She is Heaven.

Felix eased out of Hannah's embrace, the better to lie back and look at her. All the years imagining and his dreams had never come close. His fingers, his mouth, had traced every inch of her: she was known and yet new.

I won't let her go again. He gazed at the hair spilling golden threads across the pillow, at the dark wing of her eyelashes. *This will be my every morning, my every night.*

Hannah stirred, her eyelids fluttering. Light peeped around the edges of the curtain.

Felix checked his watch: six o'clock, the day would soon be calling. He didn't want to meet it. He wanted to replay last night, from the moment their lips met and Hannah led him, without speaking, through a maze of streets to her apartment.

Images swarmed back to him brighter than spotlights. The two of them bursting through the door, the key fumbled, falling against the wall, every button a barrier. Hannah urging him "this way, this way" into a bedroom where the satin shock of her skin overwhelmed his senses and left him apologizing. Where kisses became a conversation that moved their bodies back together into a dance, this time slow and exquisite...

She stirred again. For the first time, work was a nuisance—his only interest was in spinning plans that would keep Hannah by his side. He would call in sick: the thought of it had him grinning like a schoolboy. He would make her do the same and stretch the day out into another night, into the weekend; make this impossible, improbable stumbling over each other into something solid and real.

Felix got gently out of bed, pulled on his shirt and padded into the kitchen. Breakfast first—he would leave her sleeping and surprise her—and then the calls. He wondered if Hannah might be any more skilled at pretending than him.

Felix rooted through the cupboards and the small refrigerator. Eggs, coffee, milk, bread, a small jar of blueberry jam. There was only one cup and one plate, but he could improvise a bowl for his coffee and sharing the rest would be suitably romantic. The kitchen was neat and brightly colored, but he couldn't help noticing how sparsely furnished it was and how functional. There were no personal items in the drawers, no cookbooks or keepsakes on the shelves. *Perhaps she's only recently moved in.*

He put down the fork he was about to beat the eggs with, his curiosity piqued. He'd done so much talking and Hannah had told him nothing, about her background or where she'd been since the war ended. She'd brought him back here: surely she wouldn't mind if he did a little looking?

He wandered into a sitting room, which was bigger than the kitchen but equally as empty. There was a wooden-framed chair, covered in blue fabric. A green rug with one cream stripe covered the neutrally colored carpet. There was a simple teak bureau in one corner with a blue Anglepoise lamp positioned on top and a television set on a thin-legged stand. There were no pictures on the walls. If there were books, they were locked away in the bureau. There were no ornaments, no soft furnishings to soften the sleek lines of the furniture. There was no sense of Hannah; there was no sense of anyone.

Felix crossed to the window and opened the curtains, trying to ignore the sudden tightening in his stomach. The apartment was impersonal—that didn't need to mean anything. Perhaps she couldn't bear to be reminded of her losses. Except he had been in plenty of homes collecting his testimonies where the losses had been unimaginable and every surface of those had been crowded with lost faces. *She's not finished it, that's all.*

Nevertheless, when he turned back to the room and caught sight of a photograph the shadows had hidden, he went toward it with a sense of relief. Too many mysteries made Hannah insubstantial and he'd had more than his share of that.

The photograph was in an amber resin frame slightly too big for it. Felix picked it up and held it closer to the light. It was a boy, perhaps six or seven years old. He was a serious little thing, his face unsmiling but arresting: dark blond hair falling over intelligent eyes set off by high cheekbones. He looked familiar, which was absurd: there wasn't a trace of Hannah in him.

Felix decided his unease had to be hunger. He put the picture down, intending to finish breakfast, and accidentally dislodged an envelope, which fluttered to the floor. It was a pale blue airmail one. When he picked it up, a letter crackled through its onionskin covering.

Felix turned the envelope over. It took him three attempts to read the name and address written across it, although both were printed in precisely drawn capitals.

WOLFGANG EICHEL
a/c COLEGIO ALEMÁN
AV. ÁNGEL GALLARDO
SAN CARLOS DE BARILOCHE
ARGENTINA

A coincidence, what else could it be?

The envelope wasn't sealed. Felix folded the flap open, eased out the translucent paper.

My darling boy...

"Felix."

He looked up. How long had he been crouched on the floor, reading the same three words? Hannah was in the doorway, wrapped in a red robe.

"Don't." He didn't know so much sorrow could sit in one word.

She held out her hand. He tried to pass her the letter, but it slipped from his shaking fingers. She gathered it up, put it in her pocket and sat down opposite him. "I can explain. If you let me. At least I can try."

She didn't look like she could. Her mouth was so twisted, Felix couldn't see how any words could come out of it. He stayed silent. Perhaps if he stayed like that long enough, she would shake him awake and tell him this was a nightmare. Or tell him he'd gone mad, which seemed both plausible and preferable to anything else she might say.

"Wolf is my son. Mine and Eichel's." She said the last part again when he stared at her and shook his head. "I wish it wasn't true. I wish I never had to tell you. But he is."

There was an explanation here—he just had to find it and give her the right story. "This is what he did to you. This is why you still fear him." Once Felix started, his narrative flared. "He raped you. He made you pregnant. He stole the child. That's why you can't hear his name without shaking." Provided he didn't think about it, it made perfect sense.

Felix waited for Hannah to tell him he was right. She looked like she wanted to.

"No. If I could lie and tell you that and not have you hate me the way that you will, I would. But it's not true. Yes, Max Eichel stole my child, but not like that. I was married to him." Her words fell on him like rocks at a stoning. "I still am."

She wasn't crying—her eyes were too empty for that. She was staring at him like she needed something; he wished she would stop.

"That's not true." Her white face said it was. "Tell me the lie, please." She dropped her gaze and said nothing. "You can't be married to Eichel—that's impossible. His wife is the Ackermann girl, Inge, and you're..."

Her head drooped; the world fell sickeningly into place.

"Her."

Now she began to cry—silently, endlessly, as if she were broken.

He couldn't move. "Why were you there? Why did you dance with me?"

"That night was meant to be fun." He started to retch. She started to gabble. "No, listen. I was being married off to a man I hardly knew, who was so much older than me. Going to the Ballhaus was supposed to be one last adventure. And then I met you and…I don't know. Suddenly, I wanted to be someone else."

"So you made up a name." Now that he thought about it, how different she'd been, how impossible to find, the truth was blindingly obvious.

"I shouldn't have. I'm so sorry. It was all I could think to do. And I shouldn't have gone to the Tiergarten. Max—I mean Eichel— followed me: it was him prowling on the veranda. I liked you so much, but it was impossible. I thought you'd forget me."

It was all so absurd, Felix wished he could laugh.

"And then there you were, at Sachsenhausen, being beaten. I saw you and I knew, somehow, that even though I barely knew you then, I could love you, given the chance. But it was all such a mess. And I was a coward, Felix. Until then, I was a coward, or maybe a fool."

His memories were shifting, his past rewriting. "You weren't a prisoner?"

She shook her head.

"Eichel was beside you because he was your husband?"

She stumbled a yes. Felix sobbed then, a great tearing sound that almost drowned out her words.

"I had no time to think. Max was so controlling; I was just starting to learn that. If I'd pointed you out and said that I knew you, there's no telling what he would have done. So I gave your drawing to a nurse and told her to take it to Krueger. I threatened her. Afterward, well, I was sick and Max went back to the camp, to find you. I don't know why he did that—I know he hadn't heard your name and I said nothing, even when he drilled me later.

Anyway, when he got there, you'd gone. I had to believe that you weren't dead. I would have gone mad if I'd let myself think that."

"And now he's coming and you won't be here for him to collect..."

"Later I learned I'd saved you, but Max told me I'd only delayed your death."

Felix couldn't look at her—all he could see were other faces. "He took twelve men instead of me. They all died, experimented on by your husband." He scrambled to his feet, as desperate to get away as he had been to stay. "You made up a name and I made you up from it. Has anyone ever been more stupid? All that time, when I was writing to you, fearing for you, ruining my life for you, you were married to Eichel." He stopped as the enormity of that hit him. "How much did you know?"

"Not as much as you think. Not then." She had curled into a ball. For an insane moment he wanted to kick her.

"And now?"

"Everything. Maybe more than you." She dragged herself onto her knees like a beggar. He wished she would stop being so beautiful. "Felix, forgive me, please. I was blind and stupid and I was afraid. But I'm trying to make it better. And I hate him. I hate him as much as you do."

He couldn't let her make them equals in this. "No, you don't. You slept beside him. If you hated him as much as me, you'd have killed him." She tried to speak, but he brushed her away. "I don't want to hear it. Unless you tell me I have this wrong and you left him long ago, before he ran to South America."

"You don't understand." And there they were, the clues he had so blithely ignored in the sheer joy of finding her—the lilt in her voice, the sun-kissed skin—rushing back in and screaming. What was left of his heart sank. "I couldn't then—I was pregnant and he wouldn't let me go. I wanted to leave—for years I wanted nothing else. But I had a child, and no money. I know how weak it sounds, but it's the truth. I was trapped. And I couldn't leave my boy."

"So when did you finally do it?" The answer didn't really matter.

"A few months ago. I came back here in December."

"Why then? What changed?"

She suddenly looked as weary as he felt. "Because Max tricked me and stole Wolf. I thought I had finally outplayed him, but I was never even close. I left because he won. He made me go—he said he would kill me if I didn't. I believed him; he'd given me cause enough. And now he has my son and no doubt he will do all he can to make Wolf hate me."

Her head shot up; her voice hardened. "This is not what I wanted, Felix, to find you, only to lose you again. Because I know I will lose you. That is agony, but trust me, it is nothing compared to losing my son. That is hell. But I will get him back. In the end, nothing else but that matters."

He heard her misery at the mess that was now them, but he also remembered her question: "*Do you still do that? Identify Nazis?*" And he heard that louder. Those words, and the speed with which she'd dragged him into bed, crashed the last of his hope away.

"Is that what this is? You could have told me the truth before, in the café, but you went on lying. Last night wasn't some love-struck reunion: you did it so I'd help find your son. You never wanted me at all."

"No! That's not true. I've never stopped loving you, never stopped hoping you were alive. That was me, Felix. In bed with you: that was me."

The paralysis that had crept over him when he picked up the letter dissolved. The pain that rushed in to replace it was unbearable. "But I don't know who that is. All these years and there never was a Hannah. There was never anything close to a Hannah."

"There was. What you saw in me is what I could have been. And could still be." She was on her feet, grabbing for his hands. He wanted to pull away, but his skin remembered hers too well. "Last night was real. When you woke up this morning, it was real.

Isn't that what you wanted? Isn't that enough? I looked for you too. When you were writing letters, I was collecting photographs, combing through newspapers for news of the camps and the trials, hoping and praying you were still alive, although I didn't know how anyone could live through such horror. When I saw what you had suffered, what men like Max had done, my heart broke, Felix. I swear it broke. You could fix it. I could fix you. You can't be happy, whatever you've done with your life, or you wouldn't have kept on searching for me."

He couldn't answer: his heart and his mind were no longer in tandem.

She plowed on, her voice rising as she laid out this new story. "The Hannah you wrote to, the one you believed in. She's here—she's looking at you. I didn't have the courage to hold on to her back then; you think I don't have it now, but I can find it, with you. Think about it, Felix. What's been done is terrible, but it's been done. We can be real for each other. I said that I'd lose you, but what if it didn't have to be like that? What if we were brave? We could heal the past and build a future. It's here to be had. You and me, and yes, my boy, if we can do that. We can make a life that's worth having."

He longed to believe it, to share some of that feverish hope in her eyes.

"Please. Come back to bed. We were real there—you can't deny that."

He was so tired. So weary of the anger, the wrong choices, the illusions he had let lead him. He wanted to leave, to hide, and yet all the years spent searching: how could they fall to nothing so soon?

"When I found you, there was meant to be magic. You and me, both survived the worst and finally together: it was supposed to make all the horror worthwhile." He sounded like a child. He felt as helpless as a child.

"Maybe it still can. Shouldn't we try? Don't we owe it to the couple who danced in the Ballhaus to try?"

She made it sound so simple.

Maybe she'll have the strength to write this differently for us both.
He followed her back to the bedroom, praying he could be the
brave man she wanted, full of love and forgiveness. Praying he had
more than ashes to give.

He was gone. The room was silent, the space beside her cold.

There'll be a note.

Inge had whispered that three times before she opened her eyes.

There was nothing. There hadn't been a trace of him in the flat
beyond a torn-up blue envelope.

Inge had sat at her kitchen table, heart aching as she unpicked
the night. All that love. Carried by him, carried by her. Unearthed
and breathing and dust just as quickly, like a relic pulled from
a tomb without sufficient care. She had shivered, although the
morning was warm.

They had tried. They had lain back down again. He had kissed
her. He had held her and touched her in the ways they were learning.
He had tried, but his body recoiled. When he turned his back and
sobbed, she knew it was done.

Inge had called in sick that morning and the next. She had sat
by the telephone even though she knew he wouldn't call. She had
waited by the door, although she knew he wouldn't knock. She
had pulled her past apart until it was shredded and still couldn't find
a place where they could have lived the different life she cried for.

All those years, Felix had loved a girl who didn't exist, a better
girl than the one who did. *And now I could be her; now I'm ready.*
She could repeat the words till her hair ran gray—it wouldn't matter.
So I won't do it. The sudden certainty cut through the fog she was
shrouded in. *If I do, all Felix will hear is another of Inge Ackermann's lies.*

Inge hauled herself up from the cold floor she was curled on.
There would be a future, but it couldn't be this—begging and hoping

and seeing him hate her. She couldn't do that to the starry-eyed couple they'd once been or the good man he now was; the good woman she wanted to be.

Inge pulled herself down the corridor, her limbs too shaky to trust, and limped into the bathroom. She stared at her exhausted face in the mirror. *No more tears.* That would be today's goal. Tomorrow she would set another.

She nodded to herself in the glass; she couldn't imagine trying a smile. There was still Wolf. There was still Max to deal with. *One day and then the next. Small steps, that's all I need.* There was still a future, a better life waiting somewhere for her; there had to be.

"Small steps." She repeated the words into the mirror until her voice stopped shaking. "That's all I need to take until I get to wherever I'm meant to be."

CHAPTER TWENTY

June 1956, Berlin

For a month, Felix went to his office, sat at his desk and pushed papers around. He went home and went straight out again, taking walks that refused to stop the pain. He ate badly, he slept badly. Twice, a junior caught him crying. He felt, when he let himself feel anything, like a poorly tethered balloon. In the end, it was Levi who marched him to a bar far from the office and dragged the whole sorry story out.

"She was very young." Levi refilled Felix's beer glass for the second time. "Step back from Eichel and your anger for a moment. Eighteen and raised how she must have been? It's not like she chose him, Felix. It's not as black and white as you'd make it."

"She wasn't always eighteen. She stayed married. She went to South America. She was there ten years."

He wasn't prepared for Levi's sigh. "And from what you've told me, she was terrified of him. Did you ask her how he was as a husband? If he was cruel, if he beat her? It's not hard to guess. I bet you didn't ask, but you told her she should have killed him? How would that have played out? Do you think Perón would have given her a medal?" Levi's questions were making his head ache. Felix shifted and sighed, but Levi plowed on. "You're angry, you feel betrayed. Have you stopped to consider that this isn't her fault?"

Felix pushed his glass away; without Levi's restraining hand, he would have stormed out.

"Don't be so quick to run, my friend. Isn't that how all this trouble started?"

Felix sagged against the booth's hard back. "What do you mean, it isn't her fault?"

"You said it yourself: she made up a name and you made her up from it. She didn't ask to be your talisman. Although maybe you should be thanking her for that. She kept you alive, Felix, physically and mentally. She risked her life to get that drawing to Krueger. And then you clung to the Hannah who'd done that—the Hannah you invented—like a life raft. Without her bravery, you would have died. Without everything you turned her into, you would have died. *She* was your luck."

Levi drained his glass. Felix picked his up, although his stomach was churning.

"Even if all that's true, I wish I'd never found her. I was warned not to hope for it. 'Whatever you find of her, it won't be what you imagine.' That was good advice—I should have listened."

Levi shrugged. "But you didn't and that hope brought you more good fortune than harm. No one came through unchanged, Felix. And we all did what we had to do to survive, your Hannah included. Eichel is the monster. You can paint her the same or as one of his victims. Whichever you choose, you're still grieving." Levi reached out again, this time to pat Felix's suddenly trembling hand. "You lost her and now you've lost her again. Mourn that and this will get better."

He turned to a waiter, waving the empty beer jug, engaging him in conversation while Felix composed himself.

Grieving. He'd been so caught up in her lying, he'd never thought this rage could be loss. He waited until a new jug was delivered and the glasses refilled.

"I'm sorry, Levi. I should have talked to you, not buried my head and blundered about. I never know when I need help. I certainly don't know how to ask for it."

"Few of us do." Levi raised his glass; Felix followed. "But I don't think it's me you owe an apology."

"I can't see her again, whatever I owe her." Levi said nothing, and Felix reddened. "Oh, you meant Kitty."

"What have you told her? Please God you've said something. She's too good a woman to be let down again."

Felix closed his eyes. The memory of that phone call still chafed: *"I've found Hannah, Kitty, and it's bad."* He'd ground to a halt and left too long a silence.

"I'm not going to ask, Felix: I'm going to wait for you to tell me." She gave him a pause he didn't know what to do with. He could almost hear her nodding. *"Then you need to understand something, Felix: I'll wait for a little while, but I won't wait forever. And when this is done, I won't wait again. It's in your hands, Felix, but then it will be in mine."*

She'd put down the phone; they hadn't spoken since.

He nodded at Levi, who finished his drink.

"Your past is one thing, Felix—your future's another. Only you can decide what you can afford to remember and what you take forward. Choose a path and make it the right one... What?"

"You sound like my mother." For the first time in weeks, it was laughter that made his eyes well.

"You have a visitor, Herr Thalberg."

Felix looked up from his desk with a groan. He had no appointments scheduled. Given the throb in his head from the previous night's beer, his only plan for the day had been organizing the work he had thoroughly neglected.

"It's a woman, sir. She wouldn't give a name."

It was Hannah, in a full-skirted black suit and lace gloves. She looked breathtaking. Felix wanted to grab hold of her. He wanted to order her to leave. She sat down without waiting for him to do anything at all.

"I would have called first, but this way you couldn't refuse to see me."

Felix felt the air settle stuffy around him. His neck and wrists were clammy, but the intimacy of loosening his collar and pushing up his sleeves was impossible. Hannah—because that was the only name he could give her without crying—placed her bag on the floor and set a brown-paper-wrapped parcel on his desk.

"Can I arrange you some coffee?" He sounded stilted, dried up.

"No. This won't take long." She was so composed, so different from the girl begging on the floor.

Eichel is the monster. He swallowed hard.

"I'm sorry. For how I was. For leaving you without a goodbye or a note. For not behaving better."

She nodded. "Thank you. For saying that. And for trying, that night, to rewrite what we both now know can't be rewritten."

Her smile was so gentle, Felix suddenly wished they were back in the café, that he could magic them up different stories. Even as he tried the hope out, he knew it was hollow.

"Can't it?"

Her smile shivered. "We would have tried, wouldn't we? If I'd woken and seen you leaving, I would have begged you to stay. I would have told you it would be fine in the end, that we could make the impossible happen. I think you would have gone along with it, wanted to believe it. I believed it myself for long enough. I waited for you to call. I wondered if I would find the courage to come to you."

His body ached so much to hold hers he could barely remember why he had left.

"And now you have. So maybe you were right after all and we can be brave enough." *Could I do it? Could I forget all the anger? Could I let it all go and believe in us?* In that moment, staring into a face that still held the girl he had loved for so long, Felix had never wanted anything more.

As if she sensed the shift in him, Inge reached out her hand. It hung in the air for a moment, as easy to catch as thistledown. Felix leaned forward, his fingers tingling. As their fingertips met, however, she shook her head. Her hand fell from his before he could grasp it.

"No, we can't. All we would do is delay and worsen our end. I know you don't believe me, but, before you argue, think about this. When I look at you, I see you, Felix: a good man I should have hung on to. When you look at me, who do you see?"

It seemed such an easy question. He wanted to say Hannah, at the very least Inge, but when he opened his mouth, a different name altogether almost leaped out. He clamped his lips shut, but her shudder told him she had heard what was there.

"That's what I thought." Sadness flooded her face for an instant and then it was gone. Her hands were on her lap now, too far away for him to reach. "I know the name you nearly said. And I know, if we tried again, we would hurt each other. Not deliberately. There's too much love between us still for that. But there will always be a moment when you see him when you look at me. You won't mean to, but you'll never get past it. And then you won't see the Inge I want you to see anymore, the one who is all the best bits of Hannah. You will only see the woman who married a Nazi and lied." She lifted her chin and let out a long breath that whispered around her like petals falling. "I won't end us that way. So I'm glad that you didn't pretend, that we can be honest. I love you, Felix, and you love me, and we could have had a romance to write in the storybooks, once upon a time."

Her smile made him want to weep for everything she was and everything they could have been. She was so still; one bound and he could have caught her and pinned her in his arms. He ached to do it, to hold her fast and weave a spell around them that would keep the world at bay. *If we tried again, we would hurt each other.* He didn't move. How could he, when he knew in his battered heart she was right?

"Is this goodbye then?"

She nodded. "But first you deserve to know that it was me you were meant to meet in the café that day. I was the woman who called." She pushed the package across the desk, her manner switching so suddenly to businesslike it took him by surprise. "This is the information I had with me for the lawyer I didn't know would be you. Take it. There's nobody better placed to act on it."

"What is it?"

"Open it and I'll explain."

Felix peeled off the string and the thin paper layer. Inside was a set of slim notebooks and a larger volume covered in maroon-colored leather. He turned that over first, looking for a name, as Inge began an explanation Felix sensed from its speed she had practiced.

"The book is Max's. A diary of sorts. It's a list of every one of his killings, with their dates and their methods, from the clinic he trained in, in Austria, through the stamina tests in Sachsenhausen, to a cluster of rather nasty experiments in Buenos Aires. It's easy to follow. One thing you can't fault my husband for is his record-keeping. I've thought long and hard about giving you this, wondering whether it's fair to tie you to me, no matter how loosely. Wondering if I was doing it out of a desire for revenge that would eat me up and do me no good. I'm not. I know giving Max up is the right thing to do. That it will rinse away some of the stain he's cast over me and, more importantly, bring comfort and justice to the people he has hurt. That would be something I can be proud of. But, if you don't mind, I'd rather you read the details after I've gone."

Felix put the book down unopened and picked up the notebooks. Inge's voice slowed. "And these are my records, proof if you—or maybe I—need it, that I wasn't a supporter of their terrible beliefs. In there are the details of the others who are in South America with him: Mengele, Eichmann, Priebke, Kopps and a handful of other men whose names carry as many shadows.

Addresses, aliases, snatches of conversation. They're not as neatly kept as Max's, I'm afraid, but they'll do their job."

Felix sat back as this woman he could barely find a name for rewrote herself again. "If these are what you say they are, if their testimony is used and your role gets back to Max or any of the others, it could be very dangerous."

She was using the books and her distanced manner to form a barrier between them. Part of him was grateful for that, but he couldn't pretend her actions sat easily on him.

"There could be consequences for you I can't bear to think about. Aren't you afraid?"

Inge dusted her hands and picked up her bag. "I'm done with being afraid. I have a lot of life left to live and I am going to do it in the best way that I can."

His heart swelled as she squared her shoulders like a soldier readying for a battle that could be as easily lost as won.

"Besides, what more can he do to me? He's taken my son—what could be worse? You saw my letter to Wolf. I write dozens of them, but I doubt any are read. There's no way of knowing what Max has told Wolf, or what he's shaping him into. Maybe this will get me my boy back, maybe it won't. I have to carry that and not let it drown me. I have to keep hoping my decision is right. If the truth comes out and destroys Max, if it separates Wolf from him, whatever comes after is worth it. I know my son will be horrified and heartbroken." Her voice quivered, but she grabbed it back under control. "I once vowed I would beat Max, whatever the cost, but I didn't know then my child would be the price extracted. I can't stop that. But if I get the chance, and I am determined to believe that I will, then I will love Wolf enough to make up for his father. I have to believe that, Felix. And I have to believe Wolf will forgive me."

She stopped. When he nodded, she found a tentative smile.

"I hoped for a miracle once and here you are, so why not hope for another one?"

She was such a beautiful mixture of vulnerability and strength, Felix knew she would survive whatever came at her. He could imagine her, one day not too far in the distance, happy.

"You're braver than I ever was."

Her eyes were shining, but he knew she wouldn't cry. Not with him, not anymore.

"No. We are both brave, Felix. We are both survivors. Perhaps that is why we were drawn together and had our fleeting moment."

"Wolf will come back to you. There's a bond between mothers and sons that's not easily broken." It sounded like a platitude, but he meant it and was glad when she didn't dismiss it. Glad that they weren't any longer at odds. When she spoke again, her voice had cut loose its tight edges.

"There is one more thing I need from you, apart from using this information to get justice."

"Name whatever you want and it's yours."

"You should be careful promising women that." And then she laughed, and Felix caught one last glimpse of the woman he could have shared his life with.

He started to say something and stopped. His was a private pain now, as hers was; there was no place left for airing it. She waited until she had his attention back.

"The papers are talking about a new unit being set up in Ludwigsburg to investigate war criminals. I want to work there; I don't care in what capacity. Don't look so surprised. To catch your enemy, you need to know your enemy, and who knows the Nazis better than me? I want to do something good, to balance the scales my husband weighted all the wrong way. I need a reference and I need you to write it. One more letter, Felix; the final one." She smiled and wrapped a scar around his heart.

He nodded; he couldn't trust himself to speak.

"Good. I'll leave my details with that rather fearsome secretary. I won't be coming back." She stood up and crossed swiftly to the door. Then she paused. "A fresh start for us both. New beginnings. I'd wish you good luck, but I have faith you'll make your own now. We both will. We both know what love is; we've learned the best lesson. I will always love you, Felix. I will always be grateful for us. Whatever comes next will never match this."

She was gone before he could answer.

If this was a film, I would follow her. There would be a look, and a kiss, and the world would stop and wait while we remade it.

But it wasn't a film, and a world where a Felix and a Hannah could have lived and loved was lost long ago.

Felix crossed to the window and watched her walk down the street, watched heads turn as she passed. The swing of her hair was Hannah, but the rest of that shy girl was gone: this Inge commanded far more space.

In a little while, he would phone Kitty, arrange a meeting; tell her everything. *No more secrets.* She would hold on to him, or she would not: he knew which he wanted and which he would ask for. First, there was work to be done.

Felix went back to his desk and spread out his new treasure. All the words he had written and now the ones that mattered were collected by her. He pulled the book close, running his fingers over the richly worked leather. Eichel's secrets finally his.

With Inge in his heart, and Kerstin and Arno at his shoulder, Felix opened the cover and started to read.

A LETTER FROM
CATHERINE HOKIN

Hello,

Firstly, and most importantly, a huge thanks for reading *The Fortunate Ones*. I hope you enjoyed reading it as much as I enjoyed writing it.

The Fortunate Ones started its life as a short story about a meeting in a café in Berlin between a woman with a secret and a man with a dream whose paths had fleetingly crossed many years earlier during World War II. Unlike the other short stories I have written, however, Felix and Inge refused to stay quiet once I thought I was done with them.

Germany was the first country outside the UK I ever visited. I was sixteen at the time, on a school exchange, and I fell in love with it. Since then, I have been particularly fascinated by Berlin and its checkered, conflict-ridden history. My son lives there, and it is a place I visit often. I am also fascinated by quieter voices, the stories that distill wide-reaching historical events into something personal and relatable. The physical and mental impact of World War II on Berlin was colossal—there is a series of "rubble films" made at the end of the war that will take your breath away. Big-scale history is all there in the city, but what Berlin's museums and monuments also focus very effectively on is the individuals who were caught up in desperate circumstances outside their control. This aspect is particularly strong at the Sachsenhausen Concentration Camp, where I pored over photographs and found the stories that went into my Felix and also the real people, the guards and the counterfeiters, who surrounded my character. My Felix, from his first brief outing in the short story, was always an artist and a dreamer; now he had come to life.

I was also lucky enough to go to Buenos Aires while I was writing this book. Like Berlin, Buenos Aires is a fascinating city, but this is a place that deliberately and efficiently hides its past. It was while I was in the chandelier-stuffed Casa Rosada, staring at a portrait of Eva Perón set so high our necks hurt, that Inge burst off the notepad—far away from home, alone and afraid and finally all too aware of the dangers that lurk beneath glittering façades. She has a lot of growing up to do in her story; I hope you agree that she did it, in the end, with grace.

These are characters who have come to mean a lot to me, so thank you for spending your time with them—I hope you have found it worthwhile. If you have a moment, and if you enjoyed the book, a review would be much appreciated. I'd dearly love to hear what you thought and reviews always help us writers to get our stories out to more people.

I hope too that you will let me share my next novel with you when it's ready. I'm heading back to Berlin where there are a lot more stories left to tell…

Thank you again for your time,
Catherine Hokin

@cathokin
www.catherinehokin.com
Cathokin

ACKNOWLEDGMENTS

As every historical fiction writer does, I read a huge number of books while writing my novels. The ones I would particularly like to mention are as follows: *Berlin at War* by Roger Moorhouse, *The End* by Ian Kershaw and *The Bitter Taste of Victory* by Lara Feigel, which are all brilliantly readable accounts of the impact of World War II on Berlin; *Hunting Evil* by Guy Walters and *The Real Odessa* by Uki Goñi for their forensic exploration of Nazi fugitives in South America and *Blind Eye to Murder* by Tom Bower, which traces the treatment of Nazi war criminals in Germany after the war; *Krueger's Men* by Lawrence Malkin, which tells the endlessly fascinating story of the Sachsenhausen counterfeiters; and, finally, *Nazi Chic?* by Irene Guenther, which is the definitive account of fashion and womanhood in the Third Reich. The documentary *Bariloche: Pact of Silence* by Carlos Echeverría was also invaluable.

I owe thanks to many people but would like to single out some. Tina Betts and Kathryn Taussig, my wonderful agent and editor, for their insight, patience and hard work and for loving my story and helping me to tell it in its best possible way. To the whole team at Bookouture, who got behind it, especially Kim Nash for her energy and passion. To my daughter, Claire, and son, Daniel, for their crucial first reading and insightful critical feedback and for having the excellent idea of doing a Spanish degree and a German degree and, in Daniel's case, living in Berlin—it was almost like we'd planned it. To my very talented writer-support friends Julie Rea and Jools Forest for pep talks and Prosecco and the best GIF work money can't buy. And, lastly but never least, to my husband, Robert, for coping with the crazy and keeping me sane and taking me, magically, to Buenos Aires. Much love to you all.

ABOUT THE AUTHOR

Catherine Hokin writes World War II novels inspired by her favorite city, Berlin. After earning a degree in history, she worked in teaching, marketing and politics, while waiting for a chance to do what she really wanted, which was to write full-time. She is a lover of strong female leads and a quest, and is an avid reader and a cinema lover.

For more info:
catherinehokin.com
Twitter: cathokin
Facebook: cathokin

READING GROUP GUIDE

Discussion Questions

1. Does the title *The Fortunate Ones* fit with the content of the story?
2. How do the settings, Berlin and Buenos Aires, impact on/ reflect Felix's and Inge's character development?
3. Were both storylines equally engaging?
4. Discuss the relationship between Max and Inge. Was Inge powerless or complicit in the way it developed?
5. Was anything in the relationship between Felix and Inge ever real?
6. Are there any parallels between Felix and Kitty's relationship and Max and Inge's?
7. Is Inge a good mother?
8. When Inge accuses Max of being a monster, he says that is a "meaningless word." Do you agree? Do all the characters commit "monstrous" acts?
9. Does the novel have a satisfying ending?

Q & A with the Author

Q: *What inspired you to write THE FORTUNATE ONES?*

A: This was originally a short story I wrote because I wanted to explore what it means to be a "monster." There were a couple of versions, but the constant was a café in Berlin, ten years or so after the war, and a meeting between a woman with a secret and a man in thrall to a dream, whose paths had fleetingly crossed once before at a concentration camp. The original Felix was badly broken from his experiences and Inge was an unrepentant Nazi, and a far crueler character than she became. Short stories are usually complete worlds, but this one wouldn't let me go.

Q: *How did you create the characters of Inge and Felix?*

A: I went backward from the short story to find out who Felix and Inge had been when the war broke out: doing that, meeting them in their teens, allowed me to create far more complex and sympathetic characters. I knew from the start that I wanted the meetings between them to be fleeting—which carried a level of risk—because I wanted the element of a quest. Inge needed to grow up and become her own woman, and Felix needed to stay alive: making him a Mischling (a legal term used in the Third Reich to denote persons deemed to have both Aryan and Jewish heritage) and putting him among the counterfeiters was very much part of this process. This is a love story, but the characters are in love with, and in need of, love, far more than they are actually in love with each other.

Q: *Inge married a man who was not of her choosing. How did you get into the mindset of someone living with that burden?*

A: The first thing I had to do was fully accept the period in which she was living and its constraints, in both Berlin and Buenos Aires, and make those plausible for the reader. A girl from Inge's background did not have choices, and, when we meet her, she is young and spoiled and her head is easily turned. Her life would have actually been far less of a burden if she had kept her eyes shut to what was going on around her, as many undoubtedly did. What I was trying to explore, therefore, was how someone behaves when there is no easy, or safe, way out of the situation they are in and they have to put someone else first (in this case, Wolf) even when the personal cost is so high. Once I realized that Inge facing up to herself rather than to Max was the burden, she became brave. Yes, she experienced a lot of loss and fear, but I think she grew strong, and would carry on growing stronger after the last page.

Q: *Felix never gives up hope of finding Inge. Why is reuniting with her so important to Felix when they spent only a few hours together?*

A: I used Leo to try and explain that when he says "you clung to ... Hannah ... like a life raft ... without everything you turned her into, you would have died. She was your luck." Hannah/Inge is a talisman for Felix, from the blue dress to the drawing that saves his life, she is a light in the darkness that has swallowed him, and a light he has to keep following. Once he is back in Berlin, she becomes his shield against a world he is too frightened to properly rejoin. Loving again means he will lose again: the dream of the perfect girl protects him from this. She isn't real, which is why Felix can invest so much more hope in her understanding and loving him than he ever allows Kitty.

Q: *What is it like to create a fictional narrative around a historical event?*

A: For me, the biggest challenge was writing about the experience within a concentration camp. Firstly, because it is essential not to exploit the suffering, or romanticize it and make light of its horrors. As writers, we cannot use the realities of the camps carelessly, creating situations that cannot possibly have happened and blunting or belittling what could. However you do your research—and I used both the wealth of well-written source material available and visited key sites such as Sachsenhausen—you have to understand the realities and the limitations of "life" in the camps and to stick like glue to the facts. The second challenge is to keep someone plausibly alive in a camp for any length of time—this was why I chose to make Felix part of the counterfeiting team. And I really believe the old writing adage "get in late, leave early" applies here: I want to tell these stories because they matter, but I don't want to wallow in other people's pain.

Q: *What is one shocking or incredible piece of information you learned when doing research for the book?*

A: There were so many, the hardest choice was what to leave out of the book. If I had to choose one surprising thing, I would pick the Rosenstraße protests. This was an act of very vocal resistance carried out over ten days by about 200 non-Jewish women who were protesting the detention of their husbands and fathers by the Nazis. These Jewish men were, up to that point, counted as "privileged," but they had been rounded up for deportation in the brutal February 1943 purge of the Berlin Jews. Despite very real fears that the women would be, at best, arrested, their protest worked and the men were released—Hitler was said to have been unnerved by the action, as it reminded him of the 1918 protests, which led to the November

Revolution. I find the women's courage astounding—I have visited the street and it is narrow; they must have been face-to-face with soldiers whose brutality was well-known, but they didn't back down.

Q: *World War II historical fiction is incredibly popular right now. Why do you think that is?*

A: It's a good question. Being caught up in a war, either as a combatant or a civilian, must be one of the worst experiences anyone can endure, and yet, since storytelling began, we have filled up our books and plays and poems with stories of conflict and the pain that comes with it. With World War II it could be because the number of survivors is shrinking, and that brings an increased need for remembrance, a need to hold on to accounts that many people have only felt able to share in recent years. The Holocaust has also been described as an embodiment of some of our deepest fears, and that resonates with me. We can pretend such a horror, with its inescapable round-ups and removals and contempt for human life, can never happen again, but do we believe that? When we live in a world stained by rising anti-Semitism, when we have witnessed genocide in Rwanda and Bosnia and Myanmar?

Overall, I think we make sense of our world's cruelties through reading, and telling, stories. Holocaust and World War II literature is part of this: our own horror story existing still, albeit just, in living memory. We exorcise our fear of war's pain and death and separation on the page, but we also look for hope. The moments of bravery and sacrifice that change a life, the moments we want to think ourselves capable of and pray we never have to face.

Q: *What is your writing process like? Do you just let the story flow, or do you have a strict process?*

A: It's a combination of both. I am a very visual person and I cannot start to write or plan until I can envisage the very last scene of the book. Once I have that, I write a synopsis (a maximum of two pages) and then begin the research and planning, both of which are ongoing processes. I plan my books in acts and break these plans down into chapter outlines. That sounds very tightly structured but it isn't: I constantly revisit the plans and leave enough space for the characters to start walking around on their own and surprising me. I write longhand, then re-read and edit what I have written, then type up and edit again, so I am redrafting as I write and there is a lot of going back and tweaking. The "first draft" I send to my editor is usually about draft six!

Q: What advice would you give to aspiring writers?

A: Write about things that you care about. Know why you are writing, in other words determine what validation looks like for you. Find your own way through the planning and drafting process—everyone will offer you rules, but there aren't any, so learn what works for you. Learn your craft: I entered lots of short story competitions that offered feedback and it was always worthwhile. If you can, find someone you trust who will give you critical feedback, and listen to it, but also listen to your own voice. Submit things. Celebrate every success. Don't give up, keep writing, keep pushing, keep listening: it only takes one person to love what you do for the doors to start opening.

Q: What's one thing you want all of your readers to know about you?

A: The song "A Nation Once Again," which is a kind of unofficial anthem in the Republic of Ireland and was voted the world's most popular song in 1972, was written by one of my ancestors, Thomas Davis. Telling people that in Dublin has led to some very lively nights.

Walking with History: An Essay

Like most historical fiction writers, I love the research process. For me, the start of a new novel means weeks spent buried in the books and films that form the backdrop to my story. I was already aware of some of the topics covered in *The Fortunate Ones*—for example, the Sachsenhausen counterfeiters and the Nazi "ratlines" into South America; telling their stories was part of the impetus for writing it. I also, however, uncovered lots of hidden nuggets along the way and had a few neck-prickling moments, which is exactly what a writer with a story in her sights is looking for!

I spent a lot of time in Berlin and was also lucky enough to be able to visit Buenos Aires while writing this book. One thing that struck me was the very different way Argentina and Germany face their history, and present that history to the world. Berlin does not shy away from the horrors perpetrated by the Third Reich. The city is full of museums and exhibitions focused on this period, and the conversations, particularly over the way concentration camps and other "memorials" are remembered, are ongoing across Germany. These dialogues are often difficult things: the National Socialist regime has cast long shadows, and, no matter how much I think I know, there are still moments that make me pause.

The location of the Sachsenhausen concentration camp, for example, was a shock: I knew that the site was close to Berlin, but I wasn't prepared for how closely entwined the camp was with the town of Oranienburg, which flanks it. They are not separate entities. What I have written about shutters closing and townspeople turning their backs as the prisoners were marched through the streets is fact. What is immediately clear, however, to anyone walking the route from the station past the neat little houses is that, even if it was possible to block out the sights, it would have been impossible to block out the sounds. And the camp itself is not a tucked-away thing. One of the guard towers has a display directing visitors to look through a small window onto what was once a sprawling SS housing estate, an estate many local girls lived on when they married the officers who ran Sachsenhausen. Without wishing to pass judgment, ignorance in this case must have been hard won.

For all the difficulties experienced in understanding it, history in Berlin is very much part of the city's present. There is no similar impetus in Buenos Aires, however, where the past is far more carefully curated.

In Argentina, the Nazis do not exist. The National History Museum skirts over World War II, making no mention of the hundreds of war criminals President Perón's regime gave shelter to. The Immigration Museum, cited in the building that was the first point of entry for arrivals, has no publicly-available records for the period. Perón's National Ethnic Institute, where my character Max worked, existed, but I found only one internet link which mentioned it and there is no trace of it left at all in Buenos Aires.

Despite, or perhaps because of, the gaps, I had three neck-prickling moments when researching Argentina. The first was discovering the existence of the Ethnic Institute and how aligned its official task was with Nazi eugenics. The second was uncovering the history of the little town of San Carlos de Bariloche. Bariloche is now an internationally famous skiing resort; from the end of World War II, it was also a favorite residence for a number of Nazi fugitives. Reinhard Kopps, an SS lieutenant accused of organizing ethnic crimes in Albania involving the murder of thousands of Jews, ran a hotel in the town. Frederic Lantschner, a Nazi governor of the Tyrol, used the letters SS as the symbol for his Bariloche construction company. Josef Mengele is known to have taken his driving test there. Adolf Eichmann, one of the architects of the Holocaust, was a resident, as was Erich Priebke, the senior SS commander at the Ardeatine massacre in Italy, who became president of the Bariloche Germano-Argentinian cultural association and was an influential teacher at the local school.

All these men, and many like them, lived active and untroubled lives in Bariloche, although it is hard now to find any trace of them—the luxury Llao Llao Hotel makes no mention in its history that the hotel whose site it stands on was once the Nazis' favorite watering hole. Priebke, whose identity was revealed to the wider world in the early 1990s, lived in Bariloche for over fifty years until he was finally extradited to Italy to face trial for crimes against humanity in 1995. Many of his neighbors protested against this because of his good service to the community. His sentence of life imprisonment was changed to house arrest on appeal; requests for his extradition to Germany were refused. Priebke died of natural causes in Rome in 2013, age one hundred.

It is fair to say that many countries are very adept at turning away from their past. The wealth brought by slavery, for example, remains a difficult subject for many British cities, including my hometown of Glasgow. The dialogues to rectify this are, however, at least under way. I loved Buenos Aires, but Argentina, with its history of coups and dictatorships, is very definitely a country that does not want its surface pricked. It was ironic, therefore, that it was during my visit to the city's Eva Perón Museum that I discovered the clearest public link between the Perón regime and their Nazi sympathies, and had my neck prickled again. This museum is run by a Perón family member and is a truly remarkable place in its rewriting of history. There among the costume collection was one of Eva's favorite dresses. It was very pretty; it also dated from 1946 and was made by Maggy Rouff, the Berlin fashion designer beloved of Frau Goebbels and the Nazi wives. Sometimes the devil really is in the details.